Eyelash

Rev. Nikolai Kingsley

The SubGenius Foundation
Glen Rose 2021

Cover Design by Rev. Ivan Stang.
Interior Design by Rev. Onan Canobite.

First Edition: 2021
SubGenius Fountation, Glen Rose
10 9 8 7 6 5 4 3 2 1

Kingsley, Nikolai
[English]
Eyelash
ISBN 978-1-946529-01-5
1. Fiction–Science Fiction, General
2. Fiction–Religion
Rev. Nikolai Kingsley (b. 1963); Rev. Ivan Stang (b. 1953)

The World Ends Tomorrow and YOU MAY DIE! Well, no, probably
not... but whatever you do, just keep reading! Do people think
you're strange? Do you? THEN YOU MAY BE ON THE RIGHT
TRACK!

subgenius.com

Forward

L ONG before the ad-crammed, TV-like Internet of today, there was an Internet that was not at all TV-like... and only smart people even knew it existed! Emojis hadn't been invented, and the users had to type out entire words! They even used the shift key. This secret network, known mainly only by college weirdos, the military and the phone company, had no blogs, no websites, no videos, and only the crudest pornography, but it did have smart people.

Then we SubGeniuses started using it and it turned into Usenet. Not only did SubGeniuses start jumping in and writing their fool heads off to each other, but eventually (once the porn improved) the dumbest of the humans also jumped in. There was a different specialty "Usenet newsgroup" forum for every possible category of interest.

The main SubGenius one was the unmoderated, text-only alt.slack. In the end, the dumbest of the humans took over and the SubGeniuses left, but during its heyday in the 1990s it had some of the best writing, particularly either funny or angry writing, to be found anywhere, very possibly because none of us were being paid for it, and were in fact sneaking around on it when we were supposed to be working at our day jobs.

After using a forum like that for a year or ten, one starts to notice special contributors who somehow almost never say anything embarrassing, don't post unless they have something funny or interesting to say, and, most miraculously, don't get into online feuds! One such alt.slack writer was Nikolai Kingsley. All we knew about him was that he was an Australian and he was really sharp... but rarely cutting, unless somebody really deserved it.

One day, posts appeared from Kingsley that were chapters of a SubGenius novel! A whole novel, I tell you! We had published several books that we like to call nonfiction — they certainly weren't novels — and we had even published an anthology of specifically SubGenius-centric short stories, usually focused on our charismatic but elusive religious leader, J. R. "Bob" Dobbs.

There had been a few SubGenius novels written, but they were all terrible. This was very different indeed! Kingsley had obviously studied the previous factual works on "Bob" and the prophesied

End of the World, as well as the short stories in the anthology *Three Fisted Tales of "Bob,"* especially the ones written by the earliest SubGenius "Doktors" or Hierarchites, such as Paul Mavrides aka LIES, and G. Gordon Gordon. Mavrides' "World Without Slack" stories were especially rich in SubGenius mythos detail. And the SubGenius mythos had become very detailed by then.

I was flabbergasted by what Kingsley had done. The intricacies of the details! The funniness of the funny bits! The vast-ranging references across archaeology, history, pop culture, weird science, the New Age, and of course SubGenius! I'm a huge Neal Stephenson fan, and stylistically, this was right up there! Kingsley's not only hit the SubGenius mythos details perfectly, but he'd also added new and improved ones!

It was just so damned imaginative it made me jealous! To me, Kingsley's writing was easily equal to that of the giants on whose shoulders we crouch, holding on for dear life with white knuckles to the oversized weave of their immense dandruff-dusted sweaters while they stride about their titanic world.

But, dang it, I hated reading it in plain text on a little desktop screen! I'm an old man and that's no way to read a great novel. So I started printing out the pages so I could read them in my Excremeditation Chamber like I read all real books. Well, dag nab it, it was using up too much expensive inkjet ink!

I realized that if I wanted to read this thing right, I would have to publish it! For real! By then, self-publishing had become not only possible, but downright free, thanks to print-on-demand companies that were popping up everywhere. My old colleague Dr. Onan Canobite already had quite a bit of experience in print-on-demand systems, and gave me all-important advice. I also intended to reprint our illustrated old books and some new ones, but I wanted to start with something like *Eyelash* that was all text, and hence easy for beginners.

But instead, we first published Dave DeLuca's novel *Neighborworld.* I think it was because Dave was an actual neighbor and radio co-host, and also, being just laid off work, he was desperate for spare change, which is about all that self-published books make.

Then I got bogged down for two years in unexpected emergencies. Luckily for everybody, Dr. Canobite had achieved unexpected Slack, and took on the SubGenius Foundation publishing efforts. Thanks to him, FINALLY, I COULD ACTUALLY READ EYELASH! ALL THE WAY TO THE END! — and without it hurting my eyes! And indeed by the time I reached the end, my eyes were being washed with tears of happiness.

Knowing that the character Tai is based on a disabled close friend of the author may have made me a little extra weepy.

Rev. Ivan Stang
Glen Rose, TX
August 2020

For Ricky

Eyelash

2

"Justifying his turpitude with equal amounts of cleverness and effrontery, he loudly proclaimed that his poltroonery being nothing more than the desire to preserve himself, it were perfectly impossible for anyone in his right senses to condemn it for a fault."

— Donatien Alphonse Francois, Marquis De Sade, of the Duc de Blangis, *The 120 Days of Sodom*

4

THEY were waiting for the end of the world.

The precise time and date had been set long ago: X-day, 7:00 am. July 5th. After that day had come and gone it was just a matter of getting the year right; until that happened, it was an occasion for end-of-the-world parties.

Elif na Roche – formerly John Matthew Lee – hadn't taken any of it seriously until his abduction; he'd been shown the reality of the situation through the always effective medium of personal experience. He had once believed the whole SubGenius thing was a joke, a parody of millennial saucer cults with science fiction and fantasy elements thrown in. Actual abduction by honest-to-God flying saucer aliens, being kept in a cage in a rack along with dozens of other creatures, being threatened with live vivisection and having other terrible things done to him had made it all too immediate to laugh at.

He hadn't taken it well.

Once he was over the worst of the shock he'd abandoned his mundane identity; burned his credit cards, changed his name and hidden in a safe cocoon of hermetically self-contained paranoia for two years before he came across other SubGenii who'd been abducted. It was one thing to look up at the stars and think humanity would be exploring them one day and quite another to realise it was already very crowded out there, crowded with things that made humanity look like a cluster of dazed cheese mites by comparison. He dealt with it, mostly, but it was the sort of bump in the road of life that left a permanent bend in your front axle.

While most of the SubGenii around the world got drunk, danced and made a lot of noise, Elif na Roche and Tai (no surname) huddled under blankets in Tai's back yard and drank peppermint tea, anxiously watching the skies as seven a.m. drew near. Elif was a short thirty-four-year-old apprentice engineer with the rounded features of someone about to start a diet; she was a helplessly mediagenic twenty-six-year-old geek lesbian (or lesbian-geek, depending on who was to hand) studying neurology and artificial intelligence through round wire-frame glasses, her black hair contrasting with skin pale from a life spent indoors, her every movement restricted by Myasthenia Gravis complicated by a series of typically 21st century autoimmune syndromes.

Elif nervously clutched his mug of tea; Tai's cup rested on the padded arm of her wheelchair. "This is pointless, really," he said. "It won't be this year, but it will be soon. I know they all say that every year..."

"... but?" Her voice was soft, just audible over the sound of nearby traffic and sirens.

Before that day Elif hadn't spoken of this to anyone, not even the other abductees. "... but that's what he told me."

"He? Him? You actually met Him?"

He examined his mug. "Actually Him. The Man. I met J.R. "Bob" Dobbs, in the flesh. The Dealmaker. The one and only High Epopt of the Church of the SubGenius." Elif sipped his tea and swallowed, grimacing. "He told me: either this year or next year, and I could tell, at the time, he was really worried about it."

Tai hadn't been abducted but she had met some of the tentacled things that had taken Elif. She knew enough to take it seriously, knew that Elif took it very seriously and knew him well enough to want to lighten the mood. "What was he like?"

Elif laughed quietly, a series of short hisses from his nostrils, and smiled. "He's a really nice guy. You'd trust him with your life savings, and if the deal went bad and everyone lost their money you'd forgive him and trust him again. It's what makes him such a great salesman. He's a little vague at times – like he's got a lot on his mind – but you can tell he's very sharp underneath it all. And, uh," glancing away with some embarrassment, "he's probably the first guy I've ever felt even vaguely attracted to. I don't know what it was. His aftershave, I think. Or maybe the pipe smoke."

Tai laughed. "You are the most relentlessly hetero guy I know, and you're gay for "Bob.""

Elif shook his head in a slow, dazed manner, lost in thought. "It's just one of the, uh, things... about him." He stared up into the sky. "Something half-way between meme and the aroma of the pipe-smoke. It faded a little after he went back to Malaysia but it's always there. Like hepatitis. Like the Numa-numa song." He poured tea and blew gently to cool it. "It was a night like this... clear skies... about half-past six in the morning, when my phone rang – "

And as he said the words – of course – his cell phone started ringing.

He stared at her, eyes wide. She gave him an encouraging shrug. "Well? Go on – answer it! You know it has to be him."

He drew a deep breath. "I'm not ready for this. I'm really not ready for the end of the world."

She rested her fingers on the back of his hand and tapped a five-button Bat-keyboard pattern, their private code: I'm here. Go on.

With the cautious air of someone unlatching a gun's safety catch, Elif thumbed the pulsing ANSWER icon and held the phone to his ear. He didn't need to ask who it was. "Mr Dobbs. Hello".

A pause of fifteen seconds. "Yes." Another ten seconds. "Of course. Yes." Eleven seconds. "Yes, she is. One moment, please." He addressed Tai: "Are you up to a short trip into the city?"

Her eyes widened. She was plainly exhausted from the evening's vigil but at the chance of meeting "Bob," immediately said "Hell, yes!"

Elif nodded. "We'll be there, sir. No, thank **you**. It's quite an honour." The phone beeped, the call ended and a disabled-access taxi pulled up in the lane-way behind Tai's apartment, ready for her wheelchair.

THE ride into the city was mercifully brief; their driver thankfully silent (Elif had a congenital inability to get along with taxi drivers; they all held opinions diametrically opposed to his and seemed to have no problems with letting him know it). Tai locked her wheelchair's brakes and tried to ride with the bumps from potholes and stray obstacles the driver couldn't avoid. Elif gazed out through inch-thick glass, lost in memories not, for a change, of the two months he'd spent locked in the hold of the saucer but of the time after his escape, and of the support of other SubGenii who'd been there – Tai in particular – and had understood. By any regular, rational standard they were all dysfunctional freaks, but they were also survivors.

The taxi was shot at nine times, the bullets dimpling the taxi's body and leaving glittering streaks on the windows but he barely noticed. He did see Tai flinch with the first few shots so he gave her hand a reassuring squeeze. Growing up in the suburbs he'd become accustomed to being shot at.

Elif wanted to believe they weren't intentionally being sent into danger but he'd seen how peoples' lives were turned upside-down after getting involved with "Bob;" he was the classic example of someone insane things happened around. Not **to**; "Bob" seemed to exist in the eye of a cyclone. It was his assistants and employees, his co-workers, cohorts and co-anti-conspirators that felt the force of the storm, caught the shrapnel and, if they survived, picked up the pieces. It was "Bob" who'd accidentally helped Elif escape from the saucer... but it turned out that it was mostly "Bob's" fault he'd been abducted in the first place. As the taxi pulled into a narrow laneway behind a corporate office block Elif vowed to himself that whatever was coming, he'd keep Tai out of any danger if he could.

A s he guided her wheelchair down the taxi ramp he tensed with the sudden and undeniable feeling that a large window nearby was about to shatter. His breath stopped in his chest. Tai sensed it as well; she lifted a trembling arm – for a moment Elif thought she was pointing at the sky and he glanced up nervously, looking for saucers – then he saw the orange-tipped hands on her titanium Pingu wristwatch: 6:59 am. The taxi purred away and for a space of sixty seconds they waited in the laneway, unwilling to move, nestled inside a bubble of perfect silence.

Nothing happened.

The sky wasn't torn open by the wakes of a thousand Xist saucers. The buildings around them didn't explode into burning rubble. Gradually, as if God was fiddling with the volume, sounds from the real world returned; traffic from nearby city streets – car-horns, screeching tyres, garbage trucks... gun-shots near and far, police sirens, feral pigeons fighting with kleptoparasite seagulls and the gritty hiss of five hundred thousand people grinding their teeth. The only sound from the skies was the familiar, if not reassuring buzz of surveillance drone 'copters.

"Well... maybe next year," Elif sighed as he pushed Tai's wheelchair up the ramp in front of the office block.

The elevator let them out onto the first floor. It wasn't any more of a maze than most office buildings but Elif managed to get them lost within seconds. More through luck than conscious intent they found room 3013 behind a glass door, a sheet of paper with the word "SUBGENIUS" scrawled in stippled green crayon taped to the wrong side. In the middle of a room big enough for a four-hole golf course sat a single desk surrounded by heaps of crates, packages and letters; large, small, flat and mounded with suggestive shapes, bubble mail-packs, architect blueprint delivery tubes and obliquely trapezoidal and tattered cardboard boxes held together with masking tape. As they negotiated the narrow gap between tottering mounds of correspondence a voice spoke from beneath the desk:

"Uh, 'With reference to your shipment of, uh, April this year. We regret to inform you that none of the subjects met requirements detailed in our order MFBC 2317. Unless you are willing to cover the cost of returning this shipment, the subjects will be released into the general population with, and we feel we should emphasise this point, **with** their control implants locked in Berserker Mode.

"'Please contact this office before July 5th if you want to, uh,' blah blah blah, well. Too late for that. Eh eh eh." A faint crackle of crumpling paper was followed by the tinny thunk of a balled document hitting the round file.

The voice was smooth and self-assured, the odd laugh imbued with the confident, oily tones of a politician who had managed to bribe everyone within arm's reach with money stolen from their own pockets. Elif could easily imagine that voice selling time-shared condominiums in hell, and he could just as easily imagine buying two of them. Tai had an expression of such obvious and undiluted fanboy eagerness that Elif wished he'd thought to warn her beforehand; he was about to tap her hand with something along the lines of a caution when the man in the neat grey suit came out from under the desk, smiled, took the pipe from between his unnaturally regular teeth and approached, hand out, pinkie finger crooked in some obscure Masonic greeting. Despite his concern, Elif found himself returning the smile and accepting the handshake. He received a slight electric shock, like scuffing plastic shoe-soles on nylon carpet.

"John! Damn good to see you out and about. You're over the whole alien abduction trauma thing? Hope so: I have an important job for you, and it's gonna involve some saucer-folk."

THE next day while Tai was avidly absorbing the fine details buried in the notes "Bob" had given them, Elif read a few paragraphs and then decided to take a more relaxed attitude to the whole thing. They had plenty of time to prepare – four days, now; even so, Elif hadn't gotten past the second page.

Judging from the outline it didn't sound that bad after all. Ears full of loud music and lungs full of sinsemilla smoke, he paged back and forth at a rate that allowed him to take in about one word in twenty. Thankfully it began in convenient point form:

- On X-day (see: **Rupture**) the **Conspiracy** (see: "Reptilian Satanic-Masonic-Military-Industrial-Complex Bankers, Finance Sharks, Media/Weapons/Chemical Conglomerates") plan to sell the Earth to the **Aliens from Planet X** (see: "Xists").

- Conspiracy leaders to receive **amnesty/rescue** in exchange for a properly polluted biosphere and **seven billion units** of Essence (see: "Souls").

- **"Bob"** has offered them a better deal: polluted biosphere and seven billion units of Essence spiced with **SubGenius** flavour. Conspiracy escape vessels to be occupied by **SubGenii** –

(the words "plus families plus selected friends and pets" had been added in a different font; the outline continued in that style...)

Nobody wanted to leave their friends behind even if they weren't paid up SubGenii. So we added the pets clause, which means we need three times as many escape vessels. So we have to raise extra capital to pay the deposit. Which is where you come in.

Elif had heard of the Xists but had never met one; utterly non-human and fearfully advanced beings with technology so powerful and complex it was godlike. To put the situation into a useful perspective he imagined them as linebackers wearing heavy boots, and all of humanity as a spoonful of small, blind beetles beneath those boots.

The Xists were master manipulators of lesser races and never did anything in a straightforward manner when they could do it in a tangled knot of deception, fronts, multiple agents, stabbed backs, puppets seemingly possessed of their own twisted agendas which somehow always come out benefiting whichever Xist was behind it all, disinformation, set-ups, outright lies and greed followed by a cheap cover-up to invalidate the evidence and a better cover-up of the cheap cover-up. Among those who Knew, the general opinion of the Xists was Best Left Alone; nobody ever benefited from dealing with them, aside from "Bob."

Elif noted the mention of The Contract. It was a mythical document purported to detail the whole evil scheme. Dozens of versions existed, most of them lumpy with pseudo-Latinate legal terms and irrelevant human concepts. The version Elif had read had a number of authenticity points in its favour: the damn thing only barely made sense – translated from a starkly non-human idiom of nightmares and enthusiastically pursued personal greed – and it didn't mention the Vatican, the Masons, the Greys or the Trilateral Commission, unlike most editions. This particular Contract described a typical Essence deal: buying and selling souls.

The Xists had a myriad of tentacles in thousands of ventures both grand and sordid, and something they did particularly well was Essence (or "Skull") Farming:

- Drop tribes of simple apes on an empty planet;

- Let them breed out of control;

- When you have enough apes, harvest and sell their Essence.

Elif's engineering outlook on life led him to believe that if "souls" existed at all, they were complex fields of an unknown form of energy woven with memories and other elements that described the owner. He was still out on the whole transmigration-of-memories-through-reincarnation thing; similarly the ghost thing, the spiritual healing thing (which he half-believed in but had decided it wouldn't work on someone as cynical as him) and the whole concept of benevolent superior beings, either physical or spiritual. While he could accept the idea of, for example, leprechauns, on the basis of Terence McKenna's "Faberge eggs from Mars morphing themselves with Mandaean alphabetical structures" – intelligences encoded within information – he still had a problem with souls, and probably would until he could get one under a high-resolution flatbed scanner. Souls, if he had to, could be imagined as invisible heat-haze lightning stretched out, knitted into a sock and the open end slipped over the owner's head. Once he could see it he had no conceptual problems with an Xist owning an entire planet of people, harvesting the socks and selling them from a booth in the eleventh dimension. He'd decided the distinction between regular "Pink" souls and the SubGenius variety was probably something like the difference between cheap nylon socks and comfortable, chunky hand-knitted woollen toe-gloves.

Presently he got to the crunch, mission-wise:

- Authorise SINGLE pre-Rupture Essence sampling of **up to five hundred units** outside established Contractual limits on Harvesting. Infuse with SubGenius **zest** through **exposure to live SubG Essence. NO SUBGENIUS HARVEST- ING TO TAKE PLACE WITHOUT CONSENT**. Xists to process, market and sell improved product; profits split seventy-thirty in Their favour.

Elif thought about it, nodded sagely, lit up another spliff; then he frowned, muttered, "Wait, what?" and paged back to the start of the file.

TAI was watching text scroll slowly by. A pinhole camera kept track of her eye movements and adjusted the scrolling speed accordingly; recovering from the trip into the city, she didn't have energy to spare on moving her hands.

After the Conspiracy Medical system had decided they didn't know precisely what was wrong with her body, Tai had reluctantly turned, first to the alternative medical market – a raging sea of contradictions, chicanery, blithe ignorance and sadly misplaced enthusiasm – and then (after an embarrassing episode with a Tesla coil, one hundred ping-pong balls and a bathtub of yoghurt) to the Alternative alternative medical market: the dark side of the Consumer Culture Nightmare. They weren't as bad as she'd heard; generally a loose network of second- and third-hand dealers in items from the fuzzy border somewhere between Over-the-Counter, No-Name-Brand, Not Available In Your State and Item Has Been

Discontinued. Over time she read, learned, evolved, contributed; became well known in the associated social spaces, helped a lot of other similarly lost souls, found a combination of things which relieved the symptoms and the pain, but couldn't do anything about the growing vague fuzziness of her thoughts. It was slow but relentlessly progressive. She didn't want to think where it would lead. Privately she mused that eventually she wouldn't have the mental capacity to worry about it.

She was reading all of the supporting data on Essence and its users. For some – beings even further up the scale than the already advanced Xists – Essence was a drug.

How advanced are They if they have a drug problem?

It was all a lot more complex than it first appeared. After sorting through the few bits of almost-truth brought back by actual abductees, a depressing picture started to appear. Out there were societies at every level of development: hunter-and-gatherer cavemen and star travellers, grubby medieval diggers in the dirt and slick hyper-urban data miners, intelligent machines and non-sentient energy forms. Every possible way of encoding life was represented somewhere: intelligent plants and non-intelligent animals that ate them; grazers grazing wherever there was cheap energy, hunters preying on the prey, who were preyed upon by bigger hunters, and parasites to fill the niches, all arranged in order of who ate what; wants and needs made manifest, arrangements made to supply them, addictions indulged. Little guys and big players; brutally repressive oligarchies and ridiculously ornate hierocracies and dizzying, chaotic anarchies. Every manner of law and code and government and tradition, and the resulting confusion of jurisdictions and crimes, every element bumping up against the others in a hopelessly tangled and constantly shifting no-holds-barred death-match fought between mutually incomprehensible and rigidly, grimly held world-views.

The section on religion simply said:

> Oh, just forget it.
> Let's just say
> anything goes.

Every possible social problem would find expression somewhere, and the ones that could be profitably applied to other races – higher or lower – would spread in every direction. Each variation on the old games: master and slaves, farmer and cash crops, citadel and barbarians, dealer and addicts. Every kind of scam, confidence trick, insider trading deal, concealed toxic waste dump, law enforcer bribed to look the other way, rigged election, counterfeit currency, profiteer's war and plain old-fashioned genocide. Every market would be a grey market; everybody's ass would be up for grabs. You could be the mayor of the planet one day, and the next, locked inside a cheap wooden crate on your way to some alien creature's dinner table.

She tried to imagine a four-dimensional chart that could show it all in real-time and fell asleep to dream of tentacled and subaqueous Elder Gods; slime-dripping, their crusted carapaces wrinkled, ridged and nippled in dark ocean-floor grey-green. Deceptively friendly abominations of the abyss who watched through closed eyes and who burbled in a liquid language just on the far edge of comprehension and who only wanted to buy some... stuff, you know? Got the necessary right here... name your price, we're good for it...

THREE days later Elif had made a list of things to ask Tai:
Did you read the part about the Scoop, and does it mean what you imagine I might think it means? Like, don't bring the cat food – leave it at least five yards beyond the perimeter.

There are two hundred pages missing from my copy of Document 4. Do you have one and does it have a page 23?

Is there anything you need me to get from Doolan? because he owes me a lot of money and I'm going by that way tomorrow.

I don't see anything in here anywhere says they have to feed us at all. Do you have a spare refrigerator I can stash about two hundred cans of Bivalve in?

BATTERIES. Big ones. How many have you got?

He'd written one further point, then deleted it, then put it back and deleted it again. He had the impression that even if he backed out now, she wouldn't, so there was no point in asking.

He put on some light urban armour and went to visit the business associates that he felt he owed at least an explanation. His main worry was that only half of them would believe he was going overseas and the other half would want to come along; as far as he could tell from the notes he'd actually read, there was only room for two humans on this trip.

He made a brief stop at the 24-hour Pharmaceutical Market, wandering along the aisles, shopping for cough mixture, vitamins, banned food additives, soft drinks with far too much caffeine (he picked up several thirty-can packs of Bivalve Mutathing, his favourite far-too-much-caffeine tipple, imported from a country that technically no longer existed) and unlicensed knock-off painkillers so cheap they were handing them out for free. As he stacked plastic drums of cough syrup in the back of his car he noticed the bright blue contents glowing faintly under the overhead streetlights.

A portion of the glowing blue syrup was a going-away-present for his part-time boss, a dazed anarchist who was building a fully outfitted machine shop completely independent of the existing socio-politico-economic structure. In secret, down an abandoned mine, on a deserted country property owned by his parents. Elif retrieved his work tools and three briefcase-sized charge cells, maxed out his credit card to charge them at the gas station (which hadn't sold gasoline for years), then stopped by Tai's place.

She'd been making a list of things to ask him:

Does this whole Essence thing bother you much?

I don't think I know any Conspiracy Pinks. Is there an easy way to tell?

Will they stop relative to us before they use the Scoop? If not, how would they bring us up to their velocity? They do need us alive, right?

"At least intact," Elif said. "From what I read about these guys, this is a cover for something else, which is a cover for something else and so on for longer than anyone would care to look. If we're lucky we'll never need to know what they really want us for, but I think it would be prudent if we tried to find out, quietly. If things go sideways we won't get many chances to bail out."

"Can we do that? I thought they were proto-godlike, or at the very least proto-Krell. On their scale we'd be less than – "

Elif held up a hand and tried to wave the metaphor away. "I'm trying to avoid comparisons like that because once you start you never stop. From what I saw of the last bunch they have a lot of tricks, a whole catalogue of ways to dazzle the lesser creatures, but behind it all they aren't much more advanced than us. They still lie, cheat and steal and use each other in their games. Just because they can move planets about doesn't mean they do it for a good reason. Or what seems like a good reason to us."

Tai looked too tired to argue with this, so Elif guessed what she would have said and said it. "Anyway, I'm supposed to be arguing the doom and gloom side, not you." She smiled and closed her eyes. Elif continued (as he usually did until her neural activity – as reported by her computer – dropped below the level of consciousness). "Does the whole Essence thing bother me? In a way, yeah. There are several things wrong with it I can think of, and a few more you can probably list. Let's see.

"One: do we have the right to sell other humans for their parts? Well. The notes claim that Essence extraction a), doesn't kill the subjects unless they're really, badly unbalanced, b) less than three physical deaths in the six thousand previous extractions, and c) the subject goes on to lead a normal Pink life with no ill effects. I don't know how much of that's true. The notes also say only the most highly Pink types have enough Essence to be worth triggering the extractor, and the device targets the worst people in terms of maladjusted predators and the like.

"Anyway, it's not us, it's the Xists. If we refuse to do it they'll just get someone else. I don't think they're gonna change their minds because we have some moral problems with it. And I want to learn all about this business in case there's a way we can, I don't know exactly, make Essence less appealing. Reduce humanity's market value until we're too expensive to be harvested, and then hope we can get off the planet before They decide to destroy all human life and start again with the dogs. Or the bears. They look like a nice gullible bunch.

"Two: Pinks, is there an easy way to tell?" Elif thought about it for a moment before shaking his head. "It's a Bell curve. A pretty steep Bell curve, but, yeah, there are people clinging to either side, not strange enough to be SubGenii and not dumb enough to be Pink. They got tired of fighting and retreated to suburbia where it's still mostly safe. And while it's hard to tell if your neighbour is Pink... Mr Corporate Greed handing over a suitcase full of cash to have some toxic waste buried in your back yard – he's pretty easy to spot. I'd like to imagine They'll be going after him, or people like him."

Elif paused to finish his shot glass of cough syrup. "So what it comes down to, is, if we don't do it someone else will, and if we do it we might be able to do something about it one day."

Tai didn't open her eyes but added sleepily, "They want us for something. The Essence story is pretty neat, but I want to know why they chose us. There must be something they need two SubGenii for, and I can tell you're about to mention a breeding program and if you do I will hit you with this ergonomic keyboard until you change the subject."

Elif grinned. "Us, specifically? That'd be the part about 'Essence spiced with SubGenius flavour', but until I get a good idea of what Essence actually is and how it's collected, I'm not going to say any more. There is something about the Scoop I wanted to ask you about. My notes say the thing will pick up everything within about twenty yards. It's smart enough to only pick up non-living stuff so They don't collect any people who happen to be in range, except They want to collect us as well so they fiddle the settings some more and now it just picks up us and part of our houses and half the neighbour's house as well. And all of the clothes off of anyone in range, or part of their clothes if they're near the edge."

Tai gave a few brief nods to show she was thinking about it, then said "That's pretty much what my notes said. They also said they'd arrange better quarters when we were on-board but They might have to use the material of the house to make them. I guess They're up on the whole reconfiguring matter thing."

Elif pursed his lips and made an absent "mm-hmm" sound. "Right. I have stuff I need to do before they pick us up. Anything else you need me to promote while I'm out?"

"N'p."

"'Kay. I'm going to bother some citizens. I've just had an interesting idea."

"You're not going to hurt anybody, are you?"

Elif thought, then shook his head. "I don't think so. There'll probably be a fistfight, but in general it will result in a move toward social harmony. More or less."

E LIF had to drive through the bad part of town to get home; bad
in that the locals had armour piercing rounds and very short
tempers. He avoided the worst trouble spots and stopped at a local
watering hole, which was crowded with hundreds of angry, drunk,
sleep-deprived and desperately unhappy gun owners. Knowing he
didn't belong here and that with one stray word any of these people
would happily loose a round or two in his direction, he got in quick
and spoke to the door guys:

"Is the Captain in?"

They didn't even look down at him. "Nuh."

"I heared the Buy-back guy is making his move, midnight tonight."
This caught their attention. Six months ago many of the locals
had been forced to hand in their less legal weaponry to a city "buy
back" scheme. It was strongly rumoured the guns hadn't been
destroyed but were on their way north for sale to whoever was
corrupt enough to want to pay for them. Within days the weapons
and their new owner had been located; quite a few people were
waiting for him to leave his heavily fortified bunker and make a run
for it. Coincidentally, the bunker was next to a vacant lot behind
Elif's house. **Now, who else would like to join this party?**

In this town it wasn't hard to find a couple of hundred people
who didn't much like each other. It wasn't much harder to convince
them to attend what was shaping up to be a free-form riot which
Elif found himself promoting, improvising completely off the cuff
as he went along, adapting the story for the market. He didn't
want people to be hurt – at least not seriously; if he timed it right,
nobody would get shot or stabbed.

After two hours of dealing with difficult and not very bright
people, Elif decided he'd indulge in one last meal of junk food. As
a child – like most children of his generation – he'd been duped into
thinking the stuff was tasty and even healthy by a constant barrage
of Conspiracy advertisement-programming; even as an adult, he felt
the phantom tug of sub-conscious media influence telling him it was
desirable. He hadn't touched the stuff since he found out what went
into it, what They did to the ingredients in order to maximise sales
and what it did to the human body. Once, he'd been cynical; now
he just tried to be careful about what he ate and drank, and he
kept his unpopular opinions to himself. He'd discovered the hard

way that most people didn't want to know the terrible truth.

He pulled in at a Temple of Mass Consumption – they'd once had different names, but lately they didn't bother, given that they all sold the same mass-produced, deep-fried garbage – parked his car as far as possible from the main road, went in and cautiously joined the queue for the front counter. Around him were standard family units that had been eating the stuff all their lives, and it showed: parents who were angry, impatient and slightly dazed and children who raced about shrieking furiously while trying to kill each other with the edges of their plastic meal trays. Elif tried to avoid eye contact and pretended to focus on the menu, which, since he'd last visited one of these places, had been redone in pictograms showing unrealistically stylised versions of what was on offer to avoid offending the reading-challenged. The prices were represented by green rectangles; six of them for a large drink, three for a small drink and eight for... whatever that thing was. It could have been a hamburger, once, he supposed. It appeared to have been machine-moulded from pulped animal-feed-quality corn meal, lard, and processed sugar. The drink looked like old sump oil and reeked of acetone. The side dishes – or what he guessed were supposed to be side dishes – resembled bundles of bright yellow foam rubber off-cuts covered in salt. He ordered one of each thing, handing most of his money to the blank-eyed humanoid robot behind the counter (eating it was bad enough... Elif couldn't imagine having to handle it eight hours a day), and took the food over to a corner near the door; the safest place to be.

At first he thought the worst part was that the stuff actually tasted pretty good; at least good enough to want to finish it. A few minutes into the meal he'd changed his mind: the worst part was that the drink was eating its way through the waxed-paper cup. As he crumpled the packaging and tossed it into the trash receptacle – the only person in the place who'd bothered – he changed his mind again. The worst part was the kick to his system; how it made his pupils dilate and his heart race. He could feel the additives dissolving into their precursors and spreading into his bloodstream. He felt sick and hungry at the same time. He felt like biting through the metal post that supported the bright blue dollar sign logo. He felt like standing up on a table and giving a sermon about the relationship between profit, addiction and the dissolution of the social contract. He recognised the symptoms and quietly went back to his car, where he sat gnawing on the steering wheel with his hands over his eyes until the shakes, nausea and the urge to scream obscenities faded to a manageable level. Then he started his car and very carefully got back into the traffic.

He caught sight of the glossy black Conspiracy van as he came within sight of his house. They were following him; probably had been following him ever since he came out of "Bob's" office. If they kept to their regular pattern they'd stake the place out for a few hours before doing anything as gauche as knocking on the door. There were already a couple of small groups of people on the vacant lot, looking for cover that didn't exist, trying to work out the best way to ambush Mr Buy-back, who lived in a partial cul-de-sac open in two places: at the entrance and across the vacant lot.

It would be a monumental coincidence if he did make a run for it tonight, he thought. He went inside and made some phone calls, including one to the police. **Let's see how many angry, armed people we can get into one place.**

A LONG with several boxes she hadn't ordered but was too tired to argue about, Tai had just accepted delivery of enough painkillers and arcane neurotransmitter adjusters to last for two weeks. When they were finished, she expected the Xists to provide pharmaceuticals in line with the paragraph about Them keeping the SubGenii in good health. Even if the humans were less than pets; even if they were considered to be less than insects, the Xists had a contractual obligation to provide a carefully defined level of support. Smarter people had been over it all before, and it was the best deal that could be screwed out of Them, and whatever They had in the way of medical care had to be an improvement on what Earth had to offer.

They were coming for them at midnight; by eleven forty-five Tai had tidied the place to the extent her disability would allow and sent the cat to a neighbour for feeding, in the hope it would stay over there for at least fifteen minutes. She counted her supplies once more, noticed the extra boxes and shrugged; she turned off the lights, the security system and, one by one, the many small faithful machines that hovered near, keeping her alive. She lay down in the suddenly quiet darkness and watched the digits on her screen, counting the seconds.

THE familiar sound of someone putting half a brick through a car windscreen alerted him that things were getting out of hand. Another five minutes to go, and groups of local assoholics were already pulling down his back fence and securing positions in his yard. Before long they'd be at the door and on the roof. It was dangerous, but he had to go out there and try to talk them down, just long enough to delay the start of shooting. Elif knew they worked to the rules laid out in TV shows, their primary source of knowledge: typically things would be tense, then someone would start shooting, then everyone would start shooting. Four minutes, now.

He didn't recognise the man huddling next to the widening hole in the back fence but he appeared almost perfectly average and therefore the Conspiracy's primary marketing target: early to mid twenties, male, overweight, half-drunk, and not too bright; angry without knowing why and with just enough money for a loud car and some fashionable guns. Despite his occasional impulses toward street-corner ranting and proselytising, Elif had never been a fan of dealing with strangers – especially Pinks – but when sufficiently scared, his defences kicked in and gave him a confidence not found outside of six strong cups of coffee. He called out from the door to the nearest citizen: "Hey, I didn't think you'd be here tonight, man. You know it's the police laying a trap, right?"

Judging from his expression the citizen hadn't known, and now that the possibility had been raised, he clearly didn't like it. The man crept forward to discuss it with his friends, who started to discuss it with their cell phones.

Elif had tied back his unfashionably long hair with a headband that held in place a tiny LED egg timer shoved across the bridge of his nose. He could just see the digits if he crossed his eyes. One hundred seconds. If nobody else did anything stupid, they might all just survive this. He quietly closed the back door and turned around to stare down the blued-metal barrel of the pistol aimed at his head by the Conspiracy agent. Naturally, he hadn't heard him come in. Elif froze, his gaze locked with the whites of the man's eyes glowing faintly under the overhead strip-lights, through his agent shades.

Elif had gotten used to people pulling guns on him, but rarely in his own house, and never with the intent obvious in the expression of this man. Something in the shark-like grin, the confident stance; the angle at which he was holding the gun, casually half-tilted to the side as if to say **We're in charge and nobody is ever going to find out what we did here tonight**. Something in the way he wore his dark grey suit, the uniform of Conspiracy agents, or perhaps in the set of his thin lips and lumpy, scarred face. It set off that internal alarm, the cold feeling that only went with the immediate possibility of death.

Wait, I haven't done anything wrong! Yeah. Tell that to the gun.

Elif didn't dare take his eyes off the agent but the egg timer LEDs were still flickering hazily in the corner of his vision. This man didn't look like an ignorant grunt; he looked smart enough to know some of the things They weren't allowed to tell regular folk, secret Conspiracy deals so bad that no-one could ever find out. This arcane knowledge put him above most people, but especially above low-rent scum like Elif. The agent looked smart enough to want to gloat. He probably had some profound observation he'd memorised for just this situation.

Elif held off as long as he possibly could before lowering his gaze slightly and looking down at the man's tie: signalling he'd accepted defeat and was ready to hear the speech.

The agent sneered, tilted the pistol back a couple of degrees and got as far as "When you've been in this game as – "

– before vanishing, leaving a collapsing suit of clothes unevenly weighted by guns, handcuffs and 'phone. The angry murmur of people ceased; the lights went out and the green glow of the microwave oven clock faded. Aside from a faint, dying subsonic thrum felt through the soles of his feet, everything was quiet. He held his breath and waited; from somewhere outside came the faint tinkling of broken glass settling in its frame, a long, drawn-out metallic screeching that ended suddenly, then complete silence. The egg timer LED counter had ticked over and was counting down again from 5:00. He took it off and tossed it to where he knew the kitchen table was.

He fished around in his pockets for the kick-ass torch he'd bought earlier that day. It had a bank of bright white LEDs around the front, was powered by a hand-cranked rechargeable cell and looked the way a futuristic weapon should look. Two minutes later he'd worked out how to turn it on, and he checked out the house. Nothing was damaged aside from his bedroom, the familiar space halved by a featureless curved wall of dull grey metal. There were well-armed empty dark grey suits in two rooms and a rather severe dark grey midi-skirt affair draped over the side of the bathtub. There were some items of black lace underwear inside the skirt and the blouse, and Elif found himself hoping fervently it had been a female agent wearing them. He checked the ID; she had short blonde hair and the kind of angry sneer that would look good in an Imperial Stormtrooper costume. He shuddered, thinking that SubGenii must have a fear of Conspiracy agents encoded at the genetic level.

The view through the bathroom window was a little odd, to say the least. He could see the jagged edge where the mob had started dismantling his back fence; some trees in the vacant lot just beyond that were lit by a pale cyan moonlight-level glow coming from above, thousands of tiny points of light, a sweeping grid that marked out the underside of a dome. Beyond that, he could see nothing; no neighbours' houses, no sky, no stars; dark grey nothing. He went outside and shone the torch up; the spot of light leapt from the edge of the roof and vanished. He climbed up on a weathered plastic crate and peered over the edge of the fence. Nobody; the vacant lot was littered with empty clothes and guns and beer-cans and a couple of torches throwing their beams across the grass. The faint light showed sections of cars cut along the curved edge cut out by the Scoop; half a tree had fallen across the front of one car, pushing its tail into the air. He tried to imagine the scene below; a large bowl bitten out of the ground, water from ruptured plumbing, ground turning rapidly to mud, the whole thing filled with angry, naked people worked up and fixin' to kill each other. He wondered if the police had turned up yet, then walked over to where the circle of grass stopped at the chamber wall, a hard, grey shell difficult to see clearly in that light. It rose up with a curve suggestive of a space, in full, about the size of a basketball court.

Working on the idea that someone might be listening, Elif leaned close to the wall and murmured, "It would be nice to see what's going on outside," and was struck with the realisation he might be talking to a creature from another world; his immediate response was to stop breathing to reduce the chance he might say something that would get him accidentally or on purpose diverted out of an airlock as some elaborate kind of alien joke. The wall didn't reply, anyway. He decided to say as little as possible until he had a better idea of the situation, and wandered around the entire perimeter until he reached where the grey curving wall cut off the edge of his house. Peering through the broken window he saw it was his bedroom; more or less. About forty percent of it. He went back inside to assess the damage. One end of his computer's case had been cut off; fortunately it still worked when plugged into a power cell. Every single antique betamax videotape in his collection had been neatly bisected; each tape's worth now depending on how far it had been rewound. He tried to put down the rising feeling of panic at being locked inside another alien ship and went to search the perimeter for an obvious hatch.

TAI opened her eyes and restarted her computer from the power cells under her bed. Some of the closer machines woke up and started complaining quietly about not being able to connect to the net. She started a local command server, something clever enough to calm them all down, and set it to looking for local data points. She didn't expect to find any; she had no idea if the Xists offered local internet to creatures of her level but it didn't hurt to look. She accepted an origami cup of cold water from a dainty, long-armed bot, sipped gratefully and sat back in bed to wait, wondering if Elif would get here before They did.

HE'D made three complete circuits of the inside of the Scoop chamber before he decided that Tai's place wasn't in there and that the exits were either hidden underneath one of the houses, or that there were no exits and They used smaller Scoops to move things back and forth. Probably a good policy given that They were usually scooping up things that wouldn't agree with the idea. He checked out the clothing and equipment that had been scooped, hoping that nobody had brought any of those cheap homemade grenades that were so popular with today's youth. There had been a couple of Conspiracy agents in the crowd and their pockets held all kinds of interesting gadgets.

He went back to his living room, restarted his computer and looked through "Bob's" notes for anything about the aliens presumably running this show. In most places the notes referred to one Xist; in the later pages there seemed to be two of them. Beyond some stories about their perfectly self-interested business practices, there wasn't much. A few observers had noted an Xist tendency to doing things by remote control, much preferring to operate from somewhere safe. Their natural environment was physically harmful to most life-forms, so much so that meeting Them in person was out of the question. The notes didn't have any pictures or even vague descriptions beyond hints that anyone who'd ever seen Them had immediately regretted it.

He turned off the computer. One charge cell could run his machine for about four hours; he had three of them, and he hoped someone would organise some power cables, or at least greet them or even acknowledge their presence before they ran down. Hopefully he could find Tai before that.

After finishing whatever food was left in the refrigerator he took out the dividing shelves, filled the 'fridge with as many cans of Bivalve as would fit and hooked it up to a cell; good for about an hour.

Twenty minutes later he was starting to think They were deliberately ignoring him and that it might be an intelligence test. Perhaps he had to find a way out. He spread the collection of Conspiracy gadgets out on the kitchen table and examined each one carefully. Mysterious pen-shaped beeping things, magic 8-Balls displaying 404 pages, cartridges for various weapons and a couple of things he decided were detectors of some kind. He pocketed the ones he could activate and went out to examine the perimeter of the scoop chamber more closely.

He found two hatches, on opposite sides of the chamber. Unfortunately they were both partially covered by parts of houses the Scoop had picked up, along with Elif's apartment and sections of the cars that had gathered for the riot. He could just see one tantalising edge of a circular hatch, three yards across, with about two hundred hods of broken brick wall and part of a roof covering it. "Don't you guys have a system for dealing with this?"

Apparently not.

Elif collected as many weapons as he could find, looting the SUVs and the Conspiracy black van. A small electric Soccer Mom four-seater – trapped between half of a battered SUV and a tree – had belonged to Mr Buy-back himself. The front and back seats were loaded down with enough guns and ammunition to start a modest war, but nothing more exotic than might be found at any regular Soldier of Fortune convention. The Conspiracy van was loaded to the brim with more or less normal weapons mixed with some very odd alien artefacts; enticing as they seemed, Elif decided to leave them alone until he came across some documentation. Perhaps their Xists hosts would help with that.

Working on the assumption that the hull of the Xist ship would be strong enough to resist puny human explosives, Elif borrowed a few packets of the Conspiracy's C4; he read the warning labels twice, then very carefully set the detonators, attached them and planted the packets behind the brick wall covering the hatch, after spending an anxious few minutes wondering if the hatch he'd chosen led further into the ship or out into open space. Five minutes gave him enough time to get to the other end of the chamber and hide behind something. **I really hope nobody opens that hatch in the next sixty seconds**... Perhaps he should have tried to tell someone? He leaned close to the dull grey chamber wall and said with emphasis "I really hope nobody opens that hatch in the next sixty seconds."

The explosion was disappointing; a dull thump, a cloud of dust, the sound of tumbling bricks and a faint aroma of burned almonds and damp concrete. The rubble blocking the hatch had been distributed in a broad fan of bricks, wooden beams, plaster, concrete chunks and strips of carpet. A small crater of soil had been gouged out of the ground, revealing more of the neutral grey chamber wall and a broad ramp leading up to the hatch, made of wall material. Elif checked the equipment he'd felt would be of any use – a heavy crescent wrench and his thumb-drive music player – then confidently strode up to the hatch, a circular notch with a flattened base that merged with the top of the ramp. He saw no buttons or speakers or obvious places where an organism might press a tentacle or a palp to have it scanned.

He knocked and hurt his knuckles; it felt like cold stone a yard thick. He said "Door, open" a couple of times, pressed his forehead against the centre and visualised the hatch opening in several impressive ways (his favourite being where it defloresced into twenty-three long spirally nested sections which unwound and slid into the wall), waved his cell phone over the area around the hatch watching for magnetic disturbances that would make the screen jitter. He thought about how stupid he'd look if he tried to walk through it as if it wasn't there, given how solidly and impressively there it obviously was. He pushed against it with all his strength. He licked it. He considered variations of every cheap SF trope he'd ever read; he breathed on it, thought happy thoughts, sang to it, tried pressing different parts of the hatch and the wall it was set into. He tried shoving the hatch sideways; it didn't move. He tried several of the unidentified Conspiracy trinkets with buttons; they beeped or buzzed or flashed cheery candy-red indicators, but none of them convinced the hatch to open. Then he went back to the ruin of his apartment and started reading the notes again.

After an hour he turned everything off, braced himself with a cold Bivalve, cranked up his torch and went back to the hatch. He knocked again; nothing.

"Aw, come **on**, assholes," he muttered angrily. The hatch slid open, the circular section rolling smoothly sideways into the wall. A short connecting passage led to the next room, hopefully the Scoop chamber Tai had ended up in.

I T was the same disaster movie set with different props; abbreviated sections of different houses collapsed against the chamber walls, and slices of slightly better cars leaning sadly on their irregularly bisected axles. He recognised the neighbour's houses but was briefly confused by having to come at Tai's apartment from an unfamiliar direction, through part of the back neighbour's fast food franchise and over the fence. The building seemed intact; They had obviously taken more care when Scooping her place than They'd bothered with his. He knocked on the back door and called out. He heard someone moving inside and almost panicked at the thought someone else had gotten in; Tai didn't move about much under her own power. He tip-toed through the dark kitchen, bumping his hip on the edge of the 'fridge, over to the far wall. He edged past the slightly open door and peered through the narrow gap at the hinge. Dimly lit, he saw a vague blur; in outline, Tai in her bed, her attendant machines, and two people-shaped blurs hovering over her. The people-shapes were wearing hooded cloaks. Bad guys! He hefted the ten-pound chrome-steel wrench, pushed the door open and lurched in.

There was just enough light to see them turning in response to his entrance; just enough to show something very wrong about the way they looked. Ragged, loose skin that didn't cover ribcages, one empty staring eye-socket, a cheek-bone and part of a rack of grinning teeth exposed to view, as well as the torn, hooded cloaks woven from something like dusty brown hemp-cloth. A hand reduced to bones and ligaments. A couple of tufts of dry yellow hair attached to the side of the head.

Zombie Dominicans!

Elif didn't stop to wonder what zombie Dominicans were doing on-board; he stumbled as close as he dared and swung the wrench at the nearest zombie monk's head. It crumpled like an empty oil can, absorbing the force of the blow. The decayed figure jerked once, stick-thin arms flailing, then it staggered forward, pulling the wrench from his hands, bumping against Tai's bed and raising a small cloud of mildew and dust from its tattered cloak.

It reached up and behind with both hands, found the end of the wrench and tugged downward, pulling it free with the sound of metal scraping on metal. Elif stared at the torn edges of the hole in the back of its head and saw pieces of shiny multicoloured grit like coarse sand falling out. The other zombie had turned to stare, but it was the look on Tai's face that stopped him, a look he knew well: he was being stupid. She kept giving him that look even after he gave her the look that said **What did I do**?; apparently, this time he'd been really stupid.

"They're the Xists. Well, Their puppets. So," seeing comprehension dawn, "yes, they're on our side."

The less damaged zombie turned its awful face to Elif and pointed a withered and dried hand to the dusty rags draped over its chest. "Remote." Its voice was a barely comprehensible monotone buzz.

The dummy turned slightly to address them both. "New language mode of thought understood." Deciding that the last was a question they both nodded, and Tai managed to refrain from shuddering when the damaged zombie monk's left arm fell off. The thing didn't seem to notice. "New information. One thousand minutes. To avoid misunderstanding. Do you have needs is atmosphere acceptable."

Elif thought about it. "Air's okay. We need about, uh, twenty-two percent oxygen."

With some difficulty, the zombie nodded once. "Waiting for new information. One thousand minutes." It took three steps back, closed its eyes and froze. It wasn't moving but Elif suspected They were still listening. He glanced at the badly dented head sitting crookedly atop the first zombie, feeling the burn of having done something really dumb. Tai saw his expression and tried to cheer him up.

"Oh, don't worry about it. They're just remote-control dummies, really old ones. You didn't hurt anybody." When he looked up at this, she added, "You should really read the notes."

"I've been reading the notes ever since we got them. It's not helping."

"Then you should take a copy of mine. Here, give me your phone." She scrolled through some pages about the Xist ship that Elif's notes didn't have. "These dummies aren't new; they're about a thousand years old, left over from the last time any of Them came by here. They're obviously on a budget. I thought once we establish proper communication we could offer Them the spare material They scooped up with us, in exchange for more information."

Ever-practical Tai. He nodded. "More information is good. The notes are, well, there's a lot of it, but I'm starting to see some major gaps. For example, poking around out there I found a couple of Conspiracy devices with a kind of alien look. I'd like to know more about them. The Xists are pretty major figures in the field. They have to know all sorts of interesting things."

TAI spent the next few hours dozing while Elif moved everything useful he could find from the Scoop chambers into her kitchen and garage, stacking the rest in the yard; after all, it wasn't about to rain. He sorted the weapons, took a couple of them over to the far side of his house in the second scoop chamber and nervously tried them out. There were two cheap Magnum knock-offs (weapon of choice for the low-brow suburban street thug – an impressive look, but with an unfortunate tendency to jam and blow off the hand of the idiot firing it) and a couple of nasty Conspiracy specials; matte-black finish, sleek, compact and quiet. Designed to kill rather than impress; good for quietly shooting people in the back, in the dark, at a safe distance. He wandered around the new ruins in Tai's chamber, looted the fast food place for whatever was cooling on the racks, washed it down with some Bivalve and checked back with Tai. He held her hand as she woke up and, trying to keep his movements as unobtrusive as possible, tapped Bat-keyboard codes against her fingers:

Covert information deal.

She replied: Who? Us?

He gave her a frown of mock-exasperation. Them. Best interests. Give away stuff we don't need OK but at some point They won't need us. Not saying subvert their plan. Just find out.

Elif spent two more hours searching through the three and one quarter surviving rooms, seven and one half vehicles and forty-four sets of clothes over in his Scoop chamber. He collected the clothing, including the dark grey Conspiracy agent's midi-skirt suit, stockings and shoes along with anything else he thought might prove useful. He sorted the various drugs into three categories: Commercial (sedatives, painkillers, tobacco and booze), Street (weed, speed, downers and hallucinogens) and Conspiracy (heavy-duty psychotropics for the most part, out of the back of the Conspiracy Agent's van; presumably for interrogations), and hid a selection inside the dusty back of the analogue television set he hadn't turned on in ten years, now sitting in a corner of Tai's garage. He left one can of Bivalve Mutathing on the ground near the hatch as a kind of offering in the hope that the Xists might be able to replicate the stuff, then retreated to Tai's garage with his computer and dived back into the notes.

He had a copy of the files "Bob" had given Tai, but finding anything useful was now twice as hard; he found himself flipping back and forth between her files and his, trying to see a pattern in the differences. He knew it'd be much worse if he tried to merge the two uneven sets of documents. Eventually he gave up on common sense and tried bibliomancy, paging about at random with his eyes closed then seeing where he'd ended up: half-way through a discussion on the nature of Essence.

It read like thirteenth-century religious dogma. Most of the words seemed to have some subtly different meaning from the ones he knew, as if the writers had been forced out of fear to speak in obscure metaphors. He paged back to the front of that section and rolled his eyes in exasperation: the text **was** from the thirteenth century; Richard Rufus of Cornwall. "Gah," he muttered disdainfully, "as if **they** had anything relevant to say. As if they **ever** had anything relevant to say. Their concept of reality was as unfounded as any – "

He stopped, eyes darting about suspiciously. They were probably listening, or at least recording for later scrutiny. He was going to have to be careful about thinking out aloud if he hoped to conceal his motives from Them at all.

Wait – why do I need to conceal my motives from Them?
He chewed his thumbnail nervously.
Because I don't trust Them.

EVENTUALLY the last of their power cells began to run down. They unplugged everything and exchanged worried looks by the slowly blinking red indicator light until Elif remembered his LED torch. Its bright white beam showed the motionless mechanical zombie corpses in all their unpleasant detail, the badly damaged one leaning against the wall of Tai's room.

Elif sighed, located the ten-pound wrench, lifted it and brought it down on the damaged zombie monk's shoulder as hard as he could, striking at an angle which almost severed the misshapen head from the torso. It shook with the blow but didn't move. He leaned close, shouted "EXCUSE ME?", and then knocked the head completely from the shoulders, tumbling the dry body to the floor. He picked up the severed head, holding it by one leathery dry ear-lobe, and shook it. Dust and grit scattered in the light of the torch. "HELLO?"; no response. He raised the crescent wrench with the intention of knocking the zombie monk head into the kitchen, and the other zombie opened its eyes to regard him blankly.

"Don't," it said.

Elif dropped the head, tilted his own to one side and rested the crescent wrench on his shoulder. "Forgotten about us? A human isn't just for Christmas, you know."

It looked down at its broken companion, chin ratcheting jerkily in stages. When it spoke again its voice, while uninflected and neutral, was an improvement on its formerly dry mechanical intonation. "We have finished reviewing the information on your kind. Assimilating. We proceed with the Essence collection phase."

"There are some environmental requirements that need to be met before we go any further. Power. Fresh water and food," Tai said.

"Information," Elif added. Tai nodded in agreement.

The zombie stared at them motionlessly for just long enough for the experience to be uncomfortable before continuing. "Understood. Rooms: prepared, forward section of the ship. When ready: transfer possessions. Other useful mass: store in this chamber. Everything else: recycle. Budget restrictions. All available mass necessary."

ELIF preferred to work alone in the first Scoop chamber. Coming out of the front door of his disintegrating house to be confronted by a one-armed and headless corpse was something that took a while to get used to, even if he knew the thing was made of foam plastic, powergel and smart string. He stood back and regarded the broken zombie as it staggered about, scavenging metal. It had hauled debris: smaller car pieces, bricks, decayed yellow home insulation foam and chunks of concrete, dragging them, with effort, to the recycling bay next to the Scoop chamber. That effort had taken its toll; pieces kept falling off it.

After three hours of this some vital ligament snapped and it fell, awkwardly, to the ground, twitching like a burning Tickle Me Elmo doll.

Elif prodded it with the toe of his engineer boot. The zombie monk convulsed, arching its back, the empty hood flopping about like a loose sock, a dry retching sound coming from the neck-hole; then it fell silent and was still.

He peered down the ragged-edged throat; the thing's innards seemed to be made of writhing, lumpy strings of plastic spaghetti of an unpleasant military green hue. Their roiling worm-like movements slowed, then stopped. He sighed, regarding the rotted thing with distaste. Eventually he grabbed one dry-skinned, sandal-shod foot and dragged the unusually light body forward to the recycling bay.

They had learned that the ship's name was the "Trebuchet Bitchslap", a second-hand Xist Cow-Catcher-class light cruiser. The two Scoop chambers were at one end, one behind the other, like two peas in an otherwise empty pod. The recycling bay was less than two yards long and without detail aside from two tall rectangular surf-board-sized shelves, one on either side: molecular scale disassemblers and printers. Elif put his hands under the dead zombie's armpit, lifted it upright and let the board-stiff form down onto one of the recyclers. It began to gnaw away at the zombie wherever it touched the rough-textured surface. Elif knew it would take about an hour to consume the zombie completely; he'd been feeding the disassemblers with bricks, lumber and lumps of plaster and concrete long enough to learn their limitations.

He wasn't sorry to see the zombie corpse disappear into the machine. It had looked sufficiently human to inspire empathy and revulsion at the same time. The disassembler ate through a cable in the leg; it snapped and the foot twisted outwards, bending up in a hideous parody of dance. Elif drew back instinctively.

He laid a bundle of timber fence-palings on the other disassembler then took a few minutes off to check on Tai, who had set up camp in the next room: a hemi-cylindrical space almost as large as the Scoop chambers with impossibly high-definition video screens covering every surface. The end of the room nearest the recycling bay was indented by six rounded bumps; presumably, fuel or perhaps even weapons pods attached to the outside. The indentations were about three yards across; five of them showed red indicator-lights, dinner-plate sized, each pulsing slightly out of phase with the others. The sixth was dark.

At the far end of the room where the next hatch would be, a slate-coloured ring like a giant dump-truck inner tube sat against the wall. Nestled within was a sphere two yards across, the same dull grey sheen as the hull material. It hung in the air like a soap-bubble: the Essence collector. Unless there were more rooms at the ends, the whole ship was less than fifty yards long.

Elif used half a cup of water to wash the concrete dust from his hands and sat on an empty power cell next to Tai's bed. She was exploring the ship's computer systems, looking for more information. The wall around Tai's bed was overlaid with dozens of overlapping screens projected in the air, rectangular windows crowded with text and images and video flickering and changing faster than Elif could follow, although Tai didn't seem to be having any trouble with it. She noticed him, raised her eyebrows in a gesture that said "aren't I clever?" and brushed aside a cluster of screens with a gesture, exposing a single ultra-wide-screen-sized window with a view of Earth from, Elif estimated, about two hundred miles up; too close to see the horizon.

All of the images they'd ever seen of their home from low orbit were solemnly beautiful. This view was close enough to the surface to see an ugly grey and brown stain spreading out in a circle from the city below. "This is the view NASA doesn't show off," Tai said sadly. They watched angry bruise-coloured plumes mixing with the clouds. "I didn't know we had that much local heavy industry."

"Oh, we don't," Elif assured her. "That's from the cars and trucks... and burning buildings, and the generators people run when the mains power goes out. And cigarette smoke."

The remaining rotting mechanical zombie monk entered the bridge, a thick book bound in black leather under its arm. The thing smiled broadly, an expression involving the lower half of its face, managing to look sinister and unctuous at the same time. The effort of this smile snapped something and the jaw dangled loose, held only by a thin layer of skin. The monk stood there for a moment, regarding them calmly over the unevenly bulging mouth, lower front teeth indenting the torn, thin lips. Carefully it pushed its jaw back into place and held it there with its free hand. Elif produced a roll of duct tape and deftly ran a length from one ear, under the jaw and up over the zombie's patchy, balding pate. "We thank you," it said, voice only slightly muffled by the tape sling.

Tai examined the repair-work, her head tilted to one side. "He looks like a garden gnome, with that beard."

Elif nodded. "It reminds me of Sir Russell Post, the Bugtown assassin."

Tai laughed. "Unless you have a problem with it," she told the rotting zombie monk, "we'll call you Russ."

The Xist made the machine nod. "Acceptable."

Elif stood back and appraised his work. "You don't smile much, do you?"

The mechanical monk turned to look at him with such a natural seeming gesture that for a moment Elif forgot what the thing really was, felt less anxious, then remembered what it was and immediately felt worse. It said "These puppets have been in storage for more than nine hundred years; unfortunately, they weren't designed to last that long. They came as part of the package; information, ship, power cells, scoops, collector and human-interaction puppets. This ship collected the previous sample from your planet."

People sample. Elif tried to see possible implications. "Do you have any records from that, uh, venture? Video, perhaps?"

Russ appeared to pause for thought, the remote's gaze shifting from Elif's eyes, down and to the right. It blinked, slowly; the brow lifted a fraction of an inch as if to say **Oh there it is**. It gestured at the wall and a broad window appeared over the others. Flickering images faded up from dark grey. It was a little difficult to tell at first – there was no sound, and the frame rate kept changing – but quickly, they saw it; a dark room with a group of men clad in roughly sewn grey and brown clothing, seen in silhouette holding their hands out, warming them near a flat video projection of a log fire. One of the zombie monks approached; there was a silent argument and the monk was knocked to the ground and viciously kicked. One by one the men drifted back to the warmth of the video screen. The monk crawled out of sight of the camera.

"We are in position to begin the Essence Collection Phase. Please align yourselves with the Collector."

Elif stared at Russ. "What about those guys? Is that it? Don't you know anything about them, like where they were from and what happened to them?"

"We can discuss this presently; the ship is in position."

Russ gestured at the dull grey sphere floating within the stone ring. Elif helped Tai to sit up, then pushed the bed closer to the ring and sat next to her. For a moment it felt like old times, watching television together, until Russ moved the machine monk to stand uncomfortably close behind them, giving off its pungent odour of wet rot and mildew. "Before we begin this holy and devotional act,"

– Tai glanced at Elif, who replied with a covert let's-go-along-with-this-for-the-moment look – "A few inspirational words from the Good Book are indicated." The zombie monk flicked the book open, thin fingers riffling through the dry onionskin pages. It spoke in a droning monotone for what seemed like ten minutes and, despite having some familiarity with most variations of biblical texts, Elif couldn't place this one, even to within any particular testament, Old, New, Revised or Low-Calorie. It was strewn with archaic words and obscure metaphors beyond comprehensibility, reminding him of the version of the Contract he'd read. Eventually the sermon came to a halt, seemingly in the middle of a sentence. There was another long, awkward pause.

"Uh... amen," Elif murmured.

"Praise god-damned 'Bob'!" Tai said loudly. Elif nudged her with his elbow and frowned. "Sorry," she mock-whispered, obviously not very.

The floating sphere made a dull ringing sound like an underwater temple bell. Its surface rippled, resonating with the sound, and then went through a series of texture changes so quickly that Elif could barely follow them all; matted grass, rippling animal fur, chromed silver metal, asphalt, porous pink chalk and pale, veined flesh. It was flickering back and forth between bright orange spaghetti and bile-green shag carpet when Tai slapped the device, saying sternly "Cut that out." For the brief moment when her hand touched it the Collector froze, presenting the texture of porous orange Terracotta; it resumed changing when she drew her hand back. Elif pressed the palm of his hand against the side; the surface felt like cool, wet glass. The contact ignited an uncomfortable tickling sensation in the base of his brain. The only thing he could compare it to was when he'd once rested his head against the side of an active Van der Graaf generator. He cleared his throat and coughed. The Collector jumped from the look of wet, stained cardboard to hexagonally threaded lavender denim stretched over coin-sized flat discs. He glanced back at Russ's cloak and vividly imagined clearing his throat again: the Collector smoothly morphed to mimic the rough grey-brown Hessian cloth. Tai got the idea quickly and changed the Collector's appearance to a standard touch-keyboard; as soon as she withdrew her hand, the square keys drawn on the curved surface became hexagons, then interlocked Escher tiles, then seven-sided leaves in bright green which appeared to grow legs and scuttle around to the back of the sphere. Elif repeated what he'd decided was the trigger thought and pictured a cloudscape wrapped around a slowly-turning planet. The Collector changed to match his visualisation.

"We're supposed to be choosing targets," Tai reminded him, "so maybe we should be selecting territory to include. Or exclude."

"Humans are obsessed with borders and territory," Russ mused. "Exercise your other primate talent: marking other primates as friends or enemies. Review your memories for examples of suitable Essence donors. The Collector will create a template, and make its selection based on that template and suitably high levels of Essence."

Tai gave Elif a worried look. He waved his free hand, said "I can do that. I know the kind of people it wants. You're far too innocent."

"You sure you don't have any moral problems with this?"

Elif shrugged. "If they were people I knew personally and cared about, I might. If I had to sit across from them and watch as their heads imploded, I might. They're all outside my 'monkeysphere', and we can't see the process happening, so it's sufficiently abstracted for me to ignore."

Tai raised one eyebrow at this. He continued, "Above all, there's no accountability here. I'm not going to be held responsible for this, at least not by any agency I acknowledge – " Tai waved this aside, recognising the start of his familiar "accountability" rant – "so, hell, yes. Let's do this thing," trying to project a note of lightness in a situation that was becoming increasingly heavy.

The Collector's surface twitched beneath his hand. He rubbed his fingers against it; wet, cool glass. Then it felt like sandpaper; like warm, sticky rubber, like cold concrete studded with a regular grid of bumps; the heads of nails, perhaps. The cloudscape cleared and the device projected a convincing illusion of a clear glass sphere filled with intricate machinery in silver and chrome; steampunk-ornate cogs, levers, cams, rods and curved wire tracks winding in and out. It looked like an insanely elaborate and pointless Survival Research Laboratories art machine built by a deranged clockmaker; eye-catchingly beautiful, and as far as Elif could see, without any mechanical purpose beyond being eye-catchingly beautiful.

He concentrated on the trigger impulse thought, cleared his throat to encourage the trigger. Movement began at the centre of the device: clear glass marbles the size of ping-pong balls were carried up to the start of a track by an off-centre pin-wheel from somewhere within the maze of interconnected mechanisms. One by one the spheres ran down a spiral path, bounced off a series of shifting pins and onto different tracks that led them back into the middle of the structure. Elif shook his head and tried to drag his gaze away; his natural tendency to try to work out what a machine was doing made it difficult. He closed his eyes and concentrated. **Bad people**. Conspiracy People. Think, damn it.

He thought about a local politician, an arrogant and opinionated cross between Boss Hogg and the tycoon from the Monopoly board with a touch of Snidely Whiplash added. He thought of all the petty, minor government functionaries he'd ever dealt with; the ones who took a perverse pleasure in snaring people in webs of contradictory regulations. He remembered being called in to fix an air conditioner in the office of a particularly porcine defence contractor who had ignored him while shovelling cocaine off the touch-screen of his 'phone and shouting at a subordinate.

Like so many near the top of the ladder he was a white male in his fifties; receding hair; overweight, eyes bloodshot behind expensive wire-rimmed tinted glasses. His hands had twitched as he pushed the yellowish powder about on the glass surface; he gave off a stink of fear-sweat and rancid hormones. While belittling his secretary he was a bored, disdainful patriarch; while trying to push the right buttons to call his next victim he was an angry four-year-old denied a toy he didn't really want. The disparity between the two states gave an impression of borderline schizophrenia.

Elif remembered the sneering look the Conspiracy Agent had given while pointing the gun at him. The intensity of that moment was enough to give the Collector a good idea of what kind of person it was looking for: it clicked and whirred and the spheres were directed down a different series of tracks leading through a Laocoön of coils; when they came out the other side, each sphere had taken on a sullen, dark anodised metallic purple colouration. They then rolled into an ornate rack, clicking together as if magnetised.

Tai was looking at a cinemascope-proportioned screen that had formed on the wall next to the stone ring that held the Collector. It showed a night-time overhead view of the city, slowly passing by underneath. The ship's passage was marked by sporadic failures in the power grid; lights went out and then hesitantly flickered back to life. She turned to face the rotting zombie monk and asked "Russ... what exactly is 'Essence'?"

The mechanical man-shaped thing stared at her blankly. "Residue of parasitic energy-form, attracted to neurological signal complexity. Virtual-particle-informatic equivalent of–" it paused–"yoghurt."

She stared back at him in a manner that would have said, to anyone else, "I want a different explanation." Russ either didn't know enough about human expression to take the look's meaning or didn't want to elaborate; she had to prompt him with a wave of her hand.

"Neural activity generates patterns of electrical energy. If the patterns are sufficiently complex, they attract simple creatures formed entirely of energy, the same way that larger physical creatures attract bacteria and parasites. These energy creatures form a relationship with their hosts, granting survival characteristics such as consciousness, awareness, detailed memory, the ability to plan and to form models of their environment."

Tai frowned. "I thought those things were just functions of neural complexity."

Russ raised an index finger in a reflexively sacerdotal gesture; Tai supposed that the alien controlling the machine probably had a whole range of priestly poses prepared in advance, ready at the touch of a key, or whatever the Xists used. "The most basic variations of consciousness come from the emergent interaction of complex neural structures. They become more effective, in terms of survival, when that activity attracts 'Aetherics' – energy parasites. The elaborate human mythology surrounding reincarnation and 'the soul' in general is a result of misunderstanding the relationship between the physical component – " it pointed at Tai's forehead – "and the non-corporeal element." It indicated the growing stack of purple metal marbles in the base of the Collector. "There are twenty-three basic types with minor variations in size, appetite and ability. Some of the less common variety are able to communicate with each other over a distance, providing their hosts with telepathy. Some help regulate the host's body, extending its life. Some encourage feelings of aggression, leading the hosts to expand their territory and produce more offspring suited to supporting that Aetheric."

Elif stopped staring at the Collector's machinery and asked "Thought-forms?", thinking **oh, hey, someone's trying to sell me an invisible Brooklyn Bridge again.**

Russ turned to face him, tendons creaking with the effort. "Thought-forms implies origin within the mind. Aetherics exist independently of physical forms; they have, if I may desecrate the metaphor, one foot in the physical realm, one in the world of energy and one in the informatic sphere. They can pass through solid matter or influence it; they can travel between dimensions. They can be contained with the appropriate technology."

Tai gazed at the purple metal spheres. "And Elder Gods like to huff them."

Russ appeared slightly pained at the coarse expression. "More or less." The robot monk froze, again for a socially awkward length of time, then continued: "We cannot reveal the nature of our end client, but be assured you will both be well paid for your services."

Elif rubbed his lower lip with his index finger. "Added flavour."

"SubGenii carry a slightly different array of Aetherics, some of which can alter the harmonic overplurality of unrefined Essence. A few days' exposure will quadruple the worth of our cargo."

The last of the spheres clunked into place and sat with its companions, giving off a vague sensation of... something unpleasant. As if the contents resented being squeezed into little balls. Elif said "But you don't need to extract anything from us, right? We're not edible in that sense?"

Russ gave him a thin smile. "Everyone is edible to someone. Don't worry; you're worth more to us alive."

J UDGING from Russ' growing skill with the modern conversational mode, Tai felt the ice had been broken and asked, "So what was with the devotional sermon? Didn't you know we were SubGenii?"

Russ directed the remote to give a slightly embarrassed look. "We were still assimilating the new cultural information. The 'Good Book' routine worked quite well with the previous sample, except for the single SubGenius in the group." Seeing Elif counting on his fingers, Russ forestalled his objections: "Yes, that was nine hundred years before the founding of your faith; however, the genetic and Aetheric patterns that make up a SubGenius appear frequently throughout your world's history." The video window showing the men around the fake log-fire reappeared; the screen zoomed in on a young man sitting by himself off to one side. He had short, pale tonsured hair, wore a simple dark grey robe and had the general disposition of a nerd trapped in a locker-room full of jocks.

"We don't have any detailed records relating to the others, but his name was Sybrandis deVonk, Rassaphore of some minor Catholic schism. Sybrandis was considered something of a trouble-maker; inducted into the order to keep him from spreading his inadvertent heresy. The sort of person who could start a fist-fight simply by asking the wrong questions." Elif knew that one very well, and nodded. "It was that disestablishmentarian attitude that kept the others from killing him. In a way, they respected him more than they did the priest."

Tai grinned. "He was a SubGenius, all right." They watched the young man helping the damaged mechanical monk to its feet, brushing dust from his robe respectfully and glancing at the other men nervously as if expecting a beating himself. "What happened to them?"

Russ was staring at the screen, giving the impression of someone lost in memories. "They died," he said presently, with a trace of sadness. "Knife fights... one, drowned in his soup by the others. Sybrandis survived them all and died of old age at the Xist exchange point that is our destination. This once belonged to him," Russ held out the leather-bound book. Elif took it and carefully leafed through the pages.

Tai was still looking at the screen. In a deceptively casual tone she asked Russ, "So, did you fuck him?"

Russ didn't rise to the taunt. "No, but the director of the previous sample mission did, via the remote," gesturing at the mechanical monk's chest. "Sybrandis seemed to expect it. It was, at least, consensual. As much as it could be under the circumstances. He was the only one of them who understood what was happening; the others thought they'd died and gone to heaven, and were bitterly disappointed it wasn't what they'd – "

Tai looked up at the monk. It was motionless, its mouth half-open, hands folded behind its back. "Ping?" she asked. She nudged it with her foot; it rocked slightly then settled. She nudged it again, slightly harder, and it would have toppled over if Elif hadn't grabbed its sleeve.

"What is with this bible?" he muttered, not taking his eyes off the pages. "It's printed. Typeset. But as far as I know, Gutenberg didn't do that until the fourteenth century. Can't see anything that looks like a new testament... the Pentateuch is a, what," flipping through the start of the book, "a dodeca-teuch... and, get this, the page numbers are in octal. Russ, is this some kind of Xist joke bible?" There was no answer.

"Elif? I think he's out to lunch."

Elif looked up from the book, studied the still form and prodded it distastefully with his index finger. "Off with the fairies. Oh well," he sighed, closing the bible and shoving it under Russ' arm, "I guess we're in charge now. Ship: what's our heading?" The ship didn't answer. "Maybe I should hit him with the wrench. It worked last time."

Abruptly the monk resumed speaking: " – been led to expect. Excuse me. This remote is close to complete systems failure. I shouldn't have let my assistant do all that heavy lifting with it."

"Assistant? Was he the one controlling the other monk? The one Elif broke?" Tai asked. Elif blushed at the memory.

Russ nodded. "We take turns at operating this unit, and he is not very good at it. He's not my brother, but you can call him Ron. We must make a brief stop before we go much further." The video of the eleventh century peasants was replaced with an ornate map crowded with animated symbols connected by unevenly dotted lines. Russ pointed to several icons in turn. "We, here; open market, here; gap in the Convocation Exclusion zone, here."

Elif peered at the map, trying to work out which symbol meant what. "So we aren't orbiting Earth any more?"

Russ pointed to a tiny dot in the lower left-hand corner of the window. "That cluster of stars includes your planet's primary, about seventy-five light years away."

Elif glanced about the room and bounced up and down on his toes, as if testing the ship's suspension. "Of course I'd have to be completely paranoid to imagine we haven't moved at all and that you were making it all up as you go along."

"I could open the rear hatch and you could take a look for yourself. How long can you hold your breath?" Russ sneered.

Elif gave him the finger. "Convocation? Exclusion zone?"

Russ turned to face them both, hands clasped behind his back (Tai imagining the Xist had pressed the "assume a lecturing pose" macro on the mechanical monk's control panel). "As you might imagine, a civilisation's influence extends only as far as it can enforce its laws. If a problem affects more than one civilisation, they will pool their resources to solve it. The Convocation is an uneven alliance between factions of the Spree – "

Elif put in, "I've heard of them. Cockroaches, right?"

Russ stopped long enough to show his displeasure at being interrupted. " – the Abandoners, several other groups of no importance and, unfortunately, some of the more annoyingly moral Xist clades. The problem they are united against is the illicit traffic in Essence."

There was a moment's pause while they took that in. Tai summarised the situation: "So... we're running an illegal drug past a line of cops which includes some of your own people."

Russ waved his hand dismissively. "Xist society – if you could call it that – is less cohesive even than the many and varied tribes of humanity. We belong to a group known as the Emergency Xists, defined by certain preferences in physical forms and our infamous proactive attitude. Many have nothing to do with the rest of the universe, preferring to spend their time in contemplation. We prefer a more hands-on approach." The monk indicated an irregular coil of grey diamond-shaped symbols that stretched across the screen. "The Convocation has established an Exclusion zone of long-distance sensors between one of the larger clusters of Essence farms – which includes your world – and what is considered the civilised part of the galaxy. Regular patrols of warships enforce their intent, which varies in severity from confiscating the cargo to destroying anyone who passes by. While the zone is too large to detour in any practical manner, there are gaps through which a small ship can pass undetected."

Tai turned her head to one side and squinted in an attempt to see the helix as a wall. "They're only after the bigger ships. Couldn't someone use lots of small ships like this one to move the cargo?"

"Yes. It is done. However, that cuts into the profit margin sufficiently to make it impractical on a large scale."

Elif was trying to establish which of the icons represented their ship. "Can't your clients travel to the farms, shoot up and then go home?"

Russ swivelled the monk's eyes toward Elif, an expression that conveyed more than a trace of suspicion. "We will not be tricked into revealing details of our end client. All you need to know is that they prefer, in general, to remain in one place." The monk managed a wry twist of its lips. "You would not want them to visit your world, I can assure you."

Elif rolled his eyes. "You can knock it off with the client confidentiality thing. We know it's an Elder God. Or Elder Gods. Would they lose anything by having a pair of primates know their shameful secret?"

Russ tilted his head back and closed his eyes; an oddly reverent pose. "If you had any experience in dealing with them, you would show a little more respect."

Elif gave his quiet, hissing laugh, tried to think of something irreverent to say, then decided the laugh would do.

THE monk remained motionless with its eyes closed as the symbols on the map slowly shifted and rotated in a manner suggestive of motion through some notional set of higher dimensions. Some icons grew fainter, others larger, while the coil of diamond-shapes writhed and flexed but remained a prominent feature of the display. Neither SubGenius wanted to speak out loud, knowing that Russ was probably still listening.

Presently Elif decided to break the silence. "I hope we can get something to eat at this place we're going."

Staring at the display, Tai said distractedly "I'm not really hungry. There's some packet soup if you want it."

"Oh." Feeling awkward, Elif racked his brains for something to say. "Um, what flavour?"

Tai looked up from the screen, eyes unfocused, recollecting. "Green, or purple."

Elif grimaced. "I guess I'm not really hungry either." He wandered over to the Collector, which had lapsed into a dull grey metallic texture, prodded it. It felt like metal. "Do you believe any of that crap about Aetherics and energy parasites? It all sounds suspiciously like a certain other insane-religious-saucer-cult-scam-which-I-won't-name."

Tai shrugged. "It could be a metaphor for something a little more, um, grounded in what we know of the real world. Or it could be real." She closed her eyes and thought about it some more. "Would explain a few things. Magic, and why it's so inconsistent. The ability to heal others. Or influence them. Maybe even control them. Think about some of the more famous weirdos from history with magic powers. They could have had Aetherics helping them. It could even explain the myths about paradise, or that whole tower of Babel thing. The Pentecost thing. Although you'd think if these creatures conveyed any real advantage to survival, they'd still be around today."

Elif considered this, then tugged the old book from underneath Russ' arm and flipped through the pages before remembering it didn't have a new testament. He scowled. "Did you notice how that breakdown conveniently got him out of having to explain this?"

In the voice she used to placate Elif's more paranoid trains of thought, Tai said "Well, if he can get repaired at this market, he won't have that excuse any more, will he?"

Elif's scowl deepened. "He'll come up with some other excuse. Gah, he probably printed this thing out himself, as a prop to impress the Breughel crowd." At Tai's questioning look he explained, "the Dutch guys. I'm assuming they were Dutch. 'deVonk' is a Dutch name."

"But the book is in English, isn't it? He was reciting English."

Elif sighed. "Gods, I don't know. Some kind of... old-fashioned... thing... well, here, look at it."

He passed the book to her; she peered at the dark brown letters through her wire-frames and nodded slowly. "Yeah. I see what you mean. Just on the far side of comprehensible, unless you're a medieval scholar. Not a lot of use, really."

Elif considered this. "Could come in handy if we run out of cigarette papers."

Tai gave him her mildest disparaging look. He made a concilia-
tory gesture. "Don't worry, if I'm going to smoke any 'frop, I'll do
it in the far scoop chamber."

Abruptly the monk spoke: "Bathroom unit has finished printing.
Set it down in scoop one, press the black button, stand back."

They both stared at it. The words had had none of Russ' now-
practiced tones. They could have come out of a Speak-n-Spell:
completely devoid of inflection. It didn't say anything else.

Elif nodded toward the hatch leading to the back of the ship.
"Come on. This should be good."

H E helped Tai to the top of the ramp, then dragged the heavy
white foam cube down to where the soil had been cleared away
at the base. He touched the black spot on top and stepped back
prudently. Slowly the flat sides and top bulged out, inflating until it
resembled a mushroom-cap shaped footstool about a yard across. A
tree-root pattern of black lines swept over the top, faded back into
white. They waited; nothing else happened.

"That's it?" Tai peered at the shape. "I was expecting something
a little more elaborate." Elif prodded it; the surface dimpled and
smoothed over again. He looked up at Tai, who frowned. "I'm not
looking forward to having to squat over that."

The mechanical monk limped out of the recycling bay to stand
next to Tai. "Not finished," it said, in its spare telemarketer voice.
"One hour."

"Ron?" Elif asked tentatively.

The machine stared at him, its face empty of expression. "Pleased
to meet you," sounding anything but. It wavered from side to side,
then settled on its right leg; with a soft click the left leg detached
at the knee and fell to the deck, foot wrapped in dirty grey cloth.
Elif retrieved it, examined the complex knot of struts and cables at
the broken end and gave Ron an apologetic look.

Tai said "Ron... what Russ told us about Aetherics... is that
true?"

The machine turned to face her, neck tendons creaking. "Yes."

"Is there any way we can see them? Do they have a shape?"

"No. No." Abruptly the machine trembled, almost fell; the face
took on a faintly concerned pondering look: **How do I explain**

this to these primitive apes? It continued in Russ' voice.

"Consider the instructions that go to make up a computer program. Do they have a shape? If you render the program as a flow chart, yes; however, it's an abstraction only partly related to the program's function, and it's the function of Aetherics you should be concerned with, not what they look like."

Elif considered crossing his arms but decided it might look confrontational. "Demonstrate."

Russ smiled humourlessly. "Allow me." The monk beckoned to Elif; cautiously, he stepped up the ramp and stood just outside its reach. Russ held up his hand, palm out. Elif did the same, holding his hand a few inches from Russ'. The monk's smirk softened to tolerant amusement; he gently pushed Elif's hand aside and pointed his palm at Elif's forehead. Russ asked "Can you factorise the number seventy-eight?"

Elif thought. "Should be easy... two, three... uh, and thirteen." Russ nodded.

Elif thought he saw a violet flash of light; not from the palm of the monk's hand but from a point between its eyes. He felt a trace of a shock, as if remembering being slapped across the face. "I have disengaged the Aetheric that assists your inherent numeracy. It takes a few moments for the effects to show; they will only last for five minutes. Aetherics are quite resilient... now, can you factorise the number one hundred and sixty-two?"

Elif gave a confident nod, held up two fingers, then three, holding four fingers on his other hand over them: two times three to the power of four. He grinned.

Russ beckoned him closer, waved his hand over Elif's forehead as if scanning for signs of life. "You have an unusual array of Aetherics, even for a SubGenius. Your Numeracy is partly fused with Speech Generation. Can you describe how you feel?"

Elif's grin faded. His eyes darted from side to side as if examining his internal control board for alarms. His hand went to his throat, thumb nestled in the hollow above his breast-bone, his heart racing. He could almost feel the gaps in his mind where the words had been. He opened his mouth then closed it slowly, realising it wasn't going to work. He glared at Russ, hefted the piece of leg he was holding as if about to club him with it, then wrinkled his nose, dropped the leg and stalked off to the second scoop chamber with as much dignity as he could muster.

H E sat at the top of the ramp with his back against the outer hatch, idly shuffling through a pack of Tarot cards. Seventy-eight of them. He could see the symbols but couldn't say the words; couldn't even hear them in his mind. It was uncomfortably like needing to sneeze. He remembered the peasants kicking the monk to the ground, grimaced, began to understand their anger and nodded.

The first time he'd been abducted They (They were all part of Them, no matter which race They were) had treated him like a wild animal; ignored his attempts at communication, showed him what they'd wanted and threatened him with electric shocks until he'd complied. He'd thought things would be a little different this time around. He was annoyed that Russ had felt such a demonstration was necessary. On the other hand, the fact that Russ **had** felt it necessary meant that perhaps there was reason to show them the stick. That there was something Russ was afraid they might do, or not do. Which was cause for hope.

Unless, of course, that's what Russ wanted them to think.

A N hour later he went back into the first scoop chamber, still unable to speak. The bathroom unit had grown into a geodesic dome the size of a four-person tent with an arched doorway, finished in smoothly rounded white, like moulded plastic or porcelain. He peered inside; to the left, a standard toilet bowl; to the right, a bath/shower alcove large enough for two people, and ahead, a basin set at waist height. The fittings were all made of the same white material; it felt like hollow plastic when he flicked a fingernail against a wall. He could taste damp air around the shower alcove. He considered testing the materials by hitting a wall with the big wrench but couldn't summon the enthusiasm for even a token act of vandalism; besides, it would probably just grow back.

He thought of Russ' broken leg; he rooted around in the untidy stacks of salvaged building materials, found a rusty metal rod about a foot long, as thick as his thumb, spirally grooved: a spar from a section of reinforced concrete, one end mirror-bright where the scoop had cut through. He picked up his faithful roll of duct tape and the detached robot monk's foot – which was where he'd left it, at the top of the ramp – and went into the bridge. Tai was lying on her bed; Russ standing next to her, pointing to clouds of symbols on the map screen.

Elif jammed the end of the spar into the ragged end of the detached leg's knee joint, screwed it around until it was firmly seated, then strode over to Russ, knelt, pushed up the hem of his robe and grabbed the broken leg stump. He forced the metal spar up into the thigh, twisting it around until the broken ends met, then wound duct tape around the join, over the kneecap and down to the calf, until it held. The foot was pointing at about ten o'clock from normal, but the monk was able to stand on it. Russ tested the leg, stamping the foot three times; it held.

"Crude, but effective," he said. "Elif, I apologise for the mishap with your Aetherics. I should have scanned you first. There is a veterinary service at the market that can repair the fault; that will be our first order of business."

Elif gave him a forced, mirthless smirk, then gained Tai's attention, raised his eyebrows and nodded to the left: **are you coming with us**?

"I'd like to tag along, but I'm too tired," she said quietly. "If you see anything interesting, take some video. Oh, and get a souvenir if they sell them." To Russ, she said "Can we afford souvenirs?"

"We can," Russ assured her. "On top of the revenue from the sale of the raw materials we scooped, there is the media stored in your computers. While only a few races have any inherent interest in human-oriented entertainment, films and songs are very popular with humanoid slaves, even if they are in an alien language. Elif, the films on your computer will prove very popular, particularly the science-fiction action extravaganzas; there are few things funnier than the idea of humans venturing into space under their own efforts. Your pornography collection will prove quite profitable. Tai: most of your video collection is natural history documentaries, and while the images are, in their own way, interesting and perhaps even beautiful... I hesitate to distribute them, in case anyone decides that Earth is worth visiting."

"You wouldn't want people raiding the place," she agreed.

Russ nodded. "That planet and its contents belong to us." He turned his head slightly toward the rear of the ship. "We have docked. Elif, bring your computer."

THE walls were plain, undecorated grey stone framing a rectangular space the size of a two-car garage. One end closed around the ship in a circular collar; Elif was reminded of the time a Discordian had shoved a hot-dog bun into the mail slot of his letterbox. He would have liked to examine the exposed end of the ship's hull, but Russ beckoned him away.

The air was cool, damp and had a faint musty scent Elif associated with underground concrete structures. He followed Russ down the wide, dark and disappointingly rectilinear corridor, shining the torch around and trying to spot some detail, anything; an advertisement, a security camera, a ventilation slot. The corridor was bare, at least of things he could see.

Russ paused, favouring his good leg, and beckoned Elif closer. "There are some things you need to know about the social environment we are about to enter. In particular, that humanity occupies a low position, somewhere below third-class slave and just above vermin. In some places humans are tolerated, and this is one of them: a smuggler's exchange point. This is where criminals do business: pirates, thieves, drug dealers, gun-runners, kidnappers and slavers. I have told the local security that you belong to me, but I would advise against exploration. I don't want to have to buy you back from the local animal shelter."

Elif nodded. The monk seemed tired; it sagged against its bones for a moment. "Ahead, first on the right: take me there. Leave your computer there also. Six doors down, again on the right, is the specialist I have engaged to aid you. Don't talk to anyone else. Go there, enjoy your treatment, then go across the hall and straight down to the cafeteria, where I have arranged for a meal. I will meet you there when the technicians are done with – ", gesturing to itself, then slowly toppling over to one side and falling to the stone floor in a cloud of dust. Elif crouched to stare at the rotting mask that lay on the front of the machine's skull like an uncooked pizza. The eyes slowly swivelled to point away from each other.

Elif gnawed his lower lip, shrugged, grabbed the zombie by its good foot and was about to drag it away when he heard something behind them in the corridor leading back to the ship. Was Tai coming out to join them? He stopped and listened: silence. Then, quite distinctly, one after the other in a slow, uneven pattern: metallic rapping sounds, loud enough to echo; the footsteps of something with more than four legs. He waited until the sounds faded, turned to walk away again: a gentle breeze blew up the corridor, carrying a trace of the smell of almonds and swamp gas. It had to be coming from the ship.

If it was Tai, she would have called out. Was it Russ? They'd been told that the rotting zombie monk was operated by remote control, directed, Elif had assumed, from a compartment somewhere on the ship, with Xist atmosphere, air pressure and temperature. Maybe Russ had put on an Xist spacesuit and was coming out to shop. He shrugged again and hefted the leg.

Elif dragged the dead thing over to the next garage-door gap in the corridor. It led to a warehouse-sized space filled with stacks of flat boxes, each one a different colour, the sides barnacled with sensors, digital manifests, blinking lights, data ports and enigmatic-looking grilles. They were stacked seven or eight high, each stack slowly grinding across the stone floor, turning to face a neighbour and conversing with flashing indicators. He watched them for a while, and then set his computer down on the floor next to Russ' dead body, which was leaking clear fluid and starting to smell worse than before. He left with only two backward glances to see if the shifting columns had taken any notice. Judging from their movements, they hadn't.

Four of the five doors he passed opened onto empty warehouse spaces, at least as far as he could tell with only his torch to light the darkness. At the back of the fifth were two pallid figures with about eight limbs between them; one of them flung up a tentacle to protect its face from the torch's glare. Elif turned the beam away quickly, waved in a vaguely apologetic manner and moved into a small courtyard with a domed roof lit by drifting motes of pink-white light that slowly dimmed and brightened over time. The place seemed empty, his footsteps echoing from the bare walls. Nothing else moved. For a few moments he entertained the idea that the entire structure was empty except for the moving crate towers and those two in the fifth warehouse space, and that Russ intended to abandon him here. He wrinkled his nose and shook his head.

A faint whirring sound came from the other side of the courtyard. Prudently, Elif retreated into the corridor and peered around the corner. A smoothly rounded grey shape like a shopping cart wrapped in cling-film cautiously peeped out of a doorway then darted into the courtyard with the furtive speed of an embarrassed customer coming out of a pornographic florist's. Elif aimed his 'phone at it and recorded some video. The shape spun about, seemed to notice him, made a noise like a horse's whinny and fled into a side corridor.

The first door on his right was a narrow slot that extended up to the ceiling, five yards above. The pink lights made the place look like a cheap nineties retro rave; all he needed was a glow-stick and a cherry-flavoured energy drink, mentally rendering the concepts in crude pictograms in his absence of words. At the end of the alcove was a large, abundantly padded dark grey dentist's chair; above it, three thick glass aquarium walls containing cloudy water speckled with green fluorescent scum and in the middle, a squid large enough to fill the entire tank. The squid's skin rippled with silver chromatophores and iridophores drawing an evolving cellular-automata pattern on its rounded form. At least six of its many tentacles hung over the edge of a slot in the glass, rippling with green and blue stripes, below a single eye the size of a hub-cap. Compared to the mobile disco on its body, the eye was just large, enigmatic and dark. Elif wondered if this was the doctor, or part of the décor. He didn't think he'd have any trouble treating it like another intelligent being. He smiled and waved. The squid waved back with three tentacles, then gestured to the chair.

For a moment his paranoia rose up; he was in the middle of deciding whether to panic or not when a faint wave of warmth passed through him. It was barely noticeable, but enough to make him stop and –

– there was that tickling sensation again, in the back of his brain. If the squid was an Aetheric doctor, it would naturally be able to manipulate its patients through their Aetherics. His anxiety faded; he sat down on the padded chair, lay back and closed his eyes.

The squid laid a thick tentacle over his forehead, with the faintest suggestion of a caress, then it poked tentacles into his ears, right down to the ear-drum. The first tentacle held him down as he gasped and jerked up at the feeling. **Just relax**, he told himself, taking a slow, deep breath. **It's not going to hurt me but I may experience some dizziness. Let's take a look.**

More stray tentacles waved over his face, their tips glittering with iridophores. **Whoever did this wasn't very careful**, Elif thought. **What a mess. Substrate Aetherics all over the place, and the Linguistic Actuator is missing altogether. Hmm. Owner is an Xist. Why am I not surprised?**

The implications of having an owner irritated Elif more than he'd thought they would. "He's not my owner. I just work for him," he said carefully. "Holy crap!" His voice had returned.

You humanoids pray to some unusual deities, he thought. **The last one I worked on was part of a culture that worshipped those glands the females have on their chests. The round ones, you know?**

Elif knew. "Oh, yes. What's so strange about that? Streamlining, source of nourishment for the young, clear visual signal of a healthy potential partner, something comfortable to lay your head against, what's not to like?", jabbering aimlessly with the sheer joy of being able to use words again.

Obsessive. Overdeveloped visual cortex. Looking at a culture, you get to recognise the signs. I'm not sure it's such a good idea.

"You're hardly one to talk about overdeveloped visual cortices," almost stumbling over the words, leaning back to stare, upside-down, into that huge single eye. It didn't glow or try to hypnotise him with its abyssal depths or even look particularly alien, but Elif could now feel phantom feelers hesitantly probing his mind, each touch causing a successively stronger wrenching, dizzying shift in attitude. He felt a sense of being disconnected from reality – imagining his experiences of the past few days to be some elaborate kind of street theatre – followed by a rush of sadness at the few things back on Earth that he'd thought worth hanging on to. Things he actually missed. Other people, even if they were Pinks who couldn't help being irritating just by being Pink. Then it surged over him: a sense of complete trust in the squid (***Doctor Squid, if you don't mind – I am a qualified veterinarian, you know***) verging on affection, then marching right over the edge into love. He loved the squid. The warm intensity of the emotion made him feel like he was sinking into the chair's padding. He closed his eyes again and exhaled, feeling completely safe. *I don't often have the opportunity to talk to my clients. Most of them aren't able to form words. Now, in order to repair the mess your owner left I must replace some of your substrate Aetherics. This will be disorienting, but in the long term you'll be much better for it. Would you like something to bite down on?*, waving a tentacle before him.

"No thanks. It's a very nice tentacle, by the way. I really like the colours."

Thank you! Okay. There seem to be a lot of empty slots here. I'll just put in some useful modules...

He could see faint traces of the patterns he saw when he rubbed his eyes; slowly turning grids, spirals, pulsing balloons of silver light. "What do you mean by 'useful modules'?"

You're from a Crash culture, so Mechanical Affinity is always useful... Spatial Locative... Lifesense, to improve your chances of finding a partner – it's also an element of the translation array, so it'll help in understanding others... if you had the power to run it, I'd put in a Nextstep Prescience, but your low-slots are filled with bee-see-esses and... stuff... typical... so I'll throw in a Merest Hint. You won't be able to see into the Unhappening but it will let you know if something is about to kill you.

Elif was trying to remember it all in case he got the chance to ask someone reliable what it meant. "What's a... Crash culture?"

A Skull farm where the natives are allowed to use tools to make better tools. It starts with sharp rocks and ends with fission bombs and deathbeams.

Elif knew that scenario all too well. "Sucks to be us. Is there any way out of that social dead-end?"

What, do I look like an anarchist? I'd lose my license if I even suggested your kind should examine their goals and find a reason for existing beyond unchecked reproduction and territorial games. It may look like a dead end to you, but in the deeper view it's right where you're supposed to be.

"But I don't want to be just another pissed-off ape among billions of other pissed-off apes."

One of the tentacles curled, uncurled, flashed blue and green like a barber's pole. *Then don't be. Devote some thought to what you do want to be before you start looking for another rock to perch on. There. How does that feel?*

Elif paused, took a deep breath. It was like the rush he'd felt after eating at the Temple of Mass Consumption, but without the nausea and giddy, aimless anger. Slowly he said "For the first time in my life I feel like I have both hands on the wheel – uh, I mean, I'm swimming in clear water. Thank you." He smiled up at the eye with genuinely felt warmth as the squid touched a tentacle to a row of billiard-ball sized spheres set into the floor of the tank. **We're done**, with the implication he should get up and leave. He didn't want to. "Can I stay here with you? There has to be something I can do."

There was the impression of a smile in the sweeping skin-patterns. *That's the Attractant Aetheric I use to keep humanoids calm while I'm working on them. It'll wear off in a while... although you are quite attractive, for a primate.* A pause. *How long can you hold your... no, I'm being unprofessional. The Attractant works both ways, unfortunately – makes it difficult to be objective. One last piece of advice: think only of yourself. Statistically, more people survive if they think only of themselves.*

Elif raised an eyebrow. "Russ told you to say that, didn't he?"

Russ did.

"Then that's what I'll do, unless I know Russ is watching, in which case I'll do the exact opposite." Elif tried to remember where he was supposed to go next, and a vivid visualisation of where he'd been and the side-corridors he'd glimpsed on the way came to mind. The layout suggested the building was a broad cylindrical tower. "Hey," impressed, "hey hey hey. That's very useful. Is there any documentation for the stuff you've added?"

Experiment. You can't break anything, so feel free to explore. And watch out for the shark.

Slowly, "Always a good idea."

ELIF stared at the bread roll he'd picked up from the counter. It was saucer-shaped, dusted with light-blue flour and smelled delicious but was so hard he couldn't tear any off. He didn't want to risk his teeth on it. He dipped it in the bowl of cashew-flavoured yoghurt/soup; the roll wasn't at all soup-absorbent. The food had been sitting on the counter, freely available as far as he could tell – at least, nobody had asked for any money. He watched some of the other customers come up and take it before he dared to do the same. Russ had said he'd paid for it.

He wiped yoghurt off the end of the roll and gave in to his growing sense of frustration, repeatedly bashing the bread against the rounded table edge; it flipped out of his grasp, spun in the air and bounced into the personal space of the next diner. He froze, not daring to breathe.

There were a couple of obvious non-humans off to one side, non-oxygen-breathers safe inside their mechanical power-armour or environment suits, but the majority of the patrons were variations on the basic humanoid frame dressed in coarse-woven grey and brown pyjamas. Some were taller, some shorter; some with skin tinted light blue or dark slate grey, some bald, some with bright fluorescent green hair, and some with long, furry rabbit ears. The grey-skinned guy next to him was easily half again his height and at least three times as heavy, all of it in solid, broad-shouldered muscle. He didn't seem offended by Elif's careless bread tossing; he finished sipping from his yoghurt-soup bowl, picked up the roll and easily broke it into three uneven pieces, returning two and keeping the smallest segment for himself.

Elif breathed again. He had no idea what was acceptable behaviour here; the humanoids – all of them male – seemed to be primate-based, presumably with primate territorial instincts, yet nobody argued. There was a definite sense of being in a high-security prison. Elif couldn't see any guards, gun emplacements or cameras but the others behaved as if something was watching them carefully; something armed. There were no fights; no hierarchy games. Nobody spoke and despite Elif's only just having recovered the use of his voice, he didn't want to say anything until someone else did. It wasn't as if any of them would understand him, anyway, although if they did, he'd've confirmed a lot of awful suspicions.

Other humanoids came in, ate, and left. Elif finished his soup and, chewing on a chunk of bread and with nothing better to do, wandered over to gawk at the aliens. At first he thought they were playing some kind of chess; the beige-coloured beanbag-shaped one would place an object on a grid marked out on the table, and the one that looked like a heavy seven-legged mechanical coffee-table would extend a leg up and over the edge to put something down on its side of the grid. Over five minutes they shuffled the objects – cylindrical things, coin-like discs, small boxes and chrome-plated humanoid figurines – back and forth, sometimes moving their own pieces, sometimes grouping them with things that belonged to the other. Elif eventually decided they were playing a trading game, establishing a basis for exchange without a common language, without even a common set of kinesic signals or gestures beyond give, take and offer.

The beanbag slouched back with a stack of discs clutched in a fold of its integument and rolled away on its side. The coffee-table was sorting its winnings into topologically similar groups when Elif sat down across from it and set out the few things he had in his pocket: eighty-five cents in coins, a plastic clothes-peg, a small roll of duct tape, a red whiteboard marker and his now-useless car and house keys. The coffee-table stopped moving, evidently surprised that a humanoid would have the nerve to aspire to alien-trader status. Elif sat back and crossed his arms. **You don't like it? Deal with it, Jim.**

The coffee-table alien's legs were each of a different thickness, length and number of segments. It used its thinnest leg, or arm, to reach up and prod the keys tentatively. It tapped the coins, pushed them about to determine how many there were, then slowly and deliberately moved a figurine forward from its own ranks.

Carefully Elif moved everything he had to the middle of the grid, then picked up the figurine. The alien didn't try to kill him; it pushed the metallic objects to the edge and over, where they dropped onto its flat top-surface. It left the peg, tape and marker and moved off with a curiously regular (given the different length of its legs) spider-like gait.

Elif pocketed what the alien had left and examined the figurine. Some very light alloy plated with chrome, shaped like a female chess piece with softened, Venus-of-Willendorf outlines. **Too simply formed to be decorative, unless you're a big fan of Lladro... maybe a piece from a board game. Or a toy. Or a souvenir.** Whatever; it had only cost him eighty-five cents plus whatever worth could be attached to the keys for his things back on Earth, however far away that was. He didn't think he'd be too upset if he ever got back to Earth and found that alien driving around in his car.

HALF an hour later Elif peered up each of the corridors leading into the cafeteria; no sign of Russ. He sat down, considered getting another bowl of yoghurt, decided against it, twiddled his thumbs, thought about playing a round or two of Nethack on his 'phone, decided against **that**, thought about a girl with purple hair, tried not to look like he was staring at the others, wondered if he should risk speaking to them, wondered how long it would be before he was back on the moss farm –

On the what?

As a SubGenius he was used to random images tumbling about inside his head, but this was a new one; he couldn't assign it to any particular video game or anime he might have seen. Weird enough to want to examine more closely. As soon as he concentrated, the images faded, of course. He forced himself to calm down and relax, letting the sensation creep back in at its own pace. There was that girl with the purple hair; she had long, pointed ears. The moss farm was set in gently rolling moors under a huge, dim grey sun, low flat-roofed buildings made of roughly hewn wood, and stacks of grey-brown moss cut into couch-cushion-sized slices... pulling them up from the ground with his large, strong fingers... the thin roots tearing like Velcro... the grey guy next to him flexed his hands and **oh my god I am reading their minds.**

He only just stopped himself before exclaiming out loud, more from the prison environment feeling than anything else. Like being suspended on the edge of sneezing, he waited to see if he could pick up anything else, but the effect had faded again.

Elif bit his lower lip. Had he been imagining it? Had Russ told Dr Squid to give him this, or was it an accident? Above all he'd have to hide it, in case it hadn't been intentional. He couldn't see Russ giving him an advantage like this unless Russ knew it wouldn't work on Xists... of course, it wouldn't work on Russ' remote-controlled dummy... but Russ had to be on the ship somewhere, didn't he?

Or did he?

It was possible Russ was directing the ship and the robot all the way from planet X, wherever that was. Elif shook his head. No; the signal lag would be... but They would undoubtedly have a means of instantaneous communication... it fit with what Elif knew about them – puppet masters, after all... it was something he'd endeavour to find out if he got the chance. He added it to the list.

Thirty seconds after coming to this conclusion, Elif was bored again. He went through his wallet and found a dog-eared collection of business-card-sized Dobbsheads, stylised images of "Bob" with the word BEWARE at the bottom. Elif handed one to the grey guy who glanced at it, pointed down the corridor opposite to the one Elif had entered from, then dropped the card and resumed eating.

T HE corridor went on – with empty rooms to either side – long enough for him to wonder if the grey guy had been playing some kind of joke on him. The sort of thing you'd do with any stranger to the tribe... but then, they'd broken bread together, and that had to count for something, even with a non-Terrestrial culture... was there a SubGenius outreach on the station? Elif looked at one of the Dobbsheads, turned to look down the corridor to the cafeteria, shrugged and turned back and just avoided colliding with –

– at first glance it was a tall, skeletally thin and extremely ugly guy in a business suit made of black plate. The arms were attached to the torso in a way that made it look like a car had backed over it several times, but as Elif stared, the plates shifted and fluttered, the arms ratcheted forward and the face – a pleated set of chitinous shingles right out of a Jack Vance novel – flexed horribly, like the underside of an overturned millipede. It had appeared seemingly out of nowhere, perhaps dropping from the ceiling while his back was turned, without a sound, uncomfortably close; Elif stepped back involuntarily. The creature stepped back at the same time, its knees bending the wrong way. It wasn't wearing armour, rather, an artful arrangement of wing-cases and dozens of specialised antennae with flattened edges that came together like clothing seams. The plates writhed and, in groups, settled into an almost perfect imitation of a human wearing a three-piece suit, the effect spoiled only by the lack of colour. Like a giant cockroach. A Spree! At last, an alien race he'd actually heard of. Unfortunately all he knew was the name and that they were insects of some kind, which didn't give him any clues toward how he should behave. If he smiled, it might take that as aggression... spray some pheromones? Somehow, spitting – or peeing – on it didn't seem appropriate, at least until he could determine how dangerous it was. Offer to shake hands? Bow? Curtsey? The least threatening thing he could think to do was to crouch back in mock terror. While he was trying to decide, the Spree kept changing, perfecting its mimicry, and Elif understood why the grey guy had sent him down here: the insect looked more and more like "Bob" with each passing moment.

How could it know? Had "Bob" been here before? It was possible; the Epopt dealt with extraterrestrials on a regular basis. As Elif pictured "Bob" in his mind, the Spree's facial mandibles flexed to one side, making a stalk with a rounded bulb at the end; very much like a pipe. **Okay, it's a mimic... and it's getting its cues from me. Let's test the theory.**

The first thing that came to mind was a television news presenter he'd once had a minor obsession with, noted more for her cleavage than her skill at reading the autocue. Her image came to mind easily, but the Spree didn't suddenly develop the curves he was visualising; it lifted a hand and rubbed two finger-shaped claws together in... **the universal sign for "hand over some cash"? For all I know it's telling me its name. Or declaring war on all humankind. Or it wants to have sex with me.**

Recalling his recent success in non-verbal communication with the coffee-table, Elif went through his pockets, looking for something to trade; the first thing he found was the chrome figurine. He held it up; the Spree recoiled and bowed almost to the floor, completely ruining the humanoid façade. **Oh, god, what have I done this time?**

It backed down the corridor while bent over at an acute angle, still facing forward in a manner that made Elif's lower back ache just to see. When he didn't follow, it added a smooth beckoning gesture with both arms while slowly unbending. Cautiously, Elif stepped forward. The Spree bobbed up and down approvingly... **at** least I hope it's approval and not a prelude to chewing my face off. If it wanted to kill me, it could have done that while my back was turned.

It led him to a large, low-ceilinged room with five humanoids sitting on shallow pedestals. They wore collars that were chained to the walls: naked girls with long, pointed ears and purple hair. Elif realised what the figurine was a token for: he'd traded his car keys for an alien slave girl. He almost grinned before his inherent sense of decency ruined the fantasy. None of them looked very happy to be there. Alien slave girls were fine, as long as they were cosplaying and not –

The Spree made a sweeping gesture in the style of a game show hostess offering a chance at the grand prize. Elif got closer to the nearest girl. Aside from the prehensile rabbit ears she looked human enough, although her small, pouting mouth and widely-spaced eyes gave her the slightly inbred look of a high fashion model, the effect compounded by her vacant stare. He tried to get her attention, but she didn't seem to see him. Which was about what usually happened with women, in his experience.

He got a little closer. She wasn't naked; she sat in the demure pose of the Copenhagen mermaid, wearing a light beige bodystocking that showed off her slim lines. He tilted his head to one side. **Very slim lines.** In fact, judging from her narrow hips and practically non-existent breasts, she couldn't have been more than fourteen years old.

He turned to the Spree pimp. "Uh... do you..." He stopped speaking, realising how futile it was. Sign language? Could he even be sure the Spree was looking at him? It was probably going to misunderstand no matter what he did, but he tried anyway. He pointed at the girl and drew two vertical, parallel lines in the air with his hands. The Spree's head tracked the movement but it didn't give any sign that it had understood. In contrast to the first gesture he drew a set of exaggerated curves to represent breasts, a narrow waist and broad hips. The Spree didn't move. Elif rolled his eyes and muttered "Oh for the love of the fuck" in exasperation.

He sighed, closed his eyes and became aware of a kind of warmth radiating from the girls (there were five of them, all very much alike, and he could locate each one precisely, with his eyes closed, just from the feeling). He might not have noticed it except for the odd sensations he was getting from the Spree. Not coldness, but a definite absence of human warmth, like a suit of armour run by clockwork. He summarised the scene: five kittens and a black ceramic vase filled with glass marbles.

He opened his eyes. The Spree gestured, drawing its imitation hand along its side from waist to chest, then turning the hand out as if presenting a business card. It waited; when Elif just stared, it repeated the movement. "I can't believe this. We've been reduced to charades. Where's your advanced alien technology? Your translators? What kind of a – " It repeated the gesture patiently. Elif thought carefully, then imitated it, his fingers finding the figurine in his pocket. That got the girls' attention. He waved it from side to side and their gazes tracked it like hungry kittens following a fish. He smiled slowly and moved the figurine to within inches of the nearest girl's snub nose; she almost went cross-eyed. She came fully awake, fixed her attention on him and gave him a double-barrelled shot of the Attractant Aetheric that Dr Squid had teased him with. His blood pressure dropped into his boots and he stopped breathing.

When she saw his pupils dilate she gave him a prim little smile that said **it's working** and at the same time **males are so predictable.** Ordinarily the disdain would have put him off, but at that moment she could have kicked him in the balls and he would have smiled back. He stood there, eyes wide, his hand out, the figurine forgotten. Her eyes narrowed a fraction; she sat up and reached out to take the token. He would have let her take it, but another hand reached around from behind (his peripheral vision had narrowed to about five degrees) and took it first. The girl glanced up at whoever it was, her sly smile vanishing. Elif got a vague impression of someone's fingers closing over the figurine and the intensity of the attractant feeling faded, leaving the same kind of affectionate after-glow that Dr Squid had inspired. The girl lost interest, lapsing back into her former lassitude. Elif's consciousness slowly seeped back into his skull from somewhere south of his belt-buckle. As the elf-girl went back into her waking sleep, he woke up.

He could still sense their warmth and the Spree's spring-loaded precision, but whoever was behind him gave off no sensations at all other than the usual primate peripheral senses' **there's somebody**

behind you alert. Even more machine than the Spree, it had to be Russ. With an effort he forced his attention away from the elf-girl and noticed that Russ had had a manicure – long, oval nails, dark burgundy nail-polish, smooth pale skin over the knuckles in contrast to the gnarled brown tree-roots on the rotting zombie monk...

Oh. This is going to be bad. He took a deep breath and turned around.

Russ' new remote-controlled toy looked like a serious business-woman in her early thirties; short, red-blonde hair, stern expression behind designer framed glasses, dressed in the Conspiracy agent's dark grey midi-skirt suit, black mesh stockings and the jacket, which was buttoned over a pair of breasts just a little larger than that news-reader's had been. His shoulders slumped.

Russ cocked a grin at him. "Well?"

Was that a trace of a Dutch accent? Elif glared at her. "You really don't think very highly of me, do you?"

Russ sniffed. "I'm sure Tai will like it," pocketing the figurine and turning to leave. When Elif didn't follow she turned and looked back over her shoulder. "Come on. We have to go. The police are after us."

Elif ignored the implicit threat and looked pointedly at the girl. "She's coming with us, right?"

Russ pretended to consider this. "No. We can't afford to keep another primate on board. These," regarding the purple-haired elf girls with a hint of disdain, "are even less intelligent than your kind and are extremely high-maintenance. Mainly decorative. Besides, Tai isn't that much into guys, and neither are you."

Guys?

He couldn't help it: he looked back at the girl. His Aetheric-enhanced new sense was good enough to tell she wasn't male; was Russ only lying, or testing him as well? **Think quick, think quick... if Russ doesn't know I can tell and is trying to find out if I can tell that she's bullshitting, uh, you're taking too long, damn it, I need a diversion – wait, what did –**

"Police? But we haven't done anything wrong yet!... have we? Aside from running Essence?", muttering to himself "God. Why am I making excuses for your behaviour?"

Russ led him into the corridor. "We both know the police never need a crime, or even a reason; if they want to involve themselves, they will." She walked away, expecting Elif to follow. He remained in the doorway of the purple-haired elf girls' showroom partly because he didn't want to leave, but primarily to mess with Russ' assumption that he was going to obey without question. Russ had to stop and turn around. For a fraction of a second she looked through the doorway at the slaves, then at him, with a brief narrowing of her eyes. It had the impact of a subtle threat, then she gave him a tolerant smile. It was a good smile; Russ had been practising. "As a SubGenius, you know the value of avoiding the attention of the authorities, so please, take your time... weigh your desire to stay against your desire to avoid being interrogated." She drew the last word out to emphasise the unpleasant implications. He conceded the point and followed.

ELIF'S newly-installed sense of direction showed him the best path back to the ship, but Russ led him away from the human's cafeteria, along a corridor parallel to the one he'd arrived by, then off at an angle. Initially, her gait was an economic, brisk pace; the Conspiracy agent's shoes were more for efficiency than show (although Elif was certain Russ could make this new body run at full pelt even in six-inch stiletto heels, if necessary). At what Elif saw as the first significant departure from the quickest route back – when, if he was going to ask, he would have – she began experimenting, adding a subtle sway of her hips with each step. **It's a test. It's all a test. She wants to know if I know where we are. She wants to know if that ass is having the desired effect. Whatever. I want to see some tourist sights before we go. Let us see where this leads.**

He didn't bother to hide that he was staring at her – after all, it was an attractive shape – but he did remind himself frequently just who was controlling it. He appreciated that she didn't go overboard with the hip-swaying; she didn't descend to sashaying, or god forbid, flouncing, but the thought that she might... that she had an array of subtle assets (and a rack of unsubtle ones) to manipulate him at an elemental level simply made him more determined to remain aloof. That didn't mean he wasn't going to enjoy the show; it just meant he wasn't going to buy the popcorn.

At the next intersection of three bare, unmarked stone corridors that looked exactly like all the others, Russ stopped and looked about, as if unsure of the way. It was a good performance, but Elif didn't buy it. She turned to him and raised an eyebrow. The left turn would take them back to the ship; the path ahead, eventually, to the room with the moving stacks of crates where he'd dumped the rotting zombie monk and his computer. He pointed to the right, down the path that led further into the asteroid.

"Are you sure?"

He snorted derisively. "No. Aren't you? Never mind. I know you have a complete map of this place to hand, or claw, or pedipalp or whatever it is you things use, so spare me the elaborately contrived bullshit answer and let's just go this way."

She gave him a frown of mild reproach (about two point five, on a scale of one to ten). "We are going to have to work on this complete-lack-of-trust issue."

He gave her his warmest and most sincere smile. "You can't buy trust. Not even with a body like that. Particularly with a body like that. You were more credible as a rotting theocrat, disgusting smell and all."

She grinned. "I still have the robes. Want me to dress up as a nun?"

He gave her a superior look. "Not my fetish."

"I know," she said easily. "What you want to know is why we are wandering around out here instead of going back to the ship. Several reasons, but principally, two: we have to collect some supplies and, at the same time, avoid the corporate compliance officers that are looking for us." She turned and walked down the right-hand corridor. "Come on. I'll take you to see the night-life."

After a few steps, he risked asking "So I'm straight, and not into nuns. What makes you such an expert on my sexual orientation?"

She glanced back, bemused. "I've seen your porn collection. All of it. I read between the lines. You're straight."

He looked off to one side as if trying to remember. "When did I show you my porn collection?"

"I had to review it all before I could sell it." Before he could object, she continued. "Yes, I sold the contents of your computer. Technically, those copyrighted files belong to my corporation, which owns the Earth."

Elif looked at Russ' body from a new perspective... that hairstyle, the cheekbones, the smile, the sultry, heavy-lidded eyes... not to mention the generous breasts squeezed into the Conspiracy agent's white shirt. A suspicion formed somewhere in his back-brain, but he'd need those files to confirm it. "You copied those files before you sold them, right?"

"Of course. They're in the Bitchslap's memory. Your machine was... eaten."

"What, data transfer is beyond your technology?"

"That's how Abandoners work," she said, defensively. "They eat things, they examine them, they understand them and then they excrete them again."

"So I'll get my machine back?"

"It belongs to them now. We couldn't afford it. We can get the ship's indentured Abandoners to build a cheap machine and copy the files to it."

"Human technology?" Russ gave the impression of thinking about it, then shook her head. Elif was momentarily taken by how attractive she could make that simple gesture look. "... an Xist computer?"

She favoured him with a benignly tolerant smile. "No. A Sheydal media player will do... video, audio and olfactory."

But with no computing power. If Tai still has her machine, she can check this for me. She's good at that sort of thing. Elif let his attention wander toward Russ' curves, telling himself it was research for his new suspicions. It wasn't as if there was anything else to claim his attention; if there were any advertisements about, they weren't directed at humanoids. Perhaps more advanced races thought the entire concept of advertising somewhat gauche, or as pointless as Elif regarded it, or, more likely, it was being distributed in a medium he couldn't sense. **Aetheric advertising. What a horrible concept.**

THE alien quarter was a huge, multi-levelled lounge packed with a bewildering variety of things, only some of them immediately recognisable as life-forms. From long hours spent arguing with serious hard-science-fiction fundamentalists Elif knew that the definition of 'life-form' could include almost anything from clouds of steam to piles of rocks; confronted with the possibility of offending a sentient alien throw-rug by stepping on it, Elif decided to play dumb and, if challenged, to refer them to Russ, who, he thought, should have warned him first.

Remembering Tai's request he recorded some more video with his 'phone: columns of rainbow-edged crystal shot through with shoals of multicoloured lights (it didn't matter if they were alive or just part of the décor – they looked cool); a pair of those slowly moving ornate tower-stacks; several different sized beanbags like the one that had been trading with the multi-legged coffee table but with translucent skins filled with viscous, fluorescent green goop. He might have sat on one if they hadn't been actively playing the trading game with something that had an almost human profile but which, when it turned around, proved to be about half an inch thick. Elif wondered if it had room for internal organs.

Russ seemed happy to let him stumble into a possibly fatal indiscretion; he was almost tempted to deliberately interfere with someone... perhaps get up on a table and deliver a good old-fashioned hellfire-and-brimstone SubGenius Rant. Somehow, he didn't think any of the usual Rant themes would apply here... "Quit Your Job And Slack Off"? Did any of these things even have jobs? Would any of them understand his language? Would they take him to be an annoyingly chattering pet monkey and have him caged?

At a table in a corner booth, perched delicately on tall stools, sat three thin, graceful creatures with their hands held flat six inches above the table-top. They had a roughly humanoid aspect, faceless angels carved from pale bone, elaborately webbed wing-like vanes attached to angular shoulders. Everyone gave them a wide berth, as if respecting their calm, contemplative poise. For a moment Elif imagined slapping one on the back and, in a loud, good-ole-boy po'bucker voice, shouting "Damn! How the hell is ever' little thang, son? Round of drinks for the thin white dudes here!" Perhaps anticipating this, Russ took him by the hand and led him past a particularly large grey guy bearing a platter the size of a bathtub. A roasted orange lobster as large as a motorcycle was stuck to the tray with a thick glaze of congealed grease. Carefully, the grey guy slid the platter under the angels' upheld hands and quickly backed away. Russ sat Elif down at a table nearby; Elif kept recording as unobtrusively as possible.

For a few peaceful moments it appeared as if they were praying over the roast. Then, all at once, they began pulling off claws and legs with ragged chunks of steaming, bright red flesh attached; jagged-edged diagonal slits opened on their faces like giant Venus fly-traps and they crammed the food into them, making sickening squelching sounds, casually tossing pieces of half-chewed food over their shoulders and spitting out any fragments they didn't like. Some of the chunks hit other nearby patrons; nobody objected, although when a foot-long segment of greasy mandible landed in front of Russ she picked it up gingerly and dropped it on the floor. A puddle of something oozed up, around and over the morsel, picked it up and carried it away, too quickly for Elif to frame with the 'phone. "What the hell was that?" he asked, too surprised to worry about the implications of what Russ might say.

"Abandoner colony," Russ said absently, her attention on the crowd. "Organised, intelligent bacterial slicks. Around here, they do most of the mundane work at the molecular level... recycling, assembly, and so forth. They're everywhere; there's no escaping them." Russ left off her scanning of the crowd to check his reaction.

He was unconcerned. "Oh, I got over that. Time was I couldn't sleep at night, worrying about bacteria. Around the time I was reading Greg Bear's work. Gave myself an ulcer, ironically." Russ was giving him the look interviewers gave when they wanted their subjects to keep talking. "Uh... you know, 'If the eye could perceive the demons that people the universe, existence would be impossible'."

Russ appeared to think about this. "That was said before microbiology was an established discipline on Earth, wasn't it?"

Elif snorted. "The hell if I know. I think it's from the Talmud. They could have been talking about bacteria, or Aetherics, or unhealthy sexual practices."

"So, you just don't think about it."

"There's no point. Isn't much I can do about it – human life is too deeply mixed up with bacterial life. I don't think we could – " he stopped, listened to the background noise; buzzing, high-pitched squeaks, hisses, metallic clanks, cello-sounds modulated to the point of almost being like speech, and a familiar drum-beat. "Damn it, I know that song."

"You should. It's from your collection." She pointed to an oval screen on the far side of the lounge, which was showing an unlikely computer-animated six-person orgy on a trampoline.

Elif recognised it, but refused to allow Russ to embarrass him. "Ah. These guys into that sort of thing?"

Russ laughed. "Hardly. It's something they've never seen before, so they'll buy it, but mainly for their human slaves. Humanoid cultures as technologically advanced as yours are rare, so when a new supply of media becomes available it's snapped up quickly. It paid for our ship's fuel and for this body," touching a slender finger to her throat and running it down towards her cleavage. Elif wasn't paying attention; he was continually distracted by the endless parade of unfamiliar alien creatures passing their table. It wasn't just the strangeness or the differences in height or form or motion; he was used to seeing things keep to the horizontal, more or less. Some of the lounge patrons hooked legs into niches in the ceiling and crept past overhead, while others slithered along the ground. A copper caterpillar made up of dozens of large-dog-sized segments did both, arching over their table, legs clicking, continuing on its way above the crowd.

Russ spotted someone at an entrance; she stood and led Elif through the crowd, around trading game tables and eye-watering pools of ammonia to an entrance where a hulking grey guy stood, holding a battered, rusty and undeniably terrestrial shopping cart loaded with ten-gallon-sized containers of thick pink liquid. Elif leaned back, shaded his eyes with one hand, peered up as if over a vast distance; the man's head almost touched the ceiling, twelve feet up. Russ nodded to the grey guy who deferentially set the cart down just outside the lounge's entrance. She smiled, reached up and patted his ass. He gave her a nervous grimace, made a brief, ducking bow, shot Elif a surprisingly human look – part contempt and part sympathy – and left.

Elif stared after him. "They sure do grow 'em big down on the farm, don't they?"

Russ nodded absently, checking the containers. "He's got a few years before he reaches his full size. The market uses teenagers for delivery work; it helps them deal with their rebellious phase. Gets them used to servitude, rewarded by occasional visits from your purple-haired friends."

Elif didn't say anything. Considering something as small as a purple-haired elf girl partnered with Andre the Giant's bigger brother there made him feel uncomfortable. **Uncomfortable? How do you think she'd feel?**

He tried to push the cart. It was from Earth, all right; one of the wheels was stuck. The containers were so heavy that the only way he could move them was by lifting one corner of the cart and shoving as hard as he could. "Damn... cheap-ass human... craftsmanship... couldn't they steal them from a Crash culture that has a sense of pride in what they make?", throwing in the phrase that Dr Squid had used in the hope that Russ would give something away.

She deigned to walk by his side at the best pace he could manage, but gave the impression of not listening. "Mm-hmm," she murmured, "she's going to spend the rest of her life on her back with a series of extremely large grey guys on top of her... legs spread wide... trying to breathe in between the thrusts."

"That's nice," he retorted sarcastically. "Maybe I could get a job on the moss farm."

Russ grinned. "You wouldn't last five minutes down there." Her grin faded a little. "Where did you hear about moss farmers?"

Elif blurted the first half credible thing he could think of. "They were handing out samples at the cafeteria – damn it," cursing the shopping cart wheel, which had locked up completely. "Can you give me a hand with this?"

Russ held out her hands apologetically. "This is a display model. It's not very strong. If overloaded it'll break down prematurely, like the last one did."

Elif was remembering how strong her grip had been when she'd led him about the alien cafeteria. To head off his inevitable objection, Russ took a deep breath, her breasts swelling against the white shirt material. He glared at her again and knelt to examine the faulty wheel.

Russ said "As for cheap-ass human design... you might be surprised to learn that Earth has the most advanced primate culture within a thousand light-years."

"Well, less surprised and more OH MY GOD that **sucks.** Really?

We? Are the most advanced... wait a minute... there." He thumped the wheel with the palm of his hand and forced the bearings back into place.

"Next to the Spree, the Abandoners, even the Sheydal... well, there's no comparison. But, yes, Earth has the most advanced primate-developed – well, **mostly** primate developed – culture, and the highest population/lifespan ratio, of any skull farm in this part of the galaxy."

"You sure you have the right planet? Concentration camps?" Russ nodded. "Atomic weapons? Unchecked environmental rape? Billions starving, gross disparity between the rich and poor, fundamentalist faiths that eat their young, global communications network yet almost zero empathy for the starving billions?" He wasn't entirely sure where he was going with this, but he thought he might force Russ into defending what he saw as the worst excesses humanity was capable of. If she actually did work for the corporation that owned Earth, perhaps the awful conditions were partly her fault.

"I didn't say it was pretty. Or fair. Or anywhere I would choose to live. I did say 'most advanced', qualified with 'primate culture'. And your hostile response to what I intended as a compliment is simply a symptom of the low place your kind have within the greater population. The Anointed," indicating him, "have always been outsiders, condemned as heretics, yet necessary. In a social structure supposedly founded on stability, the random element is a heresy, but without heretics the power structures have to generate their own victims, or risk looking incompetent."

Elif pushed the cart forward. The wheel wobbled and squeaked and would probably pop out again eventually, but it did the job for the moment. Conversationally he felt like he'd just run into a brick wall, so he backed up to the last part he could follow: humanity as the most advanced people in the vicinity and deciding, for the moment, to accept it as true, then branching out to another of his more pressing concerns: "So in terms of finding better medical care for Tai, we're screwed."

Russ dismissed this with an airy wave. "Oh, no. Think of it in terms of Earth's varying levels of pet care. Poodles receive better medical attention than most chickens, for example. Better than some people. If it came to that, I'm sure we could locate a... poodle breeder... who has invested sufficient effort in keeping their pets alive to be able to help her, although by now you should know that humans are seen as an expendable commodity in general. We Xists know a great deal about how to breed humans for profit, but medical conditions with a neurological basis are... tricky. Your lives are so short, it's usually easier to simply breed such faults out of the gene pool."

This opened up several conversational avenues that Elif wanted to explore, but Russ stopped, her eyes turned to one side as if listening. For a few moments there was silence, then Russ' eyes turned to him and, despite her completely neutral expression, Elif knew he was about to be conned. Her mouth opened as if to speak; she paused, looked away and then continued.

"I have just come across an opportunity for us to make some money on the side. Contract work, three minutes, no more." She slowly raised her eyebrows, an effect creepily on the wrong side of the uncanny valley.

Exasperated, "Oh, what is it? Some horrible thing with tentacles wants to have sex with me?"

"No tentacles," adding, after some thought, "and not strictly what a primate would consider to be sex. More like a handshake." Eyes looking down, "Look, we have to make this quick, or I'd explain the situation in more detail. We go in, one of them comes up, takes off its clothes, you hold hands for thirty seconds, we get paid, we leave. Are you up for that?"

It didn't sound dangerous, and Elif was emboldened by the thought that at some point Russ needed him for something important, and that this wasn't it. The whole thing sounded like a last-minute side trip. Besides that... alien sex! That would look good on his resume. He nodded. "No involvement, no weird-ass Aetherics. Wham, bam, thank-you, whatever you are. Let's do this."

Russ led him down a side corridor past empty grey storerooms to a space the size of the docking collar he'd seen around their ship. A stack of flat boxes – an Abandoner high-rise building – stood in one corner, levels coloured in blues and pinks like a packing crate full of baby food. Four other things stood next to the Abandoners, wearing detailed body armour over a more or less humanoid shape.

Big and broad shouldered, while not in the league of the grey guy who'd brought the shopping cart, they were much taller than either Elif or Russ, and looked like they could kick a car over. They didn't have faces, or they hid them behind enigmatically detailed helmets. Either that, or the top part wasn't where they kept their heads.

Nobody moved. Elif waited until it occurred to him that other cultures might have different ideas about appropriate response times; if someone moved too rapidly, that might be taken for aggression... but if you didn't respond quickly, something faster would attack... perhaps these guys came from a culture that was so advanced, their sense of personal safety so entrenched, they'd lost any need to make defensive gestures of any kind.

This took about a minute, then Elif held out his hand to the nearest armoured form. **What's the worst that could happen? I proposition the wrong one? Maybe they're waiting for me to choose somebody. If one of them paid for this then they should say something. Wave an arm. Flash some lights. Whatever.**

One of them stepped forward heavily and the armour split open on uneven jagged lines, recalling for a moment the faces of the bone angels in the alien quarter. A foot-thick layer of translucent jelly drew back into the suit, revealing another suit which opened and "There isn't anything in there at all, is there, Russ?" standing there with hand out and feeling silly even if nobody else there cared if he looked silly or not. Eventually enough layers peeled away to reveal a creature as thin as a broom, its skin textured like ruby over polished chrome. It stepped clear of the suits and held out a hand with pencil fingers. Elif took it and returned the hesitant squeeze, wondering if he should be looking at the end of the broomstick where the head would be, or even if anyone cared where he looked. He felt a faint Aetheric tickling, but it wasn't anything to be alarmed about. Aetherically, they didn't look like anything special; a faint blue water glow around the middle of the broomstick with occasional cinnamon green flickers and a suggestion of pneumatic hissing in its movement. It resembled something from an up-market executive-toy store, fifties chrome styling, expensive red inlays and no readily apparent function. **Was that an Attractant Aetheric? No, that was just a Bulldada alert.**

While waiting for it to finish Elif considered its form purely from the perspective of Bulldada, the class of low-brow artwork that cannot be accepted as art. Elif could readily see someone paying to have one of these creatures sitting on his desk for no better reason than as decoration, except for the ethical dilemmas this posed. Elif thought about asking Russ how much they would cost, and then thought better of it.

The creature released its grip and moved smoothly back into the suit, which closed up one layer at a time, and, inevitably, the theme music from the television show **Get Smart** started playing in Elif's head. The suit shuffled backwards to rejoin its friends. It lifted an arm and pointed at Russ. It spoke in clearly accented English, a gravely electronic-synthetic twang like a wasp theremin: "You'd better not screw us again, or we'll kill you. Again." Whoever they were, they wanted Elif to know this. **Thanks for the tip, guys, but I already know Russ can't be trusted.**

The suits opened a circular door in a wall at the end of the docking collar, got in to their ship and left. Elif had just enough time for a glimpse of tantalisingly complex alien machinery, banks of dark green indicator lamps pulsing enticingly through a fog of cerise steam and even just for a fraction of a second a Jacob's ladder arc doing a crackling hot pink belly-dance – and the door was closed.

"How come **our** ship doesn't look that cool?" Elif said after a suitably respectful pause.

"Because we're not a bunch of smarmy yuppie investment banking poseurs in rented suits, might have something to do with it, I expect," Russ said, leading him away.

"And how many times have those guys killed you?"

"Once is generally enough."

"... so how much did we make?"

"Enough to buy a second power cell."

"No, how much did **we** make?"

"Enough to buy a second power cell with enough power to make fifteen thousand cans of Bivalve Mutathing."

"That's better."

NEARING their ship, Elif smelled a faint trace of marsh gas and was taken with the idea he shouldn't let Russ know he could smell it. Deciding instead that he'd let his paranoia dance around naked long enough, he risked saying "Can you smell that?"

Russ lifted her delicately shaped nose and inhaled deeply, straining the shirt again. "Methane, with traces of phosphorus trihydride and tetrahydride. Most likely a faulty seal on an environment suit. Quite a few people here breathe methane. Incidentally, where did you get that whore token? They don't hand them out with the bread rolls, generally."

"Oh, I traded my car keys to someone I met in the human's cafeteria. Environment suit, lots of different length legs, didn't say much. Until I found out what it was for, I was going to give it to Tai as a souvenir."

Russ smiled. "And now that you know what it's for?"

"I am definitely going to give it to Tai as a souvenir, along with all the unspoken implications of such an act. Just shut up, you wouldn't understand." While he was being reckless he decided to risk another question: "Look, I'm completely lost, here, but even taking into account the occasional act of prostitution, we seem to be taking a lot longer to get back to the ship than it took to get to Doctor Squid's place."

"As I inferred earlier, there are several people we are avoiding... police informants, mainly, although there are a couple of corporate compliance officials I wouldn't want to have to explain my presence to. We're almost there."

Elif had a look about with his Lifesense Aetheric, but couldn't feel anybody else nearby. He thought about his next question for about twenty steps, then asked "Do I want to go into the question of police jurisdiction, the boundaries of interstellar law, why the cops are after us – aside from the prostitution, and the Essence running, and the selling copyrighted media – and what they can do if they catch us?"

Russ made the remote's mouth do a prim, slightly mocking thin-lipped smile that said **if you only knew.** "Boundaries are a limitation of primate thinking. In this reality there are no borders drawn between one system of law and another. Each pushes up against the others, mixing in different ratios depending on their relative strengths, usually not to anyone's advantage. Aside from the lawyers, of course."

"Strengths as in military force? The ability to bring big-ass weapons to bear on a problem?"

Russ shook her head, waving one hand with frustration. "This is another point where your language has insufficient precision to describe the situation accurately. 'strength' can mean how many destroyers your society can effectively put in the field. It can also mean what kind of incentives you can bribe your enemies with. It can mean how effectively you can subvert their social systems. It can mean feeding disinformation into their intelligence apparatus. It can mean bringing into contact two societies who have never met before and who would rather fight each other than you. There is an Xist word for it, but it has no simple terrestrial equivalent."

Elif quietly smiled to himself. **We're back to ragging on the primates. All is well.**

Apparently not; Russ stopped, frozen in the pose of someone listening carefully, one hand held out in a gesture that said, plainly, "wait". More by habit than by considered disobedience Elif deliberately kept pushing the cart until Russ grabbed it and forced him to stop, giving his arm an insistent shake to emphasise that she'd noticed his deliberate disobedience. He had another look around with his Lifesense and, perhaps getting better at it by now, caught a hint of something in a corridor somewhere ahead.

"As to why the cops are after us," Russ whispered, "what we are doing is not highly regarded. If we are caught, you and Tai will most likely be killed and I will be put in stasis for a couple of thousand years." Seeing Elif's distraught look, she assured him "Don't worry, my financial standing wouldn't suffer. Oh, and your killing would be done very quickly and ethically. You wouldn't feel a thing."

Elif started to ask "So what are we d-", then pretended to be listening for whatever Russ was avoiding while trying to focus on what the Lifesense Aetheric was trying to tell him. The creature approaching had a curiously plural aspect, like a group of different animals, or people; he closed his eyes and for a moment the feeling intensified with painful clarity. His mind translated the sharp sensation into images: a monster made of the severed parts of others, sewn or tied together. A sled driver holding onto choke-chains attached to a dozen different, injured wild animals, all frantically tugging in different directions. A... dinosaur? With smaller animals tied to each leg, like some misconceived three-legged race... a silent crab-thing tied to its head (or perhaps to its tail), claws sunk into the dinosaur's sensitive ears, driving it, whipping it on with a pair of white-hot antennae, hating the dinosaur and the dinosaur hating it back. Moans of pain from the animals tied to its legs.

Whatever it was repelled him with the same unthinking intensity that the purple-haired elf girl's Aetheric had drawn him. He wanted to back off and find a dark corner to hide in, but Russ had grabbed his wrist. He settled for not moving or breathing until the shambling thing had passed out of range, although the telepathic cries echoed for some time after Russ indicated it was safe to proceed. When they reached the corridor that led to the ship – the corridor that thing had come down – the swamp-rot smell was stronger.

Russ wasn't visibly spooked by the encounter (if she had been, she wouldn't have showed it) but kept her voice low. "Unload them into the second chamber," pointing to the containers. "If we stole the cart, market security would come after us, and we have attracted enough attention as it is."

Elif was too nervous to argue about who had originally stolen the cart from whom; he started moving the jars, pausing only for a moment to observe that most of the building debris was gone from the scoop chamber. Each jar was extremely heavy, and the exertion was a welcome distraction from the psychic stench that was clinging to his brain.

After stacking the jars next to the ramp leading up to the hatch, he stuck his head out for a last look around; Russ was staring down the corridor. She turned to him. "The one you traded your keys to, for the whore token; did it smell anything like that?"

He shook his head.

Russ' expression was blank for a moment, then she nodded. "Let's go."

Russ directed him to feed the bottles into the recycler, and, in response to his put-upon look, said, "I'm going to have a shower." When he kept giving her that look she continued, "To wash off the nano-scale fabrication residue. Assembly scaffolding, stray Abandoner factories and the like." She picked up one of Elif's favourite towels from a pile of clothing that had been inside his old wooden chest of drawers, disappeared into the first scoop chamber. He looked around, cataloguing what had been left and what had been taken. The canvas bag he'd filled with recovered guns, explosives and Conspiracy agent devices was gone, which wasn't surprising. All the bricks, chunks of concrete, pieces of roof tile and sections of lumber had been taken. Whoever had done it had even swept up after themselves.

While trying to work out how long they'd been away, he was struck by a sudden pang of regret: he wasn't going to see Dr Squid again. That feeling led to another, relating to the purple-haired elf girl. He wasn't going to see her again, either. He put his hand on the slight bump in his pocket: his 'phone. At least he had some video, which he could store on his computer – except that was gone also. Well, he'd store it on Tai's computer, unless Russ had traded that away.

He carried the first jar of pink fluid to the recycling bay, past the bathroom dome, resisting the temptation to peek through the doorway and see Russ naked. He rested the jar on the recycler's rough surface while trying to work out how to open it; the device began chewing away at the base of the jar. He watched until the pink fluid started draining out of the gnawed-off end, ensured it wouldn't fall over, then left it and went to check on Tai. She was asleep, lying on her side, one hand resting against her keyboard, surrounded by dozens of floating rectangular windows displaying text, pictures, graphs, and visual representations of audio waveforms. He smiled, then wrinkled his nose and sniffed. The smile faded; a faint trace of swamp rot. Had that thing been in here, or had the smell blown in while the hatch was open? The first possibility was too horrible to consider.

He assumed Russ was still watching in one way or another, then shrugged and went back for the rest of the jars. The recycler seemed to love the pink fluid, sucking it out eagerly. "Ah, poor ship. Russ doesn't feed you very often, does it?", stressing the pronoun, trying to disassociate the ungendered alien creature from the exaggeratedly feminine puppet in the shower. He could hear the water hissing as it bounced off her shoulders. its shoulders, damn it. Still, Elif suspected Russ had overplayed its hand a little with the new toy; he'd had years of experience in ignoring the Conspiracy's temptations. They had a generalised kind of base appeal but always proved to be disappointing once you got the fancy wrapping off. He appreciated the need for a comforting deception – life on Earth would have been impossible without it – but he much preferred to, as the SubGenius aphorism said, pull the wool over his own eyes.

Thinking of the Conspiracy's fancy wrapping reminded him of the purple-haired elf girl, and the effortless way she'd grabbed his attention. It was a far more effective demonstration of the power of Aetherics than Russ' crude club-to-the-speech-centres had been... so why didn't Russ use that technique on him? If what they'd been told about Aetherics was true, Russ couldn't use them directly; they needed to be attached to a living primate mind. This did raise the possibility of Aetherics that attached themselves to an Xist's mind but if Russ was running this puppet show remotely from planet X... if the Xists had Aetherics that could work over interstellar distances, they wouldn't need starships: they'd rule the galaxy. Unlikely. Elif nodded to himself and patted the end of the first empty container as it sank into the recycler.

He went back onto the bridge, closed his eyes and felt around inside his head for the trigger that uncovered his new senses. Slowly, the imaginary eyelid lifted... that dim, red cinnamon-amber pulsing hum to his right was Tai, asleep; behind him were two small, hard white points of hissing salt water... he opened his eyes, turned to look: before, there had been five red indicator lights on the six outboard pods. Now there were only two, and for some reason, they were registering with his Lifesense. Perhaps the ship itself was alive, or parts of it were. Or maybe just the engines.

An unpleasant crawling sensation behind him made him turn back: the stone ring at the end of the ship, with the Essence capacitor floating inside. He closed his eyes and noticed for the first time a dark grey background fog, in contrast to the ring, which was completely black, cold, silent and smooth. The Essence capacitor looked like a slow-motion synchronised swimming carnival of fireflies, their fitful dance constrained to the surface of a sphere. It grumbled and occasionally made thin, faint screeching sounds in his mind like a violated pig, and the longer Elif stared at it... weren't there more points before? Had some of the trapped Pink Aetherics died? Did they have a shelf life?

And what was that grey-green shadow behind the capacitor, the one that vanished as soon as he concentrated on trying to see it clearly? Imagination, or was there something on the other side of that wall? The brief glimpse he'd caught had all of the furtive air of that alien shopping cart he'd seen. If there is something there, and Russ doesn't want me to see it... then right about now would be a good time for another distraction. Right... about ... now.

"All hands, brace for cruising speed," Russ said as she entered the room. Elif opened his eyes and nodded. **Right on time.** Russ was dressed only in the Conspiracy agent's white shirt, and was towelling her hair dry. Elif manfully resisted the urge to stare at her bare thighs, looked about for something to hang on to, but aside from Tai's bed and the stone ring around the Essence capacitor, the room was bare. "I'm kidding. There won't be any stray acceleration, and you won't be forced to lean to one side if we go around a corner." She tossed the chrome figurine to him; awkwardly, he fumbled at it, batting it from one hand to the other before catching it.

"Then how can we tell we're moving?"

Russ tilted her head slightly to one side and a broad window appeared at the end of the room, neatly covering the Essence capacitor, showing blackness, hard white points of light and part of a rough-finished, irregular grey shape with narrow vertical pits let into the surface; a grey potato with archer's slots, or docking ports. A tiny rod-shaped shadow rippled over the light side. The shape – presumably the market – slowly receded. It could have been simulated. If it was faked, at least Russ didn't insult his intelligence by having the stars shift past as they moved.

The map they'd seen earlier appeared next to the display, packed with confusing detail like a cubist fish-tank in four dimensions. Russ pointed to a place on the map that didn't look any different from any other part, as far as Elif could tell. "The gap in the Convocation Exclusion zone is here, about an hour's journey away. Until then, relax, stay near the capacitor, and do whatever it is primates do to pass the time."

Tai was awake. "Watch some videos?" she said sleepily.

Elif gave Russ a disparaging look. "We could watch some cartoons, except Russ sold my computer."

Russ opened another window in the air with a list of files. Addressing Tai, she said "I copied them all to the ship's memory first. Most of it seems to be pornography of some kind."

In a stage whisper, Elif said to Tai, "Russ is trying to embarrass me."

Tai was unashamedly staring at Russ' breasts wobbling while Russ vigorously towelled her hair. "We could always watch some of Russ' videos. I found some interesting things in the archives."

Russ stopped drying her hair and peered out from underneath her fringe. "I don't recall giving you access to that."

Tai arched her eyebrows in mock-innocence. "If you wanted to keep me out, you would have put some kind of security on it." When Russ kept staring at her, she continued, "Some kind of serious security, anyway. It wasn't that hard to find, although you guys have some weird ideas about video codecs." With an effort she sat up and pressed some keys on her keyboard, opening another window with harshly lit, jerky video of Russ's old monk body and Sybrandis deVonk sitting on the floor, away from the others. Elif recognised the round indentations in the wall; they had been in this room. Their lips moved, but frustratingly there was no sound.

"I remember having that conversation," Russ said. "'You believe this to be true. On what evidence?'" she translated, speaking over the old robot monk's lip-movements. Sybrandis' pale face looked confused. " 'I saw it. Not a dream and not a vision. That man must come one day, not as a saint – if what I saw was true, he will be a fornicator, a blasphemer, a liar and a cheat, but he will come to save us. Some of us. Not them,' glancing at the peasants near the fake fire, 'but the ones like me. The ones who think as I do. That man will come... and smoke and fire will come from his mouth. No, not from his mouth, but from a cup held in his teeth.'"

Elif produced a tattered Dobbshead from his pocket. "They didn't smoke pipes in the twelfth century, did they?"

"No," Russ said. "At the time I thought he was hallucinating – something primates are quite good at – but after some investigation I found Sybrandis was host to a rare Aetheric that allowed glimpses of the future. It's something we Xists are quite interested in."

"What, you guys can't see into the future? So much for god-like technology," Elif said scornfully.

"We can view near-future events, but not consistently, and the process requires an inordinate amount of energy. So much so as to make it unfeasible. Sybrandis managed it with only the power available to his primate brain, which made it worth investigating."

Elif was remembering what Dr Squid had told him about his new Aetherics. "Next step something-or-other?"

Russ nodded. "I asked the doctor to install one if she could, but I understand that your brain is rather under-powered, so she probably only managed to squeeze in a Merest Hint. We should probably test it."

Elif grinned. "Think of a number between one and a hundred. Twenty-three! Was I right?"

"About as right as you usually are, which is to say, no." Russ unwrapped the damp towel from her hair and draped it over Elif's head. Before it covered his eyes he saw she had a length of timber – a two-by-four – in one hand. **Where did that come from? Wait** –

"Russ, is this a good idea?" Tai asked.

"I'm not going to kill him," Russ replied, "and besides, it's fun." Elif tried to sense, but all he got was a bright, fuzzy glow from Tai, the angry bee-drone of the Essence capacitor and the two white pinches of concentrated ocean-smell behind him. They served as reference points, but he couldn't sense Russ's robot body at all. The towel smelled faintly of shampoo perfume and freshly-rained-on earth.

A gentle tap on the back of his head startled him. Having seen more samurai movies than most people even knew existed, he didn't immediately turn to face that way, but the Aetherics weren't giving him anything useful. He listened for Russ' bare feet on the floor and tried to see which way Tai was looking, but the image reported to his brain by the Lifesense Aetheric was too blurry. Another tap, this time on his right shoulder; if Russ had seen the same films, he knew the next one wouldn't be as gentle. He calmed himself and tried to open the unfamiliar channels that the Lifesense reported through.

The two points of light behind him suddenly buzzed much louder. Instinctively he turned to look, casually swatting away the two-by-four as Russ swept it at the side of his head, realised the towel was blocking his view and impatiently pulled it loose. Russ aimed another blow at his behind but before it could land he twisted the towel into a loose rope and lassoed it around the middle of the lumber, depriving it of momentum. He held up one hand in a not-now-this-is-important gesture, listening; sensing.

The white lights weren't getting bigger, but there was a feeling of increased pressure, of something – two somethings – being contained in uncomfortably tight quarters. Those somethings were alive in there; by now he could identify the Lifesense's signature. Trying to see them clearly made him dizzy, like watching a regular film through 3-D glasses with his eyes crossed. Whatever was inside those round nacelles on the outside of the ship was –

"Cheeses **Kite!**" The spike of pain through his head made him drop the figurine and squeeze his eyes shut in sympathy, but he opened them again and turned, hearing Tai's cry. **"OW!"**

Russ was at her side instantly, one slim hand resting on her forehead. The buzzing ozone pain grew briefly stronger, then faded back to a tightly held hiss.

"I hadn't expected that," Russ said. "The power system is interfering with your Lifesense. I've cut our speed to one-quarter; is it less painful now?"

Elif was about to reply when he saw that Russ wasn't concerned about him; she was entirely concerned about the effect on Tai. "God-like technology," he muttered, his words slowing as a trace of meaning filtered through the sensory noise. "... can you turn it up again, just for a few seconds?"

"Why?" Russ asked in a slow, patronising tone.

"I could almost hear what they were trying to say."

There was a pause, just long enough for the insinuation to be apparent. "They who, Elif?" Tai asked quietly.

"The engines... that's... they... who," seeing the look Russ was giving him, "A-HA! See? That's just what she – " and seeing Russ take a deep breath, the shirt tightening across her breasts, " – stop that."

"What's she doing? Can I see?" Tai asked.

"You can touch them if you want," Russ said with a sultry, sideways glance.

"Hell, yes," Tai said eagerly.

Elif rolled his eyes in exasperation and turned to leave. "I am going to practice holding my breath for when I throw myself out the airlock."

Russ was sitting next to Tai, leaning over her. "Hatch."

Elif stopped but didn't turn around. "What," with undisguised impatience.

"It's a hatch, not an airlock. If you manage to get it open, you'll decompress the entire ship."

Elif picked up the figurine, thought about presenting it to Tai, then decided to leave. He didn't stamp out; he'd played the petulant teenager far enough. If he didn't think about it too carefully he could pretend he'd arranged the situation to give Tai something fun to play with. **Anyway, what kind of spaceship doesn't have an airlock? God-like technology. Hah.** As he stepped down the ramp into the first scoop chamber, he heard Tai giggle "My god, they feel more real than mine."

*T*ai *has a Lifesense? Probably born with it, poor guy.*

ELIF sat at the top of the ramp at the far end of the second scoop chamber, his back against the outer hatch and, behind it, the infinite emptiness of space, admiring the reflection of the dim overhead lights on the figurine. He wasn't anywhere near as perturbed by Tai and Russ' symmetrical docking than he'd led them to believe. He knew Tai wasn't taken in by the jealous prude act; they'd played that one so often in the past that Tai referred to it as their "straight man / funny man" routine. What concerned him was whether Russ believed it or not. Elif's acting ability wasn't commercial grade but it had fooled a lifetime's worth of Conspiracy drones, even the supposedly smarter higher echelons. They weren't as smart as They liked to think – "we know all about you and your dirty little secrets" was an old part of the dominance game – but Russ was another order of intelligence entirely; vast, cool and unsympathetic. Or was she?

Ever since the incident with the Discordian and the hot-dog bun Elif had routinely examined his preconceptions with a view to overturning them, even more so after discovering Robert Anton Wilson's Zetetic perspective: question everything. It tended to complicate his life – shopping was a nightmare – but it gave him a view of the world he believed to be superior to the one encouraged by the standard Conspiracy line. Was Russ really that much smarter? She had this ship, after all. **Doesn't mean she built it.** She picked up modern English pretty quickly. **Clever, but not godlike. You could do the same with a capable translation app in your 'phone.** He was about to counter himself with Russ' striking him dumb before realising he'd already condemned that as crude. Was there any other evidence of Russ' superiority? Anticipation of their actions? **How hard is that when you're all trapped in a tube fifty yards long?**

In the past, when dealing with Conspiracy drones who thought they were "more than clever", Elif waited; gave them time to make mistakes. They always did. "It just takes longer with the ones who are smarter," he murmured.

He looked about the scoop chamber, cyan twilight and a faint scent of concrete dust. It was possible that the ship – if it really was a ship – was much bigger than the four rooms they'd seen, although his Lifesense gave the impression of complete emptiness beyond the walls. He'd been through the hatch behind, seen the market, sensed emptiness there now; in terms of what direction to explore next, this left forward. Behind the Essence capacitor; behind that stone ring. Grey-green fog. If he sat up straight, he could see all the way through the ship, through three doorways, to the dull copper gleam of the capacitor. A faint hint of the buzzing Aetheric fractions drifted back to him. Mouth drawn in a line of grim disapproval, he glared at it. **That thing worries me.**

It wasn't just that he'd colluded with Russ on the collection; it was the suspicion that Essence harvesting wasn't as benign as Russ had implied. What exactly had Russ said? He couldn't remember.

Idly he reviewed the 'phone video he'd captured at the market, smiling at the memory of the purple-haired-elf-girl's cute, kitten-like grab at the token as if seeing it for the first time, and the sudden bathos of the thin white angels' table manners. He closed his eyes, wondering how long it had been since he'd slept, and dozed off.

WHEN he woke, Russ was standing at the bottom of the ramp. "We have a small problem," she said. Elif tried to conceal his glee. **This is where the lie begins to emerge. Careful; watch for the lie. Let's see... I'm supposed to be angry and jealous.** "Is it anything I can fix? No? Then why tell me?" he said, sullenly.

"You want to know what's going on, and I want to be as accommodating as possible," smiling and leaning forward slightly to emphasise the point.

He stood, stretching his stiff legs. "Oh yeah. You are just about the most accommodating suit I've ever met. Something decent to sleep on would be nice, but I don't imagine we'll be here long enough to need a bed. Will we."

"That depends if the Convocation has covered all of the other gaps in the Exclusion zone. Additional patrol ships have reinforced the first. We are detouring to the next."

Elif yawned, shook his head, trying to wake up completely. "And what if your information is hopelessly out of date and the next gap is closed as well?"

"Then we proceed to the next. And the next."

"Until we die of old age?"

"The Convocation can't cover them all. They don't have enough ships. Nobody does."

Elif stepped down the ramp, stood uncomfortably close to Russ and looked her in the eyes. "Russ... they don't need to cover them all. Just the ones we're trying to get through."

Russ shook her head. "You have an exaggerated idea of our importance. We're nothing. We are less than the bare-foot hippy with three seeds in her back pocket."

Tell that to Corporate Compliance, you liar.

Russ continued. "Something big is going on – something unrelated to our activities – and we just happen to be on the wrong side of the fence." She turned to leave, then paused and turned back. Elif had sensed that Russ would make an appeal to a deeper understanding between them eventually, and had been dreading it. Simply deciding that everything she said was a lie wouldn't work, and it was getting harder to sort out the truth from the lies and the half-lies. This was just going to complicate things. "I'm afraid I haven't been entirely candid with you about Essence extraction," she said, avoiding his gaze. "It is... mostly harmless. However some-

times it can result in physical side-effects, and in some rare cases
– the very far end of the bell curve – it can result in catastrophic
structural failure."

Elif's eyes widened and a slow grin spread across his face. He
couldn't quite believe Russ would actually confess to something this
nasty. Russ gave a small frown; she hadn't expected that reaction
and was willing to let him know it. "Their heads implode," she
said, with emphasis. Elif's grin got bigger. Russ' frown grew apace.
"Have you ever seen a head implode? It's not pretty."

Elif was trying not to laugh. "No, I haven't, and I wouldn't want
to have to clean up after it. But still, you have to – ", seeing Russ'
stern, chiding expression, " – well, okay, I guess you don't have to.
Never mind. I suspected it wasn't as benign as you made it out to
be." Russ nodded and did the avoiding-his-gaze thing again. **Okay,
here we go. This is the big one.**

"Elif... do you think Tai likes this shape?", sweeping a hand
from cleavage to waist.

He stood back a little and regarded it as if appraising Bulldada,
which, in a way, it was. "I think she likes it better than I do, which
is saying something."

Russ appeared relieved. "Humanity has changed a great deal
since Sybrandis' time. Socially. Culturally. Everything I know about
your culture was learned by watching your media and observing the
things it can't or won't mention. For someone without any innate
sense of primate nature, understanding this is not easy. Thank you."

Wow. That almost sounded sincere.

Elif followed her through the first scoop chamber, scenting the
faint scented moisture in the air around the bathroom cubicle. "So
we're getting mixed up in something big. You seem remarkably
calm about it," and, yes, her ass was swaying in a confident manner.
He shook his head; it was an extremely nice set of curves. **Focus,
damn it. No, not on that. Focus!**

"Large upsets in the natural order are perfect. I love them. We
can slip through in the confusion. We can even appropriate materiel
from the unprotected edges of the conflict. The advantage of being
one small fish in an inordinately large ocean full of bigger fish."

R USS consulted the map on the bridge, with Tai and Elif looking on. "Yes: the first available gap in the Exclusion zone is closed. Also, there is a Spree scout following us."

Sarcastically, Elif said, "It's a good thing we're nothing. Less than nothing."

Russ dismissed this. "They were following us from the station, along with three Xist destroyers. Two from Corporate Compliance, and one from Due Diligence, from the signatures."

Tai frowned. "So some of them are trying to stop us, and the other is making sure that what we're doing is being done according to, what – corporate regulations?"

"Sounds a little schizophrenic to me," Elif put in over her shoulder.

"You know what large corporations are like," Russ countered. "It's probably just some greedy middle management taking the ships out for an unauthorised spin around the cluster. They won't shoot at us." She paused. "At least, not in any serious way." Another pause. "As long as we don't give them reason to."

"What you mean 'we', white man?" Elif asked, slowly, cautiously, knowing he wouldn't like the answer.

"Well, that was **your** pirated media on the public channel at the market." His jaw dropped at the effrontery of this. Russ grinned. "Don't worry. I wouldn't throw you to Corporate Compliance. I like you, Elif." Tai matched Russ' grin with her own impish variety.

He came close to turning pale at this. "I would much rather you didn't," he said quietly.

Appearing genuinely curious, Russ asked "Why not?"

"It's not consistent with our relationship. I have a hard time trusting anyone in a position of authority. True communication is only possible between... equals..." His voice trailed off as Russ gave him the works: staring into his eyes, her pupils dilated, head tilted forward to focus her attention on him. She inhaled, cleavage swelling, and slowly smiled, giving him That Look. She didn't use any Aetherics; she didn't have to.

"You understood that, didn't you?" she purred.

He swallowed. "I understand how; I just don't understand why."

Russ tilted her head slightly to one side while keeping her eyes on his. **Dear god, is this leading to a kiss? No. No way in hell.** He shook his head once, a matter of a fraction of an inch's

movement each way. Russ blinked slowly to indicate she understood
and even managed to look disappointed; Elif felt apprehensive at
how quickly she'd developed her puppetry skills.

She'd probably had a lot of practice with Sybrandis.

A N hour later they were examining an expanded version of the
map with, respectively, annoyance, despair and a sense of I-told-
you-this-wasn't-going-to-work. In deference to the humans' limited
visualisation skills the map now covered the end of the bridge; a
section of a sphere fifteen yards across with even more icons than
the previous version. Elif could just about grasp a notion of where
they were headed, and that each gap in the Exclusion zone they
might have squeezed through was being closed off. Several times he
was on the verge of pointing out a likely detour, only to see a dozen
red plus-signs outlined in flashing yellow converge on that spot. "It's
enough to make you think it's a conspiracy," he muttered.

"Conspiracy theories grow in suspicions," Tai chided. "So, Russ:
alleviate our suspicions."

Russ peered at the map. "They are distributed evenly over this
area," pointing, "in effect, closing off eighty percent of our possible
routes. At the moment our best course is... here," indicating a long,
flat loop around the edge of the Zone. "Travel time: six hundred and
seventy-nine hours." Elif and Tai shared a glance. Russ sighed. "I'll
have Ron print out a bed for you, Elif." The robot's face went blank
and it left the bridge without any of Russ' distinctive mannerisms
or gait.

Elif called out, "Hey, Ron? Can you make some more Bivalve?
We're just about out," meaning there were only one hundred and
ninety cans left.

"Yes," it said in a monotone over its shoulder, without turning
around.

Elif nodded, pleased. "That's what I like about Ron. Straight
and to-the-point," muttering, "also I like to think Russ can't spy on
us when Ron is at the controls." He thrust his hands into his pocket,
found his 'phone, and remembered, "Oh, hey, souvenirs: video of
the asteroid market, and an actual alien artefact."

"Gimme!" Tai said eagerly, reaching for a data cable. When the
transfer was complete she displayed the images on a new window

hovering over her bed.

Elif discovered she'd sent a file to his 'phone; while she examined the figurine and watched Dr Squid have its way with him, he watched a palm-sized patch of harshly-lit sepia where three beefy peasants pinned the arms of a fat human priest – Sybrandis' mentor, he guessed – and forced him to kneel before an ornately detailed chest made of glittering bronze: the Essence collector, disguised as a tabernacle or some such piece of ecclesiastical furniture. Elif frowned. The view zoomed in on the priest's face, anger and disbelief drawn in unflattering diagonal cross-hatching, motion-blurred by his struggles and the irregular frame-rate. The peasants pushed him forward until his forehead touched the tabernacle; he fought back as if his life depended on it, almost winning free.

Then the top of his skull caved in as if struck by an invisible bowling ball. Fuzzily rendered dark liquid jetted from his eyes and ears. The peasants dropped him; blood seeped into the collector's carving. "'Ooh, that **had** to hurt'," Elif quoted.

"I doubt he felt anything," Tai said casually over her shoulder, her attention on the video of Grey guys eating yoghurt... "Nothing left to feel with."

"When did you find this?" Elif asked.

"Just before you woke up. A file that had been partly deleted."

"Uh-huh," **about the time Russ was apologising for misleading us about Essence extraction.** He turned off his 'phone and gazed thoughtfully at the places where the chrome finish had worn off the buttons. "I wonder if the Collector could make **our** heads cave in." Tai didn't reply; she was watching Elif's encounter with the purple-haired elf-girl, filmed from the vantage point of the floor; he'd dropped his 'phone without realising it. He was about to explain the situation when Tai silently mouthed "ahh" and nodded. "Aetherics?" she asked.

He nodded. "Oh yeah. I was completely helpless. If Russ hadn't turned up I'd still be there, kneeling in a puddle of my own drool."

"Or worse," she joked, then, in an envious tone, "what was it like?" Elif ran his hand through his hair, opened and closed his mouth four times without finding the right words. "That bad, huh?" He nodded, relieved that she could see it. She sighed. "I suppose it's too late to go back there?"

"Once we're done with this," waving a hand at the Essence capacitor, "we'll hitch a ride. We still have that token. And I think you'd really like Dr Squid."

Tai laughed. "If that dopey grin on your face was any indication, I'm sure I would."

"Very likeable. I just wish the 'phone could've picked up both sides of the conversation." Elif frowned, then remembered. "Oh, yeah. Telepathy."

"I thought you didn't believe in telepathy."

Forthrightly, "I didn't believe in flying saucers, either, until I ended up in one."

"RUSS, what does this symbol mean?" With an effort Tai got down on her hands and knees and poked her finger through a glowing amber bead near the floor.

"Why?" Russ asked tersely, slightly narrowed eyes glancing about the map, looking for a way through.

"Because it seems to be at the centre of the filled gaps in the Exclusion zone."

Experimentally, Russ zoomed the map back, rotated it. "I do believe you're right. Imagine that." The map expanded until the bead became a teapot-sized Klein bottle drawn in lines of glowing gold. "It's one end of a transit corridor, what you'd call a stabilised wormhole. The Abandoners run them between lucrative economic gradients. When the lucrative runs out, they move the generators at either end through regular space." She folded her arms beneath her breasts and seemed to think that was all the explanation they needed until Tai stared her down. "What?"

Elif counted on his fingers. "Where's the other end? How much does it cost to go through?", faltering when he realised he only had two points – not really enough to justify enumerating.

"And is there an information service, like a toll-free number?" Tai added. Elif nodded, encouraged.

A row of dinner-plate-sized white discs appeared in the air before them, spattered with black spots linked by crooked, hair-thin tracks like ant trails. Russ pointed to each in turn: "Dual carriageway; emergency traffic only; far end is at reference blah blah blah, hazard level so-and-so, standard fee scale, turbulence minimal, time dilation zero point zero two plus or minus seventeen seconds."

Tai looked at Elif, whose expression said **see what she's like?** He asked "How far from the other end to our destination? Flight time?"

Russ looked uncomfortable. Tai turned up the intensity of her disapproving stare. "... ninety-one hours," she admitted grudgingly. "But I don't think they'll let us through."

Tai was almost exasperated. "Not if you tell them we're running Essence, obviously! What if you say... you've got a desperately sick human pet on board. You have to get home in time to record 'Galaxy's Funniest Temporal Anomalies'. You know these people. Think of something," Tai said, looking to Elif for support.

"Tell them Corporate Compliance are on our ass," Elif put in.

Russ inclined her head towards him and raised her eyebrows, joking, "**That** might work," then continuing pensively, "I can convince the ship to demonstrate the signature of a Sheydal Emergency frigate... nobody ever stops them..."

Elif asked "Who are the Sheydal? You mentioned them before." Tai waved her hand in annoyance. "We don't have time for a – "

"THE SHEYDAL," Russ interrupted jovially, "are one of the galaxy's saddest tales," seemingly enjoying Tai's angry glare, "a very spiritual people. Dedicated, even fanatical philanthropists; they live to serve others. They maintain a network of aid and rescue stations that spans a third of the galaxy."

Despite her annoyance at the diversion, Tai had to ask "Why is this sad?"

"Because of the extent to which everyone exploits them. Everyone. Elif, do you remember the thin white angels in the alien quarter?" Elif nodded slowly, thinking that they had looked like the type who might be excessively spiritual. "They were eating a young Sheydal. Yes, I know what you were thinking. You can't judge a race by their looks, but you can always judge them by their table manners."

"So, let me get this straight... they are so selfless... that they allow themselves – they allow their children to be cooked and served up on plates," Tai said hesitantly, not quite believing it.

Russ nodded. "Excellent means of population control. Humanity

could benefit from their example." She thought for a moment. "Come to think of it, they have, in some places."

"W̲E can go faster than this," Elif said, tracking their progress across the map display with his nose.

"Of course," Russ said, "But if I run the engines at full, you might hear what they were trying to say, and they might give away my evil plans. And we don't want that." Elif's only response to that was the disdainful look that Daffy Duck had borrowed from Jack Lemmon. "We are proceeding at this relatively sedate pace for several reasons... primarily, to spare Tai the pain of having to sit near the engines – "

" – it wasn't that bad," Tai interrupted cheerfully, "more a surprise than anything else. Ramp it up slowly and we'll tell you when it gets too much to bear." Russ regarded her warily then gave Elif a brief look that told him just how little his opinion in this mattered.

Elif shrugged. "Crank it. I'm a guy, so I'm not going to give in first, and she has a pain threshold like a cliff of obsidian rock fifty miles high."

Russ continued, "... but also to keep a reserve of energy in case we need to leave the area quickly. I don't like the look of this."

Elif gently kicked the underside of the Essence capacitor, which rang like an empty oil can. "Sell 'em some of this. Maybe they'll set up a little wormhole just for us."

As the itching hum of the engines slowly became more uncomfortable Russ aimed a particularly sour look at him. "Don't kick the capacitor," she said with a trace of annoyance, which Elif picked up on immediately. **If we could damage it, we wouldn't be allowed near it.**

"Can it be? Is there something the Xists regard as sacred after all?"

Patiently, "It's my cargo. It's why I'm out here. Show a little respect."

Respect? Oh my, no. Elif was casting about for the least respectful thing he could possibly say when he caught Russ' lack of expression. In a deceptively casual tone, she said "When you were scuttling about your filthy, monkey-infested back alleyways, trying to buy a drug that might let you forget your dismal, pointless existence for a few minutes... did you show the same casual lack of regard for the subtleties of the dealer-addict mystique as you do now?"

Defiantly, Elif matched Russ' serious tone. "Always. I insisted on it." He leaned against the capacitor, draping one arm over the top. The bronze sphere swayed as if supported by magnetic fields. "There is nothing so sacred that it can't be laughed at. Nothing. A mother's love, the most refined social dance, God, addiction, profits, your place in the pecking order, life, death, spontaneous observed proton decay – **nothing.** If you aren't allowed to laugh at it then you damn well should."

He stopped, realising he'd gone a little further than he'd originally intended to. There was a moment's respectful silence after this outburst, which Tai defused by saying, quietly, "Praise 'Bob'!".

Was Russ smiling? "With that attitude I'm surprised you didn't cop a shiv between the ribs."

"Oh, he did, on more than one occasion," Tai laughed, "and he usually ended up on my doorstep afterward."

Russ accepted this. "I sometimes forget how cheap life is to the lower orders of existence."

During all of this Tai had been typing and glancing up at a window hovering directly over her bed. She caught Elif's attention and beckoned him closer with a subtle eye movement. The display showed picture thumbnails which he recognised immediately: his computer's image collection, specifically, a subset of the vast accumulation of soft-core pictures of women he'd ever thought attractive enough to keep on his computer. **Yeah, and, so, what?** he said with one raised eyebrow. They'd talked about this before; Tai regarded it as a mostly harmless guy thing, and Elif defended it as an approximation of the neurological imprints he'd acquired during adolescence: signposts pointing the way to the archetypal goddess of his dreams, which, he'd said, didn't really exist outside of his mind. Then he remembered his previous suspicions about Russ' interest in his porn collection and tried not to give it away with his expression.

As he watched, the pictures paired off and merged, coalescing into fewer and fewer images until there was only a single screen's worth. With a flick of her index finger Tai dismissed the hopelessly confused ones and then caused the remaining few to combine. The final result looked enough like Russ for the meaning of the procedure to be immediately obvious.

Elif took a few moments to absorb the import of this. **Which is why Russ really wanted my computer.** He sighed. "Sometimes I feel like I've got a big old suitcase handle bonded to the top of my head," he said.

"I could think of worse places it could be attached," Tai said reassuringly. "By the way, you didn't mean any of that about holding nothing sacred?"

Elif made a sour face. "Hell, no."

Russ was stalking around the map display, watching the gathering clusters of red plus-signs which were being joined by long convoys of octothorpes and six disturbingly large inverted ankhs, slowly taking up positions around the Klein-teapot. "I don't like the look of this at all. Gate control says they'll let us through, but they won't say why there are so many military caste Spree ships here." She sighed. "At least they haven't deployed any – " and here, each octothorpe released hundreds of red dots – "fighter... swarms... very well, they **have** deployed fighter swarms. No. I won't risk taking the cargo through that gate. Not without any good information on what's at the other end."

"Well, let's review what we do know," Tai said. "If we don't go through, we'll be stuck here for, what? Twenty-eight days. Nothing personal – it's a very nicely appointed ship – but I don't want to spend close to a month in here. My medication won't last that long."

From an unfamiliar edge in Tai's voice, Elif got the feeling than a bad argument was in the making; in a rare moment of clarity he tried to cut to the chase. "What do we know about the area on the other side of the gate?" Russ gestured, opening six tall column-windows filled with writhing maggots in unpleasant shades of yellow. "It's... full of worms," Elif said with sarcastic approval. "Let's go there right now."

Russ pointed to each column, translating (although she could have been making it up as she went along): "Two red giant suns, almost dead. No planets. No stations. Informatic complexity close to zero. No regular traffic. What concerns me most," indicating the last column's noticeably slower worms, "is that this report is not at all reliable."

"It is so hard to get good help these days," Elif joked.

"Actually, that data was collected by an Xist," Russ said.

"It's so hard to find masters you can trust these days," Tai said with uncharacteristic spite; she was getting angry.

Elif walked around to the other side of the map and peered through the glowing symbols at Tai and Russ. "So we don't know what's on the other side, there's a huge military force on **this** side; they'll let us through, but they think we're an ambulance or something... if they need ambulances, maybe we don't want to be there."

"This is a drug run, not a mission of mercy," Russ reminded them.

There was a few moments' silence. Elif said, "Russ, why don't we just ask them what's really going on? Speak plainly, admit what we're up to, and ... uh... " He stopped when he saw the look Russ was giving him. "Oh."

"If negotiation was going to work, they wouldn't need that many warships," Tai said.

"It's always good to negotiate from a position of strength," Russ pointed out.

"Can you get your corporation to threaten them with economic sanctions?" Elif asked.

Russ shook her head. "Given that the Spree are the basis for manufacture in this – "

"Russ, we are going through the wormhole," Tai cut in, "and until we do, I'm on strike. No more SubGenius flavoured essence." She grimaced with the effort of getting to her feet. "It's always good to negotiate from a position of strength," she added and, using Russ' two-by-four as a cane, slowly made her way to the scoop chambers.

Elif glanced after her, then back at Russ; he shrugged, said "I need to think about this," and followed Tai.

SHE had continued on to the second scoop chamber to get as far as possible from the Collector. Elif got the idea she didn't want to talk just now, so he ducked around behind the bathroom cubicle, went straight to the old television set which had been stashed there, pried the back off and retrieved a bag of weed. Within thirty seconds he'd made a water pipe from an empty Bivalve can and the television's volume knob and was getting as stoned as possible. The usual anxiety over being caught faded quickly; he didn't know how far away the cops were, but he didn't think the local authorities would be concerned.

He believed that being whacked on suburban back-yard ditch-weed made it easier for him to work out what was going on. "Tai wants to get this trip over with as soon as possible. Easy to see. Russ wants to avoid the militia. Understandable. Russ admits we don't have a reliable idea of what's on the far side of the wormhole... avoiding responsibility for the consequences? I can't imagine as big an asshole as Russ coming out here without a very good idea of the threat... but she's not really here, is she, and if she isn't, all she stands to lose is her Essence and two SubGenii. And her ship."

Elif inhaled another shot, lay on his back and blew a plume of grey smoke up at the grid of cyan lights overhead. "Okay, let's drop the pretence that we know who's where and what they want. If Russ can't keep Tai healthy for the next four weeks, we don't have any choice; we'll have to go through. Now, if I was **really** paranoid, Russ would use this as a bargaining chip to make us do something even worse than sit around listening to her exaggerate her importance."

This time he heard Russ approaching and had time to think of a little mind-game he could play. Sitting up against the back of the bathroom cubicle, he drew his legs up in an exaggerated panic when Russ peered around the corner. "Gah GAH-DAMN IT, don't you ever knock?" Russ almost had time to protest before he added, "I mean, I didn't interrupt when you were masturbating in the shower, so for the love of whatever the hell it is you respect, show some god-damned manners."

Patiently, "Are you quite done?"

Elif packed some more weed into the makeshift pipe and blew smoke in her face. "Well done."

"We are going through. Against my better judgement. With regard to Tai's declining condition, the only other option is a procedure that I don't think she'll readily agree to."

"What, something worse than sitting around listening to you

exaggerate your importance?"

Russ crossed her arms. "Well, I don't know. She might like the idea. I'll have to ask."

Elif took a few seconds to shift mental gears from contemplative stoner paranoia to active Russ-baiting. "I'm not exactly thrilled with the prospect of another month of your bullshit, so I can't imagine Tai would like it any better." He knew Russ had been referring to that ominous-sounding procedure, but he couldn't pass up an opportunity to... what? With the ditch-weed's characteristic abruptness he realised he was exhibiting classic primate behaviour in response to a threat. Insults were just the modern equivalent of monkeys throwing poop at each other, and Russ was no monkey, even if she looked and smelled like one and even occasionally acted like one.

While generally accepting that people were monkeys and that he was a person, Elif tried to avoid the more pointless excesses of habitual monkey thinking... **and, frankly, the amount of monkey-poop that I need to throw at Russ doesn't exist. So how would an Xist deal with this?**

Sweetly, Russ said "Elif, I can hear the cogs in your head grinding against each other. Don't bother. Keep throwing monkey-poop. It's what you do best."

To his credit he didn't panic at hearing how well Russ could follow his thoughts; his SubGenius Do-Something-Unexpected instinct took over. He stood and handed the pipe to Russ. She accepted it, looked at it, then shrugged and took a hit, exhaling through her nostrils. Elif didn't try to conceal it this time; he stared in slack-jawed appreciation of Russ' curves, then "Wait, can you actually get ripped on this? Give me that," retrieving the pipe with a frown. "Get your own damn drugs."

"If I had anything worth sharing, you know I'd offer you some."

Elif turned to look, significantly, down the front of the ship at the capacitor, then, on a hunch, craning his neck to one side as if trying to peer around the bronze shape, before turning back to stare at her. Deliberately, but not so deliberately that Russ might think it was deliberate, his expression gave the look of someone trying to put two and two together while wearing boxing gloves. Without turning around he put one hand back to intercept the end of the two-by-four just as Tai was aiming it at his ass. Seeing the looks Russ and Elif were exchanging, she pushed between them impatiently, muttering "Oh, get a **room**, you two," and marching back to the bridge.

The front end of the ship was now completely filled with a realistic view of the area ahead, but at this range it was all just faintly coloured white dots on a black background. The general light levels on the bridge were lower, a subtle, muted effect that was only missing a red flashing bulb. Tai stopped before sitting down, turned and gave them both a stern look. "I don't want to hear **anybody** say 'red alert!', okay? Unless you're going to let Elif drive, there isn't anything the human complement can do in an emergency except sit here and trade witty Blackadder quotes until we die horribly. So, just, you know... don't." She waved Russ forward. "You may proceed."

Elif was at first swaying from side to side, then moving slowly from port to starboard and back again, peering intently at the panoramic display. Tai asked, a little wearily, "Elif, what are you doing?"

"Looking for the parallax... trying to see if this thing does realistic 3D. It's all too far away. Zoom feature?"

Russ actually got as far as starting to raise her hand for a magical gesture when she stopped and looked at Tai, who had pressed a single key on her keyboard. Six empty targeting circles appeared, expanding into close-up shots of each ship, adjusted for what little stray light there was out there and outlined in rippling golden false-visual grids: tumbling, gnarled black lumps, charred lengths of pine log. The largest ship – a matte black peanut fifteen miles long, conveniently scaled by a row of wire-frame Eiffel Towers drawn beneath – appeared to have a faint halo; a closer view showed clouds of smaller ships covering every possible attack point. Tai pressed two more keys and the view zoomed in on one of the smaller picket ships: an irregular cylinder detailed in what looked like black candle drippings. A wire-frame school bus appeared next to it to show the scale.

They checked out a few other ships, all disappointingly bare of ornament or blinking lights or even threatening-looking gun emplacements of some kind. After Tai pressed another key and gave each ship on the display a curved line showing its speed and projected course, Russ was plainly giving Tai a suspicious look. Oblivious to this, Elif pointed to the halo of picket ships around the biggest vessel. "They're protecting that one. Looking at the courses the others are following, I'd say they're all protecting it. From some threat ahead of them. Coming from the wormhole. If there's nothing on the other side, why all the goons? Is this how they usually travel?"

"Why all the ships, the hell if I know. Because they can?" Russ snapped. She pretended to speak into a headset microphone. "'Ahoy there insect swarm, this is the Trebuchet Bitchslap. We're Xist **drug runners.** Could we please speak to the **bug** in charge? We'd like to know what you're doing with all of these – well, what do you know? They hung up. **Puh-lease.**" This last was delivered with as much scorn as she could deliver.

"Yeesh, what got up your skirt?" Elif asked.

Russ gave Tai a sideways glance. "Tai is better at systems infiltration than we'd expected," she said darkly.

Tai tried to look modest. "Oh, utter twaddle. Those access points were just sitting there. Look, would you like me to put in some serious safeguards in case you actually need to keep people out? It'd be easy."

Russ held up her hand. "No, please, thank you. That's how it begins, and then one day you find you've been locked out of your own room."

They were close enough to pass by the outer layers of the picket ships, coasting by on long, thin tails of blue fire, moving in convoluted knots reminiscent of William Latham's computer-generated organic forms, efficiently maximising their coverage. Behind them a series of thin metal hoops that must have been at least a mile thick and fifty miles in diameter sat in ranked rows, forming a tunnel to nowhere. "Since their defensive orientation is toward the front, we shall follow behind the largest ship, at a respectful distance," Russ said. "If we offend, they will be sure to let us know."

Elif put his hands behind his back and idly paced about. "Russ, this display is getting a little dull. Can you make it at least aesthetically pleasing?" Russ shrugged and a cute kitten icon drawn in large square white pixels appeared and happily frolicked about the display before falling asleep beneath a trail of Zs. Elif had to laugh before thinking **This is what she wants. She's trying to build up a relationship of trust based on barely concealed hostility, unconcealed cleavage and amusing adventures. Remember the car breakdown theory?**

"Oh, yeah," he mused. **You don't really know someone until you've both been stuck out in the middle of nowhere when your car breaks down.** "Observation and crisis", as the Bene Gesserit would have said. If Russ was trying to win their confidence then she would probably have arranged for their car to break down somewhere ahead, and anywhere with more than a thousand Spree warships was a good place to do it.

Elif didn't see the conduit activate; one moment he was trying to see some detail on the back of the largest Spree ship and the next, the space inside the hoops had silvered over and the first Spree pickets were diving in. There was something subtly wrong about the way they moved; once through the first ranks of hoops they slowed down while shrinking into the distance much faster than one might expect. The space around them glowed like phosphorescent dust, then the largest ship lumbered into the first hoop and the Trebuchet Bitchslap followed. The hoops flashed by too quickly to count, but Elif was sure they had passed a lot more hoops than he'd seen, and they kept passing by until they made a bright blur all around, the various coal-black Spree ships showing in stark contrast. Some of the pickets moved ahead and began to elongate through some bizarre hyperspacial perspective until they were just black looped threads.

The Bitchslap drifted closer to the rear of the largest ship, just within the outer layer of pickets, the huge silhouette ahead blocking the view down the tunnel. Even the cutest animated neko couldn't liven this view; nine-tenths abyssal blackness with a narrow band of fluttering silver and gold lines rushing by at the edges. Elif caught Tai's attention, nodded slightly at the back of the Spree carrier and pantomimed pulling his head back. She nodded and started typing, groups of two keys pressed with careful deliberation. With an uncharacteristic lurch, the Bitchslap began to drop back into the trailing picket ships, which smoothly detoured around them.

Russ appeared frozen, staring at the ass-end of the Spree carrier as it moved away. Quietly, "I hope you can steer this thing back into real space. That rather unsubtle command pointer substitution has locked me out of the control halo. If I try to grab the steering wheel we will spin out through the side of the conduit and die instantly."

Tai was confident. "If I can get into your personal email, I can fly a Cowcatcher." Seeing the look Russ was giving her, she laughed. "You guys don't use email. Chill out." She was steering by the display on her computer, which, as best as Elif could judge from that angle, had rather more moving skin-toned shapes than he would have expected from a navigation interface. When they had backed off to where they could almost see around the carrier, she told the ship to hold them at that distance, leaned back, steepled her fingers above her head and stretched. "It's all in the wrist action," she admitted modestly. "We're coming up on the half-way point in twenty seconds, so if you've got a bucket, now's the time to start wearing it on your head."

Russ crossed the bridge and sat on the end of Tai's bed (rather closer to Tai than Elif was comfortable with) and covered her eyes. Tai was pointedly nodding towards the display while Elif feigned ignorance.

"What? Oh, I get it. It's the old Don't Look Directly At Hyperspace Or Your Brain Will Explode thing. Oldest trick in the book, that one." Defiantly, he crossed his arms and leaned forward attentively as the nearer ships elongated into black spikes and the spiralling silver lines burned moire patterns into his retinas. "Wish I had some popcorn," Elif sighed as the lines of light danced in the standard hyperspacial conduit passage effect with just enough subtle bobbing to give the impression of rapid movement. "Oh, yawn! You almost expect to see Margaret Hamilton riding by on a bicycle. In black and white."

Quietly Tai asked Russ, "So, nu?"

"Any second now," Russ assured her. Elif rolled his eyes and turned back to watch the display. An ugly black lump like a conifer seedpod drifted close, an attached text label identifying it as Spree Heavy Bomber [S4]; it sped ahead to join the others, dwindling into a long spiral of glittering black. Then –

– it started as a brilliant purple-white flare at the extreme far end of the conduit and faded to dark violet as it spread, edges subdividing into hairy fractal writhing, black chain lightning moving almost too fast to follow, growing along the length of the tube in an uncomfortably organic way. The whole thing wobbled like the bottom of an unbalanced spin dryer, and for one moment – barely long enough to register – something clawed aside the entire spinning weave of accelerated light, something big, the same colour as a camera flash after-image, something with claws and one huge eye. Elif stared, horrified and fascinated. That thing moved the universe aside as easily as he might open some curtains, and it saw him. For that intensely painful moment they each looked into the other, the human and the hideously eager sentience from the outer darkness –

That moment was brief enough for him to realise that he would survive it but long enough for the thing to attempt a parting shot: the furiously active hair lightning strands began to weave themselves into thicker fronds, arching about and starting to look like something very familiar... almost like the patterns formed by the tiny veins around the edges of his retinas. It was trying to **match his eyes**, and if it only had a little more time it would have a perfect match and they would be together, the human and the thing from the abyss and it would know what it was like to view the world from inside a cave of thin bone through a tangle of wet nerves...

... and he would know why it wanted so badly to get in. He closed his eyes and didn't dare move for a while. Not thinking about anything wasn't hard; he was quite literally scared witless. Damned if he was going to let Russ know it. He counted to twenty-three, then opened one eye cautiously. It was gone.

Barely managing to control his shakes, he moved closer to the display and waved angrily at the back of the Spree carrier. "Oh, come on, MOVE OVER, you great, big... thing...", still shaking, momentarily lost for an appropriate expression. Tai pressed a few more keys and they began to move back from and around the carrier. There was no trace of anything trying to match anybody's eyes lurching at them from the far end of the conduit; just looping whorls of energy and the nested black spiral needles of the Spree fleet. The carrier was still close; it looked a little bendy around the far end but at close range the visual distortion was minimal. The clear view allowed Elif to see the end of the carrier sectioning open like a seed-pod, almost like something about to deploy a horrific weapon.

Elif didn't need to ask; Tai began to back off as quickly as she could without running into any of the pickets. The carrier turned slowly as the end opened, giving them an excellent sense of its size; it was as large as a good-sized city.

"I can't say I'm particularly happy with this," Russ said. "Would any of you consider making an emergency turn off the conduit? There's a four percent chance we'd survive intact, but of course we'd be hopelessly lost. We could end up anywhere."

"Anywhere in the galaxy?" Elif asked, already suspecting the answer.

"Anywhere in the universe," Russ said. "You have to expect that kind of thing when you start messing with higher dimensions."

"And a four percent chance of survival is preferable to... what, exactly?" Elif asked.

Russ pointed at the carrier. "That is a Spree Seedship. It is assembled from trillions of living elements intended to colonise a dead planet and cover it with atmosphere and a ten-foot-thick layer of bugs inside a week. There are more living things in that ship by a factor of a hundred million than there are humans on your planet, and this sophisticated and very expensive commodity is being flung into an area of space with two, count them, two dying stars and a surveyed average of exactly **zero** planets."

"As far as we know," Elif had to put in. "Why didn't you mention this before?"

Russ snapped in angry, clipped tones, "It was Tai's idea. Anyway, if there is anything bigger than a banana waiting for us there I promise to put on my environment suit and get out there and have sex with it. Does that make you happy?"

"Ecstatic," Elif said with satisfaction, despite not believing that Russ was on board in any meaningful capacity. **She probably meant she'll make that robot go out there. Heh. I hope there is something bigger than a –**

One of his Aetherics tickled his sensorium with a faint glimpse of what was waiting for them. A fish. A big fish with big teeth. What had Dr Squid said before he'd left the market?

"Ah." he said to himself. "We're gonna need a bigger boat."

IN an all-too-sudden logarithmic rush, a circle of real space shot up the conduit and surrounded them, half the sky obscured by the Spree Seedship with eager clusters of smaller craft pushing on ahead and then exploding in a gout of sickly green radiance. Just looking at the aftermath made him physically ill. **Must be one of those fate-worse-than-death deals. Even Russ had to have felt that.** The same nauseating thing was happening to ships all around; whatever was shooting at them was on the other side of the Seedship, which would perhaps give them enough time for – yes. Russ gently pushed Tai aside and started typing on her keyboard. The Bitchslap turned end around in space and began to move away from the fighting while keeping the Seedship between them and whatever was firing beams of green death at everything else. Elif was still receiving distant impressions of the clockwork he'd first sensed in the Spree pimp at the market, but they were being silenced in great numbers all around him, and the sensation was unpleasantly like shards of broken glass being crushed together.

"The conduit is still open. I think this would be a good time to leave and I sincerely apologise for not making a space in our schedule to put this to a democratic vote." They were halfway to the gate entrance by the time Russ had finished saying this, and the engines were starting to howl.

A second wave of Spree ships slowly floated to the end of the conduit and surfaced. The watery impression was reinforced by the six Abandoner ships that followed, one large fluoro-green sac filled with fluids and five clusters of smaller sacs, each darting about rapidly and oscillating in a confident manner. For a few seconds the Bitchslap played chicken with the largest Abandoner before Russ prudently dodged out of its way; they got close enough to see faint outlines of vacuoles within the Abandoner's flexible hull, and a host of smaller bodies floating about inside the vacuoles, squirming with frenetic biological activity.

The Abandoner rippled and flung itself out into a broad doughnut shape leaving a gap just large enough for a green beam to pass through harmlessly, barely missing the Bitchslap, then the beam widened into a bilious searchlight splashing off the front of the Abandoner. A broad patch of the vivid fluorescent green fluid darkened to a morbid slate grey and began to fragment like dried clay.

Almost too quickly to be seen, three flickering silver indeterminate shapes – each registered briefly on Elif's vision as clusters of origami squids made of silver foil – darted in through the gate and promptly faded into the background. "Xists," Russ said. "Due Diligence, I'm pretty much certain of, and possibly a covert operations scout from one of the Fire Xist corporations," adding, almost happily, "this is turning into quite a party."

A needle-thin beam of white hot plasma edged in red cut a hole through the Seedship, again narrowly missing them. It ran off into the void and struck the closest of the conduit rings. The beam splashed like water and began devouring the rotating structure, sending huge fragments flying in all directions. As the beam faded thousands of red sparks remained. In close view, they looked like ornate metal crosses, slowly cooling to black. When they hit the ring they came to life, scuttled off like ticks and began chewing holes in the structure.

The display canted to the right as Russ brought the ship around on a different heading. Ahead of them were the fragments of the first ring and a loose cloud of glowing hot crosses, machines busily attacking anything and each other. The enemy on the other side of the distressed Seedship was firing them in streams, one after the other, at the rings. A Spree beetle bomber shot past them silently, spreading explosive mines in its wake, giving Russ several dozen more things to avoid.

As the bomber deposited a track of pulsing pink triangles across the display, the whole scene took on a dizzying air of unreality for Elif. He could feel the crackling sensation of Spree ships dying around him and sense a distant moaning whale-song from the Abandoners as they froze in the vacuum. He could even feel the ship rocking from side to side slightly as they dodged the mines and the fighting machines, but it still looked like a video game projected onto a wide screen.

"Now?" Russ asked Tai.

She nodded reluctantly. "Keep your distance though. But don't look like you're trying to keep your distance."

Elif almost smiled at that, and considered saying something in Wookiie to complete the quote, but the sense of cheap tropery overcame him. Russ wanted them to think they were about to die, so they probably weren't. Any curiosity about the outcome of the battle disappeared when he considered that it might just be, or in fact probably was, a simulation on the screen. He shook his head and wandered back into the recycling bay. It still smelled like a bakery from when Ron had fabricated the new bed.

He paused and considered swallowing his pride a little; most of his irritation was jealousy, based in the knowledge that Russ and Tai had formed a bond that he couldn't share... to where they were using conversational short-cuts and even code phrases. Weren't they supposed to be conspiring against her? It was good to know that Russ thought they were too dangerous to be allowed to conspire. Or perhaps that Tai and Russ had more in common than he could ever have with either of them.

"Well, she got there first. She's smart, alright," he sighed. The engines suddenly screamed much louder, and instinctively he tried to cover his ears, and when that didn't work, his eyes. One scream was a slightly higher pitch than the other; **maybe if I stood in the right spot the beat frequency would shatter my skull.** The thought briefly distracted him from his growing feeling of misery, and the engines seemed to understand. **Yes, it hurts. It's supposed to hurt. Your ability to endure the pain makes you one of the –**

A loud bang cut off the words, jolting the ship and knocking Elif off his feet. One of the engines screamed briefly and died; the other wailed off into the distance, somewhere ahead, in the direction of the gathering storm-clouds. He got up and examined the round engine mount; the grey hull metal was buckled around a sharp, crescent-shaped bump, looking for all the world as if someone had tried to shove a banana through the wall. It didn't seem to be leaking air; briefly he thought about going back to the bridge and telling Russ and Tai, but he suspected they already knew, so he went to the second Scoop chamber.

A flat mattress-sized square of white plastic was sitting in the middle of the room with their remaining furniture and boxes of books scattered about. The plastic square was slowly puffing up like rising bread dough. He went over, prodded it, then recoiled slightly, rubbing his fingers. It felt uncomfortably like skin.

He walked up the ramp and sat with his back against the hatch that led outside. If Russ was putting all of this on – if they hadn't actually gone anywhere – then the asteroid market should still be behind him. If they were out in space somewhere, then the hatch shouldn't open. If he could get the hatch open – if Russ would let him – then some of his suspicions would be confirmed. **If Russ doesn't want me to find out, then she's hardly likely to let me open the hatch, is she?**

"Gods damn it, I have to do something." He stood up, turned to face the hatch and took a deep breath, summoning the concentration to tell the door to open, perhaps onto the asteroid market, maybe onto empty space and vacuum, possibly onto something else.

The ship shook as if being struck by large rocks, then a force began to drag him backwards, down the ramp: they were slowing down. He tripped over the edge of the bed and fell to lie on his back, slid across the mattress, fell to the floor on the far side and rolled all the way over to the other ramp. A grinding shriek came from outside, metal scraping against metal, ending in a slow, sad groan as the ship came to a stop.

Elif got to his feet, muttering "Who's driving this thing?", then remembered who. "Oh, crap," truly concerned now, rushing back to the bridge, half expecting to see everyone lying in a heap around the Essence capacitor, and not symmetrically docked.

The recycling bay was eerily silent after the tortured moans of the engines. When he stepped onto the bridge, the lighting was almost as dim as in the Scoops. The end of the room was filled with a sheet of hazy static in horizontal red bands. It flickered brighter now and then, to give the impression of damaged or disconnected sensors; an old SF film standard. Tai was sitting up in her bed and typing, naturally enough, with Russ looking over her shoulder.

Russ looked up. Tai stopped typing, awkwardly tried to get up without thinking and would have collapsed onto the floor if Elif hadn't caught her. He helped her back to her bed and reassured her that he wasn't hurt, then dragged an empty power cell over and sat on it, chin resting in his hands, elbows on knees, regarding them both owlishly.

Presently Russ said "I expect you're wondering what happened and where we are now."

Elif sat silently, waiting until it became uncomfortable; Russ didn't seem to be showing any signs of impatience, so he gave in and said "Yeah. Okay, I'll bite."

Russ stepped to the side of the broken display window and clasped her hands behind her back. The room's indirect lighting faded completely to that comforting kind of warm darkness only found in the classier cinemas, and the red static formed into crisp black with silver shapes chasing beige shapes around a mountain of dark grey: the Spree Seedship and its attendant swarm.

Russ pointed to a grey-white spot at the centre of the display. "That's us. We came in behind the Seedship, turned back to the gate; the gate was destroyed." The display zoomed in on the painfully bright red and white beam as it lanced into the side of the conduit generator ring. The oddly cross-shaped red sparks were slamming into the ring and pushing it off station, spreading out on impact. Russ pointed again, and the display centred on a cross as it hit the ring and then came to life, crawling away like half a spider. Any hopes that the situation might have some sort of peaceful resolution vanished when Elif saw what the cross-shaped machines did to the conduit generator rings with their claws.

Several more beams sliced through the middle of the Seedship, carving a hole several miles wide lined with fragmenting chunks of structural forms, debris, liquid and dying Spree clades. Fire-hydrant geysers of orange gushed from main arteries. The Bitchslap hung back prudently until a squadron of Spree beetle-bombers dared to dive through the hole, then cautiously followed. Great splintered spars of white bone stuck out from the burned edges of the thousands of compartments inside the Seedship, all of them disgorging atmosphere and clumps of dying Spree, creatures of all sizes, dying in their millions. Another beam of red-white struck through very close, enlarging the hole and clipping a beetle-bomber that spun out of control, strewing glittering black ordnance in a widening corkscrew path as it went. Amidst the chaos, a smaller Spree cruiser blundered into a beetle bomb and exploded. A black shard of casing flew at them like a shuriken and hit the Bitchslap's engine pods, destroying one and knocking the other out of its nacelle and off into space. That had been the first impact.

The Bitchslap came out of the far side of the Seedship, and Elif's eyes grew wide. He stood up to better appreciate the sight: the metal walls of an immense tunnel stretched out before him, hundreds of miles deep, lined with an eye-wrenching degree of insane mechanical detail; guns firing shells, beam weapons in several colours slicing targets in two, clusters of X-shaped machines of every size and configuration flinging themselves into the middle of the tunnel to attack the Spree ships that had blundered in, giant mechanical arms swinging out from the sides to grasp at pieces of ship as they tumbled by. The distant end of the cavity faded into clouds of dark grey occasionally lit by white flashes of lightning and the long, slow burn of atomic weapons. It took a few seconds for Elif to realise that there was just as much furious fighting along the walls of the tunnel, between the various machines, as with the Spree. The insects' strategy didn't change noticeably with the destruction of the conduit rings; the tiny fighters seemed as enthusiastically suicidal as before, throwing themselves down this thing's throat at the slightest chance of delivering their payloads despite being out-gunned, massively, overwhelmingly, hopelessly game-over-guys-game-over.

Abruptly the Bitchslap changed course. The display canted up to follow, thousands of tiers of complex machinery and pipes and weapons bays sliding past as they tried to fly out over the edge of the tunnel. It seemed to take forever; when the leading edge finally came into view Elif almost fell over from the release of the tension. Tai grabbed him. He grabbed her.

The front edge of the tunnel was dotted with large spherical structures anchored in place on a web of struts, each sphere a different size, smaller ones set to fill the gaps between the larger, all the way down to relatively tiny globes. The larger of them seemed the size of a city, each with the gleaming, polished sheen of thick glass over a core of abyssal black. Like spider's eyes, ringed by a faint fringe of irregular spines set into the supporting struts, curving up and around the eyes like thin claws, or eyelashes.

One of the smaller Abandoner ships pulsed in a determined way for the largest eye. A long, spiky fragment of Spree destroyer spun past and slashed through the side of the Abandoner, releasing a torrent of bright green liquid that broke into millions of globules, still headed for the eye.

The spray of liquid abruptly changed direction and flowed toward the nearest eyelash. The green goo stretched into a line of droplets with the eagerness of capillary action on a grand scale, spattering the grey metal stalk with smears of green. Russ gestured and grids of dots appeared around the eyelashes, indicating intense, localised gravity fields pulling the stray debris away from the eyes; spent ammunition, dead picket ships, wildly flailing X-shaped robots, pieces of destroyers and cruisers and large, slowly spinning chunks of the Seedship.

And them.

Another grid of dots replaced the gravitational markers, extending around the visible structures. "These are graded by estimates of survivability," Russ said. The dots within the tunnel were all bright red; near the eyelashes they were indigo, and near the bases of the eyelashes where they joined the supporting struts, the grid was almost light blue.

"So you went for the base," Elif said.

"We went for the base," Russ agreed. As they got closer the eyelash grew into a gigantic tree-trunk with a sparse cover of what looked like mushrooms or cocktail umbrellas, glowing in cheery neon reds, greens and yellows. They passed over a particularly large variant that pulsed bright pink and dragged them almost straight down. The ship tumbled end-over-end before plunging front-first through the side of the eyelash as if it were made of foil, leaving a neat round hole. Elif almost winced as they hit before remembering sheepishly that they were watching a replay.

"Does this explain where we are in some way that I'm not grasping?" Elif asked, unable to keep the sarcasm out of his voice.

Russ inclined her head slightly to one side as if acknowledging his confusion and the view pulled back from the hole. The surface of the eyelash was made of millions of overlapping plates, a random patchwork strewn with broken vessels swarming with X-shaped machines busy tearing the ships apart and patching the holes. The view pulled back further, revealing the other spines cupping the eye-sphere, the web-like mass of struts supporting it, then back further until the entire front of the tunnel could be seen through a haze of smoke, vapour, debris and dust. The detail of the machinery gave it a sense of immense scale at first, then it blurred into scabrous dark grey lit by occasional nuke flashes: a decayed metal bucket hundreds of miles across, drawing in the remaining pieces of the Seedship and its fleet.

Russ stood in front of the display and faced them. "A Yacatisma. And we've crashed into one of it's eyelashes." She gave a game-show hostess smile and raised her hands, palms out. "Well, here we are!"

Tai laconically raised one eyebrow. "Yacatisma. Imagine that." "Big-ass killing machine, right?" Elif said. "Huh. I'm going to heat up some noodles with the soldering iron. You want some?"

Russ stared at both of them, aghast. Tai returned her stare. "What? You want us to panic? Elif, some panic, please, and make it convincing."

Elif suppressed a grin and appeared to concentrate for a few seconds. "... there, I've peed my pants. How's that?" Tai grinned and gave him a shaky thumbs-up.

Russ shook her head slowly. "Perhaps you'll regard this situation with the gravity it merits when those machines tear through the hull and pull your arms and legs off."

Tai's expression fell, but Elif wasn't having any of that. "Coming here was your idea, Russ."

Her head jerked back a fraction of an inch as if to get a better look at him. "I recall vigorously arguing against using the conduit."

Without a beat, Elif continued, "Which means you wanted us to argue for it, and to take the blame when it went sideways." Aside, to Tai, he murmured "Paranoia. It's great! It's always somebody else's fault." To Russ: "So, how long do we have before we die screaming?"

"The ship's camouflage system will adapt to the local environment in about three minutes, but I doubt we'll have that much – "

Three loud knocks sounded from the front of the ship, metal on metal. " – time before they find us. Oh, well. We're dead. Tai, it's been good working with you. Elif, you've been a medium-sized pain in the ass." Russ sat down on the end of Tai's bed and folded her hands in her lap.

Elif rolled his eyes. "You give up far too easily. I'll go out there and distract them until the camouflage kicks in." Before Tai had a chance to protest he ran to the second scoop chamber with Russ following.

"You won't last thirty seconds out there, Elif. The Yacatisma is driven by hatred of anything that isn't it, and that hatred informs all of it's systems, right down to the repair machines."

Elif retrieved the LED torch, tested it. "Yes, well, if you're right we're dead anyway, and if I go out there at least I won't have to listen to your lies for a few minutes." When Russ didn't reply, he looked up and saw an uncharacteristically put-upon look on her face, almost as if she resented being – "Oh, crap. Look, you go back there and reassure Tai. I know she's taking this badly, and I want you to convince her that this whole thing is your fault, because, you know, it is."

"Assigning blame isn't going to change the situation – "

" – no, but it'll make her feel better, and in our minds, that does change the situation. You should know that." He looked about the room. "Did you sell the guns?"

Russ appeared to come to a decision. "Very well. If you're going to try this, I can advise you. No weapons; don't attack anything. Don't even threaten anything. Your best chance is to distract them, then run and hide. Above all, don't speak or call out. Make as much noise as you want; just no sounds with any degree of intelligence behind them, or they'll swarm you. They're machines, but they are well adapted to the environment." Elif was still searching for something. "Don't bother. I got rid of the weapons."

"I'm looking for my 'phone. It has a camera with a flash."

Russ looked angry. "This isn't a Disneyland ride, you idiot!"

Elif sneered. "And I'm not Mickey Mouse. You go make Tai feel better," waving his hand dismissively. He took a deep breath and stepped up the ramp to the outer hatch, which opened just enough for him to squeeze through, then closed behind him.

THE area around the ship resembled an underground car park made of steel plates, with supporting columns set at different angles. The only light came from what looked like scattered blast furnaces, flickering red glows with occasional yellow highlights, hundreds of yards away. The furthest of these vanished below the horizon, which was close enough to show that the structure was curved; the inside of a multi-level pipe. The air was freezing and stank of industrial fumes and rotting meat, reminding him of the nauseating effluvium of arc welding in a confined space. The ceiling was made of more sheet steel, with a ragged-edged hole where the ship had entered; through the hole he could just make out another level with another hole, and another, and beyond that darkness. An explosion somewhere above flared white, and briefly he saw several further levels with more neatly punched ship-shaped holes leading to the surface. He wondered what was keeping the air in. Perhaps those gravity generators that had pulled them down in the first place.

The ship was set into the floor at an angle of about thirty degrees, just enough so that the difference between the Bitchslap's internal gravity and the outside made him feel like he was standing on the edge of a cliff. The bulging end of the second scoop chamber was sunk half-way into the floor, three yards below; whatever was knocking on the ship was at least three levels down. He dropped to the floor-plates and shone the torch around, aware that if anything was watching he'd be making a nice target. He knelt and examined the plates, which were unevenly joined with poor-quality welding. If this had been done by machines, they weren't very accurate; the seams were crooked and intermittent with inch wide gaps and thumb-sized beads of metal along the edges. Looking at them made him want to do them properly, but his first priority was to get down to the lower level and distract the locals. It only took him a minute to find a broken plate at the edge of a support column, which, he realised, was a stray piece of machinery – a gun barrel or a reaction drive tube, perhaps – that had been drawn down to the eyelash, crashed through the upper layers, then welded in place. He squeezed into the gap and slid down the column, which had enough surface detail to permit hand- and foot-holds for when he had to climb back up. He climbed down until he heard sounds, then dropped to the floor as quietly as possible and peered through the darkness in the direction of the Bitchslap. He listened; faint creaking sounds of stressed metal, a distant clashing sound, and much closer, the clack of metal against metal. Whatever it was banged against the ship's hull again.

Elif edged around the column and shone the torch away from the ship. Nothing, aside from a couple of stray metal plates and a loose coil of rusty cable. The next column was a dozen yards away. **Get into that first-person-shooter mentality,** he told himself. **This is what games train you for – total paranoia. He peeked around the edge of the column and shone the torch at the ship.**

There were two machines standing under the nose of the Bitch-slap. Forty gallon oil drums with four legs attached at the sides by complex-looking ball joints, the legs dividing into claws big enough to be considered legs in their own right. Made of scarred and rusted metal with loose wiring, standing on two legs, or four claws, each as big as a good-sized forklift, they gave the impression of serious heavy-duty industrial machinery. Just looking at them made Elif think of Einstuerzende Neubauten. One of them was pressing a claw against the underside of the ship, rotating at the wrist as if trying to carve a manhole-sized chunk out of the hull. The other – he had just enough time to see it was missing a leg – was aiming its free leg straight at him. Elif slipped his hand into his pocket and, finding only the roll of duct tape, threw it at the machine trying to cut into the ship. The tape bounced off and rolled back, perversely negotiating three heavily welded seams to stop at Elif's foot. The three-legged machine started crawling towards him, moving with the sinister grace of a tarantula. **It's a trick. It can move a lot faster than that.** He grabbed the tape, waved the torch beam at them wildly, then turned and ran for the next column. When he dared to look back, they were both following him and, as he suspected, they were gaining on him. Panic gave him a burst of speed and, as Russ had suggested, he ran, dodging nimbly around a column and thinking **I really should have planned this better. I really should have planned this.** There weren't any good places to hide. The closest machine slammed into the column with a deafening clang, rebounded and collided with it's partner. Elif reached the next column, saw a gap where it joined the ceiling and started climbing easily; the artificial gravity seemed lower. That, or his fear gave him the power of flight.

He crawled up to the level he'd started on, slipped through the gap and backed a couple of steps away from the column, wondering if they'd keep chasing him. More crashing sounds came from below, along with arc-welding flashes and the whining of over-driven motors. Something slammed into the column hard enough to loose a shower of rust flakes, then again and again. The plates attached to the column's base split and sagged. Elif glanced back at the Bitchslap – it looked the same as before, and in no way camouflaged – then he edged around the column and walked away, stamping his feet to draw the machines. They continued to beat against the column until enough plates had parted to let them through. At first he thought one had climbed up on the back of the other, then he saw the four-legged one was being dragged against it's will, and protesting vigorously. It got a good grip on the column with two legs, then picked up the other machine and – his Merest Hint sense warned him to dodge just in time – threw it at him. The three-legged machine fell, denting the plates, rolled and splayed its limbs out to stop, then stood on six claw-feet and ran back at the other, colliding and scraping across the floor with a hideous screech... towards the Bitchslap. **I can see why this place is going to hell.** That tickle in the back of his mind goosed him again, making him look up, then further back, to the point where he almost fell over backwards. **Ah-ha!**

He put his fingers to his lips and blew a loud, piercing whistle, then shouted "Hey! ZA WARUDO!" The machines stopped tearing at each other, scrambled apart and darted straight at him, the three-legged one tripping in its eagerness. He laughed and ran, stumbling over uneven plates, then tripped and rolled for a few feet, bouncing through a pocket of low gravity. The machines slowed and appeared to be examining him, assessing a different kind of threat: one capable of speech. Elif crawled backwards, closed his eyes and covered his face with his forearm.

With a deafening roar, a pointed chunk of metal the size of a large luxury yacht crashed through the ceiling, crushing both machines into the floor. It kept moving, tearing out plates, looking like a subway train going the wrong way, then slowed and stopped. Vapour, dust, rust and smoke obscured the view for a minute, but Elif didn't wait for it to clear; he ran back to the Bitchslap, climbed up the top of the ship, leaned over the end and was trying to think of a pattern of knocks Russ and Tai might recognise when the hatch opened and Russ dragged him inside.

ELIF was laughing so hard that he collapsed onto the bed. Russ stood with her arms crossed, regarding him with disapproval.

"Oh, wow. That was fun. Are we safe?" He sat up and felt his upper arm, where a piece of shrapnel had cut him badly. He picked the torn edges of his T-shirt away from the spreading blood-stain. "Have to sew that up." He sighed and lay down again. The bed had fully deployed and the surface didn't feel as creepy as before.

Russ examined the injury. "I don't think you left a trail of blood. The camouflage system is still adapting, but we should be hidden by the time their friends turn up. Shouting at them was a mistake. They will know something out of the ordinary is about, and they'll keep looking until they find it. This gives us less time to establish a means of escape."

Tai stumbled down the ramp into the scoop chamber and Elif made room for her on the bed. She prodded it, then gratefully lay down. Elif gave Russ a sideways glance. "You told Dr Squid to give me that Aetheric, didn't you?" Russ didn't reply. "Very... far-sighted of you."

Tai gave a small exclamation. "Elif, you're bleeding."

Offhandedly, still wired from his brush with death, "Yeah, yeah. You should have seen the other guy."

Tai laughed. "We did. We were watching. How did you know..." She paused, seeing his grin.

"I knew you were going to say that. Well, actually, no, I didn't. This thing in my head tells me when something life-threatening is about to happen." He sat up, pulled off one of his boots, removed a sock and wrapped it around the injury.

Tai frowned. "That can't be very hygienic."

He sniffed the sock. "Not life-threatening." He frowned. "It should smell a lot worse than that; I've been wearing these socks for, like, a month." He pushed his upper arm towards Tai's face. "Here, check this out."

Tai recoiled, wrinkling her nose. "No, thank you."

Russ wasn't listening, her attention elsewhere. Elif tried to catch her attention, snapping his fingers at her. "Hey. You at the controls? Russ? ...Ron?" He had some suspicions about Ron as well, and if he was right, there should be another distraction along any second now.

"Ah. Here they are," Russ said. She gestured and a display

window appeared in the air above the bed, angled so they could see it easily, showing the area immediately outside the ship where the Spree scout ship had crashed through the outer layers of the eyelash. Four machines were cutting irregularly-shaped panels from the side of the scout, reaching inside the ship, pulling out wet, lumpy cables and throwing them aside. "With any luck they'll think you're in there."

"Ah, it'll take them ages to salvage that... thing..." Elif's voice trailed off as a dozen more machines scuttled out of the shadows and joined in the disassembly, occasionally taking swipes at each other. He shook his head. **"Chort vosmi."** He considered this. "Hey, we should call 'em Chorts. Unless they already have a name."

Russ was watching them breaking up the scout ship. "They don't need names. After compensating for scale, they're the local equivalent of bacteria. Chort is as good as any other label." She saw Tai's questioning look and added "It's a Russian word, meaning **devil**." The machines sawed through a pressure bulkhead and one of them dragged a struggling, spiky, many-legged beige brown shape out of the ship; a Spree warrior. The machines pulled off its legs then tore the carapace apart, dropping brightly coloured and bulging organ-sacs and trampling them underfoot. They continued dismantling the ship for almost thirty seconds before a vicious fight broke out among them. More machines arrived, some attacking the Spree ship, most joining the main fight, which was rapidly assuming the proportions of a riot. It reminded Elif of the scene around his house just before they'd been scooped. Some of the losers were being thrown dangerously close to the Bitchslap; then, a single Chort the size of a bus stomped into the irregular patches of light that leaked around the edges of the hole. It grabbed two smaller Chorts and slammed them together; the others scattered in all directions, one of them running directly at the Bitchslap, bouncing off and scrambling into the darkness. The big Chort picked at the Scout ship's exposed innards, then, evidently not liking what it had found, wandered off, pausing only to stamp on the Spree warrior's detached head, which was still twitching.

Quietly, Elif said "Well, that wasn't the smartest thing I ever did."

Tai countered, "It worked. Didn't it, Russ?"

Russ sighed, not even bothering to show off her cleavage while doing it. "We are camouflaged, but I don't know how long we will stay camouflaged. Eventually something will work out what's going on. Individually they aren't too bright, but they do network – when they aren't fighting – and it's only a matter of time before the anomaly is reported to something higher. Something smart enough to organise a more detailed examination, or, far more likely, a focused Deathbeam barrage."

Elif said "Well, then, we should consider leaving as soon as we can." He glanced at Tai, who was looking at Russ, then at Russ, who was looking at him. "Right? Right right?"

Russ nodded. "As soon as possible." She waited until Elif was about to protest, then said "Of course, it isn't that simple. We lost both engines, and one was destroyed. I tracked the other as best I could and I know roughly where it is. It's useful, so the Chorts won't destroy it... but, since it's useful, they will have incorporated it into the general power grid, and they won't want to give it back."

Elif said "Then we'll have to steal it." He paused, then added, "They'll be guarding it, of course?"

"Necessarily, and not just from us. This level of the Yacatisma's being hosts an entire economy of power based on units like that, including trading, stealing, forgery, deception, banditry and outright war. The only thing that moderates this behaviour is an overriding command from above; on an eyelash, those commands come from the eye." Russ gestured and a wire frame image of the eyelash floated before them: a curved, elongated cone made of nested ring segments strung on a line of power conduits feeding warty gravity generators irregularly dotting the surface. The eyelash was connected to the rim of the eye-socket by a bulging refinery and factory section where the bulk of the salvaged scrap was recycled. The surface was studded with chunks of crashed ships, more so towards the end, which was splintered and obviously in need of shampoo and conditioner, **and, yeah, but who shampoos their eyelashes?** The frayed look matched the impression of general decrepitude he'd seen outside; the Yacatisma obviously valued function over form.

Elif leaned closer and peered into the glowing image. "Where are we on this?"

Russ pointed with a perfect oval fingernail. "Here, just inboard of that gravity generator. Our engine landed... here, but has most likely been moved. I'll try to tap into the Chort network and get some free telemetry."

"Can you convince them to go fetch the engine for us?" Tai asked.

"No. Like humans, they don't take orders very well. And, like humans, most of the information they pass between themselves is biased or deliberately false, and generally for the same reasons. I will have to weight each datum for intent."

"Like that Xist friend of yours who surveyed this part of space?" Elif tried not to sneer.

"Nobody lies like an Xist," Russ smiled. "Getting a useful truth out of these can-openers will be easy." She began opening windows in the air, displaying encoded machine signals in a variety of formats, none of them familiar to Elif. Tai seemed to recognise them right away.

Elif found a box of adhesive medical strips he'd won in a school competition back in the third grade, peeled one off the roll and removed the blood-stained sock from his arm while Tai rearranged Russ' windows, discarding two empty ones and summoning three replacements filled with grids of flashing grey squares. "Octal, duodecimal and, what's this one? Variable base. Plug that into the patternator for a few minutes."

Elif slapped the medical pad over his injury, winced, then cocked his head to one side. "I know you're good with computers, Tai... so you hack into Russ' systems and steal video... then you take over the ship and fly it... and now you're going to eavesdrop on an unfamiliar machine network with an alien protocol."

Her eyes turned to meet his with a cold look he'd never seen before. "I'm disabled. I'm not dumb."

Elif froze. She'd never brought him up on that before. He knew her condition better than most of the doctors she'd ever consulted; he understood her physical limitations, and she knew it. They'd joked about it frequently. He stared back at her, waiting for her to smile and make it into a joke, but she didn't drop her gaze.

In the face of that kind of confrontation Elif usually retreated to work out what he'd done wrong. He dropped the bloodstained sock onto the bed next to Tai, said "Be careful. These guys are

Serious Business," and left for his private smoking lounge behind the bathroom cubicle. As he stepped up the ramp Russ called out, "We'll call you if we need anything damaged or broken."

"Up yours," he muttered.

H E tore a page out of Russ' faux bible and rolled a cigarette with it. When he went to light it, his hands were shaking. **Crash into an alien spaceship? Why not. Chased by a crowd of industrial killing machines, no problem. Tai is angry at you... and that's something else.**

Tai never had a problem with letting Elif know when he was being dumb. He expected it. They were as close as two people could be without actually having slept together. They didn't just finish each other's sentences; they finished each other's thoughts. **So what was all that about?**

"She..." he began, then stopped, suspecting that Russ would be listening in. **She wasn't really angry at me. She just wanted me to leave the room for some reason. She's keeping Russ busy while I... while I do what?** There wasn't anything interesting happening in the recycling bay, which left the bridge and the Essence capacitor.

Elif finished the weed, dropped the roach into half an inch of flat soda in the bottom of a Bivalve can and idly shook it to make sure it was out, then quietly went to the bridge. The absence of the engines at the end of the recycling bay was almost painfully obvious. The lighting on the bridge was still low, and the flat holographic screen at the end of the room was inactive. The Essence capacitor floated within the stone ring, looking as it had before... perhaps a little smaller.

He went up to it and peered into the dull surface, his reflected silhouette outlined in faint red; he leaned closer and pressed his forehead against the cold metal. He couldn't sense anything inside. **Empty?** It moved reluctantly when shoved, as if full of water. He grasped it with both hands and dragged it out of the ring, let go; it stayed where he left it. He turned around and was about to sit inside the ring with his back against the front of the ship when a thought came to him.

Did Tai want me out of there because she's up to something with Russ?

Just because they were supposed to be conspiring against her didn't mean that Tai couldn't... what? Conspire against him? To do what? he didn't care if Tai took over the ship and deleted everything. What else could she want? Hold the ship hostage in exchange for... as far as he knew, Russ wasn't withholding anything either of them wanted. If the Abandoners in the recycler could fix her medical problems, it made no sense for Russ to refuse to help her, unless Russ was trying to coerce her into doing something, and that depended on whether Russ had originally intended to bring them here or not. He was still undecided about that.

Instead of sitting in the ring, Elif dragged the Essence capacitor back into place, then went to the recycling bay. He glanced toward the second Scoop chamber; Russ was still occupied. Feeling a little stupid, he leaned close to one of the shelves and whispered "Hey. You guys. I need to talk to you privately."

Slowly, over a period of thirty seconds, a tiny billboard emerged from the recycler, ten inches long and three inches high, edged with pin-points of light that flickered in marquee patterns. Elif stepped back and saw the other recycling bed had produced a similar sign, facing the first.

Words appeared on the first billboard, black text in English:

> THE WHOLE BILATERAL SYMMETRY THING
> WAS A MISTAKE.

Elif turned to check out the other sign:

> IT'S A CHEAP DESIGN HACK, GRANTED, BUT
> IT SAVES A LOT OF TIME.

He turned to where he could see them both.

> IT ENFORCES A RIGID, SINGLE-PERSPECTIVE
> VIEW OF THE WORLD. IT MAKES THE DRIVER
> THINK ALMOST ENTIRELY IN TERMS OF
> FORWARD OR BACKWARD.

> THAT CAN FACILITATE ESCAPE FROM A
> PREDATOR, BUT AGREED; WE SHOULDN't

BE IN THE POSITION OF NEEDING TO ES-
CAPE A PREDATOR IN THE FIRST PLACE.

PREDATORS ARE OUR FRIENDS.

The texts faded and the billboards slowly sank into the recycler
beds. He wasn't going to get any help from the Abandoners in the
recyclers.

E LIF lay back in the empty bathtub, one booted foot draped over
the edge, idly stopping and unstopping the plughole with the
bare heel of his other foot, considering his situation.

He'd rarely had any problems spotting and avoiding the usual
Conspiracy traps; various addictions, mortgages, Keeping Up With
the Joneses, Trying To Kill the Joneses – tribal conflict... and the
Merest Hint very handily warned him when a giant chunk of ruined
spaceship was about to crush him like a bug (and he had to wonder
if the Spree pilot had appreciated the reversal of the traditional
roles)... but he'd walked right into this one, and, what was worse,
he couldn't see any way he might have avoided it without giving
away whatever game Tai was playing. If it was a game. Her reaction
had seemed, to him, so out of character that he was surprised Russ
hadn't been suspicious... or perhaps she was but didn't show it,
which was easy for her. Russ always did play her cards close to her
chest. As close as that was possible, given the size of those –

"Busy?" Russ asked, poking her head in through the bathroom
doorway.

"Yes," appropriately surly, "I'm having a bath. Whatever it is,
get Tai to do it."

Russ paused and put on the most convincing portrayal of concern
she'd managed yet. "It's not your fault."

Elif couldn't repress a cynical snort. "You know even less about
women than I do."

"I do know more about deception than either of you. I can
usually tell when you're being less than straightforward – " **Liar** "
– but, frankly – " **Liar!** " – I don't know why she even tries."

Elif mused on this. "Perhaps she didn't like to feel left out.
Perhaps she's better at this than either of us suspect." He paused
dramatically, then continued: "Or, perhaps as I do, she has some

concerns about the nature of your stake in this. We're risking our lives here, and the most you stand to lose is a ship, two SubGenii, a can of Essence and a robot who can't see her toes."

Russ entered the bathroom, not taking her eyes off his. He was expecting another distracting flash of cleavage, but instead she sat on the floor next to the tub and hugged her knees, "I have the significant portion of my assets involved in financing this venture," she said quietly, evenly. "If this fails, I won't be able to renew my Existential Licence, my right to occupy space-time will be revoked and I'll be harvested for my organs and peripheral systems. Ron will assume control of whatever's left once the Tax office have sold my brain-lobes and genitals. So, you see," with a brittle smile, "I need this to succeed just as much as you do. More so, if, as most do, you believe an Xist's life to be worth any number of briefly-lived humans'."

Ignoring the put-down (he'd been expecting it), Elif thought about their situation; the Chorts, the murderous presence of the Yacatisma, having to retrieve the engine, getting away without being detected. "Do you think we stand a chance?"

"Oh, definitely. Our strategy has many places where sudden and dramatic changes in immediate objectives allow us a satisfactorily broad range of possible paths to success. Some longer than others; some riskier. Our greatest advantage is in being able to adapt rapidly in response to any unforeseen eventualities." She arched an eyebrow. "And we have an unexpected and well-placed potential ally, if we can make contact."

"What, the Convocation? I'm glad they're on our side. They know how to commit mass suicide in style."

Russ' arched eyebrow shifted subtly from confidentiality to disdain.

Elif blinked. "Not the Convocation? Well, I'm glad you don't have to resolve this situation with only a ship, two SubGenii, a can of Essence and a robot who can't see her toes."

"IN my youth, I made a study of Chorts, like many of my peers. They were our generation's Pokémon." Russ was in the mood to be voluble, or to disseminate some more crafted disinformation. "We observed them from a distance, and, when we thought our guardians weren't watching, we'd build fast sampling probes which could swoop in and grab a few real specimens from the outer edge of the cloud of debris the Yacatisma tend to leave wherever they go. You know those films, a giant robotic killing machine drops from the sky, threatens the city and is destroyed with electricity. This is where those robots come from; stray Chorts flung off into space at some long-dead target, disappearing into the void only to be captured in a gravity well and to drop into the middle of Tokyo.

"We studied them, forced them to fight, gave them resources and energy, watched them breed. It was all conducted on a test world far from X, so we never got into trouble, although on at least one occasion they got out of control, consumed the entire planet and flew off to, we suppose, evolve into a full Yacatisma. But I can assure you: nobody on this ship knows them better than me. I need to teach you as much as I can about dealing with these things, and our first objective is to obtain a live specimen so I can examine it for regional differences and evolved modules we may need in order to build you a camouflage profile. I'm afraid our current plan for escape requires you to spend a dangerous amount of time out there, and we need to provide you with every possible advantage." She paused at the top of the ramp to the second Scoop, where Tai was still conducting an orchestra of windows. "Tai wants to discuss something with you, so I shall reconfigure the Essence capacitor to shield its emanations completely. There are things nearby which would love some essence right about now, and we can't risk them smelling it."

Russ turned to leave, and, although Elif detested the cliché, he waited until she was almost out of the room before saying "Russ...?" She paused and looked back. "You're about to ask me to do something horrible, aren't you?" She didn't deign to answer, waving him away before leaving.

"Russ said you wanted to talk about something." Tai waved a finger at the screens hovering in the air around her. "You're right. I can't do this."

Elif tried to think of something reassuring to say. "I don't think anybody could do it. It's... well, look at it. These things have been evolving for millions of years. Their security must be insane."

Tai was staring at a blank screen directly in front of her. "What I can do is ask Russ to give me a neural implant that can connect me to these systems directly."

Elif was at a loss for words at this. She knew what he thought about alien implants; he'd been forced to wear a shock collar for two months. "You know Russ will use it to control you. You'd be giving up any freedom y-"

"Russ needs this as badly as I do. As badly as we all do. She may or may not be on this ship in any meaningful way, but her ass is on the line just as much as ours. Otherwise, what possible reason could she have for bringing us here? I read in the notes that the Yacatisma hate the Xists more than anything. There was a very colourful metaphor."

"I must have missed that page."

"It said something along the lines of, if you saw a spider on your nose, you'd flail about and swat it away. If a Yacatisma saw an Xist sitting on its nose, it would," she spoke slowly, for emphasis, "blow its own head off with a multiple Deathbeam barrage. They **really** don't like Xists. And we are in an Xist ship."

"So why **did** Russ bring us here? I don't believe this was an accident."

"Why is less important than how to get away from here in once piece, and I can't do it without help. Russ would be doing it herself, except she's paranoid the Yac will be able to tell what she is. It won't be so alarmed if it catches me sneaking about. On top of all this, I'm just going to fiddle with some of the Yac's sensors. I don't want to go out there any more than you do."

"If you look at it as 'get the engine back, then get away unde-tected', it sounds simple."

"It's going to be tricky. Getting the engine back is do-able, but getting away afterwards is going to be very tricky. Russ came up with a plan that involves a minimum of risk, but it means she'll have to use almost all of her Essence stash, so we'll have to go back to Earth and get some more."

Elif sat back on the bed. "Well. While it is encouraging that Russ is making plans for afterwards, I'm not sure I'm happy with the degree of... um, collusion, that I'm getting hints of here and there."

Rather sharply, Tai said "There's nothing like the threat of imminent death to put things in perspective, Elif."

He bit his lip and grinned. "If you're using my name, I must be in so much trouble that – "

Tai's expression softened. "I'm going to do this whether you approve or not, if for no better reason than it'll give me more time. It does a lot of maintenance, hormone levels, neurotransmitters, tanks the immune response. It's not just a fancy network card."

Elif's grin faded. "No. It's not." He sighed. "If we're going to do any more conspiring, we'd better do it now, because once Russ has that dongle in your skull you won't be able to hide anything from her."

Tai nodded. "I'll be acting on the assumption that she'll be watching everything I do, hearing everything I hear. Feeling everything I feel... reading Bat keyboard codes tapped onto the back of my hand. It puts a big boulder in the middle of our covert information flow pattern, but we'll just have to work around it." She took a deep breath and sat up. "Can you help me back to my bed? This is a very nice surface, but I need my machines."

ELIF glared at the undetailed black headband Russ was holding, fresh from the recycling bay. It didn't look like much, which implied it was worse than one with spikes or flashing blue LEDs. "Do I want to watch this happening?"

Russ gave him a mild you're-an-idiot look and placed the headband on Tai's forehead. It didn't sink into her skull or sprout wiry tentacles or anything immediately alarming, but Elif could imagine nano-scale feelers growing through her skull and doing screeching burn-outs on her glial cells. He winced, but couldn't look away. The worst part was that there was nothing he could do if it went wrong, not even punch Russ. He was coming to a better appreciation of Sybrandis' friends and how they'd felt about her, or him, as she was at the time. He almost grinned.

Tai met his gaze. "You're thinking of the Breughel crowd, aren't you?"

Elif's eyes grew wide. "That was quick. You can read the tiny electrical signals that form patterns of memory in my – "

Tai gave him a slightly stronger you're-an-idiot look. "No. I can't read your brain." A small smile. "I just know you that well, is all."

"Is it indexed?" Russ asked. "... understood. Co-processors; I'll give you tiers one and two. That should be – "

Tai pantomimed stealing cookies from a jar. "And I'll take tiers three, four, five and six as well. I'll leave you tier seven so you can run that walking blow-up-doll and keep an eye on the ship's sensors. Now... we're gonna need a tiny Chort. What would be the best way to get one?"

Confident from his first encounter, Elif grinned and said "I'll be back in a minute."

HALF an hour later he staggered through the hatch in the second Scoop chamber, bleeding from a series of puncture wounds and dragging an ugly chunk of metal the size of a Volkswagen engine. Tai was lying on her bed, curled up on one side, staring at a display window about the size of a playing card hovering in front of her eyes. "Sorry it took so long. Hell of a crowd out there." He held up one hand and examined the ragged holes in his skin. "It, uh, turned into a fight." He grinned. "It's a leg! Sorry I couldn't get a whole one. They were all a lot bigger than me."

Russ knelt on the floor and ran her hands over the shape, delicately testing the sharper edges with a finger. She stood and smoothed the hem of her business skirt. "This is enough, but it's still active. Take it to the bridge and we can drain the batteries into the capacitor."

Elif was too tired to go through the routine of trying to make Russ feel awkward about making him do all the work, but he did make a mental note to find a way out of this master/servant thing she was setting up. If they got into the habit of thinking that way he'd be less inclined to mess with her plans, if he ever worked out what she was really doing.

He grabbed the bunch of torn cables at one end of the thing, bridged two wires with his hand and got an electric shock strong enough to make him yelp and jump back. He shook his tingling fingers and was only mildly concerned when he saw a shower of hot pink sparks flowing from where he'd been zapped. They curled away from his skin like shoals of tiny fish, fading into the air with a faint ringing sound. Tai had seen it too. Russ tilted her head to one side a fraction.

"I thought you were an engineer. Don't you know anything about Namronics? Never mind," briskly, in a way that said **you're an idiot but we don't have time for a lecture,** "I'll put together some notes. Grab it there."

Elif bent at the knees and managed to get the whole thing off the floor. "Can't you do something with the ship's gravity? This thing weighs as much as a V-"

Russ stalked off to the bridge. "The gravity is fixed. It's part of the ship. Stop complaining."

Elif staggered after her, glancing back at Tai for a moment. She seemed preoccupied. "I thought it was a perfectly valid – "

"If you'd read the notes carefully you would know about the gravity. Once the batteries are drained I want you to take it apart and locate the IFF transponder. You don't need to worry about toxic dart guns or the like; this leg was part of a Maintenance Chort."

"Fine," Elif muttered, thinking that if he reduced his sentences to single syllables Russ wouldn't have as much opportunity to interrupt. **Now, where has she hidden my tools?** "Ru-"

"I've added a few tools for the more complicated sections. Their operation is self-explanatory. You can keep them, because you're going to need them." She presented a folded bundle of grease-stained white cotton, lifted one edge; Vernier, Dremel, heatpoint, 'pliers, soup-spoon, wrench, multimeter, a socket driver and bits, and a ham and cheese sandwich wrapped in cling-film. "If you need a hammer, you're doing it wrong."

Under Russ' direction he held the loose wires against the side of the capacitor. Pink sparks flowed into it with a faint humming sound like a vibrator just as the batteries go flat. Elif shook the leg awkwardly, as if draining it of fuel, then set it down a few feet away – just far enough from the capacitor's Creepy Feeling zone so he could work without distraction.

Russ noticed the sandwich and took it. "That's Tai's lunch."

"She's vegetarian."

"That's not real ham," she called over her shoulder as she entered the recycling bay.

"'You'll all be eating roach crap by the end of the century!'" Elif quoted under his breath, kneeling to examine the machinery.

At first he thought it was a solid block with a pony-tail of wires at one end. After a few minutes' scrutiny he decided it was an articulated metal beam with three elbow joints, folded up flat. In contrast to the workmanship he'd seen on the floor-plates outside the seams looked very professional, if a little over-detailed; it had ridges along the sides that didn't seem to add anything other than, perhaps, making the casing stronger, in the manner of intricately folded cardboard egg-cartons. The surface seemed entirely free of screws, bolts, tabs or any kind of mechanical fastener he knew of. Maybe it was held together with glue. **If I have to bash this open with a claw hammer Russ will crow about it. So I have to do this the Rewardian way. Path of absolute least resistance. Don't push your mind and it will –**

Wait, I have an Aetheric for this.

HALF an hour later Russ came back in to the room and stood with one hand on her hip, favouring him with a look of mild disdain. Elif was sitting cross-legged on the floor next to the Chort's leg, staring at it, his face empty of all expression. The bundle of tools sat next to him, the multimeter reduced to a lump of smoking, blackened yellow plastic.

"Well?"

Elif said nothing for a few moments, then reached out with his right hand – also a little scorched – and rapped twice on the side of the casing with the second joint of his index finger. The leg unfolded, straightened out; dozens of small, irregularly-shaped panels popped open, exposing a mass of intricately woven machinery, rounded modules of bronze and red gold connected by curved rods with tiny spinning fly-wheels running into thumb-sized casings for linear motors. It had the look of something that had been grown rather than engineered.

Elif pointed to the end of an old radio valve filled with mercury, nestled within the works. "I think that's what you're looking for." He flicked it with his index finger and it ejected from its niche; he picked it up carefully with the 'pliers and laid it in the bowl of the soup-spoon, then passed it to Russ. "Careful. It's hot."

Russ took it to the recycling bay and tipped it on to one of the disassembler panels. Elif followed her and leaned close to watch. The Abandoners didn't start eating it; whatever they were doing was making the mercury jump about in a rapid waltz time. Of all the weird-ass alien effects he'd been exposed to in the past few days, this was the most entertaining; he could almost imagine it happening to music when suddenly the liquid metal inside the valve smeared itself out against the inside of the glass like a screaming face pressed up against a window. Elif recoiled slightly.

"That's it," Tai called out from the far end of the ship. Russ smiled. Elif wondered if the smile was part of the display or if she was genuinely pleased with their work, but couldn't think of a good way to ask aside from the obvious one, which would probably result in a low put-down of some kind, and Elif didn't want to spoil the mood of accomplishment.

The mercury suddenly began a frantic, arrhythmic Tarantella and Elif's Merest Hint flashed him a warning; he grabbed the nearest thing to hand – which was Russ' arm – and pulled her awkwardly around in front of him just as the valve popped, scattering glass shards in all directions. He crouched there for a moment, looking up past Russ' breasts to her face, which bore a pained expression. "Sorry."

She flashed him a mirthless smirk. "I'll just get Tai some tweezers so she can pick the glass fragments out of my ass."

Elif thought for a moment, looking off to one side. "Yeah. That's not really something I'm anxious to see."

Russ looked surprised and turned to look over her shoulder. "Really? Is there something wrong with my ass?"

"Yeah. It's connected to you." Elif found a piece of the transponder in a corner of the bay, picked it up and blew on it; it was still hot. "What does this get us?"

"A degree of immunity to attacks from some of the Chorts. Some of them will accept you as a maintenance machine. Others, unfortunately, will see you as a valuable source of material and will try to pull your arms and legs off," when she saw Elif's expression, she continued, "because that's usually where they keep their sensors.

It's a worthwhile trade-off; you will just need to learn which ones are friendly and which ones want to dismember you. Hopefully you won't be out there long enough to need to know."

Russ moved closer to him and reached past; he shrank back, at first thinking **oh my god she's making a move on me**; fortunately she didn't catch his horrified expression and instead picked up a flat grey case that the disassembler panel behind him had extruded. She opened the case, selected the tweezers and passed the case to him. "When you're ready, there's an implant in there for you. Knowing your aversion to such devices, this one attaches to your forearm, so, if you deem it necessary, you can remove it."

Without opening the case, Elif tossed it over his shoulder onto the disassembler panel. "I don't think so."

"It will transmit a signal that will convince some of the more common Chorts that you aren't a threat. It will allow you to sense variations in local gravitic, magnetic and Namronic fields, something you will most likely need." Russ pursed her lips. "You haven't been more than a hundred steps from the ship. You don't know how bad it can get out there, particularly when the gravity generators are actively sweeping material from the surface of the eyelash into the Yacatisma's mouth. Trust me, you do not want to end up in there. Things go in. Nothing comes out."

"I wouldn't make it into the mouth alive. No air out there, right?"

Russ gave him a long, disapproving frown and then shrugged. "It's your decision. I would have hoped that the severity of the situation might have convinced you."

Elif picked the case up, opened it. A flat black coin with a grid of grey dots on one side lay within. "The terminals refer signals to your visual cortex via peripheral nerves. It's completely configurable and can be turned off."

Elif met her gaze with suspicion plain on his face. "Why didn't Dr Squid install an Aetheric to do this?"

As if addressing a small child, "Because we didn't know we'd end up here. Anyway, there isn't an Aetheric for sensing subatomic particle fields. The Lifesense works by detecting other Aetherics. We don't know how the Nextstep Aetheric works. I can't force you to use this, but I would spare you the embarrassment of being proven wrong by losing an arm."

Elif began to consider the reverse-psychological angle and all of its variations. Seeing his attention turn inward, Russ added in a low, sultry voice, "I don't need to use an implant to make you do what I want," then turned and left the recycling bay.

Elif went to the toilet, dropped the implant into the bowl, peed on it and then flushed it. As he passed the recycling bay on the way back to the bridge he saw the implant, or one just like it, emerge from the disassembler bed in front of a tiny billboard. He leaned close to read the words:

YOUR PEE SMELLS FUNNY
CUT DOWN ON THE BIVALVE, MAYBE?

"DID you read the notes I prepared on Namronics?" Russ asked quietly.

"You didn't give me a lot of time. I skimmed it before we left the ship. Sounds like Grade A horseshit to me." Elif squinted and peered through the grid of holes in the side of the reaction chamber they'd hidden in. Russ had insisted on coming along.

"**Eppure si muove**," Russ muttered. "Just memorise it. They use a lot of Namronic wave-guides, and if you just stick your paw into one you'll learn more than you ever wanted to know."

"Okay. I can see how Richard Rufus of Cornwall might not get the idea of electrons, but... intelligent electrons is a little too, you know... well, it's kind of Disney."

"They're not intelligent. They're just capricious. They're even programmable, which I imagine Tai will appreciate. She's got quite a control-freak complex going there."

"Says the alien who runs my planet like a free-range chicken farm."

"Shh. They," indicating with a toss of her head, "have very good hearing."

Russ was referring to the Chorts guarding the nearest gravity generator, periodically docking with it to recharge their batteries, running patrols around it. In quick glances through the grid-holes, Russ estimated there were around a hundred of them, constantly coming and going. They were on the lowest level of the eyelash, just above the power core; the air down here was hot and dry and static charges made Elif's hair twitch annoyingly. The only good thing about the area was an abundance of broken and partly salvaged machinery to hide in. It was packed down like Permian fossils, full of interesting things that the Chorts had discarded as too hard for them to take apart. "It looks like a monochrome version of Robert William's 'Land of Retinal Delights', except full of robot assholes who want to kill us."

Russ sniffed the air with her eyes closed. "Get ready to move in. We'll need to open the access panel as soon as it's clear."

"It won't be clear unless someone turns off the gravity generator, and we can't do that until we get access to the panel. How about that friend of yours?"

Russ looked surprised. "Friend...", trying the word out and evidently not liking it. "Friend?"

"That well-placed ally you mentioned."

"It's not a friend, and it's too well-placed to waste on a problem this small. I have other... friends, that I can throw at this."

Elif was suddenly very conscious of the short distance between them, and felt an urgent need to increase it. "You want to elaborate on that?" he said carefully.

"Oh, not you," exasperatedly, "Thousands of Spree survived the incursion. When they smell the right chemical signal, they'll attack the Chorts. They won't win but they'll distract them long enough for us to get in, throw the signal switch and then get out. Toss that can at them."

Elif held the half-full Bivalve can between thumb and middle finger and wiggled it slightly. "I had to pee in that."

"I know. Throw it. Down there, on that ramp."

"Great. We begin the attack with a deadly pee bomb."

The gravity generator's fields became a little confused down at this level; the can bounced down the ramp, curved off to the right, flew through the air and then resumed its original course, a trail of droplets spiralling out of the ring-tab hole as it rolled to a stop against the foot of a Chort. The machine didn't pay much attention beyond stamping the can flat, spraying the rest of the contents about.

The base of the generator was a pipe five yards across, narrowed down from the mushroom-shaped bulk that sat up on the surface six levels above. It lanced into the power conduits at the core of the eyelash like a thumb-tack jabbed into an artery. The Chorts were spread out in a rough ellipse, those with low power levels wandering in from one side and, when fully charged, departing by the other, moving through the clearing around the generator like patrons at an unpopular night-club.

"You're gonna need a lot of Spree to do anything with these guys." Elif swayed from side to side, trying to build up a better picture of the parade through the grid-holes.

"If the Spree had come to attack the, uh, structure we are visiting," Russ still didn't want to say the name out loud, "they will have been crafted toward fulfilling a particular objective. The Spree design a warrior to fit the enemy and set it loose. They're cheap, so enough can be made to form an effective suicide attack. Less than one in a million survives the first five minutes, but biologically speaking, those are very good odds."

"The problem with this is that there can only be a limited number of Spree who survived. The Chorts can always make more Chorts. We can't win."

With a trace of exasperation, "Consider a more specific definition of 'win'. Our objective is to get to the access panel of the generator. It doesn't matter how many Spree die in the attempt. They're just insects."

"Do they have a problem with being used as suicide troops?"

"They're Spree. They don't have problems. They have objectives and an unusually strong mating instinct."

"Okay, does your using them as suicide troops interfere with their objectives?"

Russ smiled. "If it did, they wouldn't be doing that." She nodded obliquely toward the next level, where a circular balcony hung over the concourse. Hundreds of shadowy shapes had gathered there, moving in perfect mimicry of the Chorts, smoothly rounded broad noses like the heads of old chisels, swaying from side to side, testing the air.

As one they leaped down onto the Chorts connected to the generator, forelimbs slashing down, catching in the indentations in the machines' casings, knocking them sideways. The Chorts responded with frightening speed, punching holes in the Spree warriors' cara-paces and spattering pale yellow fluids in all directions, picking them up and hurling them, wriggling, across the concourse and onto jagged pieces of metal that stuck out of the packed-metal-scrap walls. The Spree's only advantage was that they were united; the Chorts began fighting with each other, turning the scene quickly into a mecha version of the Great Pie Fight. Once this happened, the Spree began scrambling up the side of the generator, jumping to the balconies like giant fleas, trying to lead the Chorts away from the concourse. Elif could almost see that exasperated Jack Lem-mon expression in the way they held their forelimbs and antennae, peering down at the growing mass of Chorts who were now only fighting with each other. **You're supposed to be chasing us!** The Spree jumped from the ledges onto the generator column and began chewing through the wall, carving bright slashes in the grainy metal with their chelicerae; that got the Chorts' attention, and the ones that were still capable of movement began to climb after them, pausing only to take awkward one-legged swipes at each other.

Russ was watching the broken Chorts clustered around the base of the generator, feebly waving legs and claws, reaching for each other. The machines entering the area were climbing after the Spree, leaving the space relatively empty. "Now," Russ hissed, beckoning, climbing down the uneven scree of metal scraps that led to the base of the generator. Elif followed, slipping on the uneven surface, weaving unsteadily through changing gravity fields and sprawling on his hands and knees at the base of the generator. He crawled to the access panel while Russ kept a look-out.

The panel was held in place by three different kinds of self-locking bolts; he undid two of them without bothering to work out how, and rotated the panel aside, revealing a tunnel edged with a rat's nest of cables, rods, pipes and vents, just large enough for a person to crawl into. Unpleasant flickering orange-yellow light. A feeling like a heavy magnetic field sitting on his brain.

"They're coming back. Get inside," Russ urged.

Elif looked at the tunnel. "Those're live cables! Do you r-"

Somewhere above, a Chort tore open a Spree warrior, raining thick fluid down, drenching them both. Russ grabbed Elif's waist-band and collar, forced his head down and shoved him into the access hole, scrambling in behind him, pushing him over sharp edges and hot cables. "Ow, ow, ow, ow!" he yelped, trying to minimise his contact with the components that gave off sparks when touched, recoiling from one shock to the next, tumbling into an open vertical space about the size of a shower recess. Russ scrambled in after him and held an index finger up to her lips, looking to one side, listening. All Elif could hear was the hissing of the Spree blood they'd tracked into the machinery, dripping onto hot bus-bars and furry radiator fins. It smelled like ripe bananas. Russ was half-covered in the stuff, and it wasn't an attractive look; there were tiny mustard-coloured lumps in it, like overcooked rice.

Russ reached into the mass of cables, pulled one out and touched the exposed end to a bank of open bus-bars; a bright purple flash blinded Elif and he resisted the urge to grab onto something, given the choices available. The feeling of compression lifted from around his forehead, an oppressively unpleasant sensation that seemed to rise and wait up near the next level. There was something up there he didn't like the feel of.

"Don't move. Don't make a sound." Russ murmured. Elif's nose tensed as the smell of burning Spree goop drifted up, but he'd die before he would allow himself to sneeze. It would be such a cliché.

The tightly packed machinery that made up the generator's walls must have been yards thick; he could barely hear the Chorts outside, fighting over the recharge points, which were now useless, Russ having shorted them out at the base level. Most of the few faint Spree sensations were gone, like shards of shattered glass lying still now. Sixty seconds passed before Elif's vision had returned and Russ was polishing her glasses on a handkerchief, not a trace of bug guts on her anywhere.

She met his appalled gaze, and he shook his head. "No. Don't tell me. There are some things man was not meant to know. Write it down in Enochian and we'll bury it deep underground in a stone crypt and tell **no-one**."

She shrugged her eyebrows and pointed to the black scorch-mark on the bus panel. "Relay from the core," pointing to the floor, "to the next tier. The red cable is the Namronic Left channel," waiting for an opportune spark to provide an approximation of white light, "yellow is Right, red and yellow striped is Nasty. Pull that out, touch

138

it there, blows the breakers, this tier's charging array shuts down, the Chorts leave. Eventually," scowling. "Maintenance Chorts are rare, so the array will be down for at least... four hours, possibly as long as twelve. You climb up, short out that level, the Chorts move further up, we wait until it's clear, then leave as quietly as possible. Does that sound like a plan?"

Elif had to think for a few moments before he could come up with an objection and an insult combined; it seemed like a pretty good plan. "If we can trust our lives... I mean, my life, to your knowledge of Chort behaviour, then, yes. Although I really don't want to climb up there. It hurts. You go. You don't feel anything."

"The inhibitor field interferes with this body's control signal. I could lose contact." Russ gave the impression that had settled the matter, and Elif's head was starting to ache, so he decided it was quicker to do as she said. He chose his hand- and foot-holds carefully, testing each surface with his knuckles in case of shock. The gravity fields were weaker now, which helped. He climbed up as high as he could stand to be and found the Namronic leads.

The Nasty cable came out easily, and the broken stub of plaited wires at the end was corroded under a diseased-looking foreskin of melted insulation. He squeezed his eyes shut and stabbed the cable at something that had looked like the bus panel. The flash was so bright he could see the bones of his hand and the coil of the cable through his eyelids. The gravity fields wobbled and vanished on the right side, throwing him off-balance; it felt as if the entire generator tower had been bent about forty-five degrees. Aside from the distant clatter of Chort footsteps outside and the buzzing of the transformers, it was quiet.

Then a growling sound came from a gap in the machinery, less than a foot away from his face. He could feel the sounds with his own eyelashes. Suddenly he didn't want to be up there; it wasn't the possibility the machinery might suddenly kill him... there was something alive in there. He could sense it dying. He tried to dull down his Lifesense, but perversely it wouldn't.

It hesitated, took another breath; the growl came back louder, rose about a semitone and then died with a wet gurgling sigh and a very faint hiss of exhaled breath, its last. He felt it die. For the briefest moment, a stray spark lit up the cramped chamber the creature had been forced into and Elif saw something wet and organic, a confusion of grey-green flesh and gnarled stick limbs with raw, weeping wounds. He averted his eyes and backed down to the first level, relieved to be out of the unbalanced gravity field and away from the chamber. Russ didn't have to warn him to be quiet; he didn't feel like talking at all.

Russ was listening for the Chorts, so Elif had time to think about what he'd just encountered. It had felt very much like the engines on the Bitchslap just before they'd been shot away. He hadn't felt any words, but there had been something... half-way between relief and gratitude. If he'd been able to feel sorry for ending the thing's life, that feeling dispelled it, yet what did settle over his shoulders, and down into his stomach, was a sinking feeling of misery, a depression so profound he felt like reaching out and touching the burned bus panel just to end it. He actually lifted his hand, but Russ reached out without looking – her attention was still on the distant clank of machine feet – and grabbed his wrist.

"First of all, that panel isn't live," she murmured, "and secondly, get over it. It's being sourced externally. Can't you tell when you're being emotionally influenced yet? The effect will fade, and you have more important things to do."

Elif struggled to get past his ingrained scepticism of anything Russ told him. It was much easier to run away and hide from the whole thing. If it happened again, he didn't think he'd be able to deal with it adequately. The only fall-back he had was to blame it on Russ. She must have known. She'd paid to have that Aetheric put in him. Blinking back tears he tried to speak as quietly as possible while conveying his anger; he wasn't able to keep the catch out of his voice. "Was that really necessary?"

She looked at him in disbelief. "They aren't going to go away just because we ask nicely." Her gaze flickered up, then left and right, as if scanning for them. "They are starting to leave, but it won't be safe for at least half an hour, so install the transponder then make yourself comfortable."

Elif felt the corners of his mouth beginning to turn down in a sneer. **Did Sybrandis and his friends have to deal with this?** How had they managed to restrain themselves as much as they had? He felt like pushing Russ back onto the remaining live cables, but the depression was beginning to fade and he thought he could control himself now. He took a deep breath, felt a small bump against his collarbone; the cloth bag on a cord around his neck, with a pair of IFF transponders inside. He'd eventually found four of them in the broken Chort leg back on the ship. Russ had given them to the Abandoners in the recycler, and they'd come out encased in dull grey metal with five pins at one end.

The machinery around them was completely unfamiliar to him, but he knew if he twisted a particular pipe it'd slide open and there'd be a niche inside for the transponder. Elif awkwardly turned around inside the confined space, burning his elbow on a flanged heat exchanger – which partly explained why there was a semblance of atmosphere at this level – and found the correct conduit behind a loose bunch of wires which sparked pink whenever they touched. He tried to get his hand behind the wires, bumping his elbow into Russ' back. Her attention was still on the Chorts. "Hey. Move over."

"What? Oh. Excuse me," trying to give him more room, taking a deep breath, as if that would help. He hardly noticed, trying to work his hand behind the wires, a single hair on the back of his wrist brushing against a bare lead and vanishing in a tiny puff of luminous pink smoke. He pushed the outside of the conduit with the tip of his middle finger, slid it open. The niche inside had six holes, and the modified transponder had five leads. He had that Jack Lemmon expression ready, but Russ pursed her lips and shook her head, a movement of a fraction of an inch. "Doesn't matter. It'll still work, and when in place, they auto-configure. Go on. Poke it in. You're enough of a primate to remember how to do that?", raising one eyebrow.

Elif concentrated on getting the transponder – a peanut-sized module held between the ends of his index and middle fingers – around the live wires and into the niche. It sat unevenly; when he tapped it down it snicked into place and the metal surface began to crawl unpleasantly with tiny ripples like wrinkled skin. He knocked on the conduit with his fingers until the cover rotated closed and then carefully edged his hand away from the wires. There were a few moments of silence, with only distant crashing sounds from above to interrupt, then Russ exhaled. "It's working. I have a low-bandwidth carrier signal from the ship. Tai says congratulations and hurry back."

It was the best news Elif had heard all day. He grinned. "She's all through your systems now, isn't she?"

Russ closed her eyes with a contented look on her face. "I can trust her to behave responsibly with them, which is more than I can say for you."

Elif thought that having Russ trust Tai explicitly was useful, so it was time to change the subject. "Are we just going to stand here for the next half hour?"

She gave him an arch, bemused look. "What did you have in mind?"

His face fell. "Not that. Give it a rest." He cast about for something to talk about, anything, to get off **that** topic.

To his surprise, Russ came to his aid. "Would you like me to tell you about Planet X?"

He managed to conceal his glee beneath a chintzy drape of low-level hostility before asking himself why she wanted to change the subject so readily. "I suppose so," wondering just how much of it would be factual. "Tell me of your homeworld, asshole."

"IT's what you would call a gas giant. No sun. Mostly frozen methane. We live in tunnels carved in the core. If you could survive at that pressure and temperature, you wouldn't see anything; very little free energy of any wavelength... " seeing his expression, "we prefer it that way. It's much safer. Terrible things happen on planets with too much activity. X-quakes, storms and the like."

Somewhere above – perhaps three levels up, near the surface of the eyelash – a Chort slammed into the generator wall, making it shake, metal shavings raining down and striking sparks off the exposed cables on the way.

"How the hell did life even begin under those conditions?" Elif asked.

Airily, "Oh, we got our start somewhere else. It doesn't matter where; it was destroyed a long time ago."

"Sucks to lose your home planet. I'm sorry, I guess."

"Don't be. We destroyed it ourselves. In fact, we had it carved into slices and sold. We've always been commercially astute, compared to the lesser races."

A thin shriek of metal tearing far away resonated unpleasantly and made them both wince momentarily. Elif waited until the sound had faded. "Is everyone lesser to you?"

"Oh, no. We know our place in the scheme of things. We've never thought our world was the centre of creation. Some races are served, with humility, lest they destroy you. Some are avoided, like the, uh – " Russ gestured about her. "Everyone else, you enslave. It's one of the greatest achievements of the Xists; we have found a way to work with every race we've ever met, even with monkeys, crustaceans and bugs. Even with the Abandoners, and they are notoriously difficult to tempt, in that they require so little to exist." She smiled evilly. "We found a way."

Elif was thinking of cold corridors carved from methane ice, completely black and silent, with awful things dragging themselves along the polished floors, sneering soundlessly at each other as they passed. Thousands of miles of darkness above pressing down endlessly. "I'm not sure I like the idea of living there... but, we wouldn't be living on X, would we? Or in it. Right?"

"Of course not. We don't allow the lesser races anywhere near our homeworld. And, besides, I'm sure you've worked out by now that the whole Tribe Going to the Promised Land Thing is an idea left over from the hundreds of thousands of years that primates spent as nomads." There was an uncomfortable pause while Russ let this sink in, and Elif tried in vain to put a positive spin on it. "Don't look so worried. We value the SubGenii. Life won't be so bad on the reservation." Russ peered through the wires at the transponder niche. "There's always a use for a good set of prehensile monkey fingers, even if they did evolve primarily for picking peanuts out of poop."

Elif was starting to see Russ' snide comments as a kind of companionable, good-natured ribbing; then he realised she was only giving him the kind of hierarchical-dominance games that a monkey would need to feel secure. If he'd been a Spree, she probably would have been licking him. For a moment he almost found the idea attractive, before remembering what Russ really was, and then he saw he hadn't hidden his first response quickly enough. She was giving him that look. They were going to have that conversation. He'd already decided to tell a good approximation of the truth in the hope Russ would think he was covering something up; it wasn't much of a strategy, but this was the first time he'd tried it with an alien more intelligent than him.

"Why won't you sleep with me?" she asked quietly.

He looked her in the eye, their noses barely inches apart. "It's never a good idea to sleep with your employer. It makes you disposable." Russ pretended to look confused. "You have to have something to hold over them or they'll throw you away when the relationship is no longer to their benefit." He smiled tolerantly. "'True communication is only possible between equals', you know."

"Nobody is equal."

"There are... degrees of inequality. The less equal we are, the more likely it is you'd be doing it **just** to control me."

"Just to control you? Are you trying to trivialise the idea?"

"It means you think I need controlling. It means that our paths are going to part ways at some point, and you want to be able to stab me in the back before I can stab you in the back."

Russ glanced down at her breasts. "And so, when my evil plan is finally revealed in all its evility, you will recoil, hold up your hand dramatically and declare 'No!', and then... I pull open my shirt, your rational processes stop and I win."

Elif matched her sarcastic look. "No. You're all about distraction. Just enough to keep me from seeing the truth in time to do something about it."

"If there ever was a point where you could do something about it, I wouldn't be much of an evil genius, would I?"

"So there **is** an evil plan, isn't there?..." his face fell. "... and working out that there is an evil plan is part of your evil plan."

"It wouldn't be anywhere near as much fun otherwise, and if you're not having fun, there's no point in getting out of bed in the morning," her smile modulating slightly, "unless you're having more fun in bed."

Elif was starting to get irritated. He didn't believe Russ had any intention of following through with her teasing, and he half-suspected that this impression had been made deliberately to induce him to force the point to where it would appear he had initiated it. He was an old hand at this kind of paranoid sparring. "Don't you Xists have any sense of pride? I would expect doing it with a human would be comparable to a human doing it with an ant." They exchanged looks, then recited together "Lots of lube." Impatiently, he continued, "No, seriously, won't the other Xists laugh at you?"

Russ' smile looked earnest. "We don't need to play the endless social games humans play. There is only one game, only one measure of an Xist's worth: how much money they have. It doesn't matter how they got it. It doesn't matter who they had to screw in order to get it. The closest thing we have to a sexual taboo involves not giving advanced technology to the lesser races. That's just extremely poor form. Those notes I gave you on Namronics could be considered the equivalent of a brief flirtation with a barnyard animal in some ways, although given that you haven't taken in any of the details, it hardly matters." She looked down at her body. "And after all the trouble I went to."

Wait, what? She can't be giving in that easily! "Too much trouble. I'm a SubGenius! We're – look, you can knock it off with the pheromones, because you're doing it wrong. It smells like old.. socks..." He slowly looked up, then closed his eyes with a pained expression. **Oh, shit.** "'Drake, we are leaving!'" he mimicked shouting faintly. This was, whatever it was, potentially, very bad; he was unable to move for a few seconds. Once his Merest Hint had unwrapped its tail from around his brain-stem he grabbed Russ' shoulders as if to kiss her enthusiastically, performed an awkward little dance in the confined space – only just avoiding the remaining live power-lines – until he could get to the exit. "Race you back to the ship!" he whispered, slapping her shoulder and ducking into the gap. He crawled as fast as he could, forgetting the access panel until he ran into it head-first with a dull clunk. As the sharper edges underneath began to dig into his hands and knees he pressed his forehead against the coiled striations – the metal had been ground flat with some kind of router or CNC miller – and shoved it open with a sideways movement of his head.

The area around the generator was clear of intact Chorts, although the loose debris underfoot had been glued together with Spree blood, lymph and unfortunate, torn chunks of flesh and sharp sections of carapace. He noticed dark worm-like lumps in the muck, writhing fitfully; new Spree warriors were growing in the fluid remains of the old. Russ followed him out; as they sprinted for their previous hiding place they left taffy-sticky footprints in the goop. **Can't be helped.** As they climbed up to the reaction chamber, a pounding bass drone came from somewhere above, like an H-4 Hercules with eight badly-synched engines, louder, so loud that dust began to rain down from the balconies and the broken Chort bodies began twitching and jumping within the layer of goo. Elif made it into the reaction chamber with his hands pressed to his ears, but it didn't help. He slid down against the inside of the shaking chamber, wondering if whatever it was had found them and was about to destroy the entire generator. Over the heavy feeling of oppressive confinement that the generator gave off, far above, two sharp notes of agony slid by, one following the other, both slowing, turning, hovering over the generator like the motors of a dual-blade police 'copter. He almost expected to see a search-light, but there were several levels of plates between them and the outside.

Then – almost as if his imagination had conjured it up – he did see a search-light, or something similar; a truncated conical beam of sickly yellow-green radiance that flowed through the metal ceiling, cutting an arc across the floor, drawing a slow circle around the generator tower. Just as the hum became too painful to bear it began to pull away, the points of pain turning end over end as the thing departed. A couple of Spree warrior bodies fell from the upper levels of the tower, bursting into beige dust as they hit the support struts that ran from each level to the generator walls. The green beam had completely desiccated them.

Then he turned and saw that Russ was lying on the floor of the chamber, not moving.

This just gets better and better.

IT all hit him at once; having been dragged away from Doctor Squid and the purple-haired elf girl, seeing that otherdimensional thing inside the conduit, sensing millions of lives being extinguished around them as they crashed into the eyelash, confronting that horribly deformed (assuming that it didn't ordinarily look that way) dying creature imprisoned in the walls of the generator, and now this. Elif slumped to the floor of the chamber in total despair, unable to decide what to do next. Had the Bitchslap been destroyed? Was Tai dead? Could he find his way back to see for himself? The depression sharpened to where it felt like his head was being squeezed in a vice made out of cemetery clay; then the feeling popped and vanished. He blinked, mouth hanging open in surprise. He shook his head to clear it, got up and peered through the grid of holes at the gravity generator. The Chorts hadn't come back, and there was a grey-green liquid with lumps, oozing from a gap in the generator wall, up near where that thing had died, drying out – or coagulating – before it reached the ground. Elif's tongue shuddered over his back teeth with nausea. The depression was gone, leaving a giddy kind of relief. Subconsciously he understood that if he tried to get back to the ship in that state of mind he'd probably end up trying to hug a Chort, so he went over to examine Russ, lying on her side. She wasn't breathing; eyes closed, a neutral expression on her even features. Elif brushed a strand of hair aside and pushed back her left eyelid; the pupil was unresponsive, still. Dead, even. He took her hand. It felt limp, and the fingers bent as a sleeping human's would, with the expected degree of resistance. No pulse. The skin felt cool, perhaps cooling to ambient. Slowly, inevitably, his attention drifted towards the hemispherical breasts nestled between the jacket's lapels. His mouth opened a fraction of an inch, smiled faintly and then closed. **It's a trick. If I touch her, she'll wake up and do that screaming pointing thing from the end of "Invasion of the Body Snatchers"... or, worse, she'll just give me that superior smirk. Still...**

He leaned down and placed his ear against a point two inches below her left breast, facing down. Nothing; no heartbeat, no intestinal gurgles, no breath. Offline. Mechanical failure? The thing was less than a week old. Probably still under warranty. Something was interrupting the signals Russ used to drive it. That thing with the twin engines and the green beam... if the Chorts were the local equivalent of bacteria, that flying Deathbeam platform could be part of the Yacatisma's immune system, its attention drawn to a critical system under attack. It hadn't actually hit Russ with that beam, so perhaps this was a local or a temporary interruption. It might help if he got her back to the ship. Ideally, a fireman's carry would have been the appropriately heroic thing to do... **the hell with that.** He grabbed her jacket collar at the back of her neck and dragged her up the sloping floor of the combustion chamber towards the conduit that led to the level where the end of the Bitchslap was parked. It was awkward going; her body weighed more than the old rotting zombie monk's had, almost as much as a human's. Fortunately the gravity varied a great deal from one place to the next.

He'd dragged her for almost half an hour, through narrow crawl-spaces between supporting walls, under stores of unevenly sprawled floor-plates awaiting the repair Chorts; nervous, precarious runs from one safe spot to another, before realising that the best way to get Russ to wake up – via Murphy's law – would have been to grope her breasts. It still felt like the wrong thing to do. **Why? She's not human. She doesn't care. Tai doesn't care. Are you worried she might tell someone that you're a sleaze? Who is she going to tell?**

He was crawling through a pipe just too small to stand up in, crooked sections joined end-to-end in poor quality wrist-thick welds that caught on the back of Russ' skirt. Freeing it, dragging her six steps, catching it again and freeing it became so annoying that he began to suspect she was feigning unconsciousness and was doing it deliberately, and he reconsidered his plan to force her into waking up. "Yeah, well, I **am** a sleaze," he muttered under his laboured breath.

A hideous metallic screech startled him so badly that he tripped and fell against the side of the pipe. Something had heard him speak and was trying to cut its way in; a patch of the wall began to glow dull red with the friction from a saw as he hooked his free arm around Russ' waist, scrambling away on one hand and knees, resolving to keep his mouth shut from now on.

When the twin-engine Deathbeam platform had fumigated the area around the gravity generator, the local Chorts had scattered in all directions. They were everywhere, ambushing each other from niches that Elif would have liked to have been hiding in, pulling arms off and clubbing each other with the heavy claw-ends. He'd never seen machines with that degree of eager enthusiasm for mayhem, not even in films, where they were usually presented as calm, methodical killers. The Chorts had few inhibitions in the name of personal welfare, more often than not sacrificing themselves for a chance to dismember an opponent. Either they'd never heard of game theory or they were playing by a set of rules he hadn't quite grasped yet. His own options were limited; having to drag Russ' limp body around meant he couldn't get any closer to the ship than the nearest blast furnace, and he'd have to vacate that and climb back into that pipe if anything found them. At least he could see the ship, even if the Chorts couldn't, and it looked intact.

The furnace was inactive, rows of finger-thick induction coils sitting cold and dark, loose beads of metal grit underfoot, stacks of floor-plates to one side and piles of broken metal pieces up to the ceiling on the others. The basic mechanism looked very simple; scrap went into the letterboxed ceramic collar, heat was applied and sheets of metal were squeezed out the other end, although there was no apparent way to turn it on or off and, naturally enough, no safety features. He sat Russ up against a stack of plates and cautiously peeked through the gaps in the loosely packed material. His Merest Hint kept jabbing him in the back-brain, warning him against going out there, and it didn't look like the Chorts were going to leave any time soon. He grimaced and nudged Russ' ass with his foot. **If you were awake, you could call up some Spree.**

He looked down at her and slowly smiled. It took a few seconds to get into the proper frame of mind – he knew it was the sort of thing that would only work if taken seriously – biting his lower lip to suppress the grin, he knelt and took the robot in his arms, leaning her head back and giving her a look of tender concern. He'd seen the hero do this in films; not motivated by the standard primate urge to get some, it was noble, gallant and entirely justified under the circumstances. "Russ... please, **please** wake up," he whispered urgently, then leaned down and gently brushed his lips across hers. As he'd expected, the puppet came to life at what ordinarily would have been an embarrassing moment, jerking back from him, glancing left, right and up with insectoid speed, slowing down to normality once Russ had taken in their situation. Elif's look of concern vanished immediately. He dropped her to the floor-plates and whispered "Right, whatever you did to call the Spree – do it and arrange another diversion or we're gonna get stomped." He glanced up nervously, trying to see if he'd been overheard, cowering reflexively as half a Chort skidded across the floor-plates nearby, one leg dead, the other slapping the floor with clonic fury. "Come on!"

Russ blinked, pretending to consider his request, then inclined her head towards the ceiling behind him. His skin crawling – this was the point in the movie where something horrible would leap down on him – he turned his eyes slowly and looked up. If it wasn't the Spree pimp from the asteroid market, it was from the same family, clinging to the overhead plates, its carapace mirror-surfaced. If he hadn't known where to look, he would have missed it.

The lanky creature dropped smoothly to the floor next to them, long limbs scissoring to absorb the impact without making a sound, crouching low and motionless. Elif leaned back slightly, trying to keep it in view, then he said "It's not going to be much of a distraction if they can't see it."

Russ opened her mouth as if to speak to the Spree, then turned to Elif. "You don't have any moral qualms about sending it to its death?"

Elif shrugged. "Don't you?"

Russ snorted; of course she didn't.

"Look, if you want I can go out there while you and your new friend scuttle back to the ship in safety. Tell Tai I said goodbye." He even moved a couple of steps towards the gap in the stack of plates before Russ grabbed his foot.

"Get back here, monkey-boy," she muttered. "New Spree can be grown in under thirty minutes – "

" – or they're free – " Elif couldn't help interjecting,

" – but I need something with opposable thumbs and an expensive set of implanted Aetherics." She turned to the Spree, opened her mouth and made a brief clacking noise at the back of her throat, then she spat at the creature. The Spree bobbed twice and extended its limbs, reaching up to the ceiling, then crawling along the plates, a rippling patch of subtlety. Its unquestioning willingness to die for the cause seemed more mechanical than anything he'd seen the Chorts do. Russ turned to one side with a sinuous flexing movement, stood and stretched with her eyes shut, thrusting her breasts out. Elif stifled an impulse to reach over and touch them and instead peeked through the gap in the pile of metal scraps, establishing where they'd have to run in order to reach the ship quickly.

"Elif?" Russ whispered. Irritated, he turned to look and missed seeing the Spree light up like a magnesium flare. He half-turned back and then turned away again, wincing at the sudden brightness. The bioluminescent pulse faded quickly, by which time the decoy was scrabbling about in circles on the ceiling, upside-down, dodging thrown punches from the Chorts, some of the more eager machines leaping up to land blows with more force. The Spree managed three more flares, each progressively dimmer, leading the Chorts away from the ship. As soon as the way was relatively clear with only broken machines spasming feebly about them, Elif and Russ ran for the back of the Bitchslap, climbed the ship's spine and jumped into the open hatch. Russ closed the stone-solid door and stood at the top of the ramp, listening to the faint clashing sounds outside for sixty long seconds before deciding they were safe.

Elif stumbled down the ramp to the bed, his legs suddenly rubbery. "We have to find a better way of getting in and out of the ship. There can't be a lot of Spree left out there."

A single decisive and heavy clang sounded from outside. "One less," Russ observed. "However, as odd as it might seem, you're right. I'm open to suggestions, if you have any."

Elif fell onto the bed, lay back and regarded the overhead grid of cyan lights. "Why the hell don't we use the Scoop? That's what it's for, right? Let me guess, we don't have enough power without our engines."

"Wrong, as usual. The Scoop requires a great deal of calculation; at least a month's worth of processor time. We'll only need to go out there once more, hopefully; once we understand the codes we can ask the generators to report the status, configuration and location of their power cells."

There was another of the unpleasant silences that were becoming a feature of conversations with Russ. Elif got the idea she'd been avoiding discussing this because of the nasty implications, but it had to come out eventually. "Yeah. Power cells," he muttered. Russ sat down on the edge of the bed – close enough for a semblance of amity but not close enough to appear overly familiar – and looked down at him with a solemn expression. Suddenly he thought: **why not ask Tai?**

It seemed like a good idea; Tai would be less likely to lie to him... unless she was in on it as well, and if she was, he didn't want to know. It would be over. He could possibly dance around Russ' misinformation, but the two of them working together would be the end. He didn't want to go there just yet; he still considered Tai to be his closest friend.

Good idea or bad, Russ was already speaking. "There is a kind of Aetheric that has appendages in several different universes. It can open a channel from one universe to another and allow small amounts of energy to flow along those appendages. It feeds on information; specifically, neural firing patterns. More specifically, patterns relating to a brain's appreciation of pain. If you attach these Aetherics to a living creature and then hurt it, the Aetheric will reward you with energy."

Elif thought about it. "Appreciation of pain. So it doesn't have to be pain from injury. It can be simulated so the host doesn't die in the process. And that's what I was sensing inside the gravity generator."

"Yes."

"And... that's what I was sensing from the ship's engines."

Russ even appeared reluctant to admit this, as if she was actually ashamed of it. "... yes, although to our credit, we Xists use Sheydal volunteers in our power cells. The sensations you were receiving were – "

That didn't make it any better, in Elif's view. He had to re-state it, to make sure he'd understood: "You torture living creatures to power your ships."

"... yes."

Elif managed to force something like a smile, although he didn't feel like smiling at all. "Just when I think you've gone as low as you can, you manage to surprise me. I suppose you have farm planets full of Sheydal, bred just for this purpose, like you have planets full of primates bred for Essence."

Russ was being carefully neutral. "It's what we do. One of the... things we do."

More than ever, Elif was convinced that letting Russ know what he was thinking wasn't to his advantage, so he matched her neutrality while trying to put down a rising panic. **What's to stop Russ giving me one of those power Aetherics and shoving me in a pod? Or Tai? She's in constant pain. More so, once her medication runs out.**

Holy crap. Is that why Russ had brought them? Spare batteries? He needed more time to consider this. "I really should see how Tai's doing," levering his legs over the edge of the bed and sitting up, pointedly, as far from Russ as he could get. **This is bad... worse than concentration camp bad... but I don't think it's the worst bad that Russ could aspire to. I think there's something even nastier waiting, and I need to see what it is before it's too late to dodge.**

Inappropriately – given Elif's current mood – a peal of laughter came from the bridge. Evidently, Tai was feeling better. Russ got up and ran to the first scoop. Elif followed at a more Rewardian pace, noting without surprise that Russ could move quickly when she wanted to.

He paused in the recycling bay; Russ had moved into the cloud of shifting holographic displays that filled the bridge and floated about like a swarm of tall, thin hanging banners. The predominant colours were red and orange, with occasional flashes of eye-searing – even at this distance – hot pink. He leaned down and whispered to the disassembler panel, "So, I heard you guys like viruses," thinking specifically of bacteriophages, the most tasteless thing that came to mind at the moment. At least, tasteless to a bacterium.

A billboard grew from the panel and lit up with a stylised image of a Rotavirus and the text: VIRUSES ARE OUR FRIENDS.

Elif tilted his head to one side. At least they were listening. He gave them a thumbs-up and went to see what Tai had found funny this time.

THE first thing he noticed – once he'd managed to filter out the visual noise from the drifting windows – was that Tai wasn't in her bed. She was sitting on top of the Essence capacitor which was bobbing about, a foot from the floor, her legs dangling, message windows opening and closing around her like winking eyes, the hot glow of the text painting her face with light. The second thing he noticed was the sloppy drunk grin on her face, a look he'd never seen on her before. She opened five windows with a sorcerer's apprentice gesture, spun them about with a turn of her wrist and cast them aside. They swam away and hovered eagerly at the edge of the luminiferous cloud.

Tai saw Elif and waved him over, pointing at the main window before her, but something didn't feel right. He took a moment to sense the area, but it wasn't until Tai jumped down from the capacitor and hugged him that he noticed her implant headband had grown into a scarf that wrapped around her head and extended part-way down the back of her neck. He only just managed to repress the urge to push her away when he saw it, then –

"You're looking mighty... uh, enthusiastic today."

She raised her eyebrows modestly. "I'm getting a boost from the implant. It won't last, and I'll pay for it eventually, but for the moment I'm running at one hundred and fifteen percent efficiency."

He didn't get to give her That Look very often, and he never enjoyed doing it, but he did it anyway. "Who was it once told me that overclocking was a bad idea?"

"In the long-term, it is. This isn't long-term. Anyway, I may not need to, for long – these systems are so **easy**! They're wide open. The whole thing is routed through a single set of – "

"I believe," Russ put in, managing to sound laconic and foreboding at the same time, "you were just telling me it's not as easy as it first appears." Both SubGenii turned to face the robot. Russ cocked a sardonic eyebrow at Tai, who slumped a little, just enough for Elif to feel. Automatically he hugged her a little tighter, for reassurance.

"Well," Tai began, but seemed reluctant to continue.

Elif scowled at Russ, as if this latest development was her fault. She spread her hands, pantomiming **it's not up to me.** "The transponder doesn't have the bandwidth we need. The codes are coming in, but slowly; it could take days before we have enough data to ask the right questions safely, and I can't guarantee that the camouflage will hold up for that long."

"More transponders?"

Russ considered this. "Each additional tap would increase the amount of information we're getting, but we don't have enough Spree soldiers left to mount that kind of diversion again. You would have to find another way in and out of the generator, as well as another, safe way back into the ship."

Elif thought about it. "Yeah. I would. Me, alone, because dragging your sorry ass along was a big mistake, last time, Spree auxiliaries or no." His attention lost focus as he let loose the strategising part of his mind. "I could drape some scrap over the end of the ship, disguise the fact there's a hatch, that'd make it easier to get in and out... as for the generators... what if I entered them from the surface?"

Russ appeared to look shocked. "That's not an option. Sub-zero temperatures, little or no consistent atmosphere, no protection against gamma radiation, but beyond that you would be – "

Elif was getting an inordinate amount of pleasure from interrupting Russ. " – out there just long enough to duck down into the generator and out again. The Chorts that are there for recharging keep to the lower levels, and the ones that are being fired off into space hang around the edges. I'd be sneaking in under the cap of the mushroom and then down the stalk." He wanted to cross his arms defiantly, but he would have had to let go of Tai to do it.

Another long, awkward pause. "I'm not happy with this plan."

Elif nodded, as if the decision had been made. "Until you come up with a better one, you'll have to learn to live with the disappointment." In a mock whisper to Tai, he said "Personally I think she's just miffed she didn't think of it first."

Russ tilted her head disdainfully. "Nobody's plans will be advanced by your dying stupidly."

Elif grinned, his induced depression gone. "I've got better things to do today than die for your plans. Now. Transponders: how many?"

ELIF crouched inside the end of a broken ship that had, years ago, plunged head-first into the surface of the eyelash. Its tail – six yards long, shaped like one end of a canoe – was riddled with torn lengths of metal and studded with chunks of stone. Peering out of a small hole, he could just see the point where the gravity generator met the surface, also festooned with sections of broken machinery. There was a nice, big gap where he could climb down inside... guarded by a Chort the size of a double-decker bus. Evidently he wasn't the only one who'd considered this way in.

This generator was at least four times as large as the one he'd been in before, and it attracted a correspondingly larger clientele; the lower levels, all the way down to the core, had been crowded with all manner of machines, each struggling violently for a place at the charging bays. What he'd expected to see as a larger pie fight was a full-scale riot. Getting inside via the lower levels was out of the question, and getting past the four-legged bus up here on the surface didn't look any more promising, but it was at least one opponent rather than hundreds.

This generator was on the inside curve of the eyelash, facing towards the eye; the bent tail of the wrecked ship created an overhang which hid him from view. He suspected if he stepped outside, the Yacatisma would see him, and would notify the locals. Probably one of those twin-engine variants with the green deathbeams. He could feel one of them somewhere nearby, hovering just around the horizon as if waiting for "The Ride of the Valkyries" to start playing before it attacked.

His immediate problem was getting past the bus. He'd seen half a dozen smaller Chorts try their luck, only to be seized and thrown out into space. Guarding that gap was important enough to require the presence of a reasonably competent machine, and Elif didn't think he'd have any better luck than the little guys; the big Chort's reflexes were uncommonly fast for a machine that size. He wasn't silly enough to imagine he could just walk past it, getting by on pure charisma. "Bob" could probably do it, but he couldn't, outside of the context of a Marx Brothers film.

He found a loose spar of ceramic-metal composite shaped like roof guttering, set his 'phone to record and placed it in the end of the spar. Moving as slowly as he could, he edged the 'phone out of the hole, underneath the overhang, a matter of inches, then just as slowly dragged it back. The cold plastic casing stung his hand as he viewed the recording. He saw a jet-black hemisphere with a faint violet halo, three threadlike towers behind it; other eyelashes. He sat back and breathed with difficulty, trying to charge his blood with as much oxygen as he could get, thankful there was any atmosphere at all. At least it didn't smell of death like the lower levels; exposure to radiation from open space would quickly denature any organic molecules into things too simple to register as scent. It would also burn his skin to crispy bacon if he went out without any protection. He'd picked up a couple of pieces of scrap that would do the job, but he'd been here for almost half an hour and couldn't see any way past the double-decker bus and its legs thicker than his waist and its claws that could pop an engine-block like a peanut. It couldn't see him in his hiding-place, but it had no problem seeing the little Chorts desperate enough to challenge right-of-way.

He ran his finger over the edge of the hole. It was perfectly round, smooth, scalloped as if someone had chopped a sphere out of the hull. It reminded him of something, but he was too distracted to think about it in any depth. He stared out at the humped and buckled plates under faint moonlight-strength radiance, sharp black shadows that looked like a mall car-park at one in the morning... or perhaps the concrete flats around one of the factories he'd worked in, late at night, dead washed-out yellow acetylene glow on empty parking spaces. If he let it, a sense of desolation would start to fur the back of his mind until he forced himself to remember the pain cells arranged around the generator shaft below. Each time he pushed the feeling down he got the idea it wouldn't work next time; the air was getting colder and knowing there was an infinite volume of emptiness only a hundred yards above was starting to exert an hypnotic attraction. All he had to do was step outside and all of his problems would be over.

Just when he felt the situation couldn't get worse, a twin-engine Monitor Chort flew up, orbiting the underside of the gravity generator's mushroom-dome, its two-tone scream like something out of a hospital's burns ward, making him want to crawl back inside the broken ship and cover his head with his arms. It flew overhead, cast a faint shadow on the double-decker bus Chort, which tracked it as it passed and for a second Elif saw a scattering of cyan points of light set into the floor-plates.

The damn thing was standing on a fragment of a Scoop.

He stared at the surface where it met the edge of the generator shaft. It was a chunk of the same material that the Bitchslap's hull was made of, grey stone like a permanent magnet, embedded in the general metal-plate matrix. God alone knew how it had ended up here.

There is no way in hell it would still be working. And less chance of me figuring out how to get it to work...

Yet the cyan lights were on. If he waited for the faint, shifting overhead light to arrange itself, he could see them. That had to mean something. It was even possible that the hole he was peeking through had been carved out with the Scoop; it had that perfect finish he'd seen in the edges of the remains of his bedroom. Almost without thinking, he carefully backed into the ruined hull and climbed down to the level below the surface. It was completely black down there aside from slices of violet light that made it in through the edges of the badly buckled plates, less than a yard deep around the generator shaft – pounded flat by projectiles dragged down by the gravity generator's miles-wide fields – but by crawling slowly and lying on his back he could feel the underside of the scoop fragment. He risked running his fingernail along the underside; it felt just like the Bitchslap's hull. He pressed his cheek against it, expecting to be frozen, but the material didn't conduct heat at all.

Recalling the embarrassment he'd felt in trying to get the Bitch-slap's hatch open by thinking happy thoughts, he tried to sense something... anything. It was nothing like using his Lifesense to locate living things, but immediately he could feel it with his mind; a node, an irregular sphere set inside the Scoop wall, free to rotate like a gyroscope. If he concentrated he could make it spin on any axis, could push it against resistance that increased logarithmically. He knew that if he imagined squeezing, it would activate. For one precarious second he almost did it before realising it needed to be set properly or it might scoop a chunk out of him and then shove it somewhere impractical. He closed his eyes, took a deep breath, clenched his teeth and tried to convince his Mechanical Affinity to tell him how to make it work. He could use the Lifesense almost as well as his eyes or ears, and he could understand the warnings given by the Merest Hint, but Mechanical Affinity operated at a sub-conscious level. Convincing it to give him specifics was like trying to get a dog to fetch only the Sunday supplement out of next door's newspaper. Using sign language.

A clashing sound from above, followed by a metallic screech and then the generator came on-line, reversing the local gravity field, slamming him against the underside of the Scoop fragment. The already thin atmosphere began whistling out through hundreds of tiny holes and the plates creaked and shifted about six inches before the generator reversed direction again and dropped him to the floor-plates in a storm of dust. He tried to gasp as quietly as possible. **How am I supposed to concentrate under these conditions?**

It wasn't working. If the control node was pointing at anything, he couldn't see it. He wasn't even sure if it worked on a point-and-click basis, if it worked at all. To top it off, he couldn't see the Chort on the other side of the plates, couldn't sense it... this wasn't getting him anywhere. In exasperation half-borne of a lack of oxygen he mentally spun the control node and then imagined squeezing it like a trigger. There was a jarring sensation and a spherical chunk of floor-plate about the diameter of a family pizza disappeared, less than a foot from his head. His Mechanical Affinity sense worked out the details and understanding flared behind his eyes, erasing the shock of seeing how close he'd come to giving himself a really bad hair-cut.

"Hah!" he shouted, then, in a subdued voice, "uh oh." The Chort had heard. In its eagerness to reach him it stamped on the Scoop fragment with enough force to push it down by six inches. "Oh, **crap.**" Frantically Elif tried to re-aim the Scoop – it seemed to work by visualizing a tube reaching from one place to another, chopping a spherical piece out of either end and swapping them – while the Chort, realising it couldn't punch through the Scoop fragment, began clawing at the edges where it met the floor-plates. One leg poked through the hole he'd just scooped and peeled back the plates like the lid of a sardine tin. Elif frantically imagined spinning the control node about, setting the range and triggering it; silence. Despite being close to the point of blacking out, he didn't dare breathe until he heard a crash from above. The end of the leg poking through the hole twitched and pulled the plate out of the matrix, tearing the Scoop material loose at one end, then was still.

Painfully, he pushed against the plates and the underside of the Scoop fragment until he'd edged back into the ruined ship. He looked out of the gap. The Chort was resting on its underside, legs splayed out awkwardly, a hole the size of half a bowling ball chopped out of its leading edge. Resting in a niche formed by the intersection of three bent floor-plates was the piece he'd excised with the Scoop, gleaming copper and silver mechanisms slowly spinning down.

Not wanting to waste the opportunity he waited until the twin-engine Chort had flown around to the other side of the generator's city-block-sized mushroom cap, then he held a piece of thin scrap hull-plating over his head in one hand and ran for the generator entrance, grabbing the chopped-out Chort section as he passed. He almost dropped it again when the exposed flywheels – still spinning – slashed his hand and forearm; the twin-engine Chort came back around faster than he'd anticipated and he threw himself into the gap at the base of the generator, dropping his makeshift umbrella and crouching in a pile of very sharp metal pieces, his eyes squeezed shut against the psychic screams that buzzed overhead. It was only then that the uncomfortable thought occurred to him: if he could sense the flying Chort, perhaps it could sense him. The thing's shadow fell over the gap and he jumped back so quickly that he rebounded from the far wall and slid towards the gap he'd just entered by. He slammed both hands against the walls on either side of the gap and dropped to the floor, retreating more carefully until the fingers-across-the-blackboard feeling from below matched the silent, hateful paired screeching that was circling the generator. He swallowed in the dry air, examined the parallel gouges across the palm of his hand and poked at the Chort section with the end of a Phillips head screwdriver, the only tool he'd brought with him aside from his 'phone. The gears whirred furiously and chewed about an inch off the end of the screwdriver. He dropped the piece of Chort and the screwdriver, recoiling with a nervous Charles Nelson Reilly laugh, then looked around.

This generator was much bigger than the first, and didn't have that makeshift jury-rigged look. Aside from the drift of scraps that had blown in from the gap leading to the surface, it almost seemed... neat. There was no mistaking the sensations rising from below, however; there were living things trapped here, and they were all suffering. As his Lifesense picked up more detail, a sense of nauseous revulsion began to rise from the pit of his stomach. There were dozens of living things trapped here, and if the layout was the same as the smaller generator, he'd have to go down past them all to plant the transponder.

Okay. As quickly as possible. No need to stand around gawking. This isn't a Disneyland ride.

A N iris hatch set into the bottom of the spherical entrance-space led down into the nastier area. A few solid kicks knocked off enough rust – more rust than on anything he'd seen in the past few days – to allow him to force it open. The area below was as clean, white and unobtrusively lit as a Stanley Kubrick set, the walls and floor mostly made of a kind of metal-ceramic composite. He poked his head down and looked around before dropping to the floor, slowly, under about half a gravity.

A broad circular space, undetailed, empty, aside from the good-sized collection of alien bones and scraps of leathery flesh scattered all about; a less welcome change of pace from the torn pieces of metal he'd gotten so used to seeing everywhere. An open and less rusted iris hatch in the floor led to the next level.

Set into the walls: a series of round glass windows, like coin-laundrette clothes dryers, about a foot from the floor. One was open, as if someone had just taken their towels, socks and underwear and dragged them down to the next level, leaving a trail of yellow slime. Elif scuffed his boot-toe through it, ready to abandon boot if the stuff was aggressively acidic; it was still wet but more or less inert, aside from smelling like rhinoceros urine.

About half of the windows set into the walls glowed Cherenkov blue, pulsing on and off, each one slightly out of phase with the others and accompanied by a faint growling sound. Standing in the middle of the room, pressed on all sides by radiating, almost palpable waves of misery, Elif felt trapped and not at all reassured by the sudden clacking sound from the next room down, as if someone was kicking the bones about. As a way of avoiding dealing with whatever was on the next level, and knowing he really didn't want to, he slowly approached the empty cell, taking care not to step in the slime, then he peered into the cavity.

It was about the size of a shower stall laid on its side, with a heavy stone seal for the glass door, the insides smeared with splashes of that yellow liquid. A round, dark orb like a translucent VW hub-cap was set into the far end. He looked inside a few other windows, but couldn't see anything; the door glass was cheaply finished, more for keeping things in than for visibility. There was nothing else to see here unless he got closer to an active cell; he went back to the iris hatch and dropped down into the next level, trying to get back into that first-person-shooter mode of dealing with things.

It was a room like the first, but with all of the pain cells active and glowing angrily. Aside from a lot more bones, the only other notable feature was a large dog-like creature with six or seven legs and long, shaggy, matted beige fur; it was trying to retreat into a corner and discovering there weren't any. Shaking and barely able to stand, scratching feverishly at one of the cell windows with dark grey clawed fingers, it gave a particular impression of acute panic. **If it's been outside lately... well, I can understand that. If it lives here, well, shit.**

Still, the thing had the build of a small horse, easily equipped to kick his ass several times if it came to that. Elif was hoping it didn't; he was almost happy to see something that wasn't a machine or an insectoid and that didn't seem to have any immediate intent to disembowel him. There were other living things here, free agents... or, perhaps, less than free; this creature might have escaped from one of the cells. Or perhaps it had been brought here by some Xist asshole for the same reason Russ had brought him and Tai.

His first impulse was to try to communicate with it, get some background story, if possible. His communication with the Spree pimp had been ambiguous for the most part but he'd managed a kind of rapport with the alien inside the seven-legged coffee-table machine-suit. **Let's face it, all we have going for us is opposable thumbs and inane chatter.**

He looked around the room. Whatever was inside the cells wasn't going anywhere and he needed to find the Namronic cables leading to the charging array, somewhere below. The next iris hatch was rusted open, so he shrugged apologetically to the creature – which wasn't paying any attention – and said "Look, I'm sorry. I don't have time for this. Take care, huh?"

The creature howled, a mournful ear-splitting wail with the penetrating force of a factory siren, its floppy mouth outlined, via Elif's life-sense, in an aura of vivid green. Elif made as if to cover his ears with his hands, then shook his head and dropped through the next hatch.

Now, this looked more promising. The cells on this level had been ripped out, leaving jagged gaps, bunches of bare cable and sections of circular stone switching elements. More cables dangled from the ceiling, and most of them twitched as if alive; if they were

Namronic conduits, they probably were alive in some sense. The light was dimmer, and there was a sour acidic reek from the floor directly underneath the hatch; that creature might have been using it for a toilet.

The broken-fingernails-on-sandpaper feelings from above were softer but still strong enough to make him want to keep to the centre of the room. It was more the desire to get this job over with than the smell that gave him the impetus to start sensing for the Namronic junction he needed. His Mechanical Affinity told him he'd found it, although it looked completely different to the other one; the transponder slotted itself into a hole just as readily as before, presumably auto-configuring itself. He waited for a few moments, but nothing obvious happened. "Guess we're done here," Elif muttered, hoping that Marmaduke up there didn't come down and piss on the transponder any time soon.

He found a stone cell collar that still had its door attached, by a clever arrangement of three swivelling ball joints. There was no latch visible; the window swung open easily. He couldn't see anything keeping the prisoners in, unless whatever happened to them inside left them unable to move.. or that these cells were the only way of staying alive in a place with no food. Unless you got so hungry you could eat the other prisoners. "Russ," he sighed, "you take us to absolutely the best places. No question of it." He scuffed a cracked set of wavy ribs with his toe, listening to the sad clack of old, dried bones. "It can only get better," although he wasn't sure if he meant that cynically or hopefully.

He took a deep breath and waited until the local gravity field shifted, then he jumped up, grabbed the edge of the iris hatch and climbed back up to the next level. As he got his leg over the edge, the large dog creature saw him and twitched nervously, then went back to pulling pieces off a bundle of claws and other less-readily-identifiable things it'd just dragged out of a pain cell. For a moment Elif considered trying to establish communications again; **I have to be able to learn something from this guy. Everyone has a story.**

It turned all four eyes towards him and managed to get one of the clawed feet into its large, toothless mouth, the sides of its head bulging with the effort. Thirsty, Elif imagined it saying.

Elif tried not to think about his almost-full bladder. Like most SubGenii, he was always up for new experiences, but even he had to draw the line somewhere. "Okay, so you're not a narrative kind of guy. That's," a tickle from his Merest Hint, "okay with me, " he turned to look at the far wall, trying to see beyond the buzzing interference caused by the pain cells, "but now we should run, okay?"

Run where? imagined sarcastically, just before the twin-engine Chort slammed into the side of the generator tower with enough force to knock the floor out from underneath Elif's feet. The big dog-creature howled again and scratched at the wall as if it could dig through the stonework. The duet of screams coming from outside abruptly became a solo. With the slow inevitability of a nightmare, Elif lost his balance and fell over to land in the puddle of rotting flesh and sticky fluids. "Oh, I need to know this can get worse," he gasped, "'cause right now I don't think it can," trying not to vomit.

The Chort was hovering outside, limping, its single engine labouring to keep it moving, a wounded wasp the size of a railway car. Lying on his stomach in a puddle of alien puke, Elif squeezed his eyes shut in anticipation of the Deathbeam and then he brushed muck from one eye and glanced upwards as if he could see the thing. If it fired a Deathbeam through the generator, it'd kill most of the pain-cell occupants, which would deprive the gravity generator of a good portion of its power. Slowly he grinned; the grin faded when he sensed that the Chort had landed right where the other had been sitting; at the entrance to the generator. The telepathic screaming sound dropped to a moan, and then to a whimper. The creature trapped in the flying Chort's pain cell wasn't dead, just idling, or perhaps changing gear; its voice, or what Elif's brain was interpreting as a voice, joined the general chorus of misery from the other pain cells.

Even the dog-creature knew something bad was about to happen; it crouched low, making furtive movements as if to crawl closer to the centre of the room but not wanting to get near Elif. From above: a hissing sound, a thump, and a thread of dark red liquid trickled down, forming a spreading puddle in the middle of the yellow vomit. Then, after a few seconds, the unmistakeable back-brain tickling of an Attractant Aetheric.

Elif's eyes widened. This was new. It meant the Chorts – at least the ones large enough to have their own pain cells onboard – could use Aetherics through organic proxies, even if the result was unsubtle and coarse, like trying to whisper after screaming for an hour. The feeling wasn't as immediately sexual as the purple-haired-elf-girl's efforts had been; closer, perhaps, to I-think-I-left-a-tap-running. It wasn't strong enough to counter the fear he felt from knowing the Chort wanted him to go up there and take the dead pain-cell occupant's place. For a few moments, that fear overrode his desire to stay away from the active pain-cells. It was getting harder to tell the awful choices from the merely bad ones.

Little Big Dog was more receptive to the idea; the dripping red liquid sealed the deal. Warily keeping two or three eyes on Elif, it got as close as it dared, scooped sticky, drying blood from the floor into its mouth, then positioned itself to catch the drips in a flexible, furry-edged toothless mouth the size of a toilet bowl. The drips slowed; the Attractant Aetheric pulsed again, stronger, and the creature leaped for the edge of the hatch, displaying at least as many stumps of limbs as whole ones but falling short, to land awkwardly in the puddle. It tried again, and again, reaching the edge with one hand, dangling there.

Elif considered the situation. He wasn't about to go up there himself, but helping the creature up didn't seem like a moral thing to do, even if the big dog wanted to go, particularly if it didn't understand that it was being lured up there. He had a vision of twin-engine Chorts zooming about above the surface of the eyelash, dragging broken and crippled creatures around on invisible Aetheric leashes; for a moment it reminded him of something repellent he'd seen recently, but the bad things were starting to run together in his mind, and at that moment Marmaduke took the opportunity to howl again. **Thirsty! Thirstier than you!**

Not at all convinced it was a good idea, Elif got closer and tried to grab the nearest leg, or arm, which kicked partly as a reflex against being touched, but mainly from an urgent need to climb. The local gravity field shifted again, carrying them both up through the iris hatch, past the next level and up against the ceiling of the spherical entrance chamber, along with a quantity of blood and bile and dried skin and bones. The gravity field resumed its customary direction and Elif dropped half-over the iris hatch to lie next to a dead purple-haired-elf-girl, presumably the former occupant of the twin-engine Chort hovering outside. A gap in the machine's nose had opened like the jaws of a mantis, revealing a compact space similar to a jet-fighter cockpit, lined with different-sized flattened glass plates which glowed blue; a pain generator. Elif stared into the jaws of the Chort, momentarily overtaken with the signals from his brain that said this was another spot he could place a transponder. He grinned and deftly tossed the metal peanut into the Chort's mouth; his grin faded when he realised the dog-creature was crouching behind him, and –

Thirsty, but never that thirsty, rearing back to kick him through the gap, into the Chort's mouth. One furry foot came down on the hemisphere Elif had cut out of the bus-Chort and the malevolent machinery whirred into life, tangling the long fur between its cogs and wheels. Marmaduke howled, shook its foot wildly and tried to kick the thing away, failed, then jumped back, slamming against the back of the chamber and bouncing forward just as Elif had before. The dog-alien sailed neatly over him, head-first into the cockpit; the jaws closed and the twin-engine Chort pulled away. The foot with the hemisphere tangled in its fur was trapped in the jaws of the hatch, twisting around, still trying to dislodge the sharp cogs as it receded.

Elif crouched there, staring wide-eyed. The whole thing had taken less than five seconds, with the kind of smooth, deranged ballet found in a Warner Brothers cartoon. A fading shriek from the dog-alien told him all he needed to know about its fate.

Resting against the back of the chamber, not daring to breathe, he glanced at the dead purple-haired-elf-girl then recoiled as a furry foot attached to a whirring metal hemisphere fell from the sky and bounced through the gap. "Ngyah!" The twitching foot came to rest against the dead girl's side, the cogs still eagerly winding fur into their works. Elif glared at it. "We done yet?" He noticed the girl's wrists ended in smooth, rounded stumps and shook his head with disbelief. "I think I've had quite enough of this for one day."

HE made it as far as the inactive forge near the ship before the shakes caught up with him. He crouched in the spot where he'd laid Russ' body down previously and let the tremors work their way out. The sight of the dead purple-haired-elf-girl had hit him harder than he'd thought it would. He'd seen dead people before, but not that close, and never in those circumstances. These machine-things were serious. They trapped living creatures and tortured them for energy, and then threw the bodies away when they were used up, and he'd come within an RCH of finding out what it was like from the inside. He tried to breathe slowly, and, as always out there, quietly, but the panic got worse. He bit the ball of his thumb as hard as he could, which helped a little.

There was a SubGenius discipline known as Surfing the Luck Plane but he'd never learned how to do it. He knew if he kept taking these insane risks, eventually he'd come up against the ugly side of the law of averages.

A s he carefully replaced the sheet of scrap over the end of the Bitchslap, Elif was hoping nobody was going to leap out and shout "Surprise!" when he got inside. He didn't even want the conquering hero's welcome; he just wanted to scrape the dried alien puke off his clothes, take a shower and then get about ten hour's sleep.

Russ and Tai were on the bridge, in the middle of a discussion of mitochondrial Aetherics. Tai was back on her bed, and looking like she was paying the price of overclocking; pale, thin, with bedraggled strands of hair plastered to her sweaty forehead.

Elif stood in the doorway. Tai made an effort to get up, but he waved her back. Russ seemed... uncharacteristically vacant. She was lacking sufficient body-language cues to make him think Ron was in control. Perhaps she was stoned. He suspected that if he asked, he'd just get the run-around, so he didn't.

Nobody seemed willing to speak. Eventually Elif asked "We get signal?"

Tai stared at him blankly for a moment (were they both stoned?) and then deciphered his allusion. "Oh. Yes! We've got two permanent feeds and there's a third one, dips in and out all the time, but it sends more data than the other two put together. We'll have enough clues to start asking questions safely in a couple of hours. The unlinked interval is about five microseconds, on average, and it – " she took in the state of his clothes – "uh... you look like..."

Elif held his arms out, proudly displaying the stains. "Yeah. It's kinda post-modern out there. Lots of deconstruction going on." He inhaled through his nostrils but didn't smell any weed smoke; Russ was still staring off into space, so he added, "You okay, Captain? We're supposed to be having a meeting, you know."

Russ summoned a hint of disdain. "I'm fine, thank you, Susan."

Elif had to laugh, just a little. It told him that Russ had been through their video archives, at least as far as watching "Red Dwarf". "Right. Ima sleep, me. Wake if anything interesting happens, otherwise... don't."

He found some clean clothes and a towel in the first Scoop and entered the shower, occasionally frowning at the odd sensations from the bridge via his Lifesense. "Weird night... and gettin' weirder," he muttered, realising he'd have to keep a lid on the pop-cultural references; Russ would know them all by now. He was starting to think he preferred the paranoia inspired by the immediately life-threatening environment outside, compared to the paranoia of not giving anything away to Russ. He still had no idea what the Xist was working towards, but he knew with absolute certainty that he wouldn't like it when he found out. He started spinning possible outcomes but the results were so depressing he decided he'd let Russ surprise him and try to be resilient enough to deal with it when it happened. This had never worked for him in the past, but he was always willing to try.

He stood under the shower fully clothed until the worst of the dried muck had softened and washed down the drain, presumably to be filtered and recycled by a horde of specialist Abandoners, then he stripped naked and piled the clothes in the hand-basin. They'd need a proper wash at some point, but he couldn't see Russ fitting out the ship with any more human household appliances. There was probably some highly efficient and essentially repellent alien technology that would do the job; perhaps a mobile bacterial slick that oozed onto the clothes and absorbed all the dirt. He wasn't prepared to leave his best jeans in the recycling bay in case the Abandoners ate them.

Getting all of the chunks out of his hair took almost half an hour.

He towelled himself dry, got dressed and threw himself down

on the bed in the second Scoop chamber, physically exhausted, his mind racing like a hamster wheel with three hamsters. He was still receiving unfamiliar Aetheric flashes of some kind from the direction of the bridge and his mental state didn't make understanding any easier. He was still trying to verbalise or even visualise the feeling when he fell asleep and dreamed of Dr Squid.

It was one of those awkward dreams where nobody spoke but everyone else acted on some unspoken consensus that he didn't share. On top of that he seemed to be underwater, yet breathing easily; the water smelled like the scent Russ was exuding after her shower. Dr Squid was perched on a conical rock, tentacles waving about in movements suggestive of a Balinese dancer, chromatophores flashing in bands from its base, splayed out on the rock, to the vestigial fins at the top. The display gave the impression Dr Squid was trying to

—

Elif woke with a start. He felt he hadn't been asleep for more than a few seconds but it had apparently been longer, because in the interim Tai had joined him on the bed and was sleeping nestled in his arms, facing away. He didn't have to wonder if he was awake or still dreaming; that repulsive implant had grown until it covered the back of her neck and shoulders and, as far as he could see, half-way down her back. Despite the thing's evil slick black intrusiveness, he hugged her closer. She felt cold but was still breathing evenly. He tried to think warm thoughts.

Feeling an uncomfortable tickling sensation in his peripheral vision, he turned to see Russ standing at the end of the bed, staring at them, arms crossed below her breasts. Elif tugged the largest towel over his shoulder, draped it over Tai's arm and tried to ignore everything else.

"Disgusting," Russ muttered and walked away. Underneath the towel, Elif grinned, but the feeling faded quickly. He thought about the next part of their supposed mission; rescuing the engine, assuming they could find it. Assuming it was accessible.

This wasn't going to be like in the films or the games; none of that lone hero sneaking into the stronghold of the bad guys and rescuing the princess stuff. He'd pulled out all of his tricks getting this far, and he'd only just made it back from the last excursion; the next step was going to be worse than anything he'd been through so far. The Chorts obviously weren't happy with living things wandering around in their territory, but they would pull out all the stops if he actually stole a valuable component from a generator, even if it belonged to Russ to begin with. They wouldn't just buzz around like angry termites; they'd chase him all the way back to the ship and then peel it open like an orange. He'd have to run all the way, dragging the engine, and as soon as they were close enough, Russ would have to scoop them both into the ship at the maximum range, whatever that was, and then hope the Chorts couldn't work out what had happened. If they knew someone was running loose and stealing engines, they would mount a thorough search. They were at least that smart. On top of that, the Bitchslap would have to make its escape from the midst of a horde of angry machines. Not just the four-legged variety, either; there'd be those twin-engine Monitors with their deathbeams, and possibly even larger ones. The heist might even attract the attention of the main guns mounted on the edge of the Yacatisma's mouth. Elif wasn't happy with the idea of re-enacting the last ten minutes of "Butch Cassidy and the Sundance Kid" but unless Russ had some subtle plan involving a wormhole or some other hyperspacial trickery, it all depended on their being able to move faster than the Yacatisma.

Could they do that? What was stopping the Yacatisma from dragging them back with its gravity generators? Did the Bitchslap use something similar to move about, and would it devolve into a contest of who had the biggest engines? He didn't know enough about this situation to be able to make a reasonable kind of assessment of their chances, but if Russ thought it was worth trying, there had to be at least a possibility...

... unless Russ had other plans, and Russ always seemed to have other plans, with no provision for excluding plans that didn't involve the humans' survival. It suddenly became vital that he establish whether Russ – or even just part of Russ – was actually, physically onboard or not. The activity in the Essence capacitor had been dropping steadily; either the stuff didn't have a very long shelf life, or someone had been snacking on the contents, and he didn't think it had been Tai. That stone ring was interfering with his ability to sense inside the front of the ship... so he'd have to go outside again. Not now; he'd check it out in passing, on his next and hopefully last excursion. He hugged Tai again and as he went back to sleep, he felt her snuggle closer.

He didn't see the faint smile that gave her a somewhat conspiratorial look, but Russ did. Russ saw everything.

From limited personal experience Elif knew code-breaking was a long and tedious task; it usually involved waiting for a computer to say it had found a password.

Tai had constructed a holographic map of the phase space, translucent red hexagons floating in the air, representing the thousands of commands that could be sent to a gravity generator, with attached beads of white light to show the ones that had been identified. As the information trickled in and was examined, the beads lit up in patches and strings. The panels formed the inside of a torus that reached from the floor to the ceiling, and with the bridge lights down, the flickering red glow gave the room the feeling of a military command bunker. Elif thought all they needed was a table with a map covered in little ships that they could shuffle about using those little wooden rack things on sticks, and perhaps a Perspex panel lined with a grid. Something they could make squeaky notes on, in magic marker. He knew he had an harmonica somewhere.

Tai and Russ were entirely absorbed in a second holographic panel, drawing on it with their index fingers and apparently playing some kind of strategy game involving duelling circles surrounded by clouds of dots. Presently, Tai's arm got too tired to hold up her hand and she began directing her moves through her implant.

Elif poked his face close to a panel, saw horizontally-banded laser light draw ripples over his nose. He looked around at the surrounding frames, each with a mystic glyph in the centre drawn in black, although he couldn't work out how you got black, in mid-air, with a laser. "Are these, like, commands you can type in somewhere?"

Tai stared off into space, looking for an appropriate metaphor, then shook her head. "More like library functions. You set them off in bunches, they call each other and do stuff and they report back. Some are for setting up shots, others trigger them, you can set the generators to track things, catch them, throw them in a particular direction, you can build routines and macros and stuff. Reminds me a little of Perl 23, structurally. It's pretty neat."

A wave of bright yellow swept through the panels one by one, chasing itself around the torus twice then fading. Tai laughed. "Oh, yeah, there's a whole bunch of them for imaging; the Yac uses the eyelash gravity generators to bend light, focus it onto the eyes. Adjustable contact lenses." She nodded towards the torus. "That yellow stripe means the eye is looking at something and needs a close-up."

"Is it looking at us?"

Russ shook her head sadly. "Not everything is about you, human."

Angrily, "No, us. You, me, Tai, the ship. My sock collection, what's left of it. Do they know we're here?"

"When they find out, we'll learn about it very quickly."

Elif said nothing for about a minute, then, absently, "I'll be right back." He left the bridge.

HE stopped at the outer hatch again. Was this really such a good idea? If Russ was going to screw them over, she wouldn't do it before they had a chance to get away, hopefully, depending on what she had in mind. He reached out to the hatch, drew his hand back, reached out again and then an Aetheric warned him that the ship was surrounded by dangerous things he couldn't quite see; probably Chorts, on their way to destroy something. Was he game enough to go out there anyway and use them as cover? No, he wasn't. It was just the kind of stupid thing that happened all the time in the movies, something that, in real life, would get you killed. He decided to go back to the bridge and see if he could get close enough to the stone ring to peer around it, in a manner of speaking.

Perhaps it was Russ' intention to keep him wandering back and forth from the bridge to the second Scoop until they needed him to go out and die for the cause. He stopped, again, near the recycling bay. If he died out there, what would Russ and Tai do? Did they have a plan B, and was it better than plan A, and, if not, was that why they hadn't mentioned it? Russ' body wasn't reliable out there, and even if the engine floated about like the Essence capacitor, Tai wouldn't be able to drag it back to the ship by herself.

The recycling bay had produced another implant. Elif picked it up by his fingernails, took it to the bridge, marched up to Russ and pressed it against her forehead. It stuck there for a moment then fell off into her cleavage, Russ going cross-eyed following it. She glanced down, then up at him, preparing a typically disdainful look. On an impulse, Elif lifted his index finger to a point a foot from Russ' nose. Her eyes tracked his hand as he moved it up to about two o'clock then around in a semicircle. Her expression showed she was waiting for an explanation, so he gave her one: "Remember that. Those eye movements mean you're lying."

Russ rolled her eyes. Elif continued: "And that one means you're losing patience." Russ' next expression wasn't hard to interpret, but the idea that an alien was pressing buttons on a console somewhere, faking all of it, robbed the experience of any sense of achievement. "Ah, you're no fun any more."

"You don't really feel safer out there, do you?" Russ asked.

"And stop pretending you can read my mind, you, you... thing from another world, you."

"I'm not pretending, and a particularly unimpressive – "

Wearily, Tai interrupted, "Can you two shut up for just a few minutes? Half an hour. I need to sleep. So if you just have to do this, do it in the far Scoop. Quietly."

Elif said "Didn't you just wake up?" but she was already unconscious. He glared at Russ, silently mouthed the words **this is your fault** and pushed past her. He needed to smoke some more of that ditch-weed. He needed to get out of the ship and do something productive, like get one of those crude metal forges going. He needed to fix a motorcycle or a refrigerator. At the very least he needed to get away from the bridge.

His steps slowed as he entered the second Scoop chamber with his improvised pipe. **Wait a minute... I know that feeling.**

Years ago, after his abduction, the idea of procreation had become irrelevant and his libido had vanished completely. The antidepressants had contributed. In his more desperate moments he'd come to believe that was why Tai liked him.

He hadn't missed it. Being without it had made his life a lot less complex, and he'd even come to regard his situation as superior to all those poor saps who couldn't control themselves. You saw what happened to them. Whatever the cause, he'd come to regard it as permanent.

His libido was back. He immediately suspected Russ. The level of paranoia required to stand motionless in the hold of an alien spaceship while trying to work out who was trying to make him feel horny, and why... **Well, you never worry about being too paranoid when you're being paranoid.**

Aetherics? This wasn't coming on like the purple-haired elf-girl's glamour; that was like being sidelined with a perfumed baseball bat. Besides, Russ' body couldn't sustain an Aetheric unless it actually had a living human brain built into it, which his Lifesense would detect, and it didn't. Was Russ coercing Tai into doing it? Did Russ give Tai that Aetheric, or, as Elif suspected, did all women have it?

He didn't think it was an Aetheric, or at least not one he'd been exposed to before; it wasn't dragging him in any particular direction.

It might just be a reaction to having almost died at least three times in the past few days, with a high probability of dying in the near future. He'd read about soldiers going through something similar. It was far more likely this was some trick of Russ', perhaps through the Abandoners, which, he suspected, were all through his body by now. "Bob" alone knew what they were capable of. "Bob," and Russ.

Was Russ able to do this with just pheromones and subliminally provocative movements? She'd put on a pretty good show so far, and Elif wasn't above enjoying it at some level, but he still believed he was too smart to fall for it, as well as the memory of the wormy goo he'd found inside Ron's zombie Dominican body when it fell apart. Just thinking about it made him feel queasy. He swallowed, his throat suddenly dry, then he sat on the end of the bed and idly packed lumps of herb into the pipe. He put the pipe down on the floor when he realised he'd put his lighter down somewhere, and he couldn't remember where, and he wasn't about to lower himself to asking Russ unless he thought he could annoy her by doing so.

The feeling was fading slightly, but still definitely there, and the social arrangements in the ship didn't give him any avenue for doing anything about it. That, above all the other reasons, was why he suspected Russ. It was the sort of thing he'd come to expect from her. Pheromones... what could he do about that? If he'd had any habañeros, he'd have shoved one up each nostril.

Why was she doing this? How could she possibly benefit from his being in this state? Did people fight better when their flünads were engaged? Could he rig up an oxygen mask out of the bits and pieces he had lying around?

"If you're thinking about holding your breath, don't bother. It's not me. It's you."

Russ was leaning casually against the edge of the hatch, not looking at him, as if that would give her any credibility. **Maybe I should just forget about trying to hide my thoughts, since it's obviously not working.**

"I can understand if you're worried about surviving the next forty-eight hours, but yanking on my chain is just immature."

"Xists don't get worried. Our nervous systems are far too advanced for that kind of nonsense. You have to wonder how many humans ever worried themselves into an early grave for no very good reason."

"I have to wonder how many humans have been pushed into early graves by Xists with hidden agendas."

Russ simply smiled. **Because who cares what happens to a human?** At least she didn't come on to him.

ELIF peered over Tai's shoulder at the display she was studying. It was a whirring, buzzing mass of confusion, thousands of tiny icons chasing each other about, eating each other, mating, producing offspring, evolving. They swirled in tight spirals and broad loops, flowing like dust particles caught in an afternoon sunbeam.

Tai faced the screen, her face blank; her eyes were pointing off to one side and occasionally her dry, cracked lips moved. She needed a good meal and a bath and about a week's sleep, and probably another bath after that. Elif tried not to let his nose wrinkle at the smell.

"I'm gonna have a bath when this sequence is run," she said.

Elif scowled. "Why is it everyone on this ship can read my mind, but I have no idea what's really going on?"

Tai exhaled. "I know how bad I smell, but this is important."

The conversation plunged into a muddy pit, so Elif tried to drag it out. "Wha'sis? Are they gravity generator commands fighting over who gets the next CPU cycle?" He paused, struck with the idea. "I wonder if that would work... the programs would be made of the toughest opcodes, and they'd all be – "

Tai spoke slowly, carefully enunciating each syllable. "Systems intrusion strategies." She made a limp gesture with one hand, and a group of icons formed into a spherical defensive structure and began consuming the strays. "Steep learning curve, but it's kinda fun. It's good to know there are strategies beyond fight or flight, for example."

Elif tried to spot two icons that were the same. They kept changing. It didn't seem to follow any particular set of rules from one moment to the next. Humbly, he asked: "Can I play?"

For a moment Tai looked terrified. Her eyes darted about and, alarmingly, one pupil dilated. It passed quickly, and she looked apologetic. "I don't think you could learn enough of the rules before we died of old age."

"Well, you seemed to pick it up pretty quickly."

Tai gave him that look, then tapped her implant with a badly-split fingernail. "Oh." His eyes turned the merest fraction towards the recycling bay, and the possibility of getting his own implant. Tai managed a brief, croaky squeal of laughter.

"You'd actually do it. After all that ranting about being controlled by alien implants, you'd get one just to play a game."

Hastily, "I'm not going to." He thought about the benefits Russ had mentioned. A Chort-specific friendly signal would improve his chances, and being able to see gravity fields would be handy...

Tai **was** reading his mind. Gently, she said "If Russ wanted to control your brain, she'd've loaded you up with special ops Abandoners and they'd be – "

Hastily, "Yeah, yeah. I know. I assure you this isn't teen rebellion, doing the opposite of whatever Mom says – " he paused, horrified. "Okay. Pretend I didn't say that. But, yeah, I don't like very much of what Russ does," glaring at her across the room, "but that implant... 'look, I have a bad feeling about this'."

Tai nodded, looking serious. "I had a look at the structures on that thing. I can't see anything immediately suspicious, but..."

But... you know... Xists.

He nodded sourly. After a few moments' silence, Russ said "I'm right here, you know."

Elif suppressed a grin. "We know." Before Russ could reply, he continued. "Can you make an implant for me like Tai's? Could I learn to play that game?"

Russ's expression froze, her mouth hanging open slightly. She stayed frozen for almost twenty seconds, then said "No." Seeing Elif's reaction, she added "Your brain doesn't work that way. And I think one primate knocking around inside the... those systems, is more than enough; we don't want to attract any attention. That's why I'm not doing this myself."

PRESENTLY Tai and Russ exchanged a glance significant enough to make Elif notice. He looked up from the piece of Chort leg he was listlessly disassembling. "We're ready," Tai said.

Elif's mood picked up. "What exactly are you going to do? Should we get ready to run, or something? Although I have no idea where we'd go." He thought about the dog-like alien. **Run? Run where?**

Tai waved her index finger at the web of white lights. "We're not dumb enough to send a search into the network from here, so we've arranged for the command to come from the first generator you visited; the results will be dumped there. So if it goes wrong they'll be shooting at the generator, and not us." She paused. "How far away is that thing?"

Elif pointed up and towards the nose of the ship. "Couple of hundred yards, if you could move in a straight line. It's between us and the base of the eyelash, so if they decide to blow it up, this end of the eyelash could float free... until they blow **that** up as well."

Russ shook her head. "The generators are very unreliable; they frequently send out mistaken commands. The network wouldn't function at all if it didn't have a massive amount of redundancy. The eye won't report anything wrong unless it has an excellent reason."

Tai asked, "Are we going to try a single, quiet ping, or do you want to risk a full status report?"

"We'll learn from either one, so ask for a full status report. If the eye is forced to destroy the generator, we'll get something before that happens. Anything would be helpful at this point."

Tai cradled a fist-sized model of the holographic map in her hands and moved her fingers like a spider stroking its egg-sac. Hexagonal panels on the model and the main display changed colour, red to yellow to green. She spun the model end-over-end and then raised her middle finger so the map balanced on the tip. She made a popping sound with her tongue and pulled her finger out of the doughnut's hole. "And... off we go."

They sat there, anxiously glancing up in the direction Elif had indicated, listening for an explosion. Elif turned to Russ and asked "What did you mean by 'if the eye is forced to destroy the generator'?"

Russ held an index finger to her lips. "Shh. This is a dramatic – "

The ship rocked slightly and the sound of stressed metal came from all sides. All of the floating hexagonal panels went dark.

Elif said "I didn't hear an Earth-shattering ka-boom."

Tai grinned. "Doesn't matter. We got results. I'll put them into a diagram... there." The holographic hexagons were replaced by a wire-frame image of the eyelash with the gravity generators marked in white. Clusters of tiny icons like tadpoles hung from each one, each marked with more mystic glyphs.

"So where's our engine?" Elif asked.

"It's not there," Russ said.

*T*his should be a complete disaster moment. Why doesn't anyone seem surprised? Why don't I feel surprised?

Elif knew that shouting 'It has to be there somewhere!' was counter-productive; he was left with listing the possibilities. "So. Either it's been destroyed... or it's not in – or near – any of the generators..."

"... or the network is lying to us," Russ added.

"Why would it do that?" Tai asked.

"Entrapment."

"And you thought I was paranoid," Elif muttered. "Okay. This," waving at the display, "is what the generators can tell us. Could the engine be hidden away somewhere else, out of sight? Maybe transferred to the main body of the Ya-"

"It's not necessary," Russ interrupted hastily, "to name it."

"Then maybe it's time you contacted that well-placed ally you mentioned. Unless you don't think this is important enough," Elif said.

Russ appeared to think about it for a moment, then let her mouth drop open with a sigh of resignation. "All right. Let's do this. If we have to." She looked around the bridge, which had taken on rather a lived-in look; Tai had reactivated some of her spindly support robots, and Elif had been disassembling stray Chort limbs, the pieces arranged in order of how cool he thought they looked. "Dealing with an Elder God isn't like talking to anything you've ever met. It requires ritual, and preparation, and a degree of humility that, to be frank, isn't your strong point. Elif: clear all of this junk out into the first Scoop. Move Tai's bed out there as well, then have a bath. Both of you." Seeing their expressions, she added "You know what I meant. Go."

It wasn't said with the emphasis of an order, but nobody was really in the mood to argue; Elif helped Tai up, stacked some of the larger Chort pieces on her bed and then assisted her off the bridge.

TAI sat in the bathtub as it filled while Elif found the few remaining clean towels. **Really have to get some kind of laundry thing going here.** Neither spoke until she was settled, fully clothed, in steaming, fragrant water up to her chin. She peered up at him from beneath the (evidently waterproof) implant. "Elder God, huh?"

Elif sneered. "Just another of Russ' alien asshole associates. I say 'associates' because I don't think Xists have friends. Might adversely affect the profit margin."

Tai leaned forward until the water just covered her lower lip, then a bit further. She blew some bubbles, then said "I think you're being a bit hard on – "

Outside, something crashed through the upper levels, struck the side of the ship with a deafening clang, glanced off and scraped across the floor-plates. " – her. Really, this isn't anywhere an Xist would go by choice." She exhaled through her nostrils, stared at the ripples.

Elif glanced at the hatch that led forward. "I thought it was clever, how she arranged for all this to seem like your fault. Deciding to go through the transit corridor. She didn't leave us any other options. I think this ship can travel a lot faster than she lets on, and she told me there are... uh, people, I guess you'd call them, who could give you the medical care you need."

Resignedly, "Yeah." A pause, long enough to indicate a change of subject. "Um. How do you feel?"

"Me? Fine. Never better." He held up one hand, turned it over, flexed his fingers. "Injuries are healing a hell of a lot faster than they ever have."

"Abandoners. They do a good job. Sometimes too good." She paused, trying to find a nice way to say something bad. "I know if I say this the wrong way, you'll blame Russ, so I want you to keep in mind that it was my decision to get this," waving a thumb at the headband / shoulder-pad / back-plate implant, which was still spreading, aspiring to the status of an article of clothing.

Elif didn't have to think of a reason for anything being Russ' fault. "This isn't what we signed on for. You shouldn't have needed to attach that thing to your head, and I shouldn't have had to go out there and fall into puddles of alien vomit and go round 'n' round with things like pissed-off forklifts. I don't accept that this was an entirely an accident. We're here for a reason. Maybe Russ came here to sell Essence to that Elder God and it went wrong." He thought about it. "No, I don't buy that either. She could have delivered it by missile."

Tai considered the idea. "Maybe it has to be delivered in person."

"Well, if your buyer is living in a mobile war zone, they should be less fussy." Elif shook his head slowly. "Whatever. We don't know enough about Elder Gods to tell if Russ was making it up. Anyway... you were going to say something that I was going to blame on Russ?"

"I wanted to – look, not only was this my decision, but right now, this thing is, seriously, is the only thing keeping me alive."

Elif tried to swallow in a suddenly dry throat. "That bad?"

"It is that bad. It's very bad, and I'm only telling you this now so you don't think I was trying to hide it from you, later on."

"Well, how bad can it be if there's gonna be a later on?"

Tai thought about her answer for long enough for Elif to think she hadn't prepared a good reply. "Remember all those pulp science fiction stories about hotels on the moon and atomic-powered personal rocket packs?" Elif nodded. "Remember how wrong they were?"

"Well, that's a result of the collision of expectations and the technological – "

Tai interrupted, her voice burred slightly with repressed emotion. "The future is never exactly how you imagine it. 'Later on' sounds good, because, yeah, there **is** a later on. But it's always different from your expectations."

Elif nodded. "As long as there is a later on, I don't have a huge problem with different." Considering the future inspired him to check his Aetheric future-sense, and it wasn't signalling immediate danger... so if something bad was going to happen, it was some time away yet... unless the sense didn't extend to bad things happening to other people. He frowned; that sounded like the kind of catch you'd expect with being getting a supernatural ability from an Xist. The sort of catch that would trip you up fatally.

ELIF popped his head in from the recycling bay to see if anything else needed to be moved. Russ had actually been doing some manual labour; the bridge was bare, with no floating holographic displays and only the Essence capacitor and the wall-mounted stone ring remaining. She was standing in the middle of the room, measuring its limits with a machine's penetrating gaze. The "red alert" lighting scheme had been replaced with a soft, even white effusion that blurred details, giving the room the look of a vacant art space. "THX-1138," Elif muttered.

"Quite," Russ said. She handed him a spherical bottle of mauve oily liquid. "Add some of this to the bath-water. You both need to be ritually cleansed. Don't get it in your mouth or eyes."

Elif tilted the bottle, watching the stuff run along the insides. "Where is this Elder thing? Or is the idea of a physical location too mundane for – "

"I will explain everything when you're both ready. Try to take this seriously. Our lives depend on it. The recycler will print out robes for you to wear."

"Robes. This isn't a Freemason thing, is it?"

"You don't have to worry about looking silly, because humans inherently do. You just have to worry about looking respectful, probably the most challenging task you've ever been faced with."

"Hey! I can do obsequious if I have to."

"If you want to get out of this alive, then you do." Russ turned back to her examination of the room, as if looking for stray specks of dust. Elif went back to the bathroom, collecting the robes on the way. Spotless, pure white, they felt like soft cotton and had shaped ridges like rough Hessian. "Thanks, little guys," he said to the Abandoners in the recycler. "Classy!"

"'Let not the Shining Ones have power over me!'" Elif intoned in a mock-grave voice. Tai giggled, but stopped when she saw the look Russ was giving them.

"If I have to, I will zap your voice again. Making fun of the top monkey is a clever thing to do on Earth, but out here it will get you silenced very quickly, so shut up and look humble. Don't speak unless it asks you a direct question, although I don't think it will because you're both less than microbes to Their kind, but if it does, then give as little information as possible. Pretend it's from the government."

"Bad cop, worse cop," Tai said.

"Bad cop, seal-you-in-an-enclosed-quotient-space-and-torture-you-forever-cop, yes."

"Well, that sounds encouraging," Elif muttered, picking at the sleeve of his robe. It stretched easily, but playing with his clothing didn't entirely distract him from the way Russ' robe was arranged over her curves, or keep him from wondering if she was wearing anything under it. Fortunately she was facing away from him, so he didn't have to avoid looking at her breasts. "Right. How does this invoking thing go? I never understood your traditional magic ritual deal. It's not as if there's anything we have that They might want, aside from Essence, and why would anybody do that?"

Russ rested one hand on the Essence capacitor. In profile, she had a bemused smile. "Those deals usually begin with fuming incense stenchers and Latinate chants, and they usually end with screams and the sounds of bones breaking," Quickly, to cover the implication, she added "but that won't happen here because we know what we are doing. All we are sacrificing is this," patting the capacitor. "We just need to make a deal, and deliver the drugs."

"So you don't know where this thing is?" Elif said.

Russ turned to look at him over her shoulder. "Let's ask."

A circular display lit up before them, reaching from floor to ceiling. It showed a grainy view from the surface of the eyelash, a fingernail-paring-shaped slice of space sparsely dusted with dim stars around the empty black bulge of the eye, fringed in purple, as Elif had seen before. It took him a few seconds to understand what they were looking at; then he recoiled before realising it couldn't see them, hopefully.

By way of explanation, Russ said "The signal I received came from in there."

Elif thought of the feeling of emptiness he'd felt just looking at the picture he'd captured on his 'phone. "In? There?"

Russ sighed, as if having to explain something everybody knew. "The," quietly managing the word through clenched teeth, "Yac, has a strategy for dealing with parasites; it co-opts them. It imprisons them and forces them to act as sub-systems. The Elder God in question is an integral part of the optic array."

Elif said "Look, I don't trust it and I've never even spoken to the thing. How can the Yac trust it to do something as important as seeing?"

The display drew back, allowing a wider view of the rim of the Yacatisma's mouth. It showed five more spheres, ranging from the size of Wrigley Field up to the city-sized excrescence at the centre of the screen: the prison of Russ' highly-placed associate. Russ said "It has twenty-two eyes. Their input is compared and any serious discrepancies are reported, resulting in a violent reconfiguration involving – "

" – deathbeams. Right." Elif drew back from the display and squinted at the black dome. "Well, it's in character, I guess."

Tai murmured, "If thine eye offends thee..."

Russ continued smoothly, "... destroy it at the sub-atomic level. Indeed. Our... associate – "

"Our **well-placed**" – Elif interrupted, grinning, then his face fell. "Is that what you consider 'well-placed'? Trapped inside an eyeball?"

"Our **associate**," peeved at losing control of the conversation, "is under a great deal of stress and should... and **will** welcome even a small degree of analgesic distraction."

Tai zoomed the display in on the main eye; a swollen black crystal sphere mounted on a jack-straw array of beams, girders and power lines. "Doesn't look like the kind of stir they let you take drugs in."

Briskly, wanting to get past the explanations, Russ said "Well, you might find that many autonomous space-going killing machines have a remarkably tolerant attitude to anything that keeps the non-mechanical components tractable."

Tai asked "Can we talk to this Elder God without the Yac knowing?"

"We can. If the Yacatisma discovers us, it will destroy us immediately, which means no Essence for the Elder God. They don't always follow what we would consider to be rational thought processes, but they are smart enough to dissemble if it's in their best interests. So, to reiterate: don't speak to it; don't answer questions with anything more than a polite nod or shake of the head. Do not under any circumstances mention J.R. "Bob" Dobbs; he has a less than stellar reputation. If we can keep any instances of amusing sound-bites you heard on the Hour of Slack radio show, 'Ren and Stimpy', or other typically SubGenius – "

"I think we get the picture," Tai said. They both looked at Elif. He bowed.

"'Of course... **master**'," he said in a surly and exaggeratedly guttural tone. Russ raised one eyebrow. "'Death Knight', 'Warcraft 2'. I thought you were up on all that – " – another subtle suggestion from his Aetheric sense – "and, you don't know who this Elder God is, do you?"

"If knowing becomes necessary, we will ask. All I need to know is, it's trapped in the eye and it needs Essence. Take your places." Elif stood to one side, just behind Russ, and faced the display.

The video window cleared, and scattered dots of light reformed into a radial array of curved lines, gleaming chromed struts floating in the air. They appeared to be bent around the front of a hemisphere like a stylised iris, an impression reinforced by the circular gap in the middle; the lines grew and shrank like an eye adjusting to sudden brightness. The focus of the array of lines shifted about, as if glancing nervously from Russ, to Elif, to Tai, and back to Russ.

Elif desperately wanted to ask if this visitation included sound, but he was more concerned with demonstrating to the others that he could be serious than he was with possibly offending an Elder God. He shivered slightly when it seemed to be looking directly at him and thought about the empty parking lot he'd remembered when he was trying to get into the gravity generator. The floating lines presented a spare cartoon image of an empty eye, just enough detail to suggest the shape and nothing more.

Russ held her arms out and said in a slow and clear monotone, "VOVIN ZONAC OL ANANAEL – "

"Why do you disturb the work." It spoke; quiet, dryly-uninflected English, with just enough presence to interrupt Russ' invocation. The stylised eye stared directly at her. She patted the Essence capacitor, and the eye's gaze flickered toward her hand and back to her face. "What do you want in exchange," it said.

Elif completely forgot his place in the hierarchy. "We lost an," his words only slightly interrupted by Russ' other hand roughly grabbing the front of his robe, "uh, engine on the way in, and we need to know where it is." Russ' fingers loosened slightly, but he'd felt the steel behind the movement; despite her claims to having a display model body, there was strength there.

The radial lines swivelled to face him, the empty circle narrowing as if it were focusing on something beneath its dignity to notice. "SubGenius. You could be destroyed and Essence taken."

"You'd lose most of it," Russ said quickly. "We'll deliver it all if you can find the engine and tell us."

The eye remained pointed at Elif, but he sensed it was addressing Russ. "Essence first. Then you will learn what is necessary." The empty circle in the centre expanded, the lines grew shorter and disappeared. Russ exhaled and let go of Elif's robe with a sharp, dismissive motion, just short of shoving him away.

Tai sensed that Russ was unhappy with Elif's behaviour. "I think that went well."

Russ didn't bother to put on a scowl. "You almost got us killed, you dipstick." She left the bridge, presumably to sulk, or to change back into her business suit.

Tai looked up at Elif, who was only just starting to realise what he'd done. "Went well, didn't it?" she said, without a trace of sarcasm.

Elif slumped back against the wall and slid to the floor to sit next to Tai. "Me and my big mouth," exhaling unevenly. "She's right. I should have stayed in the scoop."

Tai didn't say anything for a few moments, then, quietly, asked "How did it know you're a SubGenius?"

Elif shrugged. "How did it speak English? I guess that comes with being a god, whatever that means. Probably not what we think of as 'god'. That thing wasn't even remotely anthropomorphic."

"It did look like an eye."

"If it can speak our language and know who we are, it can send an image we would recognise. If it's trapped inside the Yac's eye, the symbolism is kind of obvious." He was babbling nervously.

Tai glanced at him without turning her head. "So you don't think it was Russ, putting on a puppet show? Or Ron? Or the Yacatisma?"

Elif thought about it, then got up. "Ahh, I don't care any more. I just want to get the hell out of here. Either that, or get to the point where Russ pulls the rug out from under. This is like waiting for the punch-line that never arrives."

HE'D left his clothes in the bathroom. When he picked up his Dobbshead T-shirt, it smelled fresh, as if it'd just come out of the clothes dryer. He held it up to his nose, sniffed, then peered at the armpit where it should have been the smelliest. If it was covered with Abandoners, he couldn't tell, and there was nothing on the ship he could use as a microscope. "Seriously, you guys," he muttered. Were they responsible? Could they even understand what he was saying? One of his personal yardsticks for insanity was when you started talking to things that you knew weren't there.

He bunched the robe, took it to the recycling bay and dropped it onto the panel, where it began to melt into the surface. He leaned as close as he dared, but couldn't see any details; the material simply dissolved as it met the point where, presumably, billions of Abandoners were busily deconstructing it, stowing the raw materials somewhere inside in anticipation of making other things.

He stood and watched as the last traces of the robe vanished. He'd been giving the idea some thought and he couldn't think of any

186

aspect of it that he liked, but he leaned a little closer and whispered conspiratorially "Little guys... I hate to say this, but I think I'm gonna need that implant."

There was no immediate response, but he had the impression they were working on it. The disassembly panel ordinarily gave off a faint emanation that his Lifesense reported as a diffuse roseate glow; it was now glowing slightly brighter in the centre, a patch about the size of a domino tile. Many very small living creatures, busily building something complex. "Right," he said sourly, and went to find his last clean pair of socks.

E LIF peered out of the shadows at the end of the tunnel and held up his hand in what he believed was the universal gesture for "stop". Russ ignored it and stumbled forward over uneven metal fragments and oddly shaped pieces of stone, bumping him as she passed. She looked out. "Nothing. We haven't seen a Chort since we left the ship. Something is going on."

Elif cautiously followed, muttering under his breath, "Something is always going on." His Merest Hint sense was jolting him unevenly, as if he were crawling through a minefield of bad choices. He had the bulging essence capacitor slung over his shoulders in a duct tape harness, and the damn thing kept changing its mass, one moment as light as polystyrene and drifting around like a balloon, the next as heavy as a sack full of bowling balls, dragging through the debris. Russ had said there were only two shapes it could take, the spherical form and the tabernacle, and he chose the sphere because it had fewer corners, and he imagined there'd still be dried blood in the cracks. He wasn't sure he'd made the right choice.

They were one level beneath the generator where he'd met Dog-boy, judged as the safest option because he'd been there and back and knew some of the hazards. Russ had insisted he tell her everything that had happened – his first report had been deliberately sketchy – and when he told her about the dead purple-haired elf-girl who'd fallen out of the front of the monitor Chort, his lower jaw started trembling. He wasn't crying, but he wanted to.

"I just left her there."

"She was dead. Even if you had managed to drag her back to the ship, there's nothing we could have done for her."

"Yeah, but," Elif was visibly struggling with this, "our culture has all kinds of involuted taboos regarding death, and this kinda kicks most of them in the balls." She stared at him. "In social terms. Do you even know what I'm talking about?" Sotto voce, "You're pretty ignorant, for an Xist."

"I know precisely what you mean, but I had figured that you had played enough immersive, violent video games to become desensitised. I didn't expect you to become this battle-shocked, this quickly." Russ appeared to consider the situation. "No doubt about it. You need to get laid."

Elif's first thought was of the dead girl, and he recoiled. His second of was Russ unbuttoning her shirt to reveal a mass of gluey cyan worms doing a Russ-shaped square-dance. "Okay, I am going to pretend you didn't say that, and I strongly advise you to do the same."

RUSS led them under the gravity generator, rather than try to repeat Elif's mad rush from the shelter of the canoe-shaped fragment. "The structure you describe is a variant of a prison. One of our client species uses them to transport meat products. It has an underside entrance; we just have to find a way through."

Elif ran his clawed fingers through his hair. "I dunno. If there's a hatch in the floor, I didn't see it, and if there is it's probably full of sewage. Think this through. That's a very nice jacket, it's just been dry-cleaned and you don't want to get alien vomit on it."

"I'm able to approach this circumstance with a degree of dispassionate interest. If, in order to survive, we are required to swim through a cesspit full of wet, seeping bilious ejecta, we shall. I won't require you to enjoy it."

They had found a network of stone tunnels beneath the generator, which Russ claimed to be part of the complex. Underfoot was what seemed like a hundred years' accumulation of grit, stone chips, stray five- and three-sided bolts, nuts and scattered beads of some coppery-chrome metal, crunching underfoot like sand.

The screen on Elif's phone provided enough light for them to search for side-tunnels and eventually a hatch. He knew they were in the right place when the local gravity field shifted and threw them up against the ceiling, and then slammed them down again.

Then, like burning your fingers the same way twice, he felt the creatures trapped in the rings of pain generators, directly above. Guided by how bad it felt they located the centre of the structure and forced open the hatch. It shuddered open and released a brief cascade of loose, wet organic matter that smelled even worse than he'd remembered. There were no loose prisoners running about looking for something to drink. All of the functioning chambers were now full, and active, and Elif tried not to grind his teeth in response to the sound he was imagining. **Now would be a good time to learn how to turn this off. Tinfoil hat time.**

He stood in the middle of the room and balefully regarded the cells while scraping foul, sticky paste off his arms and shoulders with clawed fingers. "Someone's been through here and done some repairs." Russ brushed at her perfect hair briefly, not a drop of muck on her. This time Elif stared. "How do you do that? No, seriously, all Xist bullshit aside, how do you do that? Because I'd save a bundle on laundromats."

"Abandoners. These clothes are adjustable, to a degree, if you'd rather see me in leather."

Elif tore at the duct-tape flaps that held the harness together and tried to glare at Russ even harder. It wasn't easy. He was starting to run out of facial contortions that could match his mood. "Forget that. And, if we get out of this alive, I am going to take you to court for sexual harassment. Your kind has lawyers, right?"

Russ made a sour face. "Our legal professionals are a form of parasite. They've evolved off in their own direction, mostly, and as long as they are kept distracted they don't bother anyone. I wasn't joking when I said you need to get laid, and, since this expensive body revolts you, we'll have to hope that purple-haired elf-girl had some friends."

Elif was openly incredulous. "I know you were messing with me back on the ship, well, hell, you've been messing with me since before we met. I'm not stupid. That," pointing to his crotch, "is a pretty simple binary indicator. On, off. Not that hard to read, particularly if it's your own. So if I'm going all thousand-yard-stare, don't suggest..." he struggled for an appropriate term, and failed, "really dumb solutions to problems that you caused." He unstrapped the tape and let the capacitor float free. "I am starting to hate this job." His Merest Hint told him that the gravity field was about to invert, so he dragged Russ over to stand under the hatch and they floated up to the next level in style. All of the cells were occupied and active.

At the top they found that the jagged gap in the tower wall where he'd entered before had been blocked with the end of a dead Chort, partly melted and forced into place. The purple-haired elf-girl's body was gone. Again, Elif slumped to the floor, chin resting on his knees. "Well, that sucks. We can take the capacitor down, through the tunnels and up through the sheltered place I told you about."

Russ was staring at him, giving him that look. He returned it. "What? You have an oxyacetylene torch? A laser?"

Russ looked up. "We could always use that hatch up there."

Elif's cheeks burned with embarrassment. **I should have seen that before. Although I was kind of busy at the time.** It was a circular plate with radial slots just large enough for him to get his fingers into. He paused, then smiled as his Mechanical Affinity prompted him: push up, twist widdershins five degrees, push up again. The plate shot upwards with a rush of air, sucking him off his feet, and he panicked, thinking he'd opened a hatch into vacuum. He snatched at the harness holding the capacitor and spread his arms and legs to prevent being dragged up the tunnel. The wind drew Russ up towards the low ceiling to bump against him; he pushed her away and dragged the capacitor towards the hole. Looking up – or down, now, as the direction of gravity had changed again – he saw shallow spirals of rifling that led to a hole in the top of the generator, aimed right at the eye. He glanced at Russ; she nodded, and he let go of the tape harness. The capacitor shot up the tube with a hollow "thooomp" sound, but the wind picked up speed, threatening to drag him into the barrel of the generator and shoot him off into space. Russ had cautiously hung back.

"Tai's controlling this?" Elif shouted over the whistling scream of escaping air.

"Yes, but she won't shut it off until the capacitor reaches its destination," Elif trying to grab the edge of the dead Chort and climb down it, "and she can't tell you're in the breech, so – "

"So? Any advice for this kind of situation?"

Russ allowed the gravity to pull her up to the hatch where she wrapped her arms around Elif, forming an object too large to fit into the barrel. There was nothing intimate about it; like being hugged by a bicycle. Abruptly the hatch closed and the gravity resumed its regular orientation, dropping them both to the floor in a tangled pile. Elif sensed a Monitor Chort approaching – probably investigating an unauthorised use of the generator – and they scrambled down to the tunnels below.

He stopped in an offshoot of the main tunnel, principally because it had a low ceiling and he was getting tired of being thrown about. Russ joined him and stood with her back to the wall, leaning forward slightly and exposing her cleavage. He sighed and closed his eyes. "Is this going to work?"

"We're tracking the capacitor; it's on-target. Affa will get Her drugs, and, hopefully, with a promise of more, will tell us what She knows."

"Affa?"

"Tai has been chatting with Her, discreetly, through the gravity generator network. They're getting on quite well, as much as a human and an Elder God can."

Elif muttered, half to himself, "I get to paddle about in alien vomit, and she gets to talk to the Elder Gods. I think I want to see my job description again."

"You might be surprised how similar your tasks are. Anyway, Elder gods are over-rated. They're end-customers. One track minds, seriously. You'd be better off playing fetch with the Chorts." and why did that make the hairs on the back of Elif's neck stand up?

With his eyes closed, Elif could almost imagine he was somewhere else, floating in the middle of a snow-cloud, perhaps, his head gently bumping against the ceiling of the tunnel. There was a slow, surging shift in the gravity, and the buzzing, moaning psychic chorus of pain from the array of pain cells above them rose in pitch, then faded, exactly like the hush of the crowd as the film started. He almost expected to hear applause. A feeling of cool serenity seeped in and he exhaled slowly, his breath condensing to tiny points of refracted cell phone screen light. He raised his head. The feeling was coming from up there, where the generator was pointing, where all the inboard generators were pointing: the eye. The fix was in.

"When you said 'drugs... with a promise of more'... we don't have any more, do we? Unless you're planning on scraping it out of us."

"I don't think that is something we should explore until we are well away from here," gesturing towards the main body of the Yacatisma. Elif grinned; that was just like Russ. She'd screw over anyone. Privately he imagined a scenario where they escaped and Affa directed the Yacatisma to chase them, trying to get the drugs She was owed. "It'd be like the last half hour of 'The Blues Brothers', heh heh."

"What?"

"Nothing."

"What did you mean by 'it would be like the last half hour of the' – "

"Look, never mind. Won't the capacitor just smash against the eye's shell?"

"It has. The Essence is smeared against the outside of Affa's prison and She is desperately licking at the inside. Through the principle of puddle resonance, She'll get about half of it through the shell immediately, and the rest will seep in over the next few years. We've done our part. It's up to Her now."

"She's a she?"

"She has more feminine characteristics than masculine, insofar as any Elder God has humanoid gender aspects."

Elif hovered a foot off the deck, waiting for his Aetherics to warn him of the next shift in gravity, his eyes still closed. "This is the fun part," he muttered, "waiting for the pay-off." He tried to muster some cynicism, but he felt too relaxed to bother. "Affa. That's a nice name. What does it mean?"

"Nothing."

"No, really."

Russ sighed. "The most powerful Elder Gods each have a speciality, a defining characteristic they make their own. You'll find one who is The Gate, there's an Elder God with a thousand young, another one has a thing for playing pan pipes surrounded by a horde of demented insect servitors... you know the deal." Elif didn't, quite, but he was enjoying hearing Russ say something that possibly wasn't a complete lie, so he nodded. "Affa is a... younger Elder God, an up-and-coming new kid on the scene – less than six billion years old – the Elder God of Emptiness. She is present wherever there should be something, but isn't; deserts, abandoned cities, and interstellar space."

Elif remembered. "Empty car parks. Unfinished buildings."

"Yes. When you're trying to get home and you know you don't have enough fuel to make it... Affa is there. Being confined in the Y- uh, in the eye, restricts Her movements and forces Her to deal with large amounts of matter on a daily basis, so She's not at all in Her element here. The Essence should smooth Her out long enough for us to get the location of the engine out of Her."

"Smoothed out... " Elif echoed slowly.

Russ glanced up and rolled her eyes in exasperation. "She's emitting. Every living creature on all of the surrounding eyelashes is receiving, and feeling... smoothed out." She frowned. "This can not be good. Most of the local power systems are pain-based, and if Affa is radiating love, peace and harmony, they're going to stop generating. Severe power loss. Someone further up is going to notice this. When we get the information we need, we're going to have to move quickly."

Elif gave Russ a dopey, stoned grin. "I'll call her." He found his 'phone and dialled "0".

Russ hastily snatched the 'phone from him and turned it off. "You'll attract every Chort within a hundred yards with that thing. We'll wait."

They didn't wait long. Heavy thumping footsteps in irregular rhythms approached from both ends of the outside tunnel, grinding the underfoot grit and debris into dust. "Oh, dear," Russ murmured. "I was becoming quite attached to this body. Sure you don't want a quick grope before we both die?"

Elif was too relaxed to take it seriously; also, his Merest Hint wasn't reporting imminent dismemberment. He floated there, biting his lower lip to repress the smile.

A small Chort the size of a four-door sedan crept into view and was shoved back by a heavier model with short, thick legs and heavy claws. It presented its front end: scratched into its fore-plate was a set of radiating lines arranged around an empty circle. Russ glanced sideways at Elif, who waved his hand dismissively. "She's managed to subvert them. Affa Chorts."

The larger machine lurched forward then fell over, one front leg buckling as the claw joint twisted at an awkward angle. It lay on its side, the other front leg waving feebly, and they saw the rear plates had deep gouges, burns and drill holes edged in bright beads of metal. A faint pall of grey smoke drifted from an open seam. "Yeah, they're on our side, all right. Look how fucked up they are."

More machines crowded the tunnel, blocking the entrance, rising and falling slightly with the changes in gravity, each broken in some manner, the more badly damaged being helped along by the others. "That just doesn't look right," Elif murmured. "You, you should be hitting that other one. No wonder you're all beaten up – you stand out like – " He glanced sideways at Russ, then shook his head. "Never mind. Here, let's take a look at that leg."

There was only so much he could do without his toolkit, but Elif managed to fix most of the problems with the four largest Chorts by pulling parts off the smaller ones. It wasn't a simple task. While the machines were modular in design, very few of the modules were compatible, like pieces of several different jigsaw puzzles. He even had little idea what the modules did, but his intuition – or his Mechanical Affinity Aetheric – prompted him and warned him when he was about to touch something dangerous. Russ looked on with interest; she didn't care about the machinery, but she did care how well he could fix it. The Chorts submitted to his ministrations easily, like obedient pets, occasionally shoving each other aside to get closer, the larger ones forcing the smaller back into the tunnels.

HALF an hour later he wiped the back of his hand on his forehead, leaving a smear of soot and sweat. "Best I can do," he said to the Chorts, not knowing if they could understand or even hear him. "Sorry for the rest of you. We'd better get going. Does anyone know where the engine is?" Russ didn't say anything. Elif shrugged, raised his phone and dialled 0 with his thumb. Russ reached out to stop him, her arms paddling awkwardly in the low gravity, but he drew back out of reach.

The phone buzzed twice and Tai answered in a sleepy, smoothed-out voice. "Hello, who's calling, please?"

Elif snorted. "Who did you think it would be?"

"Telemarketer? Incidentally, if this call lasts longer than thirty seconds then the local Chorts will notice the signal and come looking for you. Seventeen seconds."

"Oh. Right! Um, has Affa said anything about where the engine might – "

"Too long to explain. Find a better place to hide and I'll come to you. Sort of. I'll wave, okay?" and another buzz to indicate the end of the call. Elif peered around the end of the tunnel, listening for any warnings from his Aetherics; nothing, aside from the usual bumps caused by things slamming into the outside of the eyelash. It was relatively safe for the moment. "Find a better place to hide?" he said to himself, glancing around. "Better than this?" then, as Tai's words sank in, "she's coming out here?"

Gravity re-arranged itself again and everyone settled to the floor. Elif climbed over the Affa Chorts and kneeling on the back of the largest, poked his head out of the tunnel entrance and listened. Echoes of distant fights; metallic screeches, clanging reverberations, overlaid with Aetheric impressions of agony from the creatures trapped in the pain cells above. He shook his head, trying to clear it. Then, like a slap across the face; the Merest Hint warning him of danger coming from the right. "Okay, everybody, we go... that way. Come on!"

Russ followed him, but the Affa Chorts spread out, the largest moving towards the danger and the rest forming a defensive buffer. "No, guys, that – I mean, **this** way – "

Russ grabbed his arm and dragged him away. "They know what they're doing. You could at least pretend that you know what you're doing."

Angrily, "I **am** pretending that I know what I'm doing," he shook her off and with a last glance back at the machines he'd just repaired going into battle, he ran.

Long ago, the stone corridor complex beneath the gravity generator had been jammed through the surface of the eyelash and pushed down almost to the core, tearing through the layers so that the tunnel exits terminated in ragged fangs of steel. The tunnel Elif chose to escape through ended in a flaking mess of dark brown rust. Large pieces of twisted floor- and roof-plates snapped off easily. There was an unpleasant smell in the air. Russ' nose twitched. "Something organic died here recently."

They left the dark stone tunnel complex and were back in the even darker steel-plated multi-level car-park zone. A Chort came after them almost immediately, an enthusiastic evil-looking low-slung crab the size of an SUV. They ran, Russ assuming the lead by virtue of her longer legs, Elif calling out suggestions when his Aetherics warned him of danger ahead. The Affa Chorts trailed behind, slowly sorting themselves by size as more enemies joined the fray and the larger and slower units were caught up in the fighting. After detouring around a section where the plates had been flattened almost to the floor Elif realised they were heading towards the base of the eyelash, where it met the scaffolding that joined it to the main body of the Yacatisma. He paused, glanced back, ushered the smallest three surviving Affa Chorts on, then followed them. There wasn't anywhere safe to hide, or even stop for a moment; it was like that computer game where dozens of enemies took one step towards you for every step you took away from them. They were starting to close in, and while his Merest Hint gave him just enough warning to avoid dead-ends and ambushes, the incidents were becoming more frequent as more Chorts appeared. A nauseating panic was starting in the pit of his stomach. They weren't going to get out of this one alive. **He** wasn't going to get out of this one alive.

Think, damn you, think, for once in your life don't make a stupid joke or a clever sub-cultural reference, this is it, this is your life on the line here. Think! "Uh..." **What would "Bob" do?** "He'd sell them something." **What do they need? Power? Forget about needs, what do they want?** running out of breath, now, "They want to kill us." **Well, that's not an option.** "The hell it isn't. They can..." **They can have Russ. She's expendable. She's a machine. She's not really here.** He paused behind a dented pipe that ran from the low ceiling into the floor, tried to work out where Russ was and where the main mass of Chorts was headed. "Russ!" If he called her back in this direction and then ran off to the left, they'd converge on her and he could slip away. Where was Tai? Was she going to meet them here? **Here?** "RUSS! Where the – "

"Right here. No need to shout." Russ was leaning, with a nonchalant air, against the underside of a floor-plate bent into an upright L-shape. She was watching the advance guard of Chorts as they stamped closer, slowing down, as if wanting to enjoy this to the fullest extent. Elif glanced up; no Spree ships were about to crash into the eyelash, no Monitor Chorts about to sweep the area with deathbeams. Russ was actually smiling. "Any last words?"

"Oh, who cares? I just hope it'll be quick."

The closest Chort rushed forward eagerly, levelled and spread its least damaged claw and smashed it into the pipe, framing Elif's head like the legs of a croquet hoop. Flakes of rust and fragments of grit flew about. The claws began to close, screeching against the pipe, and then a hulking shape behind the Chort seized it, pulled it away from the pipe – the claws snapping shut half an inch from Elif's nose – and threw it backwards into the others. They immediately began fighting amongst themselves.

The thing that had thrown the Chort was an asymmetric composite of six smaller Affa Chorts clinging together. As another machine darted forward, the composite leaned back, maintaining perfect balance, lifted one leg and brought it down, pushing the attacker halfway through the floor-plates. It flailed about wildly and tried to climb back through the hole. Elif didn't need an invitation; he turned and ran, not looking back to see if Russ was following.

He got about ten steps before realising he'd run into a dead end; a pipe crammed with inactive Chorts, tangled together like a robot spider sleepover. He stopped, took a few steps towards the broken machines, stopped again, shook his head as if trying to clear it; his Merest Hint was telling him to climb over them and, at the same time, telling him to wait. Russ bumped into him. "We're here."

Elif turned to give her That Look. "Here where? We? Look, are we gonna die now or not?"

The composite Affa Chort forced its way into the end of the pipe, effectively blocking it. Its left front claw – formed from an entire, smaller Chort – whirred and spun on the end of its leg, then spread out. The claw formed a rough approximation of four fingers and a thumb. The digits flexed, then the hand descended to the floor and the fingers ponderously, awkwardly began tapping out Bat keyboard codes, clanging against the metal floor:

IM IN HERE NOW ENGINE IS DOWN THERE

and the hand raised unsteadily and pointed towards the dead Chorts.

Elif crouched against the pipe wall – which was humming like an electric transformer – and tried to catch up with recent events. "Tai?"

Russ was eyeing the composite with what looked like wry bemusement. "She's directing them remotely from the ship. She can't hear you, but if you face that way and speak slowly she can read your lips with millimetre-wave radar."

Elif scowled. "Why can't she hear me? And why can't she speak?"

Steel claws acting as fingers slowly bashed out the codes on the floor: NO EARS NO VOICE, and the single arm managed a shrug that he recognised, even through that many layers of abstraction. After swallowing his panic on thinking she'd actually climbed inside a Chort, he imagined it: from Tai's mind, to the Xist implant, through the series of transponders he'd planted, perhaps even going through Affa, somehow, to a collection of hacked killing machines clutching each other. He regarded the dead Chorts. "So it's down there, with whatever killed them." He held up his 'phone and watched the screen. It held steady for a few seconds, then danced wildly, flared blue-white and returned to normal. "The magnet is no friend to the robot." He looked at the tangled heap of machines piled to shoulder height, flexed his hands, took a deep breath, then turned to the Taibot and said "Can you shift these?" He stood aside as she extended her claw to within an inch of the nearest dead Chort. The index and middle fingers shook, then kicked and pink light flashed around the edges of their joints. The hand dropped to the floor and had a small orgasm before Tai slowly dragged it back, screeching across the pipe floor. "Okay. Not the smartest thing I've done today. Maybe I should let someone else make dumb suggestions."

Russ folded her arms under her breasts. "Electromagnetic pulse. You're the only one who can go through there. The fields might drive you insane, briefly, but who could tell? Anyway, they won't kill you. Get lifting."

"Or," feeling a little more confident, "Tai can hook her damaged claw in there and drag them out of the way."

Slowly, laboriously, Elif and the Taibot pulled the dead Chorts out of the pile one by one while Russ stood off to one side, not even pretending to supervise. Infrequently a low humming noise drifted out of the casings, along with wisps of grey smoke. The first few Chorts were locked rigidly in place but as they dug deeper the leg and claw joints became easier to shift; the linear motors were looser. "Long exposure to the magnetic pulses degrades the Lorentz actuators," Russ offered, examining a blackened elbow-joint, standing well back from the hard work.

The pulses were making him go cross-eyed. "Who calls them Lorentz actuators? Some alien named Lorentz?"

"I'm translating, although I don't know why I bother. You still haven't reviewed the notes I gave you on Namronics."

"Kind... of... **busy**, lately," Elif gritted his teeth and hauled on a Chort body which suddenly came loose as the local gravity shifted. He had to wrestle it off to one side to avoid giving the impression he'd deliberately thrown it at Russ; gravity re-aligned itself and the thing crashed to the floor of the tunnel, legs settling slowly. He peered into the gap he'd just opened. "Oh. That's... uh..."

The gap led into a twisty little maze of passages on several levels, just big enough for a good-sized Chort to pass through, although none of them could, given the electromagnetic pulses flying about. As his eyes adjusted to the dimness, he saw a scattering of lights, little status indicators, round, square, triangular, irregularly shaped, blinking on and off out of sequence. The colours covered the entire visual spectrum and, he suspected, below and beyond – it was much warmer in here than out in the freezing steel multi-level car park. He looked about for immediate danger then closed his eyes and looked Aetherically. There, a diffuse cloud of sea-spray-salt-cool white-grey, somewhere inside the maze; their engine. It seemed safe, so he climbed through the gap and straightened up. Right on cue, a second life-signature – smaller, tighter, orange-tinted musty paprika red – came out from behind their engine, still inside the maze of machinery. As if it had been waiting for him. "There's someone else down here," he muttered.

"WHAT?" shouted Russ from outside.

"There's SOMEONE ELSE DOWN – " A buzzing crackle sounded, like high-tension power lines rubbing up against each other; Elif felt his 'phone jumping around inside his pocket and his semicircular canals did a barrel roll. He would have fallen over if the gravity generators hadn't been pressing him up against the roof.

Then he saw the machines that made up the tunnel walls. His pupils dilated.

He'd seen Chorts tearing up the gateway rings; they'd had no trouble pulling strips off the Spree warships, but there had to be things from very advanced races, things made of materials so dense that not even a Deathbeam could break them down. And those things, drawn into the fields of the eyelashes, would be kicked about by the Chorts... until they ended up here. Encysted. He couldn't resist the urge to poke about, looking for buttons and switches and dials, but the devices were all uniformly smooth and undetailed, probably to stop primates like him from messing with them. He placed his hand against the side of an irregularly-shaped lump of something metallic and thought about what he'd done to activate the broken Scoop fragment, then pulled his hand back again quickly, in case this thing **did** activate and tried to take his head off, or something equally disastrous.

"CAN YOU SEE THE ENGINE?" Russ called.

Elif grimaced in annoyance. This was the closest he'd been to having fun in a long time. "Yeah, it's in here somewhere. Give me a moment. Kind of hoping I don't have to fight anyone for it." His Aetheric sense of direction wasn't giving him any prompts, so he simply climbed forwards and peered around the first corner in the maze. The buzzing sound struck again, louder, but less dizzyingly; either he was getting used to it, or he'd burned out some brain-cells. In the uncertain light from the alien devices, he saw a small Chort, standing with one claw resting on the dome of their engine. The claw was holding what looked like a bent and tattered umbrella skeleton made of some coppery metal, with a translucent cable that ran from the handle down to a recessed port in the side of the engine-pod. "What the hell are you?" Elif wondered. It couldn't be a Chort, because it was alive, and it was too small to be carrying its own pain-cell.

The – whatever it was – pointed the umbrella at him; the cable glowed and the buzzing sounded again. Unlike the dead Chorts outside, Elif didn't fall to the floor. He shrugged. The thing didn't have obvious eyes, but he knew it was staring at him in disbelief. Then he remembered the multi-legged dog-alien and, from there, what the dog-alien had wanted from him above all; and that food was extremely scarce in this neighbourhood. "Oh, come on! Can't we all just get along?"

The creature shook the umbrella, as if that would fix whatever was preventing it from killing him. From a narrow gap between two alien devices behind the creature, an even smaller version crept out and waved a claw at Elif. The larger one hustled it back in the exact manner of a mother with a stray child. "You're a mimic. An organic Chort mimic. Good god, how – " Bred or even engineered for this environment? Some kind of commando infiltration thing? Why would it bring a child here? He came out from behind the corner of the maze, crossed his arms (hoping this might seem less threatening) and leaned against a cylindrical device that flashed orange and grunted in annoyance. He straightened; "Sorry," then staring at the mimic, "So, you – you've been holding off the Chorts with that thing..."

That thing that was powered by their engine. Which he'd have to take, leaving the aliens defenceless. "Oh." He thought about it, but couldn't escape the conclusion: "Well, sorry about this, but it's you, or..." feeling uncomfortable just saying it. Could they all get back to the Bitchslap intact, if he could talk it into taking point... while he carried the engine... with Russ and Tai bringing up the rear at a safe distance? Ludicrous. Would it be possible to power the umbrella from some other source? Russ? That robot body must have a power supply in it somewhere.

He turned around and stuck his head through the gap. "Russ, I need you to yank your power supply and hand it over. Got a trade situation going on here."

Russ gave him a pitying look. "I'm powered by thousands of – ", prudently stepping back as the mimic set off the electromagnetic pulse weapon again. Elif glanced over his shoulder and said to the mimic "Just wait, okay? We're not gonna leave you without a – hey!"

The mimic leaped over the engine; a long, thin strip of carapace flicked forward, stung his shoulder and withdrew, vinegar-scented fluid dripping from the end. Without thinking, his fingers closed on something in his pocket and he threw it at the mimic; the implant Russ had wanted him to attach to himself. It hit the creature's leading edge and stuck there.

The mimic reared back and opened up like a giant clam, revealing hundreds of needle teeth; then it slowly closed, tilted like a drunk, staggered to one side and threw the umbrella away. The cable jerked out of the engine and stopped glowing. Elif eyed the mimic suspiciously, probing the edges of the wound with his finger.

"Get the engine," Russ said right behind him. "It's safe. Your new friend is going to distract the locals for us."

Russ had control of the mimic, through the implant. "I **knew** it," Elif growled. "You couldn't wait to jab that thing into my brain, could you?" He'd suspected it all along, but he was currently more concerned with the weight of the engine, a hemisphere the size of a two-person bathtub that felt as if it was full of water. He could only shift it when the local gravity permitted, which made for very slow progress. The Taibot separated into its component sub-units; the largest helped Elif drag the engine across the uneven terrain while the rest scattered, distracting the Chorts. Russ sent the mimic ahead (Elif thinking **that could very well have been me**), creating a short-lived safe passage for the engine, which almost escaped their control when Tai prompted the gravity generators to lift everything. Elif spared a single glance back at the repository of strange alien devices and the little mimic, which was trying to climb out of the gap, looking for its mother. "Aw, crap."

"Never mind the empathy. We are only going to get one opportunity to do this," Russ said. "When we get back to the ship, push the engine up against any of the vacant niches, then get inside. We'll be leaving as soon as we're powered up."

"I hate this job, I hate this job, I **hate** this – " pushing the engine through the ragged tear in the metal floor, waiting until his Aetherics told him it was safe, then balancing the load on the top of the last Affa Chort and trying to steer it like a wheelbarrow. His feet skidded in the debris with a horrific dream-like futility; one moment he was shoving the engine and the next hanging on to its edges, keeping it from drifting away and trying not to flinch as one flanking decoy after another met a violent end. Most of the attackers had been gathered around the largest local gravity generator, recharging; giving this part of the eyelash a wide berth proved to be a sensible thing to do as Tai sent one command after another through the generator until the subversion became obvious, and – Elif's eyes widened as he perceived what was going to happen. "Down here, Russ, push, come on, help for once in your miserable existence – ", ducking down into a section of plates firmly held together with vertical reinforcing struts as the entire gravity generator and eight levels of eyelash were ripped out and flung into space with a drawn out shriek of tortured steel. Debris, dust, whole steel plates and angry, disoriented Chorts formed a lop-sided cloud that was immediately dispersed by the surrounding generators before any of the fragments could damage the eye. The excision of the generator complex left a gap that reached down to the core of the eyelash and was half a mile across, edged in torn plates, pipes and pieces of antique spacecraft. Most of the local Chorts had gone with the generator.

Within ten minutes they were back at the ship; there was only one large, slow Chort in the area, and it lumbered after the last of their decoys, allowing Elif to push the engine up against the side of the Bitchslap. The dome flipped over and set itself into the niche like a neodymium magnet; its faint Aetheric hiss became a low rumble. Russ was already climbing up the back of the ship and, conscious of the distinct possibility of being left behind, Elif followed her.

Tai got up to greet him and fell over before he could catch her. She knelt before the empty stone ring set into the end of the bridge, gasping audibly, framed by the banded red static of the floating display; Elif helped her back onto her bed, shuddering as his hand touched the implant which now reached all the way down her back, forming a wrist-thick ridge over her spine. She bared her teeth in what was for her a humourless grin. "How was that for a last-minute rescue? 'United as one, divided by zero'!"

Elif opened his mouth but couldn't think of anything to say. Her voice now had an unpleasant synthetic burr; her skin was eggshell pale and her staring eyes weren't tracking, as if blind. He almost reached out and waved his hand in front of her face, but instead clenched his fist and hid it behind his back. She turned her head as far as the implant would allow and faced towards Russ. "How are we for bandwidth?"

Russ took a few seconds to answer. "Nyquist by one point nine.

Say, six seconds."

This news brought a brief look of fear to her face, which she tried to erase with a laugh. It sounded like a cough. "Plenty to go around!"

"However, we only have one engine, and we will need a boost to get free of the decking. I nominate Elif."

Tai's grin faded. "Don't be ridiculous. He's too much of a guy, and you don't feel anything, so it's me. I can relax the nociception inhibitors until we're clear, but..." and that haunted look grew stronger. "Elif, help me up. You've got a window of about three minutes."

He steeled himself to put his arm behind her back and lifted her as gently as he could. She didn't weigh very much, and he felt that if he dropped her, she'd shatter. " 'Too much of a guy'?"

She waved a hand at the stone ring. "Pain generator – I mean, it generates power from pain. It'll work with you, but guys route nociception through their brains differently, and it'll work much better with me."

The nauseating panic was coming back. "And... when you say 'three minute window'...?"

She swallowed loudly and slid from his arms into the stone ring, sitting in it like very tired royalty. A flicker of her pale fingers spawned a flat holographic panel that floated around them, displaying a countdown from 177. "Then the entire eyelash gets detached and dragged into the Yacatisma's mouth. t's what happens to old structures. This one isn't so old, but Affa and I have been messing with the stress sensors so it appears old." She gently pushed him away from the ring, leaned back and took a deep breath. A trace of colour washed over her cheeks, her eyes widened and she screamed, a curiously monotone machine sound that segued into shrieking metal as the ship lurched backwards. She stopped screaming, taking uneven, gasping breaths, her lips working as if she had the universe's worst taste in her mouth, and the ship lurched again. Pinging sounds rang through the hull; sections of steel plate snapping and dropping away.

"Okay, that's enough of that," Elif growled and reached out to grab her, but before he could, she turned to face him. Her eyes locked with his, and she had a mournful expression that brought his panic to a peak.

"I really wish I could have told you. I know I owe you an explanation, and I should have said something before this, but I was afraid you wouldn't go along with it. And it's too late now. I'm going to have to jump overboard." She turned to Russ, her voice slurring with fatigue. "If this doesn' work, you're gonna have to deal with both of them, and I think he's gonna be the bigger threat."

Elif wanted to pull her out of the ring and make her stop whatever she was about to do, but he didn't know what it was, and none of his Aetherics could tell him. The panic he felt became chill as he realised she had been planning to do this for a long time; not suicide, but something just as final, just as irrevocable. The implant, reaching down her back to cover her spine, wrapped around her head – bandwidth? "You wouldn't **dare**."

Defiantly, "Watch me." She sagged back against the ship's hull and slumped to one side within the ring; the fear left her face, she closed her eyes and whispered "Ready?" The transfer took exactly six seconds. The main holographic display shut down, but aside from that there was no accompanying light show, no special effects; she was there before him, and then it was just her body, not breathing, starting to fall towards room temperature. She had jumped overboard.

ELIF stood in the red-lit semi-darkness, staring down at Tai; then he looked away. He felt a surge of grief and rage and through long habit tried to dismiss it as a primate reaction to loss, but it wouldn't go away. He swallowed, clenched his fists, unclenched them; there just wasn't anything practical or, for that matter, impractical that he could do. A gesture of anger wouldn't mean anything to anyone present; although Russ would understand, she wouldn't care. In fact, Russ hadn't moved since Tai had left, and wasn't giving the impression she would move any time soon. Perhaps the alien that controlled her robot body was busy, or it had decided this game couldn't be salvaged and had given up, leaving him to wander the ship aimlessly until the air ran out.

Rage drained away, leaving him empty inside a shell of cold, the next part of his traditional response to loss; trying to pretend it didn't matter. Distractions? Baiting Russ had lost any appeal;

getting even a small truth out of her... to what end? It was over. He didn't feel angry with Tai, because she'd had one excellent reason for this detour. She'd had to find a machine complex enough to transfer her mind into. He let his eyes unfocus and wondered if she'd made it in any sense, and if so, where. There were plenty of good-sized installations about. Thinking about the machines he'd seen here... they had the look of nineteen-fifties' heavy industry, which was rarely subtle, but as he'd seen lately, subtlety wasn't a requirement for life, if you could call the Yacatisma a living creature. Whatever directed the Yac would be sufficiently complex to be able to hold all the details of a human mind... more than sufficient. He was certain nothing mechanical on Earth had the required capacity. Which is why they'd come out here.

But why the Yacatisma? Remorseless killing machines weren't Tai's style at all. That seemed more like something Russ might move towards. Perhaps that was the nature of their deal. He spared Russ' body a sour look – which she didn't acknowledge – then reluctantly looked back at Tai. She hadn't moved since she'd left, but she looked different; no longer bracing herself against the pain.

Thinking about why they were here – in whatever sense "here" could be – was easier than thinking about what he'd do next. To be practical, he should dispose of the body, but the only way to do that was to put it in the recycler. "Too soon. **Way** too soon." Besides, he had, what, thirty seconds left? He glanced up at the floating counter display, which was flickering but still counting down: 23. Of course. He almost smiled at that.

So, what was left? Tai, gone; Russ, absent; no windows, and only one door. If he was going to jump overboard as well, now was the time, assuming he could get the hatch open... but that was no escape, because the entire eyelash was about to be destroyed.

I wonder if I could fly this thing? The control displays that Tai had used when they flew through the conduit were all dark. Besides... go where? Back to Earth? Back to the asteroid market and Doctor Squid? With the destruction of the conduit gate at this end, that journey could take a very long time.

"Well, if I'm gonna die, I may as well do it in comfort," he murmured, leaving the bridge for the second scoop and the bed, as a series of distant rumbling sounds got louder and began to overlap.

H E walked around the bed and up the ramp to the rear hatch, put his head against it; nothing. It might as well have been a cold, solid stone wall. He laid his hands flat on it then turned to look back through the doors, to the bridge... but if this was the end of the line, why had they ("they" now included Tai) bothered to pull the ship loose of the eyelash? To give him a fighting chance of survival, even though he couldn't fly the ship? Would it fly itself?

The sounds of explosions dulled by distance came from the general direction of the edge of the Yacatisma's mouth – where the eyelash had been seated in the eye cradle. The eyelash was being cut loose.

E LIF ran back to the bridge, splashing through a shallow puddle of water leaking from the bathroom. Rushing through the recycling bay he almost put his hands on the disassembler panels to steady himself but jerked back at the last moment – uncertain if the Abandoners were still friendly – so when he lurched onto the bridge he was off-balance. After some awkward windmilling arm motions he straightened up and saw: Russ still immobile, Tai's legs still dangling over the edge of the ring, and the main display now completely black, that odd light-absorbing blackness, relieved only by a handful of faint white dots: stars. **Someone wants me to see this. Guess who?**

The dots scribbled about as shocks travelled along the eyelash and shook the ship, first from left to right and then the floor dropped out from underneath, sending him sprawling. On his hands and knees, wondering what was keeping Russ from falling over, he watched in horror as Tai's body lifted slightly and fell out of the ring, kneeling for a moment before slumping forward to sprawl face down.

He looked away, then turned back just enough to see debris – Chorts, piece of Chorts, metal plates and other, less readily identifiable detritus – drifting up the screen, followed more slowly by a black dome edged in violet; the eye. It gradually filled the display, its scale only discernable in relation to the floating trash; then the lower edge of the eye appeared, two curved lines of scaffolding to either side of a torn scab lit by flickering dots of dull red where the eyelash had been torn free. Grudgingly he murmured "Huh. Look at that." It was almost impressive enough to distract him from the worst edges of his grief, for the first few seconds, although gazing out of the equivalent of a window when he should have been respectfully recycling Tai's body made him feel worse, and telling himself he was looking at the first part of the end of his own life didn't help. Still, the almost constant sound of impacts was fading, things hitting the ship or the eyelash nearby becoming less frequent. The targeting systems had decided that the eyelash was no longer important, as the entire structure slowly turned end over end, moving away from the eye, and over the chasmic, lightning-chased mouth of the Yacatisma.

It took him a few moments to recognise the eyelash, seeing it end-on at first; that last shock must have been the ship pulling free, or being thrown free as it turned. He could even see the tiny circular hole that the **Bitchslap** had made when it crashed. He had to frame his hands around the display to be sure, but with each rotation the ship was getting further from the Yacatisma... while the eyelash was not. He couldn't sense any engine activity; they were floating free like any other piece of scrap. Silent running. **All we** – he sat up and tried to get the display between him and Tai's body – **all the ship needs is a little push...**

Obligingly, a Deathbeam flickered out from the scaffolding and tore the eyelash apart from end to end, debris spreading out and pattering against the ship, small pieces and large, knocking it un-evenly, pushing it away faster. Either it had stopped spinning or the camera view of the Yacatisma was tracking now, but Elif had a ring-side seat when deathbeams fired, from all around the rim of the mouth, aimed at the base of the eye where Affa was held; first two, then seven, then more than a dozen. The scaffolding burst into flares of white plasma with the black eye-sphere nestled within, unharmed. The eye began to drift out of its nest. Affa – or at least her prison – was free.

Elif slowly got to his feet, face pale in the glare from the display, eyes wide; then he turned to Russ, his face twisting in anger, and he kicked her in the ass as hard as he could. It was like kicking a concrete pillar. He hopped back on one foot, mouthing **ow ow ow ow**, then limped aft to retrieve the heavy wrench, which he'd stashed between the head of the bed and the ramp. He didn't pound it in the palm of his hand as he returned to the bridge. This wasn't about enthusiastic machismo; it was revenge. **Doesn't mean I**

can't enjoy it, breaking into a run as he reached the bridge, raising the wrench and screaming (even, in anger, remembering that he was quoting Ren Hoek) "You've had this coming for a LONG TIME!", swinging it at the side of Russ' head. Her hand blurred up and intercepted it neatly, absorbing the impact.

She turned slightly, expression blank, and said – in empty, robotic tones – "Don't."

Elif tried to tug the wrench free, unsuccessfully. "Why the hell not?" he snarled. "You staged all of this just to free some..." Words failed him momentarily, and he half-swung on the end of the wrench and kicked her in the ass again, breaking a toe in the process. He raised himself on his good foot and hissed in her ear, "Even a pawn must bear a grudge, you articulated fuck," emphasising the word with another tug on the wrench.

The robot body said, "Wait." It released the spanner and Elif staggered back.

Ron? "Oh. It's you. Wh-" He started to ask "where's Russ" before deciding that neither Ron nor Russ would give him a good answer. On the display, deathbeams fired at the eye and were reflected back to strike somewhere deep inside the mouth.

The plasma had spread out in a dimming cloud, a thin atmosphere that extended to the ship and allowed him to hear: deep, pounding concussions as the Yacatisma fired huge chunks of scrap at the eye, which was starting to drift away. The first few bounced off the surface, knocking the eye about, and Elif saw it ripple and pulsate before it shattered, pieces spinning and stirring an oily black blot which spread inky tendrils, pushing the shell fragments aside. For a single cold moment the blackness imitated the thing he'd seen in the wormhole, its edges branching and subdividing, and a voice rang between his ears, the words like being repeatedly stabbed in the forehead with an icicle:

> TEMPLE IS CAST DOWN
> EMPTINESS IS OPENED
> AFFA, TO BE NOT RESTRAINED EVER, AL-
> WAYS TO –

Then the voice cut off with an undignified yelp as half a dozen deathbeams lanced out. The blackness curled around the beams, dodging them, contracted into a writhing knot, shrank to a point and vanished. Affa had escaped.

Elif watched the tumbling shell pieces for a few moments, then muttered petulantly, "Can we go now?" although, go where, he had no idea.

The robot body stared off into space, then said, "Not yet."

Elif shook his head slowly, placed the wrench on the floor then knelt to pick up Tai's body. It felt cold, the flesh stiff, as if cooked, although rigor mortis hadn't set in. Oddly, the body seemed to weigh more, as if her now-absent life had been something buoyant. **It's not her. It just used to be.** He took it to the recycling bay, his lower lip quivering until he bit it hard; he laid the body down and tried to think of something funny to say. Nothing came to mind. Nothing ever would; it was something you couldn't laugh at.

A yellow-green glow from the bridge drew his attention; more deathbeams. He wandered back to stand next to the robot. The Yacatisma was firing what looked like all of its primary weapons – at itself – and had destroyed another eye, the largest. Easily twice as large as Affa's former prison and made of something less reflective, the beams punctured it in several places and fluid boiled out from the ragged holes.

Elif glanced at the robot (or Ron. Most likely Ron); immobile, expressionless, and apparently not about to explain what was going on. At least Russ had occasionally dropped hints, even if they were mostly lies... but "not yet"? What was Ron waiting for? "You think she made it. She's over there somewhere, but she's hiding from you. And the Yacatisma is trying to kill her, and she's dodging it."

A long pause, then Ron said "Incentive." The display changed, switching from the external view to show a dishevelled, red-eyed maniac dressed in torn denim and a stained T-shirt. It took several seconds to recognise himself as seen from Ron's point of view.

"Wow," he breathed, "I'm gonna take a bath," but he didn't move; a compelling sense of déjà vu held him.

The sound of stone scraping on stone; a black dot appeared at the centre of the wall behind the stone ring, expanded, revealing a dark cavity with something large, asymmetric, bulbous, organic, and a smell like rotting marsh reeds. One side of Elif's mouth almost twitched in a smile.

"Hey, Russ."

The déjà vu got stronger, approaching the point of captivation, then the thing in the cavity moved, lurching forwards awkwardly. Elif stepped back to give it room.

At first he thought it was moving ass-forwards, presenting two arm-chair-sized spheres made of a grey-green translucent material about a foot thick, pressed together, filled with murky gel riddled with pale striations and bubbles. A fringe of wrist-thick tentacles dangled from the underside almost to the floor, dripping clear slime. Elif winced in sympathy as the thing fell sideways to bash against the inside of the ring, righting itself slowly.

The flattened cylindrical form shod in roughly finished dull metal stood on seven irregularly spaced simple mechanical legs; five thin, unjointed stalks on one side and two tree-stump-thick cylinders on the other, all connected by a complicated set of slowly grinding heavy gears. The whole thing was about the size of a rhinoceros, with three ugly green-tinged yard-long blisters set into its back. Moving at tortoise speed, it took almost five minutes to climb through the ring, dragging a short, thick tail that bulged at the end; by this point Elif had grown bored and had even considered helping it out before remembering who it was. He half-closed his eyes, sensed the lone Sheydal in the engine pod behind him... and one, two, three... four life-signatures before him. One of them was similar to the engine's general pattern, but fainter; weaker. The one behind the drooping bean-bag sacs felt like... putting his hand into a bag full of eels, or snakes, tied in knots, a wavering sickly-yellowish vomit smell that made him want to back away and steam-clean his brain. **That's Russ.** A third Lifesense was in the tail-bulge, but it barely registered; rapidly shuffling plates of thin glass reminiscent of the Spree pimp.

The fourth life-sense came from the middle off-centre hump on its back. Elif drifted around to get a better look, taking care to avoid the heavy plate-like feet. He pressed his 'phone against the side of the bulge, shining white light through the greenish translucent surface and caught a brief glimpse of the head, shoulders and one arm of Sybrandis deVonk, looking remarkably young for his age, suspended in gel, with empty cataract eyes, his mouth open in a permanent, silent scream, jaw moving slowly, face framed by long, dead white hair. Russ had been using Sybrandis like a cellular telephone.

Aetherics.

If Russ had been telling the truth about coming from a high-pressure frozen methane world, it must have taken Xist technology to connect a human to its nervous system and to keep him alive for eight hundred years... and Sybrandis was still alive. More or less.

The other two blisters were empty. One for Tai, if she hadn't jumped overboard... and one for him. How did Russ imagine it was going to get him inside, without arms? Persuasion?

Russ was starting to realise that Elif was no longer in front of it – slow reaction times probably came with a metabolism that ran at two hundred degrees below zero – and began pumping its legs, like someone trying to dance on seven crutches. Elif casually walked around the back of the creature, stepping over the tail and then passing up to the front. The tail twitched, several seconds too late, then a voice spoke from the point where the tail joined the trunk; harsh, mechanical, the words run together: "This trip has been a complete waste of resources so far but I will at least have the satisfaction of eating your brains."

After successfully repressing his laughter at the source of the sound, Elif said "You, in your high-pressure suit with your tempera-ture on its way to absolute zero, and you're gonna eat my brains? I don't care how advanced your technology is, that is just not going to work." He shook his head in amazement and began walking to the bathroom. He would have laughed if he hadn't had to pass Tai's body on the way.

He retrieved his make-shift pipe and the last of the weed, briefly searched for the lighter and then leaned against the door post of the bathroom and stared at the floor, carefully not thinking about anything. He'd read enough stories about advanced aliens treating humans like pets, or worse – he'd even been there himself – but to bring the situation home, you really needed to see something like half of Sybrandis in a jar.

An irregular clacking sound came from the recycling bay; Russ was struggling through the relatively narrow doorway, stick-legs waving slowly, tail sweeping from side to side as an aid to balance. Elif considered that Russ wouldn't have come out in such a vulnerable guise if it didn't have at least two or three tricks under its tail; surely it wouldn't rely solely on Sybrandis' Aetherics.

It skidded down the ramp, almost tipping over onto the thin-legged side. With a low, metallic groan, a pitted and brown-rusted probe slid out from between the tentacles, extending about two feet. The end was as large around as his little finger, and wisps of vapour drifted out. It was probably connected to a strong pump and refrigeration unit, to save Russ the trouble of having to suck on the other end of the straw.

"You will have to sleep some time," Russ said, and the feeling of déjà vu came back even stronger. Elif stared at the two baggy sacs (infra-red visual organs? Is that why Russ chose a robot with large breasts? Had it been **seeing** with them?), momentarily lost in reverie, then he nodded to himself, walked over to the wall and put his hand flat against it.

The Scoop controls were the same. He visualised a tube that ran from inside the middle hump to somewhere outside the ship, and concentrated, his eyes narrowing as the device triggered. The hump contracted, became a concave dimple, and Russ' suit shuddered as if kicked by a Chort. The eel-snake Lifesense signature coiled, knotted, hissed and gave of a smell like rotting metal and burning orange peel; an Xist scream. The déjà vu feeling cut off with a snap, leaving him feeling unpleasantly awake. **Good-bye, Sybrandis.** As a finale, Elif retrieved the wrench and pushed the end into the gears between the two large legs; they turned, caught, jammed, slowed; stopped. Russ' suit shook, but the legs were locked in place. All it could move was the probe, and that was too short to reach the floor. It rasped in and out helplessly.

"'God-like'", Elif muttered as he went back to the bridge, "What a maroon."

THE display was showing the view outside the ship again, and Elif's eyes widened. While he'd been freeing Sybrandis the Yacatisma had been in pursuit, and the mouth was about to surround them. Pointlessly, Elif looked about, but there were no visible controls. Recalling the trouble he had working out how to use the Scoop, he didn't think he would have any luck. "Ron? Can you fly this thing?" No response. "Is it too late to get Russ back? You're no help at all." He walked through the display, the horizontal bands drawing lines of dots on his face; stepped through the ring and into Russ' hideout. The cavity had a circular profile, the walls ribbed with thick copper-coloured ridges, but no visible controls. The end was an undetailed curve made of stone hull material. He put his hand against it; not even Aetherically active like the Scoop walls. He went back and sat in the ring, eyeing it warily, and then rested his chin on his fist, his elbow on his knee, and watched the display as the ship plunged into hell. He could sense a huge crowd of people – at least, living creatures – down there somewhere, and they were all screaming in pain.

Within the mouth, hundreds of deathbeams were snapping back and forth, carving ugly, glowing-red-edged canyons in the clusters of machinery, setting off explosions, throwing wreckage across the expanse; it looked like a civil war had started, but then, it always did. He saw in passing that a third eye had been destroyed, a spare lattice of metal beams still glowing yellow from whatever weapon the Yacatisma had used. The beams and artillery and gravity-generator-flung Chorts were too busy with each other to pay attention to the **Bitchslap**, although an expanding cloud of white-hot metal fragments pattered into one end, causing the ship to pitch lazily. The source of the display's image turned with the ship's motion, showing the edges of the mouth and the scaffolding that supported the remaining eyes, then a narrowing field of faint stars, and the murky depths of the Yacatisma's insides. Something shaped like a shovel blade fifteen miles long came screaming out of the darkness, blue-white fire streaming from half a dozen elliptical craters on its back, Aetherically-sensed moans of agony coming from the living creatures trapped in its pain-cells; three deathbeams caught the thing and the resulting plasma flare threw it against the inner wall, where it stuck and burned, the cries falling silent.

The pieces were getting bigger, and it was getting crowded down there. A strut about the size and shape of the Golden Gate Bridge spun slowly from one side to the other, armies of Chorts clinging to it. Elif grabbed the edges of the ring, leaned back and willed the ship to stabilise. Obligingly – or coincidentally – the Bitchslap straightened and plunged ahead. The ship passed so close to the bridge-strut that some of the Chorts leaped up, trying to hitch a ride. Baring his teeth with the effort, Elif tried to steer around the obstacles, but the safest path seemed to be right down the middle, and in the light of the increasingly frequent atomic flashes, he saw something – several somethings – directly ahead. **Bad News**. He tried to slow the ship down; it ignored him.

Four huge, distant shapes began to resolve out of the confusion, but one of them flared blue-white and dissolved into a dandelion-puff of glowing yellow fragments before he could make out any details. Of the remaining three, the largest looked like a two-legged steam shovel, a massively reinforced set of saw-toothed jaws attached to a pair of short, clawed legs, one of which was sunk into the stomach wall. The other leg had sunk its claws into a disc-shape like two bowls pressed together edge-to-edge... like a giant yo-yo. Deathbeams flashed out from where the string would have been wound, concentrating their fire on the claw, which was glowing dull red. The steam shovel arched its neck, opened its jaws and sank its teeth into the disc. White stars flared into existence along the curve of the bite, like rescue flares, and the deathbeams faded. The steam shovel shook its prey, reminding Elif of a tyrannosaur, or perhaps a feral chicken, tearing the disc into three uneven sections that drifted off in different directions. The slowness of the movements, combined with the shifting parallax as the Bitchslap got closer, told him that these things were huge; the disc had been easily as large as a city.

The third shape was something like an elongated pinecone, or a jewelled tentacle, or perhaps a slug; it was barely bigger than the steam shovel's jaw but it moved too fast for it to catch, twisting and writhing around its opponent, darting in to scrape its sides against the leg sunk into the stomach wall, sawing through it. The steam shovel – or robotic mega-chicken – spun free, minus one leg. The other leg waved, clawed at the stomach wall, missed; the jaws opened wide and the slug slipped between them and out again before they could close. A nuke went off inside the steam shovel's mouth, beams of light radiating out through the serrations, and the steam shovel froze, spinning slowly on two axes. The slug flew in closer, gouging chunks out of the steam shovel's neck, severing the jaws; the ass-end of the body bumped against the stomach wall and a treacle-slow wave of Chorts began to engulf it while the slug continued to carve pieces from the neck.

It was at that point that Elif had the feeling of someone sneaking up behind him, which, given the way he was facing, would have meant something ahead of the ship. He jumped out of the stone ring and turned; the feeling was still behind him. He turned on the spot twice, like a cat chasing its tail; his eyes darted about, then turned to the rear of the ship, where he'd left Russ. "Oh, no," he muttered, "not **this** little black duck." He marched back to the second scoop and kicked Russ' rhino-sized mechanical suit in the ass, this time with the flat of his foot. The suit wobbled, and had Elif kicked it again, it would have fallen over.

"Wait. It can't be you... unless you've got a piece of another human brain hidden in there somewhere." His Lifesense only saw the three remaining components. He thought briefly about using the wrench to pry a few pieces off Russ' suit, but that would release all of that noxious atmosphere, and at some insanely high pressure and low temperature. He leaned close to the repulsively bulging front end of Russ' suit, drew a breath to shout something, then exhaled, unable to think of anything appropriate.

Feeling even more useless than usual, he walked back to the bridge. The giant robot slug had sawed through the middle of the steam shovel's body, and the pieces floated away with a serene, pedestrian slowness that made Elif want to claw at the screen to speed up the action. The slug flew over to the other side of the stomach and delivered a nuke to the ragged edge of the largest piece of the yo-yo. The Bitchslap was so close that Elif had to shield his eyes with one hand and wonder about radiation. The feeling of uselessness compounded itself, and his gesture became a dismissive wave. As his hand moved, the edges of the display expanded until it formed a semicircle around him; a panoramic view. He waved his hand a few more times, but it didn't change. He hadn't magically gained the ability to control it. He couldn't control anything.

On the display there were dots. Amidst the now-familiar chaos, arranged around, above and below, there were dots; grey-white, shaped a little like grains of rice; hundreds of them, perhaps thousands. He saw more of them emerging from niches in the stomach wall, and, most importantly in Elif's mind, nobody was attacking them. Beams still fanned out and burned, miles-wide shuriken were launched, spinning through the dust and debris, leaving twisting trails before they slammed into the stomach walls; Chorts still clung to pieces of the losers as they slowly bumped and ground against each other, but none of it hit the dots. They would occasionally dip out of the way of some of the faster-moving pieces of debris, but they quickly returned to their positions. They were coming up from behind him, and the closer ones were cylindrical... with two bumps near the tail end. Like two golf-balls in a sock. **Where have I seen that before?**

"Oh, right." When they'd arrived, diving through the remains of the Spree Seedship; there'd only been one of them, and... "Wait, that was **us.**" He remembered the shape of the **Bitchslap**, embedded in the floor-plates of the eyelash. "They're... us. They're Bitchslaps. But if they're Xist ships... and nobody's shooting at them... okay, Russ was lying. Again. This isn't an Xist ship. It's a kind of Chort," looking up at the ceiling, as if it would only now revert to type and try to kill him. The pieces of the Scoop chamber walls he'd found embedded in the eyelash. "Camouflage". The fact that the damn thing was powered by pain. Russ saying the Xists had occasionally collected Chorts; evidently, They'd collected this one. "But nobody's shooting at them... and nobody's shooting at us..." with a self-conscious glance back at the recycling bay, "I mean, me... so, all this time, we weren't in any danger?" He would have gone back to kick Russ' suit again, except the sneaking-up-from-behind feeling was being supplemented with anticipation, and the mega-slug was now spitting nukes at anything larger than itself. There were only scattered fragments of the other three largest machines left. The giant jewelled robot slug was the winner.

He'd almost become accustomed to the idea that he was going to die soon, but this was taking longer than he'd expected. If the mega-slug was the biggest and baddest of all the giant Chorts in the stomach, then that was what he needed to deal with. He felt sick at the idea, but he willed the ship to fly closer, and the ship seemed to obey (or he was imagining it and that's where they were headed anyway)... then, out of the haze of pain that was part of the background noise he sensed them: pain-cell elements. Hundreds of them. Thousands. The mega-slug was a flying concentration camp, a suburb-sized torture machine. He was close enough to see that the flanged details along the side of the mega-slug were gravity generators shaped like knives, apparently a better tool for destructive disassembly than nukes or deathbeams. He could sense the living things in the pain cells, now, tiny pulsing orange sparks.

His eyes grew wide. "I could..." One side of his mouth twisted up in a crooked grin, and he limped to the first scoop chamber and put his hand against the wall. The sparks – the life-signatures of the pain-cell elements – grew brighter. He remembered the trouble he'd had the first time he'd tried to operate a scoop. That double-decker bus Chort had been entirely a machine, no pain-cell to power it; no life-signs to lock onto. Freeing Sybrandis from his eight hundred year prison had been much easier – he had been still alive. The scoops were evidently designed for scooping living things. He had no idea if this would make much difference – any difference – but as the **Bitchslap** pulled closer, a pair of brilliantly glowing life-signs came within range and with an effort that made black spots hover around the edges of his vision, he scooped both of them into the second chamber. "Hah!"

He collapsed against the wall, gasping, then shook his head to clear it, and then blinked. The cloud of sparks in front of him – the thousands of pain-cell elements – were flicking about, jumping short distances, then swooping away. The other Bitchslap ships were swooping in and then out again, like waves of commando bees stealing pollen, doing just what he'd done... depriving the mega-slug Chort of its main source of power. He laughed wildly, tried to high-five the air but settled for waving his hand aimlessly. The Bitchslap was pulling back from the mega-slug, further, retreating into the irregular jungle of weapons mounts and broken gantries that lined the stomach walls. Swarms of Chorts leaped from the walls and threw themselves at the mega-slug; nobody attacked the **Bitchslap**. It settled with a sideways bump and a grinding sound. Then Elif remembered: he had guests. His eyes widened again and turned towards the back of the ship. "I hope no bad people turn up," giggling nervously at the thought. So far, all he'd met here was bad people.

THEY'D landed on the edge of his bed. Grey-green translucent flesh over a stick-figure's frame of bones, too many arms, and pale suggestions of organs shrouded by a dense web of nerves. The skulls were lopsided, bulging, leaking the same sickening fluid he'd seen dripping down the side of the gravity generator he'd infiltrated with Russ. Removed from the pain cells' support systems, they had finally been allowed to die and stop hurting. He thought about rolling them up in the blanket and dumping them into the recyclers, but when he stepped forward and got a closer look at their forms – engineered to experience pain – the sight drove him back to the bridge.

He stood in front of Russ' robotic body and waved a hand in front of the glassy eyes; nothing. He was about to press his hands against those ridiculously rounded breasts and push it over onto its back before hitting it some more with the wrench when the **Bitchslap** bumped against something. Had they docked? He turned to look at the display – obligingly showing a view down the inside of the Yacatisma's stomach – and, framed by the blunt, rounded noses of dozens of other Bitchslap ships he caught a glimpse of the mega-slug Chort as it slid down and then out of the exit of the digestive system. It was twisting about slowly with not enough power to hang on to the inside of the Yac's shell; accompanied by a mist of debris, it was being left behind. They were moving, or, rather, the main part of the Yacatisma was moving away from the mega-slug.

"Ah. My baby."

He tried to turn around and jump away at the same time, and fell over instead. The rasping voice had come from Russ' robotic body, but... it sounded like Tai with a sore throat. Like a dalek, but with traces of genuine affection audible. The robot was watching the mega-slug recede to a point as the Yacatisma increased speed. "That could have been worse. Sometimes it's twins and the parent doesn't survive."

Elif sat on the floor, eyes wide. It wasn't Russ, and it wasn't Ron. He could tell the difference. Was it someone he could ask a question of and get a reasonable answer? "Who – "

Russ' body held up an index finger for silence. "Many consider this to be a precious moment. Watching a new-born child strike out for itself... the first... few... steps." The index finger dropped, like flicking a light switch; the ship shifted slightly as a dozen large missiles flashed by outside, headed down, and out. Bright blue-white nuclear flares battered the giant slug chort, pushing it further away. The robot body laughed nastily, stopped laughing with a disconcerting suddenness and then its eyes turned toward him.

"And then there's this guy," lower lip twisting as if considering a smelly stray animal. "It would be much easier for me to open the hatch and let all the air out."

So it's not Tai? Nervously, "By all means do whatever is easier. If you are going to evacuate the ship, all I ask is five minutes to drill a couple of holes in Russ' suit. Not many things I'd want to share with Russ, but that'd be one of them." Russ appeared to have heard this, because the armored suit began rocking slightly.

The robot body slapped one of the bulging spheres on the front of Russ' mechanical suit and snarled, "Quiet, you," still watching the faint dot on the display that was the largest Chort, "No. I have plans for Russ – oh, and while I have your attention, Russ? **That –** ", viciously kicking the side of Russ' suit so hard that her foot left a dent in the metal and almost knocked Russ over, "is for infecting me with that neurodegenerative virus back on Earth. I have plans for everyone. It's been eight hundred and three seconds since I jumped overboard, but once you adopt machine-referent frames of thinking, experienced linear time changes. It seems like hundreds of years to me."

So it is Tai? "What have you been doing all that time?" heroically stifling the urge to add a reference to something silly. Any mood of silliness had fled a long time ago.

"Fighting for control of the Yacatisma." Russ' robot body turned, faced him, raised one eyebrow. "We won, incidentally."

"Yeah. I figured I'd be dead otherwise."

"Or worse, in a pain cell."

Feeling as if he were walking on very thin ice laced with broken glass... for the first time in his life, when talking to her... Elif wanted to know what Tai meant about having plans for everyone, but thought it'd be smarter to risk a diversion by asking about Russ's anticipated punishment. **Oh, I really hope it's a punishment and not a promotion.**

"It can be both," Tai said easily. Elif grimaced and accepted that Tai – or the Yacatisma – could predict his train of thought just as easily as she had before. "Since Affa is no longer an active part of this concern, there's a vacancy in the optic array division. Russ will do quite nicely there. You might even go as far as to say it's poetic justice, given that Russ' people have a noted tendency for surgical coaptation of other beings' abilities," gesturing at the empty blisters on Russ' back.

"You're not worried about upsetting the Xists – of course you aren't, you're – "

"Ron is an Xist, and doesn't much care what we do. Russ isn't an Xist."

"She – " his thoughts stumbled over this. "I mean it, has to be at least working for the Xists... doesn't she?" Elif tried to think of a way of corroborating this. Would "Bob" have known? The aliens at the asteroid market who claimed to have dealt with Russ before? ... the Yacatisma? The old, familiar you've-been-gulled-again feeling made him blush.

Tai glanced around the room. "This isn't how I'd imagined this conversation going. I want to show you something more ..." her voice trailed off, giving it a faint, tantalising suggestion of Tai's spoken style, "... illustrative of the structure's intended new direction. Follow me."

Elif didn't dare snort and ask **do i have a choice**, but couldn't resist thinking it, and presumably the thoughts were read, but Tai – he was reasonably sure it was Tai – didn't answer. They walked past the recycling bay, where Tai's body was still lying on the disassembler platform. Either the Abandoners hadn't received any orders to begin recycling it, or they were too scared to. Elif thought about drawing her attention to it, but decided if she wanted to keep the body, she would have said something.

THE hatch at the back of the Bitchslap opened onto – Elif's view almost slid onto it with relief – a traditional science-fiction-starship corridor, tall hexagonal profile, the walls detailed with panels, flanges, vents, pipes and blinking lights, the effect only slightly spoiled by the tight curves it followed. He imagined they were walking along the inside of a giant vacuum cleaner hose that had been tied in knots, gradually making their way into the structure of the stomach walls. The corridor ended in a heavy rectangular hatch that slowly began opening, sliding into the floor.

As it descended Elif took what he considered to be one of the biggest risks of his life, ever mindful that he was talking to someone who could turn him into vapour in a second: "Tai... are we okay? You and me, I mean? Rightfully I should be angry at being lied to," hastily, seeing the sudden wildly angry snarl on the face of the robot, "but I acknowledge that you had the best reasons for that."

The snarl faded, again, so abruptly so as to seem disturbed. **You can't expect to put a human mind into a killing machine billions of years old and have it come out the other side without some nastiness.** "If I had asked you to come with me and help me commit suicide, you wouldn't have agreed. I needed you for this. There was nobody else I could trust. If it makes you feel any better I did spend a lot of biological time agonizing over it."

The hatch opened onto a broad, flat hangar the size of a city block. "As for you and me being okay, I will need to work out exactly who I am before I can give you a satisfactory answer. Right now you are talking to perhaps one part in thirty billion of my capacity, and those parts don't always agree. You are still needed, though. Take some consolation in that. You're still worth more alive than dead."

The hangar had the look of an engineering test bay; partly assembled, or disassembled structures the size of caravans, connected by cables that hung from the ceiling and trailed across the steel-plate-shod floor. Elif's Lifesense reported around thirty signatures, all stationary, hiding, all tinged grey with caution. Tai led him over to the nearest structure; belatedly, Elif recognised the front half of a monitor Chort minus most of its cover plates. The cockpit was unoccupied, the activity plates all dark, the sparse padding stained with trails of dark brown. Instinctively he took a step back.

"The good news about pain generators is they can be rigged to work on sensations other than pain. The bad news is, in a game-theoretic sense it's easier to hurt something than it is to force it to feel pleasure."

Elif leaned over slightly, wanting to get a better look inside the cockpit but not wanting to get within range of the doors, even though they'd been removed. "Aetherics."

Wearily, "Aetherics. Yes. They can convert intensely pleasureable sensations into power. Slightly more power than through pain induction. Same receiving hardware. It comes down to whether you want certainty - energy when you need it, by torturing the subject – or do you hope that a life-form is going to experience orgasm if it's in the mood."

Elif considered this. "Awkward. So what's the answer?"

Tai stared at him for a few seconds, then smiled slowly. "Scale. Use more generators and rely on a percentage of them coming when it's needed. Buffer the power in the short term." Behind her, a face peered around the corner of the monitor Chort frame, wreathed in wavy purple hair, then a second face nervously came out from behind the first. "And you use volunteers rather than prisoners, along with professionals... say, life-forms genetically engineered towards pleasure."

The pair of purple-haired elf-girls stared at Elif. "You'll have to excuse them," Tai said. "They were born here and they've never seen a guy before."

"I'm sure they've seen weirder things about," wondering if Dogboy was still alive, or if it had companions. He tried a smile, which broadened when it was tentatively returned; encouraged, the girls came out from behind the monitor Chort. They were dressed in something like coveralls woven from braided scarves and showed an exaggerated deference to Tai, or at least to Russ' robot body. Tai sighed. "I've tried to discourage it, but they are coming to regard me as some kind of goddess." Rolling her eyes and shaking her head, "Primates."

Once it seemed safe, dozens of purple-haired elf-girls came out of hiding around the other structures and resumed their tasks; removing plates, fitting cables, and occasionally carrying bodies out of the hangar. As the situation began to clarify, Elif tried not to grin like an idiot. "You're going to need more people in the generators to maintain the same power levels."

"A lot more, given that our strategy is no longer principally about destruction. I estimate that, to get under way, we're going to need at least fifty thousand people. I believe there's around that many registered Subgenii on Earth, so I'll be heading there first... as soon as I can re-arrange the superstructure. Make it look less like a giant flying bucket – " looking at him expectantly.

" – and more like a giant flying saucer." As the pieces began to fit into place, Elif didn't bother repressing the grin. "Making you the chief Goddess of the Pleasure Saucers," trying, for the first time, to disassociate the voluptuous fantasy-librarian body Russ had chosen, from Russ' nauseating presence. Trying to see the robot body as something other than a deception for control. Symbolic of the Yacatisma's new orientation. "The Xists weren't going to rescue all of us with Pleasure Saucers... so, you did it yourself."

"They were never going to rescue any of us! I don't imagine they'll be happy with me raiding their skull farms for humans, but if they didn't want me to succeed in their program of Yacatisma Pacification then they should have sent someone else. Solving this problem is why Ron was involved at all; the Emergency Xists are worried about the Yacatisma spreading unchecked. So I solved it for them. Once I have demonstrated the superiority of the Yacatisma Powered By Pleasure, it's only a matter of time before the other Yacatisma out there start to convert from the pain-generation system... to **my** system." Tai closed her eyes, smiled and hugged the two purple-haired elf-girls closely. "If they want to compete, the Yacatisma will have no other choice. It will be close, at first, but if this is played carefully, then our kind will triumph. We will march to victory on a road of perfumed beds!"

Some of the other purple-haired elf-girls were approaching out of curiosity. Elif whispered to Tai, "Can they speak?"

"They understand speech and can make some basic sounds, but they reserve most of their cognition for what they do best," glancing down the side of the monitor Chort, checking the arrangement of cables. "Okay, we're ready to test this set-up. Any volunteers?"

Two of the purple-haired elf-girls eagerly pushed forward, arranged themselves on either side of the monitor Chort's pilot seat, then gave Elif that look.

He opened his mouth to say something... then thought better of it.

About the Author

Rev. Nikolai Kingsley
is from Melbourne, Australia,
and was voted fifth weirdest poster
in Usenet's talk.bizarre in 1995.
His favorite chemical is caffeine.

JOIN THE CHURCH OF THE SUBGENIUS

The SubGenius material has only recently been made public. This is YOUR chance to get in on the ground floor of a huge, lucrative cult–NOW, while rates are low. You will then be eligible for all the $$$, weird sex, and SHEER POWER OVER OTHERS that go with high-ranking membership in the Church. And yes, YOU CAN PERFORM LEGAL WEDDINGS!

Overcome shyness and guilt with this fantastic replacement for a huge penis or "perfect" breasts. Read *THE STARK FIST OF REMOVAL* and learn not only the Word of Dobbs but also ways to contact, buy from, and sell to the incredible (yet real!!) network of SubGenii and subsymps everywhere. Learn of local revivals, other secret societies, UNUSUAL PRODUCTS, Other Mutants. THIS IS NO FAKE. Puts you "in charge" of your life. You'll be READY the next time your face is on fire. Quick Condown Clampspiracy release. Easy on delicate tissues... no danger of runaway infection.

This is the only way to get on the Mailing List of the Chosen, pierce the shroud of secrecy insulating the cult, join the secret MEMBERS-ONLY online forums and obtain such privileges as befit membership in a secret society of this scope. And all of it, including the surgery, can be done BY MAIL. Everything is kept STRICTLY CONFIDENTIAL (unless you want your local Clench listed). And don't worry about the diseases–they're part of the satire, too!

TURN THE PAGE *NOW* TO SEE WHAT YOU GET!

WHAT OTHER RELIGIONS CHARGE
ALL WORLDLY GOODS FOR!!!

Be a Doktor INSTANTLY. Incredible, sinister super-miniaturized fine print details all the scores of Church Ranks and Titles from which YOU can CHOOSE.

Full of rants, art, Prescriptures, doctrine, charts, filth, comics, reviews and CHURCH NEWS & CONTACTS.

YOU GET

- Pamphlets #1 & 2
- Your Own Personal 8x11 suitable-for-framing DOBBSHEAD
- Official Dobbshead/Church Logo Metal Pin
- Dobbshead Sticker, Bumper Sticker
- The SubGenius Pledge
- The Divine Excuse (signed by "Bob!")
- Doktorate of Forbidden Sciences
- Propaganda flyers to copy, Stickers
- Wallet sized, SubGenius MINISTER'S CARD
- Minister's Ordination papers and instructions.
- The *STARK FIST of Removal* online
- SCRUBGENIUS secret forum
- dobbs.town - the SubGenius Mastodobbs

(Without that membership card you have NO HOPE on July 5th!!!)

SEND FIFTY DOLLARS TO:

The SubGenius Foundation
P.O. Box 807
Glen Rose, TX 76043
United States

subgenius.com